Red Jacket

By Richard Lassin

For Barbara and Rosie

*"An invisible thread connects those who are
destined to meet regardless of time, place, or circumstance.
The thread may stretch or tangle, but it will never break."*
- Chinese Proverb

ACKNOWLEDGEMENTS

Many people helped make this book possible, and their generous assistance is acknowledged here. I am indebted to Calumet resident, Peggy Germain for her technical/artistic editing of *Red Jacket.* Her steadfast support, along with detailed information on the labor dispute of 1913, helped provide a more accurate portrayal of life in the Copper Country during the earliest parts of the twentieth century. Penny Menze and Joanne Thomas also provided background information on the copper mine strike of 1913, and I acknowledge their input with appreciation. Additionally, Richard Larson provided background information about Little Bay de Noc and Garth Point. I am also indebted to Jeanie Croope and Janice Jones for their unwavering support and assistance in editing. Thanks also goes out to Bill and Melanie Diedrich who designed the book cover along with Rick Oberle who created the map of Michigan's Upper Peninsula. The photo on the back cover is used with permission and courtesy of MTU's Photographic Collection, MTU negative 03861, Michigan Technological University Archives and Copper Country Historical Collections. Also, I want to acknowledge Steve Lehto who wrote *Death's Door,* the definitive book about the labor dispute of 1913, and Matt Bliton for his original music, *A New Morning* that conveys the essence of this novel. Finally, I want to thank the residents of Calumet, Michigan who have always made me feel at home even in the darkest of days. All errors, deliberate or otherwise, are mine.

AUTHOR'S NOTE

The first vision came in 1986, and there were others in the years that followed. But for the most part, I never spoke of the Italian Hall because the topic was so disturbing. So, I tucked it away in a far corner of my mind, trying to ignore its implications. I had another such vision recently while visiting Calumet and decided it was time to write about my experience. And so, the novel, *Red Jacket* was born out of an attempt to explain what happened to me in 1986, and these visions were used to create a fictional storyline that conveys a different understanding of human tragedy.

Recently, I stopped at a bar in downtown Calumet and chatted with the owner who conveyed a conversation he had with a customer who believed he was a reincarnated victim of the Italian Hall. I find stories like these fascinating. Yet, being raised in a Judeo-Christian culture makes it difficult for many to accept the notion of reincarnation, and I understand the reluctance many readers might have to the material presented. I offer it as a possible explanation; there may be others. At first, I didn't believe in the concept either. Yet as I age, I'm open to the idea that we are evolving as spiritual beings. Maybe in time, the notion will gain more acceptance. Regardless, I am at peace with my distant past, and I offer this novel as tribute to those who have suffered. We can rise above it and move on.

NOTE TO READERS

Characters in this novel are entirely fictional although the names of a few historical figures have been retained. Any resemblance between the main characters of *Red Jacket* to actual residents of either Garth Point or the Keweenaw Peninsula is unintended. Public places, geographical areas, folklore, and historical events are used throughout the storyline in order to convey the rich history of Michigan's Upper Peninsula.

Red Jacket is a novel that involves the discovery of a large silver mass near the Phoenix Farm Road in Keweenaw County, and in no manner does the author suggest that silver has been actually found in this area or along the lake bottom near Little Bay de Noc. These parts of the story along with the description of the 19th century schooner, *Hudson Bay* are entirely fictional.

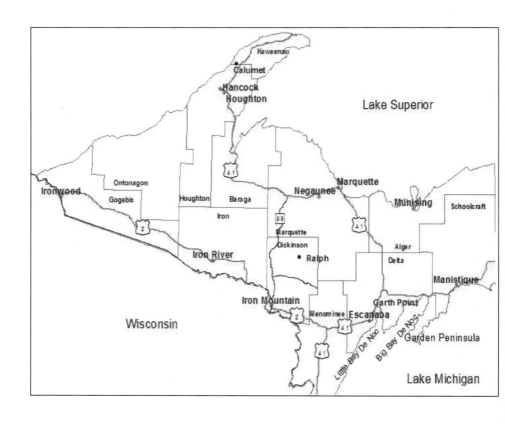

The Italian Hall is located in Calumet, Michigan. The town of
Ralph, Michigan is about 25 miles NNE of Iron Mountain. Garth
Point is at the northern end of Little Bay de Noc.

CHAPTER ONE

"We are but one thread within the web of life.
Whatever we do to the web, we do to ourselves.
All things are bound together.
All things connect."
- Chief Seattle

One billion fifty million years ago.

It was a time when the land was barren where the seed of life could find no purchase. The North American continent was being rifted apart by an upwelling of volcanic activity from deep within, depositing vast quantities of basalt, rhyolite, and conglomerate thousands of feet thick. As if the initial eruptions weren't sufficient, the land was then contorted, sending massive blocks sliding against one another. And from these ruptures, hidden chasms were formed along fault lines allowing hydrothermal fluids to percolate through every crevice and vesicle, depositing a plethora of colorful minerals like white calcite, red feldspar, green epidote, and milky quartz. As the hydrothermal solutions coursed their way through the volcanic pile, copper and silver were deposited, creating massive accretions, some weighing more than a thousand tons. But the heat that defined the area for so many years inevitably turned cold, and the land sat silent, a sentinel to Earth's evolution.

* * * * *

It felt like someone had cut her heart out. That's how Evangeline Attwood described the death of her daughter, and although it had been years since her passing, the memory of that event remained etched into her DNA. To put it bluntly, she was angry... angry with God, angry with Charlotte's father, and angry with all the well-meaning family members who offered lame excuses why the Almighty took her only child, saying she was so perfect that God had to have her for his very own. She tired of well-meaning friends who told her how Jesus didn't give his followers more than they could handle. Their assertions were nothing more than bullshit because she knew that thousands of Christians committed suicide every year, and it infuriated her. Evangeline's circle of friends couldn't understand what it was like, returning to a home that was ready to welcome an infant daughter. She had painted the guest room with bright cheery colors and had stocked up on disposable diapers and other necessities. After the funeral, she stood at the threshold of Charlotte's bedroom, looking at the bassinette, the SpongeBob mobile, the stuffed toys stacked in the corner, and the line between reality and illusion became blurred. After Charlotte's death, Evangeline drifted into nihilism.

As a result, Evangeline began therapy at the insistence of her doctor who prescribed psychotropic medication that left her feeling dull, like grey paint. As time passed, she regained some function and even started dating someone, hoping a relationship would offer a distraction from an endless grief. With the passage of time, her sorrow surfaced only periodically, but when it did, the grief would threaten to drown her as if the death of her daughter had just happened. That's how it worked for Evangeline Attwood, her life a dystopian reality; anguish beckoning like background noise, clouding every perspective through a lens crafted of guilt and heartache.

Evangeline tried to get on with life, but the simple sound of a baby crying, or perhaps walking through the infant section of a department store, would bring it all back and reduce her to tears. Recently, she saw an advertisement in the back section of a local newspaper that read, '*FOR SALE, Baby Shoes, Never Worn.*' With this simple solicitation, Evangeline relived that awful day when she donated Charlotte's clothing to a local charity and among the items surrendered were a pair of white baby shoes.

But if the truth be known, it was guilt more than anything that coursed through her veins, as if she had done something worthy of punishment in the eyes of the Almighty. Did having a child out of wedlock cause her to lose favor with God, condemning her to a lifetime of sorrow? Maybe, her punishment came from a lack of faithful service to her Lord and Savior, but whatever it was, the effect drove her deeper into darkness. And when a new wave of sorrow forced its way into Evangeline's consciousness, she pushed it back, like stuffing the clutter into an overflowing closet until the door snapped shut. With feelings safely secured, she could breathe a sigh of relief, reminding herself never to go near the door that kept the anguish at bay. Like a stubborn virus, the recollection of Charlotte's death stayed dormant, waiting for an opportunity to manifest itself when least expected.

They had met in Verona while on holiday, but Charlotte's father, who lived overseas, never replied to the numerous letters she wrote. His silence took its toll, breeding resentment. After her daughter's death, Evangeline brooded over the injustice and held onto the one thing she had control over, keeping Ulay ignorant of his paternity. After all, it seemed only fair, but as much as she rationalized her decision, there was never any doubt the source of her anger was based in grief, for she loved Charlotte's father. And that's how it worked for Evangeline Attwood, where the loss of her daughter was the measure to which all things were subsequently compared, coloring her life with an emptiness only death can create.

* * * * *

It was an ordinary summer morning. Evangeline Attwood attended an auction held at a farmhouse west of town. A recent thunderstorm had raked the area earlier that morning, and the air was heavy with moisture. While a set of curtains flapped along an old clothesline, patrons rummaged through boxes of merchandise as the auctioneer sold off the remaining vestiges of an elderly woman's estate. The owner had passed on, and the children were liquidating the home's furnishings. But there wasn't anything left of great value. Evangeline bought a box of canning jars for two dollars along with a set of steak knives that went for three bucks. She tried to open a cedar chest that sat neatly upon a plastic tarp but found it locked, and when the auctioneer finally approached, he tapped it with a wood cane.

"Now folks we have this wonderful old cedar chest. Unfortunately, it's locked, and we don't have the key. So, you're buying a surprise…could be filled with gold coins, for all we know." The auctioneer chuckled at the absurdity. "It's a real opportunity for some of you antique dealers to snatch up a good bargain." Another strong tap was followed by, "So, who'll gimme fifty bucks?"

The crowd remained silent.

"Well how about twenty then?"

Someone from the back hollered, "I'll give you ten!"

The price quickly rose to thirty-five dollars, and the auctioneer poured it on. "Now look, this chest is worth at least fifty bucks. If you don't believe me, just go over to Art Van and check out what these babies run for. I'm only asking for forty bucks." A rap with the oak cane was followed by, "I got thirty-five need forty. Forty, forty, forty…"

Evangeline raised her hand and yelled, "I'll give you forty."

After some additional haggling, the auctioneer yelled, "Sold! What's your number ma'am?" Upon eying the bidder's card, he called out, "Number twelve-twenty-four just bought herself a cedar chest."

It was heavy for its size, maybe fifty or sixty pounds, and one of the auction staff gave her a hand, loading it into the back of her Honda. A neighbor helped move it into her three-bedroom condo, and with the help of a few tools, Evangeline removed the hinges, circumventing the locking mechanism. It took a few minutes as she shimmied the top, but eventually, the lid yielded to her demand.

Evangeline lit up when she saw the colors. On top were a pair of quilts neatly folded. One was done in brown maple leaves with a cream-colored background while the other was done in small pine trees. She sniffed one of the quilts, and the scent of cedar and mothballs reminded her of her grandmother's closet where she kept her dress-up clothes. The quilts, she thought, would go well with her queen-sized bed and set them aside. Evangeline dug further through the chest, where she found a stamp collection along with several journals that dated back to the 1940s.

Once the chest was empty, she got the locking mechanism to retract sufficiently so the top could be reattached, and after a coat of furniture wax and subsequent buffing, she placed the new acquisition at the foot of her bed.

Later that evening, Evangeline donned a pair of flannel pajamas and sat in a recliner with her feet draped over the armrest, perusing various entries from the journals she found earlier that day. The earliest was from June 1942, where the author, a Miss Emma Rind, wrote about a young soldier she met at a soda fountain in downtown Battle Creek. His name was Roy, and he was going through basic training at Fort Custer, preparing for an assignment overseas. Evangeline read about how the young soldier wasn't certain where he'd be deployed as the war was raging on two continents. Emma, a mere eighteen years of age, lamented about his future assignment as Roy seemed homesick for his family who resided in northern Michigan.

Evangeline read the details of how Roy slurped the last of his soda, then walked to the door only to return moments later where he asked Emma if she'd like to go for a walk. There was a garden nearby in one of the city parks, and before long, she slipped her hand inside his upper arm.

A yellowed telegram was tucked away in one of the many journals, and Evangeline carefully unfolded it, for it was brittle with age.

Western Union

SA2 89 GOVT=PXX NR Washington DC

MRS EMMA KINCAID   JUNE 16 1945
5547 FOWLER ROAD
BATTLE CREEK MICH

THE SECRETARY OF WAR DEEPLY REGRETS TO INFORM YOU THAT YOUR HUSBAND S SGT ROY EARL KINCAID WAS KILLED IN ACTION ON JUNE 3, 1945 IN THE PERFORMANCE OF HIS DUITIES AND IN THE SERVICE OF HIS COUNTRY. THE DEPARTMENT EXTENDS TO YOU ITS SINCEREST SYMPATHY IN YOUR GREAT LOSS. ON ACCOUNT OF EXISTING CONDITIONS THE BODY IF RECOVERED CANNOT BE RETURNED AT PRESENT. IF FURTHER DETAILS ARE RECEIVED YOU WILL BE INFORMED. LETTER FOLLOWING

J A ULIC
THE ADJUTANT GENERAL

She re-read the telegram several times, then found all of Emma's subsequent entries. At first, she wrote about her despair, then went into great detail about their relationship, attempting to recapture every moment they spent together. Emma wrote about their first date when they went roller-skating and described the day when Roy asked for her hand in marriage. There were extensive writings about their love life as well, and Emma showed little restraint, writing about their most intimate encounters. Evangeline then found Roy's letters from overseas neatly tied together with a blue silk ribbon.

She spent days poring over Roy's letters and came to realize Emma had suffered a loss not unlike her own and had later fallen in love. Knowing all this, it encouraged Evangeline, offering a ray of hope to a woman who had very little.

It is said discontent often fuels the desire to change, and after considerable thought, there was no going back; only a complete break would suffice. Evangeline had planned it for months, ending her relationship with a man she had been seeing for nearly seven years. Dan didn't take it well and continued to call, but she remained steadfast. And with each passing day, the middle-aged woman with wind-swept hair felt a new freedom, as if a part of her life had been reclaimed. With a new sense of empowerment, Evangeline took another step into the unknown. She dialed the number, and when the phone rang on the other end, the secretary announced, "Pattengill Middle School. How can I help you?"

She caressed her beloved yellow lab, Lucy and squeaked, "Hi Cindy, this is Evangeline Attwood calling. Is Diane around?"

"Hang on a sec. I think she just walked in. I'll transfer you over."

As Evangeline waited, she fiddled with a refrigerator magnet in the shape of covered wagon. Following pleasantries that included an update on summer activities, she delivered the news. After seventeen years of teaching American history to middle-school children, she tendered her resignation, and the ensuing quiet felt as if all the air had been sucked out of the room.

The principal, a cherubic woman with an extrovert personality, took the offensive. "But why?"

Evangeline flipped through the yellow legal pad and found her talking points. She cleared her throat and said her heart wasn't in it anymore. Of course, it wasn't true, but if she told the truth, the decision might be subject to debate.

"Well, I'm sorry to see you go," the principal said, clearly stunned. "What will you do?"

"Not sure. Just need some time to think things through. Thought I might head north and spend a few weeks at my brother's cabin."

She ended the call with a promise to have lunch sometime, and when Evangeline pressed the 'Off' button, the former teacher sighed with relief and then cupped Lucy's face. "Well kiddo, we're on our own."

CHAPTER TWO

"Nothing ever goes away
until it has taught us
what we need to know."
- Pema Chodron

After millions of years of volcanic eruptions, the land cooled. But the external forces that rifted the continent apart now reversed, compressing the layers of basalt and rhyolite into a deep v-shaped syncline, a hundred miles across. But nothing gets buried forever. Here in the Keweenaw, beds that were folded deep into the abyss were now thrust upwards along reverse faults that extended for hundreds of miles, bringing to the surface ancient volcanic deposits along with rich veins of pure copper.

And for the next billion years, the land sat quietly as it watched the episodic development of life eternal. Vast inland seas came and went, along with new and exotic species now long extinct. The Paleozoic and Mesozoic Eras brought forth amphibians, reptiles, and birds of every kind, and the land was awash with dense forests, and insect life flourished. Vast mountain ranges were thrust upwards as continents collided into one another, then eroded away, leaving behind thick sequences of sandstone, shale, and conglomerate.

With the onset of the Pleistocene, glaciers thousands of feet thick shaped the landscape, carving out the Great Lakes, exposing the rocks below. Come the Holocene Epoch, the

14

ground became free of ice, and indigenous people came to chisel out pieces of copper from rich veins, using stone implements and fire. Here, masses of red metal were pounded into tools and weapons, then traded extensively throughout the continent. But the depth of the deposit wasn't fully appreciated until white settlers reported large pieces of pure copper strewn about various creeks and riverbeds. It was a timely discovery as the nation was astir, becoming an industrial giant. And the wealth of the land, called the Keweenaw, helped fuel an insatiable demand. Its violent origins would not be forgotten but rather manifested in the people who came here to extract its hidden wealth.

* * * * *

Her windshield was dotted with a variety of crushed insects, and as they approached Lake Michigan, the air was thick with the scent of fish and the sound of hovering gulls. Her brother's cabin was located on Garth Point that overlooked a small inlet lake that flowed westward into the bay. She hadn't been there in years, but a GPS brought them right to their destination without a hitch. It was a quiet haven, and Lucy was more than happy to explore the property, marking her presence with regular squirts of urine.

The cottage was an old, log structure from the early 1900s made from pine timber, but with the onset of the modern age, electricity and indoor plumbing were added during a renovation that occurred sometime during the 1940s. But like all older homes, problems were inevitable, and it wasn't a week before the pump died, leaving Evangeline without drinking water. In a panic, she made her way to a neighbor's home and rapped loudly on their backdoor.

Suzanne, a middle-aged woman with curly blonde hair, answered with a dish towel in hand.

"Hi, I'm staying next door," Evangeline pointed to the cabin, "and my pump quit on me. I can use lake water to flush the toilet, but I'm afraid I don't have any drinking water. Could I use your hose to fill a few jugs?"

15

Her neighbor held the door open and said, "Come on in. Didn't catch the name."

Feeling chagrinned, she offered her hand. "Hi, I'm Evie. You probably know my brother, Tom. He owns the place next door."

"Sure, we know Tom, but he hasn't been up in a coon's age. Forgot that he had a sister. By the way, I'm Suzanne. Husband ran into town to pick up a few items for dinner." After looking at her watch, Suzanne furrowed her brow. "Should be home pretty soon. When he gets back, I'll have him take a look at your service." Suzanne cupped her mouth with a hand as if conveying a secret and whispered, "Works for the power company you know, and he's pretty good with that sorta thing."

"That would be just perfect. I called a few places in town, and they can't send someone out until next week." Evangeline looked about and said, "Nice place you have here. Is it just you and your husband?"

"Got a daughter, but she spends most of her time with her father over in Pembine." As she placed a platter into the overhead cupboard, it clattered loudly. "Can I get you somethin' to drink?" she called out.

Before Evangeline could answer, a pickup roared down the dirt road, sending a column of dust and leaves high into the air. The vehicle came to a stop a few feet from the back entrance, and Richard Templeton, a formidable presence at three-hundred-and-fifty pounds, emerged with an armload of groceries. Upon entering the kitchen, his first words were a lascivious, "And who do we have here?"

"This is Evie."

Evangeline extended her hand with the palm facing down.

Richard's eyes dilated as he glanced at Evangeline's t-shirt, then handed his wife a bag of groceries without looking. As he accepted the hand, his fingers lingered until Suzanne coughed. "Honey, Evie's pump died and said you'd go take a look. She's staying next door at Tom's place."

And before long, Richard had his voltmeter out, checking electrical connections. The wellhead was a few feet below ground, and Evangeline loomed above the chasm with arms akimbo. She bit her lower lip and murmured, "Sure appreciate helping me out like this. I don't know what I would have done."

The engineer looked up with cobwebs in his hair and emitted a toothy grin. "Not a problem." Templeton continued to check various leads until he found what he was looking for. "Here we go. Looks like a corroded ground wire, that's all." He spliced in a new connection, then called out. "Why doncha flip the power back on and see what happens?"

In seconds, water was flowing through the kitchen tap, and Evangeline beamed. "How much do I owe you?" she asked, then rummaged through her handbag, hoping to find a spare twenty.

Suzanne rapped on the backdoor and yelled, "How's it goin' in there?"

"She's got water!" her husband hollered.

Lucy greeted Suzanne by placing her paws upon her belt. "Go on. Get down," Evangeline scolded as she pulled back on the dog's collar. "I'm sorry. She doesn't mean any harm."

"Well, we're old dog lovers," Suzanne replied as she scratched Lucy's crown. "Got a couple buried out back." She nudged Evangeline with an elbow and said, "Why doncha come have dinner with us tonight? I'm making spaghetti and meatballs."

"Oh, I don't know," the brunette replied dismissively. "I don't want to impose. I already chewed up most of your afternoon." She thrust forward a pair of twenties in Richard's direction and said, "Here, I want to pay you something for your time."

The engineer held his hands up as if stopping traffic while Suzanne pulled the lever to the old Amana refrigerator, then examined its meager contents. "Well, it doesn't look like you got much here to eat, and I bet you could use a home-cooked meal. We're just hangin' out tonight, and it would be nice havin' the company."

Lucy whined, and Richard scratched the dog's spine, resulting in moans and a pulsating back leg. "You can pay us back by bringing the pooch along. As da wife says, we're ol' dog lovers."

"I guess that would be alright," the former teacher replied as she stuffed the twenties back into her Kate Spade handbag, then twirled a lock of hair with an index finger. "Why don't you give me an hour to get cleaned up?"

Evangeline donned a white dress accentuated with purple orchids and checked her appearance in the hall mirror, then made her way next door with a bottle of white zinfandel in hand. As she stood at Suzanne's back entrance, Evangeline peered into the kitchen through the screen door and yelled, "Anybody home!"

"Come on in!" Suzanne hollered.

When Evangeline entered, she sniffed a couple of times. "Boy, something sure smells good." It reminded her of her grandmother who often cooked large Sunday dinners in her Detroit home.

"So how long you up here for?" Suzanne asked as she added the pasta to the churning water.

As she explained her situation, Lucy whined.

"Go lay down," Evangeline whispered. "You've had your dinner." The tall brunette caressed her companion's head and looked towards her neighbor. "I'm just taking a little time to figure out what I want to do next and thought a vacation up here would help sort things out. Brought my scuba equipment along and hope to take some pictures with my underwater camera."

They sat at the oak table overlooking the water, and as Richard loaded his plate with pasta, he added a couple of meatballs along with a slice of garlic bread. With a mouthful, he mumbled, "Don't recall Tom ever mentioning a sister before."

His wife passed a platter to Evangeline and said, "That's men for you. They can tell you all about what the Packers are up to, but when it comes to stuff like family, they don't say a damn thing."

Afterwards, the three sat about the fireplace enjoying a glass of wine when the woodpile collapsed upon itself, sending a shower of sparks up the chimney, startling Lucy who had been curled up in front.

Richard cleared his throat and turned towards his guest. "So, what do you got planned for this week?"

"Not sure. Thought while I'm here, I'd check out a few nearby towns. Was wondering if you knew any of the local history? I taught American history for seventeen years, and that sort of thing interests me."

Suzanne took a sip from a Fred Flintstone cup, then set it onto the scuffed coffee table. "Here's some history for you. After the land was stolen from the Native Americans, big lumber companies bought up everything, and once the trees were harvested, they sold off their holdings. That's how our house came to be. It's been in Rich's family for over seventy years."

"So, outside of tourism," Evangeline casually swiped a wine droplet from her mouth and thought about job prospects, "what do folks do around here to support themselves?"

"Well, there's a few jobs with the paper mill here in town along with the community college, and then, of course, there's farming."

Richard leaned forward with his arms resting on his khakis. "What she means is there's a prominent marijuana industry especially over on the Garden Peninsula. They call their product 'Garden Gold.' So, if you're out and about, you might want to take that into consideration. Folks over there are a little paranoid about outsiders." Richard glanced askew when he asked, "Didja bring a gun?"

Evangeline gasped at the notion. "You think I need one?"

Just then, a breeze made a candle flicker, and as Suzanne shut the front door, she looked over her shoulder and said, "Probably not, but then again, I'm not a single gal livin' up here all alone. We've never had a lick of trouble in all the years we've been here, but I keep a .357 in the kitchen cupboard, just in case." Suzanne laughed. "Don't let Rich scare you. This place is safer than a police station. Of course, if you come across the dope peddlers or treasure hunters..."

Evangeline cocked her head to one side. "Treasure hunters?"

"Didn't Tom ever talk to you about what's buried out here? It's a good story." Suzanne turned towards her husband and said, "Why doncha tell her about it, honey?"

Richard tossed another log onto the fire, sending a column of sparks up the flue and whisked his hands before taking a seat next to his wife on the lumpy sofa. He sipped from a Wilma Flintstone cup, then cleared his throat. "As the story goes, it started when New Orleans fell to the Yankees back during the Civil War. Apparently, a small Confederate force shipped the contents of the government mint to Georgia in order to keep it out of Union hands. When Sherman made his march to the sea, they moved their assets to Richmond which finally fell a year later."

Suzanne interrupted. "And their money disappeared."

"Legend has it, after the war, there was an attempt to resurrect the Confederate cause from Canada, and they needed gold."

"Gold?" Evangeline said as if the notion of a sudden windfall sparked an interest.

"The remaining Confederate assets were supposedly shipped by train to the southern part of Lake Michigan, where it was loaded onto a ship with its final destination somewhere in Ontario."

"But that doesn't make any sense," Evangeline argued. "The South was dead broke. They didn't even have enough money to buy their men shoes and blankets. So, I can't imagine there was much of anything left in their treasury by the time the war ended."

Richard leaned forward once again, with one hand splayed. "But their treasury wasn't the only thing they hauled out. Supposedly, they emptied all the banks in the area as well. As I said, Southern wealth was concentrated in Richmond in order to keep it from Union forces as they conquered various cities."

"But why wouldn't they have taken it by ship through the existing ports along the eastern seaboard?"

"Again, it's just a story," Richard replied with a half shrug, "and it's more than likely just a bunch of malarkey, if you ask me. But to answer your question, the widely held belief was the eastern seaboard was still strongly part of the Union occupation." A sip of wine was followed by, "There are a couple variations as to what happened next. Either a storm

20

kicked up or the crew scuttled the ship out on Lake Michigan when a naval gunboat approached. To make a long story short, they think the ship sank somewhere off the Garden Peninsula, but nothing definitive has ever been found."

Outside, the wind started to pick up while Suzanne topped off Evangeline's Barney Rubble. "Tell him honey, about the guys from downstate."

"Ah...there are a couple of nut-jobs from the Muskegon area that have been prowlin' the waters." He flung his hand as if swatting at the absurdity, chuckling softly. "Said the gold was in boxcars, and during a storm, the crew dumped everything overboard in order to save the ship. Anyways, a good story doesn't require much basis in fact in an area like this. It's just an interesting yarn that gives folks who are economically challenged some hope of makin' a quick buck."

"How much are we talking about here?" Evangeline asked with a whisper.

A slurp from Wilma Flintstone was followed by, "Tons of gold I suppose, and in today's market, it would fetch something like a hundred million or more."

"There are a lot of secrets held out in that old lake." Suzanne looked out onto the water and said, "But I wouldn't go taking any of it too seriously though."

"Like... what kind of secrets?" Evangeline asked innocently.

"Well, there've been several aircraft that disappeared in this area." Suzanne turned to her husband and said, "Tell her about it, honey."

As Lucy snored away in front of the fireplace, Richard plopped his feet onto the coffee table, then pulled an old afghan over his legs. After a giant stretch, he said, "Back in the fifties, A Northwest flight from New York was traveling near the area. Radar lost contact with it somewhere over the lake and was never seen again. No wreckage...no nothin'." He inhaled deeply through his nose and smoothed out the blanket. "Over seventy people were lost, and of course there's that incident over at Kinross."

Both Evangeline and Suzanne leaned forward with plastic cups in hand while Lucy snored.

"Back in the early fifties, a jet fighter was scrambled out of Kinross Air Force Base when they detected an unidentified flying object over the lake. Eventually, the pilot caught up to it, but for whatever reason lost communications. As the story goes, the radar image showed the two objects merge, then they both disappeared. And there was no sign of wreckage anywhere. To this day, nobody knows what happened to those planes or the people onboard."

Suzanne went into the kitchen to check on the pie that was cooling on the stove, and as she sliced it into wedges, she called out, "And don't forget the Carl Bradley."

"Who's Carl Bradley?" Evangeline whispered.

With plates in hand, Suzanne returned to the living room with a Lucy escort. "Carl Bradley was a freighter en route to Rogers City after it dropped off a load of limestone somewhere in Indiana and sunk during one of our storms back in the fifties. Rich's uncle was onboard. Ain't that right, sweetheart?"

With just a whisper, Evangeline turned towards Richard and said, "Did he...?"

Richard shook his head, and his demeanor changed. He thought about his uncle's last few moments aboard the ship and wondered how long he struggled in the frigid waters before succumbing.

"And don't forget about the Paulding lights." Suzanne said as if a change in subject would lighten the conversation.

"What are ..."

Evangeline didn't get to finish before Suzanne blurted, "It's this strange light over in the Ottawa National Forest near the town of Paulding that nobody can explain. You should go check it out if you have time."

Richard scratched an ear and said, "As legend has it, a railroad switchman was crushed to death between two cars while holding a lantern, and that's what people see today."

"Have you seen it...I mean...personally?" Evangeline asked.

Suzanne answered, "We went out there a couple of years ago. Was the strangest damn thing I ever saw. Ain't that right, Rich?"

Lucy stood before them, wagging her tail with expectation, until Suzanne let her lick the empty plates. Afterwards, the three sat by the fireplace telling more stories for another good hour until Evangeline looked at her watch and yawned. "Well, I better be going. Thanks for the lovely evening. How about sometime next week you guys come over, and I'll make something special. Do you like Mexican?"

* * * * *

Evangeline recognized the number just before she was broadsided by a strident voice. "So, you up and quit your job, huh?"

Her mother had been suffering from clinical depression off-and-on for the past twenty-some-odd years, and currently lived with her son. The seventy-year old woman stayed with her daughter for a spell until Evangeline simply couldn't take it anymore. Sensing another crisis, her brother had reluctantly stepped in and offered his mother a place to live.

Evangeline's exhalation was forceful. "Hi, Mom."

She could hear *The Price is Right* blaring in the background as her mother said, "And what are you gonna do for money? Just answer me that, will ya?" Mrs. Attwood whispered under her breath, "Just don't come around asking me for a loan because I'm not supporting no freeloaders."

Evangeline chafed at the injustice of being called a freeloader, knowing full well her mother had been living with Tom for months and hadn't offered a nickel in compensation. Instead of confronting her mother, Evangeline sounded like a whiny, five-year old when she replied, "I'm not freeloading off of anyone."

"Then why are you staying at the cabin rent free? Tell me that, will ya?"

The thought of her brother snitching raised Evangeline's blood pressure, and she quietly fumed. "I'm just taking a little break that's all." She said defensively, "I plan to find a new job when I get home."

"And what are you gonna do for money, Miss Smarty Pants?" her voice now filled with contempt. "It doesn't grow on trees, you know."

She looked out onto the backyard and watched a couple of does gently meander along the tree line, thinking she'd rather be anywhere than on the phone with her mother. "Well...I..."

"I tell ya, it's a sad day when your poor ol' mother has to talk to other family members in order to find out what's going on with their own flesh and blood. And what are you doin' up north?" she barked.

"I...I'm just spending a few days here at the cabin, that's all." Evangeline whined, "I should be home in a week or two."

"You're going to end up just like your Aunt Nora who's living in a trailer park somewhere in California with a dozen housecats."

. The years of resentment had built to such a crescendo there'd be no going back, and Evangeline was quick in her reply. "Knock it off already. I'm just taking a little break, that's all."

"You've been on break all summer! What were you thinking? Good jobs aren't easy to find."

It slipped out before Evangeline even knew it. "Maybe you're the one who needs to get a job."

"Don't you give me any of your lip, young lady." The words were now sharp, like razor blades. "You wanna end up living in some dump with a bunch of tomcats for family, that's your business. But your poor ol' father would have gone right through the roof, knowing his own flesh and blood turned into nothing but a leech."

Just let it pass. She's sick.

"You know, you're forty years old for heaven's sake, and you're acting like a silly teenager. Thought we brought you up better than that. When are you gonna settle down and have a family?" With sobs, she added, "Now that you're forty, it breaks my heart, knowing I won't have grandchildren."

Charlotte immediately came to mind, and it unlocked the floodgates, releasing years of resentment. "You had a granddaughter, but she died! Remember?"

"But let's not forget, born out of...."

24

"That's right. Your daughter is nothing but a cheap fucking whore! Is that what you want to hear?" Her voice was building and interlaced with tears. "It's always about how someone doesn't measure up to your high moral standards because you don't give a tinker's damn about anybody else's hardship other than your own!" With her outburst, the deer in the backyard raised their heads and took off. "The only reason you called was because you needed to dump on someone so you could fuel your own self-righteous indignation. Maybe if you turned off the goddamn TV, you'd have a life."

Evangeline's mother began to cry, and through her sobs, she could hear, "That's right. It's all my fault. I'm a terrible mother."

"Stop it! Your crying is just another way of diverting the attention back towards you. This is what you've done all your life. It's always about you, and you've never been there for me or Tom! If one good thing came out of Charlotte's death, it's that she never had to put up with your bullshit. If you can't be civil and act like a real mother, then don't call me any more!"

CHAPTER THREE

"The earth is not just our environment.
We are the earth and the earth is us.
We have always been one with the earth."
- Thich Nhat Hanh

Indigenous tribes opposed white settlement and sided with the British during the War of 1812, and after their defeat, Ojibwa, Potawatomi, and Ottawa tribesman were forced to turn over their land to the federal government by means of a treaty, setting the stage for massive American expansion. But the rocky peninsula that juts into the icy waters of Lake Superior is most uninhabitable with its harsh winter and short growing season. Early settlers learned this first hand as they began to survey the area with hopes of exploiting the area's natural resources. But craggy shorelines and high cliffs made it difficult for even the hardiest of ships.

Word spread rapidly. A piece of pure copper was found along the banks of the Ontonogon River, so enormous it couldn't be moved until someone hauled it out on rails. The owner hoped to charge admission to see the multi-ton behemoth. But the War Department intervened, and the 'Ontonogon Boulder' was confiscated. Copper wasn't the only mineral of interest. Early explorers also found silver, and when a large specimen made its way to Boston, investors placed pressure on Congress to open the area for mining and development.

But Lake Superior can be fickle. In calm weather, it's a peaceful body of water, but it's just a matter of time before angry, gale-force winds whip across its surface, churning the icy waters into a violent tempest. And it was here, just offshore from Eagle River, where Douglass Houghton and four others were caught in a late autumn storm. Houghton, a medical doctor and professor of chemistry at the University of Michigan, headed the State's Geologic Survey and was out on the lake, leading a group of surveyors. Ten-foot waves capsized their Mackinaw boat, sending five men into the frigid waters. Two oarsmen along with Houghton's beloved cocker-spaniel made it ashore, but there were no signs of the others. When they came across Houghton's body in the spring of 1846, he was partially buried in hard sand. For many, death on the Keweenaw came quickly and without much warning.

* * * * *

Being on the water felt invigorating, the cawing of gulls hovering overhead, the strong breeze that rustled through Evangeline's brown hair, and the tangy scent of fresh lake water.

August was an exceptionally warm month, and the waters of Little Bay de Noc were temperate, but the lake bottom was another matter. At forty feet down, the water was a mere fifty-three degrees, requiring Evangeline to don a purple and gold wetsuit that left little to the imagination. Just before departing, she spoke to Suzanne, letting her know when she planned to arrive back home. It seemed a reasonable thing to do since she was alone, and Lucy's needs had to be considered.

After her first dive, Evangeline showed Suzanne her recent marine photos. She feigned interest, but there was an image of several whitefish that caught her eye with the resolution so clear, their scales sparkled like rhinestones. Being duly impressed, a calendar was suggested whereby Evangeline pondered the possibilities.

Without gainful employment, there was ample time to think about life's larger questions, and after a few days, the routine became familiar. Every morning the train whistle echoed over the lake, and Evangeline welcomed the intrusion as boxcar after boxcar rumbled across the old steel bridge on the other side of the bay. What she liked best was lying in bed at night with the windows open, listening to the leaves rustle and the sound of the wind sweeping through the pines. The cool air drifted over her body, and the scent of lake water and seaweed evoked a distant memory of a time when she vacationed with her family near the town of Wolverine. At night, she kept the drapes open, looking out at the stars and wondering about the nature of creation. It was a time when Evangeline had no demands placed on her whatsoever, and her mind enjoyed freedom like never before.

As the morning sunshine streamed through a bank of open windows, song birds gently woke her with a melody of chirps and whistles. Evangeline lingered, savoring the moment. With Lucy at her side, she whispered, "We're the luckiest folks on earth. You know that doncha?"

But late summer also offered numerous opportunities to spend time on the beach, reflecting upon her life, wondering what would come next. Without a job or lesson plans to prepare, she was free to do as she pleased, varying her routine to meet her needs and whimsy.

Evangeline particularly enjoyed the occasional thunderstorm, and about a week after her arrival, a sudden storm blew in from the west, knocking the power out. Without electricity, there was no water. Desperate, she walked over to Suzanne's only to find the lights on, and her first words were, "You still have power?"

Richard showed her the generator alongside the house and suggested Evangeline buy one if she planned on sticking around. So, it was only a few days later when men arrived with the new equipment. As they removed the cardboard and foam packaging, one of the men said, "You the one who's been skin-diving along the point?"

"How did you know?" Evangeline asked with a noticeable edge.

"Cousin told me. Gave me a description of the gal he'd seen, and it sounded a lot like you." Curious, he tipped his head to one side and squinting. "So, did you find anything interesting?"

"I'm just taking pictures, that's all."

He chuckled, "Well be careful out there. If you find anything out of the ordinary, let somebody know."

* * * * *

It was odd. On one hand, Evangeline was phobic about confined spaces, and yet, there was something liberating about being underwater, no pretenses just oneness with all the aquatic inhabitants. Most fish were curious as to the nature of the leviathan with the purple and gold skin, and she loved capturing on camera their gills moving to and fro. The bubbles from the regulator were the only sound she could hear, outside of a stray outboard engine, and when the former teacher held her breath, the world above, with all its demands, slipped into oblivion.

It was a Sunday evening, and after a long dive earlier that afternoon, Evangeline stretched out on the old davenport and listened to the hypnotic sound of waves lapping the shoreline. As the wind kicked up, it slammed the front door against the dark pine paneling, and Lucy barked. After closing the windows and securing the door, her cell phone sprang to life, and Evangeline winced when she recognized the caller ID.

"Hey sweetheart, howya doin'?"

Her voice was deadpan. "What do you want, Dan?"

"Is that how you greet the love of your life?"

"You're not the love of my life." There was a brief pause until Evangeline said, "Look, we've talked about this. I don't want you calling me anymore. Understand?"

"So, when you comin' home?" His words were now slurred but direct. "Been by your condo, and da neighbors says you quit your fuckin' job and went on vacation. Where you at?"

Evangeline sighed heavily. "It's none of your business where I'm at. I told you before; I don't want you calling here anymore."

Once the fuse was lit, the explosion became inevitable. "Let me tell you something, sweetheart. I'm the best thing that ever happened to ya. You're forty years old and should be damn happy anybody even g…gives a shit."

Her voice elevated as she said, "Have you been drinking?"

"What's it to ya?" he barked.

"Just that you said you were going to quit."

Dan whispered under his breath, "Fucking bitch."

Click.

Evangeline walked into the bedroom, swept back the curtain, and could see the lights coming from the Templeton residence. She grabbed a coat and made her way along the windswept path that separated the two homes, pushing wet branches aside.

She spent the next two hours in front of the fireplace where Evangeline relayed the phone calls she received from her mother and Dan.

As the fire crackled, Suzanne shook her head. "Well, you're not the only one with a screwed-up family." She poured a couple of glasses of red wine into a pair of Flintstone cups and set one in front of Evangeline. "Rich's parents think I'm some sort of gold-digger, and his mother is the worst. Every time we go over there, she rolls her eyes like I don't know what's goin' on. One time, she even suggested Richard file for divorce, and if that weren't bad enough, his mom went down to the

29

courthouse and got the forms. Can you imagine? What unmitigated gall."

A sniffle preceded, "So how do you handle it?"

"I ignore it," Suzanne replied with a slight shrug, "but because of it, we don't see 'em that often. Lemme tell you somethin'. You don't hafta put up with bullshit from anyone, and from what you're sayin', this Dan character needed to be kicked to the curb a long time ago. And as far as your mother is concerned, I'd set some boundaries, and if she can't respect them, then hang up on her. But I wouldn't expect her to change any. Why doncha give it a coupla days, and maybe things will blow over when cooler heads prevail."

* * * * *

The following morning the storms had passed, and tranquil weather meant another dive was in order. The boat Evangeline used was an old rowboat about eight-foot long with a six-horsepower Evinrude motor attached to the rear end, but it served its purpose. And as it churned the water, the engine emitted a haze of white smoke along with a steady staccato rhythm: bup…bup…bup…bup.

When she arrived at the area that produced interesting pictures a few days earlier, she dove into the cold Lake Michigan water. It was only about thirty feet deep, and she quickly grabbed a couple of shots of a Coho salmon. As she was about to swim to another location, she noticed the wake of a speedboat that pulled alongside her vessel. Evangeline had deployed a buoy that spelled out 'DIVER' in large black letters and resisted the urge to surface and give them an earful. After all, their prop was churning the water into a froth, and the former teacher waited until they left. Evangeline used an aluminum ladder to gain access to her boat, and as soon as she boarded, the smell of gasoline was pervasive. In a panic, the diver looked for the source, then spotted the sliced fuel-line.

Evangeline briefly thought about Dan and chastised herself. After all, he hadn't a clue where she was, and furthermore, he didn't own a boat. She quickly checked under the seat and found the cell phone still adhered to the bottom with a piece of duct tape. It was a suggestion Richard had made, and at the time, it seemed reasonable, considering she was alone in a boat with an old motor and might need assistance. Now she realized her predicament, and her first call was to Suzanne.

About twenty minutes later, she could see the rooster-tail from the back of a fast approaching speedboat and began waving both arms frantically. Richard cut the engine, then pulled his craft alongside. As his boat bobbed from stem to stern, he shouted, "Didja get a look at the guys who did this?"

With tear-stained cheeks, she sniffled, "I was underwater when it happened. I…I saw the boat from below, but their prop was on, and I…I was reluctant to surface."

Richard hollered over the din of his outboard, "Now look, this it what we're gonna do. Got Suzanne over at the Coast Guard Station, filing a report, and I'm gonna tow you in."

She noticed the grip of his weapon neatly tucked under his belt and offered a tepid, "OK."

About twenty minutes later, she docked her boat alongside the rickety pier just outside of her brother's cabin, and as Richard tied it off, he said, "Why doncha go change, and we'll head over to the Coast Guard Station. Now tell me again, what exactly happened."

After explaining the day's events, Richard shook his head. "Doesn't make no sense. Why would someone target you? Unless…"

"Unless what?" Evangeline replied with a muffled gasp.

"Unless there's something down there they don't want anyone looking at. Did you see anything out of the ordinary?"

"Not really," she said plaintively, "Just fish and a bunch of rocks. Occasionally, I find an old bottle or a fishing lure, but that's about all."

The Coast Guard promised to check the area but offered little hope in apprehending the culprit. The Templetons also notified the Delta County Sheriff's Department along with the Department of Natural Resources (DNR), and they both echoed the Coast Guard's sentiment. And as the sun began to set, the two women sat in Attwood's kitchen, reflecting on the day's events with Lucy curled up at their feet. As Evangeline caressed her companion's ears, she talked about leaving, but after talking it over with Suzanne, her fears were ameliorated.

"Don't let this one incident ruin your vacation," her neighbor offered. "I'm sure it's nothing to lose sleep over. But if you want to continue diving, maybe Rich can go along and make sure there's no more shenanigans."

Meanwhile, Richard came out of the bathroom with his pants still unbuckled when he walked past a collection of items gathered from the lake bottom. He picked up a rock, sitting neatly along the window sill, and eyed the jagged edges. "What da heck is this?"

Evangeline walked over and stood at his side. "Just a rock I picked up. It was shiny and thought it looked pretty. Kinda cool doncha think?"

He pulled out a pocketknife from his coveralls and scratched the surface, leaving a silver streak. He looked up and said, "You have any idea what you got here?"

* * * * *

Even as a child, Evangeline was beset by night terror, where her screams would waken the entire household. By the time she was nine, it had become routine, and her father would pull out her beloved rag doll, then rock his daughter until the demons passed.

And as Evangeline aged, the nightmares never went away. Instead, she became accustom to her nocturnal cogitations. But the dreams were always thematic, where the weight of some foreign object would be placed upon her chest, making it difficult to breathe. She would also wrestle with imaginary spirits who hovered around her bed, leaving Evangeline with a heavy sense of foreboding. Medication was eventually prescribed, but even pharmaceutical intervention couldn't tame her feral subconscious, resulting in bouts of insomnia. When her body could simply tolerate no more of the tangible world, Evangeline would slip into a deep oblivion. But it rarely lasted.

Tonight, the dreams were just odd, where time wasn't coherent. In one dreamscape, it was dawn, and she stood next to her bed that hadn't been made. And with the blink of an eye, it was late afternoon, and her room was orderly. The sound of a street-sweeper caught Evangeline's attention, luring her outdoors where she used a broom to sweep debris towards the road. At the end of the drive, there was a small crevice, and when she peered into the abyss, Evangeline saw structures buried below as if there were an ancient civilization located in the subterranean darkness. It immediately reminded her of Verona, Italy. There was a walkway in the center of the old city that had been cordoned off. Here, old cobblestones dating back thousands of years had been excavated, exposing its ancient history some ten feet below the current street level. The excavation seemed curious, and at the time, she thought of the thousands of lives that had walked along this passageway, wondering who they were and what had happened to them.

Upon awakening, Evangeline dismissed the dreamscapes as nothing more than a memory of her time in Italy, but the dreams persisted, and the following night she dreamt about Emma, who was standing at a train station in a salmon-colored, car coat. Evangeline innocently asked, "What's it like being dead?"

Emma touched Evangeline on the heart with her fingertips, and she instantly felt an overwhelming sense of a peace. When asked about Roy's passing, the peacefulness she experienced was supplanted by a sharp pain, as if a knife had been thrust into her chest. Clutching her sternum, Evangeline awoke, with Lucy at her side, then looked at the clock. It was 12:24 am.

CHAPTER FOUR

*"There is a power in nature that man has ignored.
And the result has been heartache and pain."*
- Anasazi Foundation

February 14, 1913

The carbide lamp was the only source of illumination, and as it cast its light like a beacon upon the sea, it illuminated the endless walls comprised of brown basalt and rhyolite. The air was heavy with moisture from the various seeps of groundwater, and Mother Earth kept the temperature at a constant seventy degrees. Here, some five-thousand feet below surface, the world above with all its noise and commotion became a distant memory. The underground workings extended for miles in each direction, and outside of an occasional wheel screeching along steel tracks, it was quiet.

Peter was going to work on the fifty-fourth level along with a dozen other men, but today was different. When he arrived for work, he watched them load the body onto a stretcher; the white sheet stained crimson red. "Who is it?" Peter whispered with trepidation.

"Toivo," said Keinomenn, a fellow trammer of Finnish descent; his voice echoing off the rock walls. "Crushed..., but it took an hour to get the rock off of 'im."

Toivo left behind a wife of seven years and three children. Death down under was the great equalizer, targeting its victim without regard to net worth or household obligations.

Peter removed his hat as the body was placed onto a tram which was pushed towards the main shaft. Toivo's remains would later be placed onto a skip, then hauled to the surface. It was the third such death this year, and by now, it was almost routine. He had seen many injuries as well; broken bones were common as were lacerations of every kind. Work at the Ahmeek was dangerous, no doubt. Death could come by a variety of means: rock slides, falls, premature detonations. Sometimes, sudden winds would develop without warning where even the hardiest tamarack stull would succumb. But for the most part, it was dark and quiet.

As he pondered Toivo's demise, his thoughts turned towards his family, Elizabeth, his wife of six years and his beloved daughter, Mary who was now five. She'd be going to school in the fall, and the thought of Toivo's death heightened his awareness, being more cognizant of the dangers of underground mining. But mostly, death came without warning.

Peter's life underground was relegated to pushing an iron cart down a set of steel rails loaded with tons of copper ore; its destination the main shaft which at times could be more than a mile away. Once there, the foreman recorded the delivery in his log-book which was later used to determine Peter's wages. Being a trammer was the lowest of the low, reserved for the illiterate and those who spoke little English. While other miners earned around three dollars a day, a trammer made less, unless the foreman took favor. Peter was one of the lucky few because he would share some of the silver specimens that he occasionally found amongst the heavy loads of copper ore. He had emigrated from Croatia nearly ten years prior with hopes of earning enough to buy a parcel of land where he could farm, but Calumet and Hecla, the corporation that owned the Ahmeek, had other plans and paying high wages to an illiterate work force wasn't in their stockholders' best interest.

But trammers found other ways to supplement their income. Native silver, a lagniappe of sorts, was associated with large masses of copper, and they kept vigil for anything emitting a silvery reflection. One time, when Peter was by himself, he checked his load as he often did, and there amongst a pile of rubble was a mass of pure silver nearly five pounds in weight, tossing it to one side, making note of its location. Later, it would be placed into his lunch pail and sold to a merchant in town who gave store credit. But silver's presence was erratic at best. Weeks would go by without anything being found, but then without warning, a rich seam would be uncovered, and the men lined their pockets and lunch buckets. In a good month, household income could double from the purloined silver, allowing the lowly trammer an opportunity to save for a home. But more than likely, their windfall was spent in town at places like Luigi's or Vairo's Saloon. Peter liked Luigi's with its newly tiled floor because it catered to the immigrant miner. Lately, they would gather to discuss the Western Federation and their attempt to organize labor, but this young Croatian was saving his money and restricted his alcohol consumption to an occasional beer on payday.

Peter wasn't the only one trying to save money. In an attempt to cut expenses, Calumet and Hecla purchased lighter drilling equipment, claiming that it required only one miner to operate, where in the past two men worked collectively. Even though the new drill weighed a mere one hundred-and-fifty pounds, it was still too heavy for one miner to handle, and without an additional person, injuries were inevitable. In the past, a second miner kept an eye out for loose rock which was a constant nemesis, and here in the Ahmeek, several workers had already succumbed to falling material this year alone.

July 23, 1913

As new members of the Western Federation of Miners, workers on the Keweenaw Peninsula voted to strike, demanding better work conditions, shorter hours and higher pay. Management saw it differently and ignored their demands, whereby all mining in the district came to an abrupt halt. Although reluctant, Peter joined the walkout, but if the truth be known, he enjoyed his time underground and adjusting to life on the surface wasn't always pleasant. Recently, he had come home with a bloodied nose, the result of a club to the head from a security guard employed by Calumet and Hecla. Elizabeth bandaged the wound the best she could, but the beating resulted in two black eyes.

Mine management hired Waddell Mahon, a private security force, to protect property from vandalism, and a day didn't go by without a plethora of injuries, including gunshot wounds. Eventually, new workers were brought in to replace those on strike, creating incendiary conditions that resulted in the National Guard being deployed in a feeble attempt to restore order. While the largely immigrant workforce paraded through city streets with their wives and children, no one thought the strike would last, but as summer gave way to fall then winter, the matter became desperate for miners and merchants alike.

The two snaked their way along a serpentine trail where pine boughs snapped at their vehicle with every turn. As they jostled about, Sam Carter called out to his son, "Hang on!"

Travis squealed with delight as he took hold of the hand-grip attached to the door. A low spot in the road was filled with heavy mud, and when the back wheels entered, the pickup came to a dead halt. Tires screamed as the wheels spun, driving them deeper into the quagmire until Sam stuck his head out the window and cursed. He dropped the transmission into four high, and the front wheels took grip, flinging clumps of muddy debris high into the air. As their vehicle lurched onto dry ground, off in the distance they could hear the engine's growl.

The Longyear 44 was grinding away, and a cloud of white diesel fumes belched from the vertical exhaust. With the engine roaring at full throttle, it was a loud place, and one had to speak up in order to be heard. The two drillers had just boxed up a ten-foot section of core and were sitting in lawn chairs eating lunch when the pickup arrived.

Sam managed the drilling operation, and as he approached, his first words were, "How's it goin'?"

Walt, a middle-aged driller who wore a blue set of coveralls, shouted over the din. "We're down about eight hundred feet."

"What do we got?"

The two walked past the mud sump, where the driller flicked his cigarette butt that sizzled upon impact. A few feet further they came upon the stack of wood boxes, and Sam pulled out his hand lens, examining a piece of drill-core. He shook his head and shouted, "Any sulfides?"

The driller pulled open a box and pointed at the three-foot section of mostly pyrite with just a smattering of sphalerite. Sam exhaled audibly, knowing that the drilling would come to a halt fairly soon. Management would pull the plug, and not being a permanent employee, his paychecks would come to end. It was all about results. Drilling was expensive, and when the cost of assaying was included, this drill-hole would run about thirty-five thousand dollars. It was their sixth hole exploring an electromagnetic anomaly, and the results didn't warrant additional follow up. Maybe, after he had a chance to review the assay data, something might be revealed. After all, gold was often associated in these types of settings, and its presence could easily evade visual inspection. But Sam knew it was just a matter of time. Maybe, he'd get a few more weeks of consulting, but then he'd be on his own.

It wasn't like he hadn't been in this situation before, but being the sole caretaker for his son, the hardship was more immediate. With an additional two weeks of wages, he'd have enough to get through the remainder of the year, but if his assignment ended as expected, he'd need to find work elsewhere. Last winter, Sam worked at Walmart, and although it wasn't challenging, it helped pay the bills especially since Travis started seeing a therapist.

Travis had a speech impediment, and his late wife led the charge to make sure the school district provided Travis with adequate support. Sam's wife had died from ovarian cancer the year before, and this was the first summer where Travis accompanied his father into the field.

The middle-aged man with salt and pepper hair grabbed his backpack from the bed of his mud-spattered pickup and called to his son. "Get your canteen, Trav. I have a few things I wanna check."

About a quarter mile away, they found the ledge where Sam dropped his pack, then pulled out a whiskbroom. After brushing aside the dirt and dried leaves, the geologist got on his hands and knees to inspect the various structures. Travis hovered over his father's right shoulder, "Vat you lookin' at, Papa?"

"Just checking out this fracture pattern," Sam looked up and said, "and it's telling me a story."

"A stowwy?"

"You see, these rocks are quite old. They're part of the Penokean Volcanic Terrain."

Travis mimicked his father and got down on all fours, then looked up and stuttered, "Penn…Penn…"

"Say Pe…like pet."

"Pe."

"Now say, no."

His son echoed, "No."

"Ke...like key."

"Key!"

"En."

"En."

"Pe-no-ke-an."

Travis stuttered, "Pe-no-ke-an."

Sam tousled his son's brown hair. "You see, if you're a good detective, you can tell what happened out here. Why doncha hand me that hammer?" Sam broke off a piece of quartz sericite schist, showing it to his son and pointed. "See. These rocks were put down by a volcano."

"V...vol...cay...no!"

"Right," he said with another full grin, "and a long time ago hot water ran through these cracks." He pointed to a fracture in the outcrop and said, "And sometimes if you're lucky, gold and silver can be found in these rocks."

"Gode?"

As he dug through his pack looking for a sample bag, he heard his phone play the lyrics from a favorite song.

...like a child who closes his eyes
to make everything disappear,
My mind watches reruns, inside and alone...

Without looking at the caller ID, he snapped, "Carter."

"Hey Sam. It's me, Rich."

Richard had worked with Sam when he was a college student, and since then, they had remained close friends.

"Hey partner."

"Look, somethin's come up. Can you swing by this evening? Think it'll be worth your time. The neighbor girl found a rock that I thought you should look at. You know, offer a proper opinion."

"I have Travis with me. Hope it's OK to bring him along."

"Of course, why don't you guys come for dinner, and you can meet Evie. She's staying at the cottage just south of us.

Lemme tell ya, you won't be disappointed when you meet her. So, what time can you be here?"

Sam looked at his watch, then nailed a black fly, leaving a spot of blood. "We're about to wrap things up. So, why doncha give me a couple of hours. Can I bring anything? Maybe, a bottle of wine?"

"Just bring your appetite. I'll have Suze set out a couple extra plates."

* * * * *

"Unka Witch!"

"How's my little bean-sprout?" Richard picked Travis up by his arms, and swung him in a pirouette manner, resulting in a bout of squealing. Templeton continued to spin Travis and panted. "Now look... we're not trying to set you up. She's... she's just the neighbor girl... who could use a... a professional opinion, th...that's all. For what it's worth, I...I think she's kinda cute." The engineer put Travis down, then cupped his mouth so the boy couldn't hear. "To tell the truth, I think she's absolutely stunning. She was wearing this Mt. Rushmore t-shirt the other day, and lemme tell ya, Lincoln and Jefferson never looked so good." With eyes wide, Richard inhaled deeply, then wiped his brow.

Sam leaned up against his pickup with Travis in front, as if the boy offered some degree of protection. "Hope you understand. I'm just... not ready for that sort of thing." Sam looked off into the forest and whispered, "I still think about..."

His hand was big as a catcher's mitt, and when Richard placed it upon Sam's shoulder, a sense of protection was conveyed. "Come on. I think dinner is almost ready. Hope you don't mind ribs with macaroni and cheese."

Travis looked up once more and squeaked, "Macawonie 'n cheez?"

"You betcha," answered Richard with a smile as big as the great outdoors. "Come on in."

Upon entering the kitchen, Sam greeted Suzanne with a kiss on the cheek, then took a whiff of dinner cooking in the oven. "Somethin' sure smells good."

Lucy bounded onto the scene and showed little restraint, licking the boy's face, resulting in more bouts of giggling.

"So, you gotta new dog?" Sam asked as he watched the two frolic on the kitchen floor.

"Nah. It's the neighbor's. She ran home for a second and should be here any minute." Richard nudged his guest, then motioned with his hand. "Come on, I wanna show you somethin'."

The two stood before the fireplace mantel, examining the grey rock Evangeline had collected days earlier, and as Sam held a loop to his eye, he said, "Whereja find it?"

"Evie found it while she was diving off the point just west of here. Scratched it with a knife, and it's pretty soft."

The geologist pulled out his pocketknife and scraped an edge, exposing a mirror-like sheen. He looked up and said, "You got an old toothbrush?"

Richard returned from the bathroom with one in hand, and after a few moments of scrubbing, a corner glistened. "Is it what I think it is?" Richard asked, hoping for a favorable assessment.

A nod was followed by, "Mighty impressive."

"Where do you think it came from?"

"The Keweenaw," Sam replied confidently. "See this?" He held the specimen up to the light and pointed to a small reddish spot. "That's native copper, and the only place you can find this type of assemblage is in the Portage Lake Volcanic Series."

"Hmm. So, did the glaciers bring it down?"

"Nah. Too angular to be glacially transported. Had to of been mined."

There was a rap at the backdoor, and Suzanne hollered, "Come on in. Door's open!"

Suzanne stood next to Evangeline and said, "Sam, I'd like you to meet our neighbor, Evie. Evie, this is our friend, Sam."

He extended his hand and provided a solid handshake. "Nice to meet you ma'am."

She stuttered, "M…my pleasure."

After the introductions, Richard tried to tame his cowlick with saliva and updated Evangeline about her rock. As their guests hovered over the specimen like proud parents, Evangeline was conscious of her close proximity to Sam, and his cologne evoked a distant memory. In an instant, she recalled the dream she had where she explored a structure deep within a crevice out by the road. She really didn't understand why that memory surfaced, but managed a civil question, covering her vulnerability. "You really think its silver? I…I mean…what do you think it's worth?"

"Not sure," Sam answered curtly. "We'd have to weigh it, and I don't have a scale."

Suzanne was adding some grated cheese to her dish and called out, "I got one up here." Plates clattered as she pulled out the scale from a cupboard above the sink, and the five assembled about the kitchen counter with Travis holding onto Lucy.

"A little over seven pounds," Suzanne reported, donning a pair of green reading glasses.

"That would be just about one-hundred troy ounces, and its scrap value alone would be around seventeen hundred dollars. But as a specimen," Sam rubbed his neck, then proffered, "it could fetch, I dunno, maybe, three or four times that amount."

"What da hell…"

Suzanne immediately cleared her throat, then pressed her lips tight, casting a stern expression as she looked at her husband, then Travis.

Richard corrected himself and whispered, "What da heck is a piece of silver doing in our bay? It sure didn't get there all by itself."

Evangeline interrupted with, "Where do you think it came from?"

The geologist discreetly checked his zipper with a pinky finger and said, "Copper Country. With such sharp edges, it had to of been mined."

A gust of wind rustled the leaves about the backdoor, and Lucy growled at the intrusion. As Evangeline took hold of her collar, she said "Maybe, I should go back and examine that lake bottom more closely."

"Look," Richard pointed out with clear consternation, "I don't think it's a good idea you being out there all by yourself. Whoever cut your fuel-line was sending a pretty strong message."

"Someone cut your fuel-line?" Sam inquired with flared nostrils.

After Richard took a seat next to his wife, he explained what had happened, then passed a steaming bowl of macaroni and cheese.

"I wasn't aware the Keweenaw produced silver," Suzanne said as she plopped a dollop of macaroni onto her plate, then passed it along. "I thought it was just copper."

Sam grabbed a couple of ribs from the platter and licked his fingers after depositing one onto his son's plate "Actually, there was quite a bit of silver produced in the general area. It's thought the copper deposit acted as a large galvanic cell whereby the silver naturally electroplated itself."

Lucy was sitting patiently next to Travis, watching the bowls being passed until the boy slipped him a pinch of macaroni and cheese. Sam nudged his son and whispered, "Don't go feeding the dog. She might get sick."

"That's alright," said Evangeline approvingly.

"Just didn't want Lucy upchucking all over your kitchen floor later tonight."

Travis looked up and said, "It otay, Papa?"

"It's OK. Just don't give her any more." Sam wiped the orange-colored cheese from his son's mouth with a paper napkin, then calmly resumed his discourse. "Most of the silver came from the upper levels, and at the Ahmeek, it was so plentiful owners initially thought their property was a silver mine, but as they went deeper, production tanked. With industrialization, mass-mining techniques were employed, and silver production waned even further. But back in the early days when everything was mined by hand, workers are said to have packed their lunch pails with silver nuggets when they were lucky enough to find it. Who knows how much was actually

43

pilfered from those mines, but it probably was substantial. I even have a couple half-breeds back home, but nothing like what you have here."

"Half-breeds?" asked Evangeline, thinking Sam's choice of words were a slur of some kind.

"That's what they call a rock that has both native copper and native silver. Doesn't make much sense though," Sam shrugged. "Why would something like that be found here at the bottom of Little Bay de Noc? We have to be a good two-hundred miles from where this thing was deposited."

Satisfied with Sam's explanation, Evangeline casually wrapped a spiral of hair around an index finger and said, "So, what you're saying is that there's no natural reason for the rock being there?"

A nod proceeded, "That would be correct, ma'am. Hard to envision that somebody would have lost it. Maybe a ship sank nearby, but anything is possible."

After their guests departed, Suzanne approached Evangeline who was drying the last of the evening dishes and leaned up against the Formica countertop. "So, whatcha think?"

A plate squeaked as she ran the towel around the rim just before she looked up and said, "About what?"

Suzanne's words took flight as if they were lyrics to a song. "You know.... he's single."

"So, where's Travis's mom? Are they divorced?"

Suzanne placed a platter in the cupboard above the sink and said, "No, she passed on a few years ago. Lori had ovarian cancer, and it was pretty tough for Travis. The poor kid cried for months."

Evangeline lowered her head. "Geeze. What a sad story. I'm sorry for their loss."

"So, you at all interested?"

"Oh, I don't know. He's nice and all," she said with a long exhalation. "But I don't think I'm really ready for a relationship right now. B...besides, he seems to be pretty absorbed with his son and career." She finished the last of the silverware, then neatly folded the dishtowel upon the kitchen counter. "I appreciate your concern, but it's probably best if we kept our distance. Besides, I'll be heading home soon, and long-distance relationships rarely work."

As the garbage disposal growled, Suzanne hollered, "Just thought that while you were up here, it might be nice having someone to hang out with. I bet you're getting tired of having us two old farts being your only source of entertainment."

Shortly thereafter, Evangeline retired for the night, and dreams quickly rolled in, like an early morning freight train from across the bay. She suddenly found herself in a locked cellar, and in the dim light, she could see Sam's eyes. There was a woman there as well, and in seconds, she could feel the terror descend. Evangeline watched the scene unfold as Sam and the woman bound her in chains and forced her to walk in circles with a wooden yoke around her neck, slapping her periodically along the side of the head. The dreamscape was suddenly supplanted by a new vision, and the same woman was now lurching towards Evangeline. In the darkness, she scooted across the floor in an attempt to protect herself and lashed out with a knife she pulled from a pocket, injuring her assailant. Evangeline noticed the trickle of blood, and just as the woman was close enough to identify, she bolted upright, gasping for air. "What the hell!" she blurted with her hands to her throat.

CHAPTER FIVE

"Foreign Agitators Must Be Driven
From the District at Once."
- Daily Mining Gazette

"Nothing but complete annihilation
of the Western Federation
in this camp will satisfy us."
- James McNaughton
President of Calumet and Hecla Mining Company

August 14, 1913

Two men were walking along a path that crossed mine property near the town of Seeberville when they were confronted by a recently deputized security force. The two miners retreated to the boarding house they lived in, and when security caught up with one of them, a fight ensued. Someone tossed a bowling pin out the upstairs window, missing its target by a few inches. The security men, hired by the Houghton County Board of Supervisors, surrounded the building, then began firing into the structure through windows and doors, filling the home with gunsmoke so thick people inside couldn't see. The shooting didn't stop until the deputies ran out of ammunition. In the end, two were dead along with two others who were injured, including a baby.

Anthony Lucas, the prosecutor for Houghton County, obtained an indictment and subsequent conviction of those responsible. The security agency that employed these men submitted an invoice to their employer for over nineteen thousand dollars which included thirteen hundred dollars for guns and ammunition, some of it being used to perforate the Seeberville boarding house. The Houghton County Board of Supervisors paid the bill without question.

September 2, 1913

Nearly two hundred people, including women and children, took to the streets in protest of management's unwillingness to negotiate. When they reached one of the mines on the outskirts of town, they were turned back by the Michigan National Guard, and upon re-entering the city, they were met by fifteen recently deputized men. A confrontation ensued where insults were traded whereby the deputies pulled their weapons and began firing indiscriminately until their ammunition was spent. Realizing their guns were empty, the crowd charged, flinging rocks and bottles down upon them, but out on the street, a fourteen-year old girl lay, shot in the head by an unknown deputy.

December 6, 1913

There was no warning. The windows in the boarding house simply exploded as volley after volley splintered walls and window casements. It was two in the morning, and the Cornish mineworkers dove for cover. Three were killed, including Harry Jane and his nephew Arthur. Their murders ignited fury across the peninsula, especially after the shooting of two miners in Seeberville earlier that year.

Anthony Lucas, who successfully prosecuted six men for the murders near Seeberville, believed the killings in Painesdale were carried out by either local deputies or men employed by Waddell Mahon, a group of thugs hired by the Houghton County Board of Supervisors whose sole function was to break the back of organized labor. A grand jury was comprised of twenty men who heard testimony regarding the murders, but all its members owed their livelihoods to various mining companies, including James McNaughton's personal chauffeur. No indictments were issued, creating incendiary conditions upon the range.

* * * * *

A cold September rain descended upon the peninsula where Evangeline spent her day on the davenport with Lucy at her side. Whitecaps were seen out on the bay, and a steady chop of waves lapped onto the shore, depositing a fresh coat of sand and seaweed. As a flock of Canadian geese traversed the bay, the lonesome sound of a train whistle rolled over the landscape. Maple trees were shedding their leaves, and with every gust, a swirling vortex of crimson and yellow filled the air. Meanwhile, a steady pit-a-pat of raindrops pelted the front window, and a bluster of wind caused a branch from a nearby tamarack to scrape along the side of the cottage, sending a shiver down Evangeline's spine. As she added another log to the fireplace, Lucy barked, and a few seconds later, there was a rap at the backdoor. There, Suzanne stood in the cold steady rain, holding an umbrella, and Evangeline's spirits lifted.

The two sat at the kitchen table and shared a pot of herbal tea as they discussed Evangeline's dream from the night before. And when she described the attack, Suzanne furrowed her brow. "So, you were attacking yourself?"

"I think so. Please," she begged as if the disclosure caused discomfort, "don't say anything. Your husband already thinks I'm off my rocker."

Lucy barked once again, and Evangeline went to the backdoor only to see a pair of does dart along the tree line, then returned to the kitchen table. The time passed effortlessly until Suzanne spied the books on the living room sofa. "Whatcha reading?" she asked innocently.

At first, she thought about evading the question or possibly lying, but she had enough lies in her life and curtly replied, "They're journals I found back home."

As Evangeline explained how she acquired them, Suzanne thumbed through a few pages until she found the Western Union telegram. She read about Roy's death and sniffled, "Geeze, what a sad story. I wonder how Emma managed."

Evangeline thought about Charlotte. But bringing up the subject would require reliving that awful day, and she couldn't muster the fortitude to discuss the matter. Instead, she walked into the bedroom and emerged with a handful of letters.

"What's this?"

Evangeline deposited Roy's letters onto the table, and they scattered about. Suzanne pulled out a letter that was water stained and written crudely in pencil. She donned a pair of reading glasses, then gulped noticeably.

March 23rd, 1945
In the Philippines

My Dearest Emma,

A day doesn't go by without me thinking of you. If I was some kind of wizard, I'd pack myself into this mere envelope and make my way to your door. But alas, I am just your beloved Roy, and my thoughts and prayers will be all I can send. You know, the day we met I never told you, but just as I was about to leave the drugstore, I heard someone whisper, "Go ask her." I looked around, and there was no one there but you and the kid behind the counter. So, I did as I was told and am so grateful I found the courage to ask you to walk with me. I miss you so very much, my love. Be of good cheer and know that you are truly loved. I await the day when I can once again hold you in my arms. My love to you always.

Your loving husband,

Roy

Suzanne dabbed her nose with a tissue and sniffled. "Nobody writes stuff like that anymore."

"Tell me about it."

The steady rain continued to pelt the windows, and with a staccato-like rhythm, it provided a melody all its own.

"Where didja say you got these letters?" Suzanne asked.

A swig of tea was followed by, "Back home. In a cedar chest I bought at an auction."

"I dunno about you," Suzanne emitted a plaintive sigh, "but I could use something a little stronger than just tea." Suzanne swiveled her head in hopes of finding a liquor cabinet. She cuffed her mouth with the back of her hand and whispered, "Got any booze in the house?"

"Sorry."

She waved her hand with a come-hither gesture. "Well, come on, I think I got a bottle of something stuffed in my pantry, and after reading that letter, I could use a belt. Why doncha bring those journals along, and we can read 'em to one another."

The two women spent the remainder of the afternoon going over Roy's letters until they heard the truck pull up next to the back entrance. Richard walked in with an armload of groceries and noticed the fresh tear stains on his wife's face. "Ah, geeze."

Evangeline flicked a tear with her finger and said, "Well, I should be going."

Later that evening, the former teacher pulled out a notebook and penned a few lines while sitting at her kitchen table.

Dear Roy,

Even though we've never met, know that your words have had an impact on my life. As I understand, your body was never returned to your beloved, Emma. Know this: I cherish your letters as if they were written just for me. They are simply lovely.

Thank you.

Evangeline Attwood

As she held one of Roy's letters, the idea came to her.

* * * * *

The following week Evangeline refrained from diving due to rough weather and took day-trips to various tourist attractions. She visited Tahquamenon Falls, then drove to Pictured Rocks and took the boat tour that lasted for about three hours. The following day she packed her bag and headed towards Marquette, then drove west to Negaunee where she visited several antique stores. With Lucy at her side, Evangeline travelled another one hundred miles to Laurium where Roy once lived, hoping against all odds some distant relatives still resided at the address found in one of his letters.

When the red Honda pulled in front of the old two-story, she took a couple of pictures with her phone just as a silver-haired woman approached with a small terrier, no bigger than a bread-box. The dog danced about on his hind legs as he got a whiff of Lucy. Instinctively, the old woman pulled back on the leash. "Charlie, stop that!" Evangeline bent down and offered a caress just as the woman said, "Sorry, he just loves people."

The former teacher pulled a dog biscuit from her pocket, and the terrier devoured it readily. Meanwhile, a few feet away, Lucy had her head stuck out the passenger window and barked incessantly, resulting in a biscuit bribe.

"Just so you know, there've been a couple of pit-bulls running loose, and they killed a little dog named Chester just the other day. That's why I carry this." The old woman produced a chrome-plated revolver, then stuffed it back into her handbag. "Nobody is going to mess with my little Charlie."

After introducing herself, the two chatted until Evangeline asked about interesting places to visit. Bertha pointed west and said, "You could check out the Visitor Center that the Park Service operates, and then there's the museum. You go right past it when you enter town. They put up a few new exhibits I hear, and it's supposed to be quite nice. Local woman up in Allouez did an exhibit on Big Annie."

"Big Annie?" Evangeline replied with a squint.

"She was one of the strike organizers back in '13."

After receiving a history lesson, Evangeline raised an eyebrow. "By any chance, did you know the Kincaid family who lived here?" She pointed to the old house as if her finger was a weather vane. "I was wondering if they still lived in the area."

"Oh, let me think." Bertha stroked her wizened chin as she pondered the request. "If I recall correctly, they haven't lived here for a long time, but I remember 'em. Are you related?"

Evangeline explained the letters she had, but an approaching thunderstorm cut short their visit. As she opened the door to her vehicle, Bertha shouted from the steps of an old home made of red brick. "I think there's a few family members that live over on Pine Street in Calumet. Their name is Keillor, and they might like to know about your letters."

"Thanks!" Evangeline shouted. As she secured her seatbelt, the first drops splattered across the windshield. In seconds, the skies churned with black storm clouds, and the deluge began soon thereafter. So, she waited on the side of the road, and when a strong thunderclap rattled the car's interior, Evangeline pulled

Lucy close, wondering if her excursion to Copper Country was misguided.

It only took about twenty minutes before the storm passed, and upon entering Calumet, Evangeline noticed the elegant stone buildings that once housed the corporate offices of Calumet and Hecla, the primary mining company for the area, now occupied by the Park Service. She also noticed the green slab of float copper, propped up on its side along US-41, a testimonial to better times when the mineral wealth of the area fueled the local economy. But not unlike the thunderstorm that moved on, so too came the end of mining, leaving behind an array of derelict buildings, rock piles and smokestacks. It intrigued her nonetheless, and as Evangeline drove, it felt as if she were being pulled further into the town, like a piece of iron responding to a magnetic influence.

Driving down Sixth Street, she noticed the empty sidewalks and abundant old buildings now in various stages of decay. It took effort to imagine how the town looked during its prime, but what she found most interesting was the inordinate number of churches now shuttered, looking forlorn like the homeless standing in line outside a shelter during a cold winter's day.

Evangeline took the loop through town, returning to the Visitor Center on Fifth Street where she spent about an hour exploring the refurbished building that once housed the Red Jacket Union Hall. There were pictures of Calumet that dated back to the early 1900s along with several mineral displays, including a half-breed. But it paled in comparison to the one she discovered in Little Bay de Noc. Upstairs, there was an exhibit on everyday life around 1910, and she felt a certain connection with a photo of a family standing in front of a general store. The parents and children looked happy together, bringing a smile to the former school teacher, but the photograph also left a sense of emptiness as she pondered her own life now void of the one person she loved unconditionally. By now, she had become accustomed to the anguish and stuffed it away like so many other things.

Afterwards, Evangeline parked her car along the shoulder, and the two ambled along Pine Street just outside of town, kicking stones. The storm that raked the area had passed, leaving behind a distinctive mustiness, and as they walked along the roadside, the sunlight caught the facets of a few stones that glittered not unlike the scales of the various whitefish she photographed days earlier. A glint of green caught her eye, and Evangeline pulled the colorful rock from its muddy confines. Using a finger to wipe away the mud, she felt the sharp edges. It was a piece of vesiculated basalt, infused with native copper, and the former teacher rinsed it in a nearby puddle. Once clean, she held it to the light, trying to imagine its history, then tucked it away into her backpack.

It started slowly, and at first, she thought it was nothing more than a daydream. But as they walked along the blacktop, an image began to crystallize. It was a funeral procession where a steady stream of caskets filled the snow-covered roadway, some were being carried by pallbearers while others were placed in wagons. She could hear the steady clip-clop of horses along with a man calling a girl's name as he followed behind one of the white caskets loaded on the back of a horse-drawn carriage. Evangeline dismissed the vision as nothing more than an overly active imagination, but it left an indelible impression.

"What the heck was that all about?" Evangeline whispered to herself as she buckled the seatbelt. She turned towards Lucy and said, "I don't know about you, but I could use something to drink. Do you mind if we stop?"

She pulled in front of a red neon sign that spelled out, 'Luigi's' in cursive letters and found a seat at the bar. It was a saloon built in the late 1800s with a floor done with thousands of colorful pieces of tile. The bartender came over and set out a paper napkin with the PBR logo emblazoned on front. "What can I getcha?"

"A Grey Goose martini with a twist," she said smartly.

He furrowed his brow and said, "Look lady, all we got is bourbon, some cheap gin, and draft beer."

She inhaled abruptly, then sat erect. "I'll take a PBR."

The bartender pulled the lever, and the amber fluid trickled into the glass schooner like a river of gold. "It's a new keg, and it's kinda foamy," he warned. "So, when you're ready, I'll getcha a free refill."

"Thanks." She took a long draw, then whisked the foam from her lips with a paper napkin. "I'm from out of town and was wondering if you knew of any interesting places to visit?"

"Well lemme see." With a creased brow, the bartender stared at the tin ceiling. "Well, there's the Vertin Gallery which is the big building downtown. Use to be a department store, but the current owner made it into an art gallery and antique shop." He pointed in the general direction. "It's over on Sixth Street. Just hang a left as you leave, then turn right at the first street. It'll take you right there. A real nice lady, by the name of Mary Sue, runs the place."

Evangeline took another sip of beer. "Anything else?"

The bartender gazed up at the ceiling once more. "Well, you could check out the Quincy Mine. They run underground tours, and I understand they're pretty interesting, but it runs about twenty bucks."

With a slip of paper in front of her, she clicked a ballpoint open. "And where would that be?"

"If you came in on US-41, you went right past it. It's the tall grey structure that overlooks Houghton. It's just before the hill that takes you down into Hancock. It's only about a ten-minute drive from here."

As Evangeline reflected upon the day's events, it felt as if she was being pulled into a distant memory, and Evangeline thought about all the men who drank at this tavern ages ago. As she sat there contemplating the notion, a new vision unfolded and suddenly blurted, "I love you." Where that came from she had no idea, but the bartender looked up from his newspaper and said, "Pardon me?"

With a reddened face, Evangeline apologized. "Sorry, I was just daydreaming."

After quenching her thirst, Evangeline strolled about town, and for a lack of a better explanation, it simply felt like home. People would stop and pet Lucy, and inevitably, a conversation ensued. So, it took nearly an hour to make her way to the Vertin Gallery where she tied the yellow lab to a parking meter.

Evangeline slipped her another biscuit and said, "Now you stay put. I'll be just a minute. When I get back, we'll see if we can find a motel and head home tomorrow."

* * * * *

Back at Garth Point, warm weather had settled in. It was a bright fall afternoon, where the three cruised to the mouth of Little Bay de Noc in a pontoon boat. With both engines roaring at top speed, Richard hollered, "Where do you want me to stop?"

Evangeline shielded her eyes with her left hand and scanned the shoreline. "Cut the engine!" she called out. When the twin Mercury engines fell silent, the boat bobbed from side to side, forcing Evangeline to take hold of the guard rail. "This looks about right," she said as a pair of gulls cawed from overhead. "But I'm not absolutely certain. I'll have to go down and see if it looks familiar."

Evangeline stripped down to a two piece, and as she donned her wetsuit, Richard's eyes darted back and forth between his lithe neighbor and his wife who was sitting at the back of the boat with mustard on her chin. Seconds later, Evangeline fell backwards into the water, creating a splash that sent water droplets upon Richard's t-shirt. He casually racked a few cartridges into his Winchester and took a seat in back with his wife. Suzanne hung her head over the side, searching for air bubbles and muttered, "I sure hope she knows what she's doin', because I'm not a very good swimmer."

Meanwhile, Richard used a pair of binoculars to search the shoreline, looking for anything out of the ordinary.

Suzanne's neighbor surfaced about twenty minutes later, pulled out her respirator, and gasped. "You're not going to believe what's down here!"

* * * * *

The drill core was stacked into a pile of wood boxes, standing about six feet tall. There was nearly four-thousand feet

55

that needed to be split before it could be assayed, and if all went according to plan, Sam Carter would be done in a few weeks. But after that, finances would become problematic. Teaching at Bay College was a possibility, but that wouldn't be until January, and with Christmas looming, the geologist wondered if he'd have sufficient resources to cover all his holiday expenses. As he watched his son take shots with a basketball at a hoop hung over the garage door, the memory unfolded.

They were at Shopko looking at toys when Lori said, "Well, what do you think about a basketball?"

"Oh, I don't know. He's still pretty young for shooting baskets, don't you think? How about a train set? I had one when I was his age, and it was the best gift ever."

"But Travis needs to get some exercise," Lori complained. "I just don't want him to end up being a sofa spud."

"Well, why don't we get both? I think we can afford it. This way he'll have something to do when the weather turns bad."

She nudged her husband, then whispered into his ear, cupping it with her right hand. "That's how he was conceived. Don't you remember?" Lori placed an arm inside of Sam's elbow and rested her head upon his shoulder.

When the phone vibrated in Sam's pocket, it pulled him back from his trip down memory lane, and upon pressing the talk symbol, he was greeted with, "Well hey there, stranger."

"Rich...what's goin' on? Haven't heard from you in awhile."

The reception was filled with static, and Templeton had to speak up. "Look, I'm out on the bay with Evie, and she found something while diving. You around?"

Sam looked at the Shinola watch his late wife had given him for their eighth wedding anniversary and replied, "Sure. I could use a break. What did she find?"

"I'll save it 'til you get here. The girls are making Mexican tonight. Thought you and Trav might like a home-cooked meal. Why don't you guys come on out?"

"Want me to bring something? Maybe a cheesecake or a tin of cookies?"

"Nah. Just bring your appetites. The girls got enough food to feed an army."

About an hour later, the usual cloud of dust accompanied the vehicle as it roared towards Templeton's lakeside residence, and when the truck doors slammed, the occupants were greeted by a yellow lab who danced about on her back legs. Travis wrapped his arms around Lucy's neck and kept saying over and over, "I love you, Lu-tee." The mutt replied with sloppy kisses, and the boy dropped to the ground giggling with the dog on top.

Richard walked out wearing a snug Harley Davidson t-shirt with a diet soda in hand, emitting a warm grin. "How's the trip over?"

"Not bad." Sam whisked his fingers through his graying hair, then repositioned his ball cap. "There's some construction on US-2 just east of Esky, but other than that, it was pretty normal."

"Well, come on in. Can I get you somethin' to drink?"

The two entered through the kitchen where Suzanne greeted their guest with a kiss on the cheek. "Hope you're hungry," was all she said.

"What did you guys make tonight?"

"Enchiladas with refried beans. This was Evie's idea. I'm just assisting."

Sam turned toward Evangeline and nodded. "Nice to see you again, ma'am."

"Mr. Carter."

He detected the scent of perfume, and for an instant, a distant memory surfaced. At first, he thought of his late wife but realized she rarely wore perfume, leaving Sam puzzled. "By the way, my neighbor did some diving down in the Caribbean a few years back and has an underwater metal detector. Maybe we could go take a look sometime."

Evangeline squinted, "You dive?"

"Dove a bit back in college, but it's been awhile."

The dream where she was placed into a yoke came to mind, and with that vision, Evangeline inhaled abruptly. "I hope you have your own gear because you're going to need a wetsuit. The bay is pretty cold once you get under the thermo-layer."

"Ah." Her reply evoked another distant memory, and Carter wondered if they had ever met before. "Didn't think about that.

But you can still use the metal detector if you like." Sam took a sip of the diet soda Richard had provided, and then grabbed a handful of chips. "You mentioned you guys found something while diving." The geologist looked over his sunglasses with eyebrows arched. "Didja find more silver?"

"I wish." Evangeline sighed. "Instead, we found a large net that was nicely hidden. So, you couldn't easily see it from the surface. Thing must have run several hundred feet in length and twenty feet tall. We contacted the DNR and gave them the GPS coordinates."

"Said they were coming right out," Richard interjected. "Thought best not to disturb anything just in case they were legally deployed, but we didn't find any tags or marker buoys. This is the exact kinda bullshit that depletes our fish stocks, and folks wonder why the fish aren't biting. Damn commercial fishermen. I'm sure that's why they cut Evie's fuel line."

After the evening meal, the three adults took refuge about the stone fireplace while Lucy and Travis played with a basketball along the drive. Evangeline turned towards Sam and said, "Rich was telling me the story about the Confederate gold that was shipwrecked out here. Do you think that might be the source of my silver specimen?"

As an ore boat passed out on the bay, its claxon boomed over the water, and Suzanne craned her neck to catch a glimpse. Sam looked too and answered, "The Confederacy had no access to the copper mines up north. So, I can't see how something like that would make its way into their hands." Sam looked at Richard and squinted. "By the way, you didn't give the DNR your name, I hope? You know, it's rumored that a couple of conservation officers are on the take, and folks around here don't take kindly to anybody messin' with their source of income."

Richard asked his wife, "You didn't give 'em your name didja?

58

CHAPTER SIX

"Just as a snake sheds its skin, we must shed our past
Over and over again."
- Buddha

December 21st, 1913

The calendar said winter had arrived, yet the ground was still free of snow. It was just a matter of time. Folks in Red Jacket talked about winter with anticipation, but with the onset of arctic winds and blizzard conditions, the anticipation readily turned into disdain. And so it was with Old Man Winter. The first snow was a God-send as it would cover the scars of the land with a blanket of white, making the rock piles and smokestacks less ominous...less nefarious. But the wounds of the land never went away, like all things.

* * * * *

That evening her dreams formed quickly. Evangeline felt spirits hovering over her bed like dervishes and left an indelible impression of foreboding. While asleep, she had ripped off all the covers, leaving her atop of the sheets with Lucy at her side along with a couple of large pillows that were damp with sweat. A trip to the bathroom was followed by a snack where the light from the refrigerator was the only source of illumination, casting shadows long. Evangeline ate a couple of slices of cheese and slipped her canine companion a reward, then managed to fall back to sleep for a few hours until Lucy barked. In a sleep induced stupor, Evangeline rolled over and yelled, "Lucy, be quiet!" But the yellow lab persisted until she pulled back the shade.

"Christ Almighty!"

Evangeline ran out the backdoor with her pajamas flailing. The entire side of Suzanne's house was on fire, thwarting her efforts to enter the building. While the smoke and flames licked the eaves, Evangeline shouted, "Suzanne! Richard! You gotta get out!" She banged on the bedroom window to no avail, then ran to the front door with Lucy at her side only to find it locked from within. She picked up a rock from the walkway and smashed the window, then reached through the broken glass to turn the knob, cutting her forearm in the process.

Evangeline took a deep breath, dashed inside, and emerged seconds later with Suzanne draped over her shoulder. The two fell onto the grass outside the front door; both coughing and gasping for air as flames twenty feet tall, now engulfed the kitchen and back porch.

"Where's Richard!" Evangeline shouted.

Coughs were followed by, "Mil...Milwaukee!"

Suzanne rose from the ground still coughing, then re-entered the home as Evangeline screamed in protest only to re-emerge a few seconds later with a drawer filled with papers and photo albums.

"Call 9-1-1!" Suzanne coughed, her lungs tainted with acrid smoke. As Evangeline disappeared into the forest, Suzanne moved quickly. First, she moved her car away from the fire, then made a beeline to the gasoline-driven pump set up along the side of the house that fed lake water to various sprinklers. With a pull of the cord, the engine rumbled, sending gallons of water to a garden hose where she began her meager efforts to extinguish the blaze.

The volunteer fire department arrived about forty minutes later, but by then, the house was mostly consumed, except for the guest bedroom. Billows of steam and smoke rose towards the heavens as red lights pulsated from a variety of emergency vehicles that now dotted the property. Using their large hoses, firemen extinguished the few remaining embers, resulting in a wave of smoke and steam.

The property remained astir with activity as a radio squawked in the background. Meanwhile, Evangeline and Suzanne were wrapped in blankets and sat on a picnic table that overlooked the backyard. They shared an oxygen mask from a bottle the fire department provided, and both were smudged with soot and grass stains when an EMT approached with a first-aid kit. "Let's take a look at that arm of yours."

Evangeline rolled up her sleeve, exposing the gash that was still oozing blood.

With Lucy keeping a close watch, the EMT taped down the white gauze. "I think you're gonna need a few stitches. We'll take you over to OSF and getcha checked out."

She turned towards Suzanne and said, "Could you follow in my car? The keys are in the ignition but put Lucy inside before you go. The door's open."

About an hour later, Suzanne entered the cubicle where Evangeline grimaced as the physician pulled the last of the black thread through her skin. After examining his work, he trimmed the ends, emitting a satisfied expression. "Do you know when you had your last tetanus shot?"

"I'm not sure," she replied absentmindedly.

The young African-American doctor pulled out a syringe, and a whiff of alcohol was followed by a wince.

As they waited to be released, Richard pulled back the white curtain, and his first words were, "What da hell is goin' on here?"

Suzanne embedded herself into her husband's chest and sobbed, "It's all gone."

"What do you mean... it's all gone?" his words, sharp with anger.

Suzanne had used the fire department's cell phone, and all she could do was leave an incoherent message. Her husband had no means of calling his wife as her phone was lost during the fire. So, he called the sheriff's office and was informed that Suzanne and Evangeline were at the hospital in Escanaba.

"There's nothing left. It's all burned up," she cried. "If it hadn't been for Evie, I wouldn't have made it out alive."

An officer with the Delta County Sheriff's Department called out, "You decent in there?"

Richard swept back the curtain, and the deputy sheriff approached. "Ms. Templeton?"

Suzanne buttoned the top of her pajamas and replied with a tepid, "Yes?"

Richard extended his hand and said, "I'm her husband."

The officer removed his hat, whisking his crew-cut with a calloused hand. "Just so you know, we've asked the Michigan State Police to investigate. You see, there was a pervasive smell of gasoline around your home, and we can't rule out the possibility the fire was arson."

* * * * *

The following day the Templetons moved into Attwood's guest house that was located towards the back of the property. It wasn't much, just a bedroom with a bath, a small kitchen, and a space heater. Evangeline's brother built it years ago in order to provide a reprieve from his mother who visited regularly. Although it was small, it did allow the Templetons to be close to their property, as it took days to sift through the rubble. Some clothing and personal effects were recovered from the guest bedroom that survived, but for the most part, the house was a total loss. The insurance adjuster informed them that since arson was suspected, there would be no cash settlement. Instead, they'd only cover the cost of rebuilding.

When the plans for the new structure were finally approved, Evangeline spent the afternoon preparing a special dinner. Noticing there was more food than three people could possibly consume, an invitation was extended to Sam Carter and his son.

It was a few hours later when Travis ran from his father's pickup with arms opened wide. As the yellow lab raced towards the boy, Travis dropped to his knees and was rewarded with a couple of licks across the kisser.

Evangeline stood a few feet away, and when Sam Carter approached, he extended his hand. "Nice to see you again, ma'am. Thanks for the dinner invitation." A solid handshake was followed by, "I'm afraid Trav is getting a bit tired of my cooking." He looked towards the north and saw the charred pine trees just as Richard walked out of the back entrance. The air was still heavy with the scent of creosote when Sam turned and said, "Must have been quite the blaze. You OK?"

"I'm fine. Was in Milwaukee at the time, but hadn't it been for this one here," he used his thumb to point towards Evangeline, "I dunno if da wife would have made it out. Come on, let's go take a walk. I'll show you what's left."

Sam turned to his son and said, "I'll be right next door. Stay here with Lucy and don't wander off."

Travis wasn't listening. Instead, he was engaged in a game of fetch where Lucy would retrieve the slime-covered stick but wouldn't release it, resulting in a tug-of-war.

"Sorry to hear about what happened. The deputy I talked to says it was arson." As the two men surveyed the damaged, Sam turned and said, "So, who do you think did it?"

Richard glared.

"So, you're thinkin' it was the guys who owned that net? I knew it was a bad idea giving the DNR your name."

The engineer kicked a piece of charred lumber towards an area that once occupied his back porch. "No good sons of bitches." He wiped his hands onto his coveralls after tossing more burned debris onto the cement foundation. "Guess Suze will get a new washer and dryer after all. Fortunately, we carried good insurance on the building and contents."

They returned to Evangeline's cottage a few minutes later, and after stuffing himself with copious amounts of lasagna and garlic bread, Richard pushed his chair away from the dinner table. "You want help with the dishes?" he called out.

Evangeline was at the sink rinsing out a platter and turned with soap bubbles on her nose. "Just sit. We can let the dishes soak and retire to the front porch. Coffee anyone?"

The four adults sat on aluminum lawn chairs out on the patio, watching the sun make its final descent while Travis and Lucy frolicked in the backyard. The four snickered as they discussed meddling parents, and it was nearly sunset when Sam turned towards the house with a creased forehead. "It's awfully quiet back there."

He walked out to the driveway, and Richard approached a moment later with glass in hand. "Where's Trav?"

"Travis!" yelled his father. He cupped his mouth with his right hand and called once more.

Richard put a couple of fingers into his mouth, letting loose a salvo, and in seconds, both Suzanne and Evangeline gathered.

"Where's Lucy?" asked Suzanne, looking both left and right.

Richard tried to calm the storm by saying, "It's probably nothing."

They walked through the adjacent woods, and Evangeline kept yelling, "Lucy!" While Sam pushed aside dry branches and hollered for his son, Richard turned to Evangeline, and both were out of breath. "Is it like your dog to take off?"

She huffed, "Never. She roams a bit, but that's all."

They could hear Sam off in the distance calling his son's name when Suzanne said, "What are we gonna do?"

Richard turned and whispered, "I dunno, but this doesn't feel good."

* * * * *

It was nearly nine when the Amber Alert was issued along with a plea for volunteers to help with the search. Dozens of people from as far away as Manistique showed up, and out on the blacktop, parked cars extended in both directions for nearly half a mile. The Delta County Sheriff's Department organized the search and systemically combed the peninsula, sweeping north to south with a line of volunteers that stretched for a quarter mile. Hampering their efforts, an evening fog had settled in, and the various flashlights illuminated the nighttime mist with long cones of yellow light, crossing beams at times, then checking the canopy. Nothing was overlooked.

The Red Cross set up a base of operations from Evangeline's backyard. Here, they provided hot coffee for volunteers, and a bevy of heavy-set women from the Lutheran Auxiliary in Gladstone provided a steady stream of bologna sandwiches and Sloppy Joes.

By midnight, Sam was exhausted. Richard tried to get him to return to the house for some rest, but he would have none of it. Sam pressed on until a deputy sheriff intervened. "Look, I know this is difficult, but I can't have you out here in the shape you're in. Why don't you head on back to the house and get some rest, and I promise we'll call just as soon as we find anything. We got nearly a hundred people combing the area, and we'll be here all night, if necessary."

Richard took hold of Sam's arm and gave it a gentle tug. "Come on. Let's head back."

Sam's face was streaked with dried tears, and he staggered like a prize-fighter, reeling from too many punches. As he sobbed, Richard put his arm around him, and whispered, "It's gonna be alright. I just know it."

And in that moment, Sam envisioned a casket being lowered with ropes into a long trench with several others. He turned to Richard and cried, "I can't leave him. He's all alone."

"We'll rest for an hour, and I swear I'll bring you right back. You heard what the deputy said. You gotta get some rest."

As they walked back to the house, the steady chop from a helicopter could now be heard off in the distance, and its yellow searchlight swept back and forth as it cut through the heavy fog.

Back at the cottage, Sam sat in a rocker next to the fireplace, sipping cider, but sleep was out of the question. With every new arrival, he jumped to his feet only to find more volunteers.

Meanwhile, Suzanne was making a pot of coffee in the kitchen, and her husband nudged her with an elbow. "Let's step outside."

They walked about the property arm in arm until Suzanne whispered, "Whatcha think?"

"I dunno. Just hope he didn't go near the water because Travis can't swim."

"So, you thinkin' what I'm thinkin'?"

Richard blanched, and his voice elevated. "It was just a little get together; that's all. And now…"

"Don't say it," she scolded, then looked away and whispered, "What are we gonna do?"

Upon returning to the guesthouse, Richard took a seat on the squeaky bed frame and pulled out his cell phone. "Hi, is this Walt?"

"You betcha. Who's dis?"

"This is Rich Templeton calling. We met awhile back over at Hunter's Bar while I was working on the substation in your area. Maybe you remember me? We talked about you coming out to my property to cut some timber, and you gave me your number. I'm the big guy who works for the power company."

A Garth Brooks number was blaring in the background, and Walt hollered, "Yah sure, I remember. What can I do for ya dere, Rich?"

"Sorry about calling so late. You told me about the men who recovered that boy that was kidnapped over on M-95. Said they were all former cops and did that sort of thing for a livin'."

"Yah sure."

"Maybe you don't know, but my house burned down the other night. It was on the news, and the police are tellin' me it was arson." There was a moment of silence before Richard said, "Tonight, a little boy who was visiting, up and disappeared. He's only about eight years old and got half the town out here searching the peninsula." Rich gave a plaintive cry. "The boy's father is a friend, and I...I don't know what we'll do if ..."

Walt's voice rose considerably, and his words were quick. "Ya want us to come down dere and help look? I can grab a coupla guys here at da bar. We could be dere in an hour, eh? Hell, I can even get da ol' lady to come. Esky ain't dat far."

"We can use whatever help we can get, but I was hoping you could contact the men you worked with. I'd be glad to pay whatever fee they charge."

"Look, we be dere in about an hour, eh? Lemme make a coupla calls and see what I can find out."

Richard sniffled. "My wife was inside when the place was set on fire, and hadn't it been for the neighbor girl, I...I'd have nothin' left. The whole damn house went up in smoke, and now this little fella is missing. We're thinking he may have been snatched by the same ones who torched da house."

"Didja tell da cops all dat?"

Another sniffle was followed by, "Talked with the Delta County Sheriff's Department here in Esky, but they're about as useful as tits on a bull." He pleaded, "I wanna catch these sons of bitches, but I need help."

The jukebox was now playing a Hank Williams tune, and Richard could hear the crowd noise.

"One of da guys I worked wit has a camp just souta here, and he stopped in earlier dis evenin'. Lemme run out dere and see what de ol' fart has to say. Can I reach ya at dis numba?"

A few minutes later Walt addressed the patrons at Hunter's Bar and asked for help in finding Travis. Within minutes, the bar darkened, and a caravan of pickup trucks roared south along Norway Lake Road. An hour later, the entire bar along with a couple of waitresses and one of the cooks were out searching the peninsula.

It was nearly three when a commotion started, slow at first, then gradually grew in intensity. People were hugging one another, and Sam rose from his rocker, eyeing the activity outside. The police had given him a walkie-talkie, and it sprang to life, startling the inhabitants of Evangeline's cottage. The voice was shrill and scratchy. "Sam, you there?"

As he strained to get a better look, he pressed the salmon-colored button and answered apprehensively. "I'm here."

Suzanne was sitting on the sofa, took her husband's hand, and inhaled sharply.

"We got him! He's alright! I repeat, we got Travis, and he's alright! He's a little banged up," the voice on the walkie-talkie squawked, "but we're bringing him to you right now. Should be there in just a few minutes."

Sam raced outside with the Templetons close behind, and a few minutes later, the boy emerged from the backseat of a patrol car, hugging a stuffed bear an officer had given him. Amongst the crowd of volunteers that had congregated stood Evangeline Attwood who applauded as she watched Sam embrace his son. Bear hugs and sobs preceded, "Whereja go, my son?" he sniffled, "You had us all worried sick."

An officer with the Delta County Sheriff's Department went down to one knee and placed a hand upon Travis' shoulder. "Apparently, the dog went chasing after a deer, and Trav here followed but got lost. We found him in a boathouse on the other side of the point sleeping with the dog."

Lucy bounded about the property and barked several times as she ran to her owner's side. Evangeline bent down and caressed the boy's crown and said, "You had us worried sick, sweetheart."

"I'm thowwy."

The officer nudged Sam and said, "We're going to take him over to OSF and have him checked out. I'm sure he's fine, but why doncha get your coat. We can all go in my vehicle."

Evangeline looked at Sam with tears in her eyes. "Is there anything I can do?"

With the vision of caskets still fresh in his memory, his reply was terse. "I think you've done enough already. Just leave us alone."

* * * * *

They had met while in Verona. Evangeline was inspecting a box of strawberries at a farmer's market when he brushed passed, spilling a few berries that fell onto the ancient cobblestone. They both bent over at the same time, and their heads collided. That's how it started, a brief wince followed by a few mindless apologies. Then came the idle chatter, and before she knew it, they were sharing a lemon gelato at some outdoor café. Even now, she could recall the scent of coffee brewing and the cool Italian air that reeked of antiquity. He was a sculptor from Tuscany on holiday, and Ulay's arms were firm and muscular, providing a sense of security. When he took her hand for the first time, she felt an immediate connection.

They only spent about three days together, and in that short time, Evangeline felt more alive than she ever had. On their last day together, they had their names engraved onto a lock, then attached it to a wire that paralleled the old stone bridge. Just before they tossed the key into the river, they held one another as if their bond would be eternal. Although their time together was brief, it was the ending that left an indelible impression. As they walked to the train station in silence, she knew there would be no tomorrow. Evangeline recalled the streaks of grey in his beard and the wrinkle across the bridge of his nose. A deep embrace and a few words mixed with tears was followed by a swipe of an index finger along her cheek. There was some memory of a vague promise to write, but even then, she knew that was unlikely. When it came to an end, she watched the train pull away from the station, and as he pressed his hand upon the glass window, Evangeline walked next to the coach until she could no longer keep up.

And then the emptiness set in.

Returning to her tour group felt surreal, and although she was present, her soul was on a train headed towards Tuscany with a man she barely knew. That night, she walked the streets, looking for answers and left a note in Juliet's mailbox, pleading to the Shakespearian icon for another chance. That's how it worked for Evangeline Attwood, as if grief was the price for human love.

As Evangeline sat in the backseat of Templeton's truck, the radio aired, *Ulay, Oh*. She hated that song and tried to block it out by placing her fingers into her ears. But her thoughts and feelings could not be willed away or shut out. An image of Ulay's calloused hands came to mind, but it was supplanted by a picture of a lost child gasping for air. Confusion and grief vied for recognition, forcing their way into Evangeline's consciousness. And in the darkness of the backseat, silent tears coursed her cheeks.

As she wrestled with her feelings in the darkness of Templeton's pickup truck, Suzanne brought her back from her excursion to Verona when she turned the radio off and said, "How you holding up back there?"

For Evangeline, love was the most complicated emotion and preferred to keep her innermost feelings to herself. She wanted to say something about Ulay, say something about Charlotte, but instead, she pushed the memories aside, flicked the tears away with a finger, and gave a tepid, "I'm fine."

"You're thinking about Sam, arncha?"

That was the trouble with grief. What happened twelve years ago oozed into the here and now, and Sam's anger reinforced the feeling that love wasn't meant for her. She sniffled, "He blames me for everything."

Richard looked into the rearview mirror and said, "He doesn't blame you. It's just his emotions talking. You have to understand, he lost his wife, and Travis is all he's got."

Suzanne turned from her passenger seat to face Evangeline directly and said, "Give it some time, and I think the both of you will see things differently. He really is a very thoughtful person." Later, when they walked through the parking lot towards the restaurant, Suzanne placed her arm around her neighbor and said, "I'll talk to him about it, but don't let it get you down. You didn't do nothin' wrong."

The Swallow Inn was an old log structure in downtown Rapid River, and they offered a fish-fry every Friday night. As they walked past the fluorescent sign, it emitted a constant hum, spelling out in big black letters:

Friday Fish Fry
Kiwanis meeting Saturday noon
Lions Club meeting Tuesday 6:00 pm
Live Bait

Like usual, the bar was packed with patrons and around nine, a lone woman took the stage, blew into the microphone a couple of times, and said, "Hi, I'm Carol. Glad y'all came out tonight. How y'all doing?" A round of hoots and yelps ensued, and the country and western singer began her set.

About forty minutes later, the middle-aged woman with blonde hair ended her performance, and as the three were enjoying the last remnants of a perch dinner, a man approached with a package in hand. He tipped his head to one side and said, "Mr. Templeton?"

Richard looked up from his remaining french fries and squinted. "Do I know you?"

"Got a visit from Walt Pellegrini the other day, and he asked me to talk to you about the incident out on your property." He whispered, "Understand someone set fire to your residence."

"Are you at all familiar with the area?"

"Got a camp over by Gene's Pond, just north of Felch. Mind if I have a seat?" As he pulled over a vacated chair, the feet screeched over the pine flooring.

Richard coughed a couple of times. "I'm sorry. Didn't catch the name."

"Dalton. Dalton McKenna."

Richard's extended hand was big and hard, like a frozen turkey, and after the handshake, Dalton wiped off the grease with a paper napkin. "Walt told me a little about what you did over in Dickinson County. Did you really recover that boy without incident?"

"Ah, so you know about that."

"Just that a couple of gorillas from Chicago snatched a boy. Walt said they followed him from Hunter's Bar, and there was a crash..." Suzanne cleared her throat, just before she elbowed her husband. "By the way, this is da wife and our neighbor, Evie. She's the one who pulled Suze from the bedroom when de house caught fire. Hadn't it been for her, I'd have nothin' left."

Evangeline squeaked, "In all honesty, it was my dog, Lucy who woke me up. If anyone deserves the credit, she does."

"So, fill me in on the details."

After a thirty-minute dissertation, Dalton turned to Richard and said, "So you think someone at the DNR leaked your name when you reported that net out on the bay?"

Suzanne answered for her husband. "That's the only possible link we can think of. So, can you help us out?"

"For starters, I'll need everyone's cell phone number, the exact time your fuel line was severed, the approximate time of the fire, and we'll take it from there."

"My cell phone number?" Evangeline protested. "What for?"

A young waitress wearing a pair of too tight jeans sauntered over with a menu in hand. "Can I getcha something, hon?"

Dalton squinted at the stained menu and said, "I'll have the baked cod with drawn butter, baked potato with sour cream and coleslaw. Whatcha got on tap?"

As she scribbled down the order, she replied, "Bud and PBR."

"Take a schooner of PBR."

71

After the waitress scurried off, Dalton leaned forward and snatched one of Richard's fries. "You see, the government monitors all cell phone locations, and I have access to their records."

"You work for the government?" Evangeline interjected with a furrowed brow.

"Worked for the US Marshal's office out in LA, and I still retain my contacts."

The rotund engineer bit his lower lip, and his words were deadpan. "How much is something like this run gonna run?"

"Five-grand for starters."

Richard's head snapped back, and he stuttered. "Five grand? Before I shell out that kind of m…money, I…I'd like to know a little more about who you are. Just wanna make sure I'm hirin' someone who knows what dere doing. By the way, howja you know where to find us?"

"I tagged your phone."

"My phone?"

"You see, I know all about you, Mr. Templeton." Dalton McKenna opened a large manila envelope and tossed several stacks of papers onto the table. "These are your taxes over the past seven years along with your bank statements."

Suzanne poured over the various returns and scrunched her nose "Holy shit. Whereja get all these?"

"Like I said, I still retain my contacts."

Richard scooted his chair over a few inches and whispered, "Will you take a check?"

It was about a half-hour later when they exited the restaurant, and as they approached Richard's truck, a slip of paper flapped from under the windshield wiper. Standing under a street light, the engineer unfolded the note as the others looked on.

Keep your nose out of our business.
Next time we burn the place down
and nail the doors shut.

Suzanne took hold of her husband's hand when he looked up and cried, "What are we gonna do? You gotta help us!"

McKenna made a couple of calls, and by the time they had arrived at Evangeline's cottage, a list of phone numbers appeared in a lone text message. Unfortunately, the Swallow Inn was a busy place, and there were several cell phones in use that evening; seventy-eight to be exact. But when cross referenced to the location where Evangeline had her fuel line severed and the house fire, one number replicated.

Richard looked over Dalton's shoulder in order to see the screen, and his ire was up. "Let's call the sheriff and have the sons of bitches arrested. See how they like dem apples. We can go over dere right now and file a report."

"Look Mr. Templeton, we need to have an understanding." Dalton leaned in close and whispered, "You see, I'm not here to put people in jail."

Richard snapped his head back once more. "But...but how else am I gonna get some sense of justice?" Richard's voice rose noticeably as he asserted, "We lost nearly everything we own."

Dalton used his head to point towards the door, "You want to go for a ride? Maybe we can talk along the way."

About an hour later, the two parked outside a residence on the Garden Peninsula where Richard strained his neck to get a better view. The darkness was broken by a few, yellow incandescent lights that illuminated a kitchen. He could just make out an old television set, airing the weather report. "So, you're certain the person who wrote that note lives here?" Templeton asked.

"Pretty much. We have GPS coordinates placing his cell at the Swallow Inn just a few hours ago. The same phone was tracked to your house the night of the fire. You're smart, figure it out."

Richard rubbed his neck.

After retrieving a gas can from the back of his SUV, Dalton poked his head through the lowered window. "You stay put. I'll handle this."

Joe Steiner lived a few hundred feet off a dirt road and had frontage along Lake Michigan. It wasn't a showcase by any means as a couple of junked cars were parked out back that were weed bound. The house, although expansive, was weathered and in need of a coat of paint. In the front yard was a totem pole with a white rope lashed to its side where a variety of grey laundry and oversized workpants flapped in the evening breeze.

Dalton rapped hard on the backdoor, and a few seconds later, a yellow porch light came on. When the door opened a few inches, Dalton called out, "Mr. Steiner? We need to talk."

"What do you want?" said the voice from inside.

"I want three-hundred grand. That's what it's gonna take to rebuild Templeton's residence."

The door was now wide open, and there before him stood a three-hundred-and-seventy-pound specimen, wearing a worn, Green Bay Packers sweatshirt along with a week's worth of stubble. Dalton pulled out the slip of paper that Richard had removed from his windshield a few hours prior, then held it up to the porch light.

"What the…"

"Now look, it's quite simple. Either you pay up by next week or all this is goin' right over to the prosecutor. And no doubt you'll be looking at a lengthy prison sentence along with an expensive civil complaint. When the dust finally settles, Templeton will own your home and boat, and you'll be spending the next twenty years up in Marquette."

The distinctive click of a cylinder rotating into firing position could be heard, and Dalton lifted his chin. "Before you discharge that weapon, I want you to take a good whiff. That's gasoline. I've poured about five gallons worth around your house. So, when you pull that trigger, there's going to be a source of ignition." Dalton whispered, "Might want to get the ol' lady out before the pilot light on your furnace ignites the fumes."

Steiner sniffed, and his pallor faded like the setting moon. "You're fuckin' crazy."

"Doesn't matter. Three-hundred grand by next Friday! Hear!

CHAPTER SEVEN

A gem cannot be polished without friction,
nor a man perfected without trials."
- Lucius Annaeus Seneca

December 24, 1913

Without gainful employment, the Croatian immigrant enjoyed a leisure morning with his wife where they nestled together in bed like a pair of tablespoons. It was quiet in the house, and Peter was listening to the wind howl outside their bedroom window. While ice pellets tapped at the home's exterior, their daughter remained asleep. Elizabeth checked on her, then stoked the coal-burning stove in the kitchen. The house, owned by Calumet and Hecla, had gone cold, and as she raced back to the bedroom, her husband held open the covers; the bed frame creaking as she entered.

"Your feet are ice cold," he scolded. Peter pulled his wife close, interlacing her fingers with his, squeezing them tight. "You going to take Mary into town for the party?" he asked.

"Uh-huh."

"What time do you have to be there?"

"Not until two. Why don't you come?"

"Can't. Mr. Krainatz said he needed help shoveling coal. Said he'd pay me two dollars, and I'll use it to help pay for Christmas dinner. Maybe we can meet afterwards and go to mass together. Should be done by five."

Elizabeth rolled over and rested her head upon his shoulder, kissing him ever so lightly, then fell back asleep.

Later that morning, she examined the dress in the mirror and ran her fingers over the harvest-colored hues. Elizabeth wondered if it was too revealing with its plunging neckline and elegant embroidery. Her husband had found a large mass of silver while working the 14th level and sold it to a merchant in *town who provided store credit. She sighed. There weren't many fashionable choices in her meager wardrobe as the strike had depleted their household income, and their credit with the silver merchant was rapidly approaching zero. It's not like they were well to do even when Peter was working, but Elizabeth's husband had bought the dress at Vertin's for her twenty-first birthday. Although it needed alterations, the reverie of that special day warmed her spirit.*

The young woman spent the next hour getting her daughter dressed who squirmed about, making the process tedious. Mary was a rambunctious, five-year-old, but she eventually succumbed to her mother's will and stood in front of the mirror, pouting at the injustice. Elizabeth admired the fashionable white frock with the blue silk ribbon that wrapped around her daughter's waist, then cast a stern warning. "Saint Nicholas might not give you any candy if he sees you pouting like this." She handed her daughter the rag doll that she adored, now threadbare, and the two donned wool coats as they made the trek into the city from their home in Raymbaultown. Theirs was a miner's home, and its coal furnace kept the place snug during the long winter. Like many of the homes in the area, it was chopped into two flats, side by side. The Markers lived next door, and their daughter was Mary's age. The two girls went to school together, and their mothers took turns watching the children, giving each a chance to run errands or take care of business in town. But even though their home was snug and warm, Elizabeth longed for something better.

It was unusual for the streets to be free of snow especially on Christmas Eve, and they made their trek into town with ease. As Elizabeth admired the holiday decorations, she pointed to the church spires off in the distance. "Once we're done here, we'll all go to mass. Papa said he'd meet us there." Mary wasn't listening as she crunched a frozen puddle, watching the ice break into hundreds of shards. The young woman pulled her daughter's hand and said, "Let's go, lamb-chop. We don't want to be late to see Saint Nicholas, do we?" As they continued their journey, Elizabeth licked her finger, directing it into the wind. She sniffed a couple of times and said, "You know, I wouldn't be surprised if snow was on the way. We might get a white Christmas after all."

They walked past some of the finer homes as they made their way to the celebration, and Elizabeth pondered what it would be like living in an elegant home with a stone fireplace and a white picket fence. But her husband of six years was a miner, making a mere $2.75 a day. Elizabeth took in laundry to supplement their income, but it would take a miracle for them to move into a better location, and the town of Red Jacket outlawed miracles long ago.

It took about twenty minutes to get there, and after passing a noisy saloon that occupied the first floor, they made their way up the staircase where Elizabeth hung their coats alongside all the others, then took her daughter's hand. "Now you stay close, understand? I don't want you getting lost with all these people."

With fingertips to her mouth, Mary huddled against her mother's hip, as the crowd was a tad intimidating for a five-year-old. The hall was filled with hundreds of people, and they patiently waited in line as a tall woman of Croatian descent passed out treats and gifts to all the children. While they waited their turn, Mary pointed to the Christmas tree on the stage and beamed, "Pretty."

* * * * *

On Monday morning, a crew arrived at Templeton's charred property and began preparing the site for reconstruction. A new foundation was poured later in the week, and the land was heavy with the scent of concrete and tar paper. Richard was inspecting a pile of Wolmanized lumber when an SUV roared to a stop. Upon exiting, McKenna's first words were, "Well, anything?"

"No, not a word." There was a pause as Richard whisked the dust from his coveralls. "So, now what?"

McKenna walked about the construction site, examining the foundation, and Templeton followed close behind. With hands behind his back, Dalton turned and said, "How bad do you want this resolved?"

"Its not just restitution," he said with a sagging voice. "It's all the family heirlooms we lost, not to mention the threats they made with that damn letter. Da wife hardly sleeps at night, and she's keepin' my Smith and Wesson in da nightstand next to da bed." Richard thought about his grandparents who settled here nearly seventy years ago, and the hard labor they spent in building the home that was now being hauled to the landfill as charred rubble.

As Richard reminisced, he recalled the time when he was a boy out on the lake with his grandfather, and even now, he could smell the nightcrawlers and feel the rough wood along the sides of the old rowboat. Some forty-five years later, the scent of pipe tobacco evoked a distant memory of his grandfather. The thought that someone would lay ruin to his family's history made his blood pressure rise. Defiantly he said, "My family lived out here for the better part of seventy years, and we're not gonna be run off our property! So, tell me, what exactly does my five-thousand buy?"

With head cocked to one side, Dalton said, "You want 'em dead?"

A gasp was followed by, "Dead? I...I don't wanna be an accessory to murder. I just want some fuckin' sense of justice!"

Dalton McKenna opened his billfold and thrust Richard's check forward. The homeowner looked at it as if it were an unexpected house guest. "What de..." Richard said with a whiney voice. "I thought you were gonna help us?"

"That's what I'm doing, but the justice you're seeking ain't gonna happen unless someone applies pressure." With lips drawn tight, he ended his statement with a curt, "Hear."

Richard's expression went blank.

"Since they didn't meet the deadline, they've essentially told you to take a hike, and unless you're willing to make good on that threat, there's little I can do."

As the engineer stuffed the check into his breast pocket, he gulped. "Maybe it would be best if we dropped the whole thing. I...I just don't like the direction this thing is takin'."

"I understand," Dalton replied with a sympathetic nod. "But if you don't deal with it now, it'll haunt you. Maybe not right away, but surely in years to come. Besides, the men who torched your place realize you know who they are, and they're not about to let this matter end peacefully. The first time the Steiners have an accident or who knows what, they'll suspect you. So, it wouldn't be a bad idea if you kept a fire extinguisher handy."

* * * * *

Evangeline felt as if life was closing in on all sides. Between the trauma associated with Travis getting lost, listening to her mother's endless complaints, and the suspected arson of the Templeton's residence, she slumped further into darkness. To make matters worse, she felt Sam's anger, and had apologized profusely, hoping to repair the damage, but Sam Carter would have none of it. The only reprieve was spending time with Suzanne who seemed to lift her spirits. Some days they'd play gin rummy or perhaps go for a drive and check out various antique stores in the Marquette area.

On one such excursion, the two stopped for lunch at Lawry's Pasty Shoppe along US-41, and as they waited for their order, the subject of men came up, and Suzanne went into detail about how she met her husband. It was an ordinary day, she explained. Suzanne was working for the local newspaper, selling advertising when Richard came in to place an ad for a garage sale. Somewhere along the way, he asked if she'd like to have dinner sometime. One thing led to another, and after dating for about a year, Richard proposed.

As Suzanne described her wedding, Evangeline's thoughts drifted towards Verona, but there were no words that adequately described Ulay's influence upon her life. Yet, their three days together seemed insignificant and paled in comparison to the years Richard and Suzanne were together. Evangeline safely changed topics and lamented about her lack of prospects. "How come all the guys I meet are absolute jerks?"

"Well, I don't think it's fair characterizing the entire species based on just a few bad apples. I'm sure there's a lot of guys out there that would make a good partner."

"Like who?" Evangeline replied with a tone of indignation.

"Well, what about Sam? He's a decent human being."

A strong exhalation was followed by, "Are you kidding? The man hates me, and after what happened, I...I really can't blame him."

"Sam doesn't hate you. Look Ev, if you want someone special in your life, outside of your dog, you have to offer something special. I know you don't feel that way right now, but you have to believe in yourself. If you don't believe in yourself, nobody else ever will."

The pasties arrived a few minutes later; Suzanne smothering hers with ketchup. As she broke the crust, steam rose towards the ceiling, and after letting it cool, she took a bite of flank steak, moaning with epicurean delight.

"These are really good." Evangeline mumbled.

"Try it with some ketchup."

After applying a dollop, Evangeline took a bite, then emitted a satisfied, "Mmm. Is it a local thing, these pasties? I've never had one before."

"They were brought over by the Cornish when they came to work the mines. They'd wrap one in a cloth when they went to work in the morning, and it would keep warm until lunchtime. The crust really keeps the heat in."

A slurp of diet pop was followed by, "Did you think the Cornish worked up in the Keweenaw?"

"I dunno," Suzanne shrugged. "But they were experienced in underground mining, and all the towns up here utilized their skills." Suzanne looked at her watch and said, "You know, we got time. Why don't we drive up to Laurium, and you can show me where Roy lived?"

It took about an hour to get there, and they pulled right in front of the old two-story. Suzanne craned her neck to get a better view and said, "Not much to speak of. Hard to imagine such a romantic guy lived in such an ordinary house."

They snapped a few pictures, and later, stopped at Luigi's for a frothy brew. Then, it was on to the Vertin Gallery where Evangeline bought an old photograph of Calumet, showing a snow-lined street during the early part of the twentieth century. Ambling about town, they approached the museum and left Lucy in the shade, tied to an iron tram. After they paid their admission, the two women perused the various exhibits. When Suzanne came upon a pair of wooden doors, she called out, "Hey Ev! Come check this out."

The two read about the Italian Hall, and as Evangeline touched the hardware, she felt a current surge through her veins, resulting in a momentary gyration.

"What's going on?" Suzanne asked. "You look like you've seen a ghost."

Evangeline backed away from the exhibit with a hand to her throat as Suzanne ran her fingertips over the coarse wood. "It's just a coupla old doors."

Taped to the front was a sheet of paper, listing the names of the deceased who had been piled up along the staircase that led to the second floor. Evangeline stepped closer to better inspect the page and ran her fingertips over the names. Upon touching an entry, the visitor was jolted again, and this time, she staggered. All the former teacher could muster was, "I need to get some air. I'll meet you outside."

Evangeline fell into a reverie, and for a brief moment, the fog that enshrined the past lifted, exposing a barren landscape. She stood standing in the shade near the iron tram with eyes closed, and a vision of heartbreak and desperation unfolded. She could see the smokestacks off in the distance, spewing black acrid fumes and hear the rumble of a passing locomotive as it clattered across an old iron bridge. She immediately recalled the dream where she explored a crevice out by the road, and as she peered out onto the landscape, Evangeline could see the miners walking home from work. It was another time buried deep within, and the former teacher gasped for air.

A few moments later, Suzanne opened the car door and found Evangeline waiting. "Did you feel it back there?"

"Feel what?" Suzanne answered as she petted Lucy, who pawed at her purse.

"I could see..." Evangeline didn't finish her statement, preferring to keep her inner most thoughts to herself. She amicably changed subjects and said, "Do you believe in destiny?"

Suzanne snapped her seatbelt and secured it with a tug. "What are you getting at?"

"Just wondering if our lives are nothing more than random acts of chance. What do you think?"

As they roared down US-41, Suzanne stared out the window, and when Lucy poked her head out from the backseat, she took hold of the canine's neck. "I dunno." There was a moment of silence as Suzanne gathered her thoughts. "I suppose most people want to hear that destiny plays a role in their lives, but to be honest, I can't say one way or another." A heavy sigh preceded, "Maybe you're right; our lives are nothing more than just a bunch of random choices. And with all the millions of possibilities, we find comfort in the absurd notion our choices are influenced by some great power." She exhaled noticeably as if the discussion was difficult. "So, to answer your question, I'd like to believe there's some guiding force that helps us navigate our lives, but the logical part of me says, it's an insane notion. Why do you ask?"

Evangeline took a sip of bottled water, then swiped her lips with a wrist. "I was just thinking about coincidences and whether or not there's something going on besides pure chance. Want to hear an interesting story?"

"Well, sure." Suzanne leaned back into the door and pulled out a packet of M&Ms from her purse, getting Lucy's attention.

"I have this friend back home, and she's on her second marriage."

As Suzanne munched on her snack, she replied with a garbled, "So."

"You see, her first husband died in a car accident, and although it was immeasurably difficult, she found someone new a few years later and remarried. Her new husband had lost his wife to some form of cancer I believe, and it was a miracle they found one another."

"That's a nice story and all," she interrupted, "but I don't think it rises to the level of an amazing coincidence."

"I'm not finished."

Suzanne tilted her head with curiosity.

"You see, Karen's husband always wanted to talk about the past whereas Karen never did."

Lucy nuzzled Suzanne M&M packet with a wet nose as she said, "Sounds like Rich and me."

"Anyway, after years of pestering her about details of her first marriage, she finally relented. So, Karen pulled out a box full of pictures and shared memories of her first husband. She talked about how they met, and their honeymoon, and the vacations they took together. Somewhere into the discussion, her husband asked, 'Where did you guys vacation at?' And she ran off a list of places, including Lourdes. Now this is the interesting part."

Suzanne propped her head with the heel of her hand.

"Her husband said, 'Well, I've been to Lourdes. Me and my wife visited there several years ago.' So, David goes to the bedroom and pulls out a picture of him and his first wife, and there…" Evangeline sniffled as a UPS truck roared by, and when quiet was restored, she said, "So, who do you think is standing in the background?"

With head askew and eyebrows arched, Suzanne curiously asked, "Who?"

"In the background, standing right behind him, was Karen with her first husband."

Suzanne inhaled sharply.

"Sometimes I think our lives are nothing more than orchestrated madness, but every once in awhile, like when I think about David and Karen, I wonder if there's something more going on. Think about it. What are the chances of them all being together in the same place at the exact same time, thousands of miles away from home? It defies all logic."

Suzanne rubbed her hands over her biceps as if shivering. "You're giving me goose-bumps, kiddo."

"You know, when I found Roy's letters, I thought there was something important in it for me; that maybe it wasn't just dumb luck that I came across them. But then I think about Travis getting lost, and," Evangeline blew her nose into a rolled-up tissue, "if there really is a God, why would he let something like that happen? And why would he let your house burn to the ground?" As they sat in silence, Evangeline envisioned Charlotte's small face, and a lone tear descended. "I'm curious. Do you and your husband attend church services?"

"Rich never goes, but I only go because I want my daughter to have some religious upbringing. Wouldn't feel right if she ended up as a heathen, but I know what you're getting at." She nervously swept her hair behind her ears. "To me, God mostly seems rather distant, as if he really didn't give a shit what we're doing down here." Suzanne's phone rang and answered with a cheerful, "Hi, sweetheart. I'm with Evie, and we're heading home. Should be there in an hour or two. Whereya at?"

Suzanne pressed the phone to her shoulder, turned and said, "How does pizza sound? Rich'll pick something up on the way home."

"Sure, but don't put anything odd on it like anchovies or spinach leaves."

She returned to her call and said, "Pick up one of those big-ass pizzas over in Esky...you know the place...say pepperoni and mushrooms?" She looked to Evangeline for approval, and ended the call with a quick, "And I love you too. See ya in a couple."

CHAPTER EIGHT

"In the absence of inward joy,
Men turn to evil."
- Paramahansa Yoganada

December 24, 1913

The sign on top of the building spelled out in large black letters, 'Societa Mutua Beneficenza Italiana.' But to most, it was simply called, the Italian Hall. It was located on Seventh Street, a brick, two-story structure housing the Great Atlantic and Pacific Tea Company and Vairo's Saloon. Upstairs, there was a large hall with a small stage where meetings and banquets were held, and it was here a Christmas party was planned for the children of striking miners, complete with holiday decorations and presents.

Downstairs, Vairo's was packed like usual, mostly men who preferred a cold beer rather then standing in a long line in the hall above, and the bar was hot with gossip. Upstairs, Elin Lesh was in the vestibule making sure only children of striking mine workers got in, and as the afternoon progressed, she asked several men standing nearby to relieve her while she went into the main hall and helped with the festivities. With so many people coming in, the men abandoned their posts, allowing anyone to enter.

The hall was filled with hundreds of children who waited patiently for their Christmas presents. A ballerina came on stage and entertained the children and was followed by Christmas carols sung in both English and Croatian. When the presents were brought up from the basement, which included a barrel-full of chocolate-drop candies, children rushed the stage with anticipation. Elin helped restore order, telling the children they needed to settle down. With nearly seven hundred in attendance, the hall was loud, and those at the back couldn't hear the instructions to get in line.

When it came her turn, Mary beamed when she was given an orange and a pair of red wool mittens, then stood there mesmerized as she looked at the Christmas trees, steeped in ribbons and light. Big Annie, a towering woman of Croatian descent and member of the Woman's Auxiliary for the Western Federation of Miners (WFM), helped organize the event and ushered children along, hoping the celebration would infuse some joy into a rather bleak and desperate community.

When the man ascended the stairwell, no one noticed him. With his hat pulled down and a Citizen Alliance button stuck to his breast pocket, he stood at the entrance to the main hall, surveying the crowd. He then cupped his mouth with a hand, and yelled, "Fire!"

At first, folks nearby just stared, but when he yelled it a second time, people echoed the call in a myriad of languages. Panic engulfed the hall, starting first at the ticket counter, then making its way across the main room. The former Italian Hall had burned to the ground just a few years prior, and most people remembered the event vividly. Parents swept up their children and pressed their way towards the lone exit. Annie ran out into the crowd to help alleviate their fears and yelled, "Stop! Please! There's no fire!"

But her words couldn't be heard over the shouting and crashing of chairs. Elizabeth couldn't hear Annie's pleas either. Instead, she held Mary in her arms as they made their descent down the lone stairwell. The Klarich girls along with the Smuks were right behind, but the staircase was too crowded and steep. Someone fell near the bottom, and people were soon crawling on top of one another in order to get out. Screams boomed throughout the hall and then came the crush.

Pandemonium.

As the weight bore down upon her, Mary dropped her rag doll, looked up with eyes wide and cried, "Mama!" Elizabeth tried to break free, but the weight of all the bodies was overwhelming. There were people on top and below. A child's foot was near her face, and Elizabeth pushed it aside, then mustered all her strength and said, "Just close your eyes, lamb chop, and everything'll disappear." She watched her daughter close her eyelids one last time. Then came a slight grimace followed by more cries and screams from deep within the pile...struggling to breathe.... her head pinned between the wainscoting and the wooden riser. Gasping, churning, lungs afire, then utter silence followed by an impenetrable darkness.

* * * * *

The Honda twisted its way through the wooded peninsula until they found Richard standing next to the guest house, looking pale. Suzanne rolled the window down and said, "Hey sweetheart, what's goin' on?"

"Better take a look."

Evangeline and Suzanne walked into the guesthouse and held their hands to their mouth, then backed away. Their meager possessions were dumped about the floor, and someone had taken a knife and sliced up their clothing, leaving a trail of garments throughout.

Richard pointed at the bed. "It gets worse."

Someone had urinated onto the sheets and pillowcases, and Suzanne backed away once more. "We better call the police."

"Bullshit with that!" Richard pulled out his phone and flicked the screen until he found what he was looking for.

"Hello?"

"Is… this…. D…Dalton McKenna?"

"Speaking."

"Richard Templeton here. We…we had another incident at the place I'm staying, and it…it's pretty bad. While we were out, they cut up all our clothes and pissed all over the sheets we were using…I…I…"

A strong exhalation was followed by, "Have you called the police?"

"N…not yet."

"I'm on my way! Don't touch a thing 'til I get there, hear."

It took over an hour before the SUV pulled next to the back entrance, and after receiving an update, McKenna examined the destruction. He shook his head and said, "This isn't going to be easy, you know. Still not too late to bring in Delta County or the State Police."

Richard looked at his wife and said with a hushed voice, "We're done with them. We can't live like this." With his head tilted, he said, "You figure it was Steiner?"

"The GPS coordinates for Joe Steiner's cell phone shows he was here about an hour ago. Or at least his phone was."

"You're positive?" Richard asked.

"Yup."

"So, what are we gonna do?"

Dalton continued to stroll about Attwood's backyard with the Templetons at his side. "I looked at his files, and he doesn't have any kids. So, going after them isn't an option, and his boat is jointly owned between him and his cousin. As I see it, we'll have to go after both if you truly want put an end to this bullshit."

Suzanne raised her hand as if she were a student in a classroom. "I…I don't feel comfortable with all this. I…I don't want criminal charges dangling over our heads for the rest of our lives."

"Well, let me ask you this." McKenna's voice was now shrill like a preacher's voice. "How many times are you willing to put up with someone pissin' all over your stuff? If you're willing to put up with that sorta bullshit, you should start putting your hard-earned money into commercial disinfectant because you're gonna need it."

Richard and Suzanne stared at one another for a brief moment until Richard whined, "We're not killers. I work for the power company for Christ sake. I…I don't have any experience in that sort of thing." His mouth was dry, and he swallowed noticeably. "We just want it stopped, that's all." He turned to his wife and said, "Whatcha think, Suze?"

Suzanne pulled the check from her purse and thrust it forward. "Here. Kill the sons of bitches if you have to."

The following afternoon Evangeline used a broom to beat the carpets that hung from the clothesline in the backyard while Suzanne scrubbed the pine floor in the guesthouse. Meanwhile, Lucy sniffed the side of the cottage where a neighbor's dog had urinated just as Richard pulled up in his black Silverado. A slam of the driver's door was followed by a cheerful, "Place is looking nice."

Suzanne snapped off her rubber gloves, then planted a peck on her husband's cheek while Lucy walked over, seeking a caress.

"Got the comforter cleaned up and bought new pillows." Richard pulled the bedding from the back of the truck and handed it to his wife. The mattress and box spring were resting along the side of the cottage, and the engineer got up close for an inspection. "Looks like the stains came out." He sniffed a couple of times and said, "Smells nice."

As Richard unloaded the truck, Evangeline walked over. "Are those the motion detectors?"

"You betcha. Gonna place 'em out by the road, so that next time we get visitors, we'll have some advanced warning."

"But what about all the deer? This could be more of a pain than it's really worth."

Suzanne tripped over the broom she had used to beat the carpet and dropped a pillow in the process. Richard helped his wife, then turned towards his neighbor, "I can set the sensitivity to the motion detectors, and although it's crude, it's better than nothin'. So, if I have to get up a few times, it's better than having our stuff trashed."

Richard was securing the electronics to various trees when Dalton's SUV roared onto the property. After the door slammed, his first words were, "You got a full tank of gas for that boat of yours?"

As the two boarded the fiberglass boat docked in front of Richard's former home, there was a light chop out on the lake, and by the time they arrived at the marina, it was nearly dark. The *Agnes Bea* was a wooden, double-rig trawler in need of a coat of paint, and the wake from their speedboat rocked it gently from side to side. When Richard pulled next to the boat, Dalton said, "I'm gonna take a look around. Give me about a half hour."

Dalton talked to various people at the marina and afterwards, made his way to the *Agnes Bea*. The hatches were locked, and in the darkness, it took only a few minutes for McKenna to pick the mechanism. Once open, he moved quickly, using a LED flashlight to inspect the various holds and storage lockers.

When Richard pulled alongside Steiner's trawler, Dalton jumped aboard, and in seconds, their speedboat was jetting across the water at full throttle. "Whatja find?" Templeton yelled.

Dalton unfolded a handkerchief, holding up the specimen to his flashlight.

"What da hell am I lookin' at?" Templeton hollered.

"Marijuana stems. There was enough spread about the floor in one of the holds to make me believe they're using their boat for something more than just fishing."

"Gonna report it?" Richard did a double-take and shouted, "Stupid question."

The weather had taken a turn for the worse since their departure, and strong winds whipped unabated across the waters of Lake Michigan. As the boat cut through the white caps, a cold spray cascaded over the bow, dampening its occupants. Richard used a towel to wipe his face, and then handed it to his passenger.

"I suspect the growers are shipping their product by boat at least in part," Dalton hollered, "and considering it's getting late in the season, I'd think a large shipment should be heading south fairly soon."

The slap of the keel against the waves jostled the two men and made it difficult to talk. Richard shouted, "Sure glad you know what you're doing. If Steiner gets caught with dope onboard, what'll happen?"

"Coast Guard will impound the vessel, and they'll be looking at a number of years in prison."

"So, no restitution?"

"Right now, I'm focusing on neutralizing their threat. I think you'd have to agree, getting them out of the picture will make you sleep better. But as far as restitution is concerned, your insurance company is building you a new house. What more do you want?"

Richard sulked, then yanked the throttle, driving them both backwards into their seats.

Dalton braced himself using the handrail and yelled, "All isn't lost. You're getting a brand-new home out of the deal, and your family keepsakes that were lost can't be replaced no matter how much we squeeze out of Steiner."

Meanwhile back at Garth Point, Evangeline and Suzanne were working up a sweat, doing a few yoga poses. Suzanne could hear her bones creak upon executing a chaturanga, but it was a half-moon pose that caused Evangeline to stumble. They completed the session with a tree pose followed by a few moments of quiet reflection. Afterwards, the two retired to the living room, where they enjoyed the last remnants of a bottle of cheap Chianti. Suzanne had her feet up on the coffee table, listening to a Barry Manilow recording while Lucy was curled up in front of the fire, snoring away. They heard the twin outboards, and Suzanne turned towards the lake. "Sounds like the guys are back."

The women went down to the pier where Suzanne caught the rope her husband had tossed and secured the speedboat to the dock. In the darkness, Suzanne said, "So, how did it go?"

They walked up the concrete steps that led to Richard's former residence, and Dalton provided an update.

"So, how long do you think it'll be before they ship something?" Suzanne asked, longing for a favorable answer.

Dalton shrugged, then drilled the lake water out of his ears with his pinky. "Got somebody watching the marina and if there's any activity, said he'd call."

"And how reliable is this... person?"

"He's an old guy that works for the marina as a custodian and makes about ten bucks an hour. Paid him eight hundred in cash with the promise he'd get another eight when the job's complete. He's got four grandkids living with him. So, to answer your question, I think we're good."

As Suzanne spoke to Dalton, Richard stared at Evangeline's black yoga attire, fueling a fantasy until his wife took his hand and said, "I'm freezin' out here. Let's get inside where it's warm."

* * * * *

It was around this time of year when Dalton's wife died decades prior, and the solitary months that followed were hard. In order to survive, he stuffed his feelings, giving the casual

91

observer an impression he was cold-blooded, but if the truth be known, Dalton felt things quite deeply. Only when he was alone did he allow himself the luxury of vacationing along memory lane, but when he did, the former US Marshal would speak to his late wife as if she was sitting next to him. As he pushed west along US-2 through Gladstone, he turned to the empty passenger seat and said, "So what do you think we should do?"

And in his dreamscape, Adeline would reply, "I don't know, but you got to do something."

With the hum of the tires the only sound, Dalton would listen for her voice, now just a distant memory. "I miss you, sweetheart. Sorry I wasn't a better husband." He'd close his eyes for a split second and could imagine her laughter accompanied by the scent of Chanel. He had forgotten the type, but vividly recalled the fragrance, and the memories of their time together rolled in like a Lake Michigan thunderstorm.

When he showed up at Superior Aviation, Dalton tucked his dreamscape away, then tapped the bell on the counter.

"Can I help you?" asked the gangly-looking teenager with bad breath.

Dalton pinched his nose and twanged, "Jesus Christ, you got to do somethin' about that breath of yours, son. It could knock a crow off a shit pile. How you ever gonna attract a girlfriend with buzzard breath?"

The young man covered his mouth with embarrassment. "Sorry."

"Look, I need to rent a helicopter. Whatcha got?"

The manager walked out from the backroom and said, "What can we help you with?"

"Like I told the kid here, need to rent a helicopter for a coupla days."

"A couple of days?" The owner looked over the top of his bifocals and said, "You sure you can afford it? We charge by the hour, you know."

Dalton pulled out a white envelope and started counting out hundred-dollar bills. He pushed the stack across the counter and said, "How much time will that buy?"

The two walked outside where the manager put two fingers into his kisser and let loose a blast. Once he got the attention of one of his pilots, he motioned with his hands for him to come over.

"Mr...." He turned and said, "Didn't catch the name."

"John...John Mosby."

"This is Mr. Mosby, and he wants to rent one of our birds."

With cash in hand, they were airborne ten minutes later. It was loud inside the Bell Twin Ranger, and the pilot used his headset to communicate with his passenger. "Where we headed?" he squawked.

"Garden Peninsula. I have some surveying to do."

With a furrowed brow, the pilot said, "But you didn't bring any equipment."

"Just doing some preliminary inspections. Wanna take a close look at the area just east and south of Garden."

The pilot banked the aircraft sharp right while Dalton pulled his binoculars out. As he scanned the tree line, he yelled, "Need you to run some north-south lines with a spacing of about five-hundred feet. Can you do that for me?"

With a steady chop from the blades overhead, he shouted, "You're the customer. Just so you know, this area doesn't take kindly to low flying aircraft. So, the first sign of trouble, we're outa here."

"So, you know about what's going on out here?"

A nod was followed by. "Just about everyone does."

Dalton pulled out a pair of crisp hundred-dollar bills and held it in front of the pilot. "If you can show me a couple of their growing operations, we'll call it a day, and your boss can keep what's left."

The pilot snatched the currency and stuffed the bills into a shirt pocket. "You're not really a surveyor, are you?"

* * * * *

Evangeline recognized the caller ID, and her first words were, "So, you heard about what happened?"

Tom barked, "How come trouble starts where ever you go? I've never met anyone like that before."

"Don't you start with me!" The two siblings cursed only with each other as if they held a secret pact, and Evangeline continued to holler. "You had to blab to the ol' lady I quit my job, and if that weren't bad enough, you told her I broke up with Dan. If I wanted everyone to know, I would have taken an ad out in the goddamn paper! I swear, you got a mouth on you as big as a shoebox. Now she's calling up here, laying on the guilt. Says I'm going to end up in a trailer park, living with a bunch of goddamn housecats!" Evangeline could hear the chuckle. "It's not funny!"

"Look, I didn't call to argue. Talked to Richard this morning, and he told me about what happened. If that weren't bad enough, said someone broke into the guest house and trashed the place."

The former teacher sighed. "Did he tell you they slashed all their clothes, then pissed all over the fucking bed? Took days to clean the stinkin' mess up."

With exasperation, Tom said, "Christ Almighty. What de hell is going on up there? I've owned the place for over fifteen years and haven't had a lick of trouble until you showed up, and now everything has gone to hell in a hand-basket." There was a moment of silence until he said, "So, do I have to worry about the place going up in smoke?"

There was another pause in the conversation until Evangeline said, "Rich hired some guy to go after whoever did it, but there haven't been any arrests. So, you better have good fire insurance."

"What da hell happened?" her older brother barked.

"I was out diving on the bay a couple of weeks ago and came across an illegal net. Rich reported it, and before you know it, his house caught fire. The State Police determined it was arson. Since the Delta County Sheriff's Office wasn't doing much to apprehend those involved, Rich hired someone, and in no time, he identified those responsible…"

Tom didn't wait for a further explanation and blurted, "Well did you contact the police?"

"The guy Rich hired said we couldn't use the information because it comes from some government agency and supposedly all of it's considered classified."

"What the…"

"I know…I know. I thought the same thing. But Rich hired him, not me."

"Not to change the subject, but I told Rich he could use the cottage, and that you wouldn't mind moving out to the guest house. It'll give 'em a little extra room."

"Huh?" Evangeline decried.

"Said he'd pay two thousand a month in rent, and since you're not coughing up a fuckin' nickel for utilities, thought it would be a win for everyone involved." With an exaggerated voice, he added, "But if you want to pay for all the propane you've been using along with some rent, your can keep your boney-ass put." His next words were in one long exhalation. "It'll only be for a couple of months until they can get back on their feet."

"A couple of months?" she whined.

"Might be a good thing you stayed up there because the ol' lady is on the goddamn warpath, considering how you told her off last time you two talked. Should hear all the crap she's saying."

"Christ Almighty."

Tom's voice was now soft and gentle. "How you holding up?"

"It's been hard." Evangeline gulped loud enough to hear.

"I mean financially."

"I saved some. So, I'm not destitute."

"So, what are you going to do for money?"

"Oh, I don't know. Thought I'd try sales. Maybe when I get back, I'll get a job at Macy's or Nordstrom's. I think I'd be good at selling women's clothing." Lucy barked a couple of times, and Evangeline said, "Look, someone's at the backdoor, and I have to run. I'll call you next week and keep the ol' lady off my fuckin' back, hear?"

95

She opened the backdoor, only to find her neighbors standing there. As Evangeline held the screen door open, Suzanne said, "Did you talk to Tom?"

"Just got off the phone with him."

Suzanne set down a book she had borrowed and emitted a long sigh. "We'll stay put. Rich and I can get along just fine in the guest house."

"That's alright. Tom said you guys would help pay expenses, and since I'm staying here rent free, it only makes sense."

Suzanne took hold of Evangeline's hand and said, "I feel just awful about this. How can we make it up to you?"

"You can take all your meals with us," Richard blurted. "That should help with your expenses. I'd be happy to pick up the tab for whatever is involved, and with me paying the utilities, you can make your money stretch a little further."

And so, it came to pass that Lucy and Evangeline ended up in the guest house with the leaky toilet and creaky floorboards. The accommodations were a lot smaller and didn't offer a view of the lake. But it was private, and Richard had installed a double-key deadbolt, making certain the premises were as secure as possible.

It was only a couple of nights later, when the laptop, that sat upon the nightstand next to their bed, sprang to life, sending the three-hundred-and-fifty-pound engineer to the dresser where he retrieved a .44 caliber revolver he had borrowed from his brother.

Suzanne held the top of her pajamas together with her hand as she peered out into the darkness. "Who do you think it is?"

"Search me. But it's two in the morning, and it sure as hell ain't Publishers Clearing House."

"Maybe we should call the police."

With his bony knees protruding from the southern limit of his boxer shorts, he handed his wife the revolver, then loaded cartridges into his new Winchester. After racking a round into the firing chamber, Richard looked up and whispered, "Bullshit with that. By the time those idiots get here, we'll be cold to the touch." He held his fingers to his lips. "Shhh. I'm gonna go around the front. If he comes through the backdoor, let 'im have it. Just make certain you don't end up shootin' me."

As Suzanne spun the cylinders, she whispered, "But…but what about Evie?"

As the headlights illuminated the back of the house, the two ducked behind the window sill where Richard whispered, "I'll keep an eye on her. Just protect the place and keep the fire extinguisher handy."

The pickup pulled up to the back entrance, and the driver honked a couple of times, waking Lucy who started barking. Richard, by this time, was standing alongside the guesthouse in his boxer shorts, and the curtain swept back. He motioned with his finger for Evangeline to get down.

The vehicle honked its horn once more, and Templeton let loose a salvo from his Winchester, shattering the truck's back window. He yelled, "Get your hands up where I can see 'em!"

By this time, Suzanne had opened the backdoor to the cottage and fired three shots into the ground, sending a spray of dust and sand onto the vehicle. The report was an assault on the nighttime air, and the scent of spent gunpowder drifted lazily over the backyard.

"Don't shoot!" cried the driver as he held his hands high. "I…I don't have a gun!"

By now, Suzanne had the porch light on, and the driver shielded his eyes from the intrusion. Richard approached as he looked down the barrel of his Winchester, yelling all the way. "Who the hell are ya?"

"Dan…Dan Pantone. I'm here to see Evie. Drove all night to get here."

Evangeline opened the front door to the guest house and squinted to get a better look. "Dan?" she cried out. "What are you doin' here?"

Richard lowered his weapon.

Sensing the danger had passed, Pantone examined his broken back window and yelled, "Who's gonna pay for all this damage?" He then approached Evangeline with a swagger, holding a can of beer. "Just wanted to see my baby, that's all."

"Look Dan, I told you it's over, and I don't want a drunk like you in my life anymore. That's why I kicked you out in the first place. How much clearer do I have to be?"

He tossed the beer can aside, sending a spray of white foam that dotted her pajamas, then approached with splayed hands. "Ah come on. It was just a little disagreement. That's all. Now stop all this tomfoolery." Dan took hold of Evangeline by the armpit and said, "Why don't we go inside and discuss how you're gonna pay for that broken window."

He used his body to help move Evangeline towards the guesthouse, and she struggled with the restraint. "Stop! You're hurting me!"

It was dark by the entrance, and as they were about to enter, he heard the words, "Let her go." As Suzanne pulled the hammer into firing position, there was a distinctive click. She held the barrel of the .44 caliber Smith and Wesson to the side of Dan's head, and her words were slow and deliberate. "Get in your goddamn truck, and if you ever show up in these parts again, my husband will take what's left of your sorry ass and bury it out back."

Dan didn't respond in a timely manner, and Suzanne clipped him hard with the side of her weapon, sending Pantone to his knees. On all fours, he staggered, then looked up only to see Suzanne looming. He shielded his face with his hand as if it would offer some degree of protection.

Suzanne used her head to point toward the pickup. "Get in your damn truck and get da hell outa here."

With blood trickling down his ear, Pantone red-lined the engine, fish-tailing his vehicle wildly down the drive, sending leaves and gravel in all directions. And through the open window, he yelled, "This ain't over, bitch!"

As silence descended upon the property, the two women embraced. Suzanne pushed aside Evangeline's tresses and said, "You OK?"

Evangeline was shaking but managed a nod.

"Come on. Let's get you inside. It's freezin' out here." Suzanne tucked her weapon into her coat pocket and said, "I don't know about you, but I could sure use a belt."

Sam was sitting on the edge of his son's bed when Travis said, "Papa, da boys at school…day been makin' fun of me."

"Really. What are they saying?"

Travis sniffled. "Day call me r'tard."

"You're not retarded," the father replied as he turned off the lamp, leaving a lone night-light along the floorboard for illumination.

In the darkness, Travis said, "Vat does dat mean, Papa?"

"Don't pay any attention to those boys because they don't know what they're talking about."

"But Justin and Kyle day make fun of how I thpeak." With big watery eyes, Travis sniffled, "Thay I'm thtupid."

Sam caressed the boy's head and said, "You're not stupid. You have a little speech problem, that's all, and we're working on that. So, don't you worry about what others are saying, because I think you're the finest little boy I've ever known. Your Mom would be so proud."

With watery eyes and a sniffle, Travis cried, "I mith Mommy."

Sam pulled his son into a full body embrace and said, "You know, when we brought you home from the hospital, Mommy was as proud as a peacock. Must have taken a hundred pictures of you and made sure all our friends got one." He rustled his son's hair and said, "I know it's hard, but just before Mommy died, she made me promise we'd continue on."

Travis squeaked, "Why do peepa hafta die?"

He pulled a tissue from the cardboard box on top of the nightstand and held it to his son's nose. "Now blow." Travis obliged, and Sam said, "Once more." He then folded it up, inserting it into his breast pocket. As Sam placed his son under the covers, he said, "That's a good question, and to be perfectly honest, I'm not sure. But what would the world be like if no one died? We'd be filled to the brim with people. I don't think that would be a good thing. You see, dying is a part of the life cycle.

We all have a beginning, a middle, and an end. It's the way God made it."

"You die, Papa?"

Sam poked his son in the tummy, resulting in a bout of giggling. "Some day, but not right away. I'm going to be around for a long time. Someone has to make sure you do your homework." As Sam tickled him once more, Travis went into another bout of giggling, rustling the covers. "But let's not worry about that right now. It's time for sleep, OK?"

"Papa, weed me a thtory…pwease?"

"Well, I dunno. It's getting late."

"Pwease."

"Well lemme see." Sam stroked his chin, then looked up toward the ceiling, dotted with stars Lori had painted years earlier. "Have I ever told you about the Rabbit's Wedding?"

Travis shook his head.

"It's a good story from long ago. You sure you want to hear this?"

"Pwease, Papa."

"Well let's see now." Sam stroked his chin as he recalled the story. "Once upon a time, there were these two little rabbits that lived out in the country, and they were the best of friends. They played all day and ate dandelions and acorns, but the little black rabbit was always sad."

"Why wuz he thad, Papa?"

Sam whispered, "Well, he loved his friend very much and worried that he would lose her one day. So, when the little white bunny asked him why he was sad, he answered truthfully. Well the little white bunny said, 'But I'm not going anywhere.' You see, the little boy rabbit thought about all the bunnies he knew that died. Some got sick while others were shot by the farmer. So, the white bunny suggested they get married and said, 'Would that make you feel better?' The little black bunny replied, 'Well, I never thought about that, but indeed it would.'"

Travis sat up and said, "Did day get mareweed?"

"Indeed. And all the animals in the forest gathered about as the two bunnies pledged their undying love for one another.

They put dandelions in their hair and danced about with all the other rabbits. It was the best of times."

"What happen to dem?"

"Well, of course, they lived happily ever after."

"Did da momma bunny die?"

Sam sat on the side of Travis' bed with folded hands, thinking this story wasn't the best choice. He thought about how Lori might have answered and said, "She did, and although it was very hard for the papa bunny, he knew he'd see her again in heaven. Now, here is the good part. You see, just before she died, she told the little boy bunny, not to worry about her because her spirit would always be near."

Travis sniffled and said, "Tink Mommy near?"

"I just know it. You can't see her, but she's right here."

Travis looked about the room, searching for Lori's spirit.

He turned to his son and said, "But it's time for all good little bunnies to go to sleep." Sam kissed his son on the forehead, re-tucked the covers and left the bedroom door ajar. When Travis was sound asleep, Sam pulled out a photo album and began the trip down memory lane.

They had gone to the same church, but it was a chance encounter that brought them together at a bar just north of Niagara. They danced a few sets and talked afterwards. All seemed to be going well, but when he ran into her at church the following Sunday, she was occupied, talking to another suitor from the congregation. Feeling rejected, he mentioned it to a friend while ice skating, who managed to produce a phone number. He stuttered when he first called, not knowing what to expect, but Lori's effervescent personality calmed his trepidation. That first night, they talked for nearly two hours, and when he hung up, he found himself hungry for more.

There was never any doubt how much he loved her, and when she slipped her hand into his for the very first time, it was as if the world stood still. In that one instant, he could feel the wheels of destiny turning. It was as if they were tailor-made for one another, like hand and glove. He vividly recalled the arch of her back and the softness of her hands, the dark curly hair that cascaded around her face like a waterfall. And when she sang

Christmas carols, she sounded like an angel. But now her voice had gone silent, supplanted by only a memory.

Sam fingered a photograph of the two, standing next to the Baha'i Temple north of Chicago, recalling their time in the city. It was Easter, and the crocuses were in bloom. If he closed his eyes, the scent of hyacinths that were planted along the side could still be detected. Everything was coming back to life; the lawns were green, trees were budding, and the contrast between then and now was stark. He spoke to the photograph about how Travis got lost in the woods, and after a few minutes of quiet reflection, Sam Carter took the album to bed, laying it on the pillow next to him.

* * * * *

It was an overcast morning, and a light rain descended from a bank of low-lying clouds. The landscape looked like an Ansel Adams photogravure, a myriad of grays and browns. Outside, the only sound coming from the forest was the steady pit-a-pat of raindrops impacting parched soil, and its gentle rhythm was both seductive and reassuring.

Suzanne was up early, and upon hearing the car-door slam, she craned her neck to get a better view, then walked outside. With umbrella in hand, she approached the patrol car. "What brings you out so early, officer?" She didn't wait for a response. "Weren't you one of the guys that helped search for Travis awhile back?"

"That would be correct, ma'am." The deputy wore a rain slicker and gave a hint of a shiver as he pulled his collar up. "Wish I had some good news to share, but I have a warrant here for your arrest."

She jerked her head back and replied with a snarky, "You're joking of course."

The deputy flipped a few pages on his clipboard that were now spattered with water droplets and read the specifics of the complaint. "It was filed by a Mr. Daniel Pantone." The officer used his finger in a sweeping motion to find the right entry.

"Says here you and your husband put a pistol to his head and shot out the back window of his truck."

"You can't believe a word Pantone says. He's a liar and an alcoholic."

A rumble of thunder rolled over the lake just before he replied, "Doesn't matter. All that matters is this warrant." Another flipped page, and the deputy said, "You and your husband are being charged with aggravated battery and the use of a firearm during the commission of a felony."

The color drained from Suzanne's face just as Evangeline walked out from the guest house, drying her hair with a beach towel.

"Is your husband around?"

"No. He...he's at work."

"I'm sorry, but I need you to turn around and place your hands behind your head."

As the deputy applied the manacles, she stuttered, "But...but..."

"Please don't make this any more difficult than it needs to, alright? We'll get you processed, then you can call your attorney and hopefully have you back home yet this evening."

After he applied the handcuffs, Suzanne was read her Miranda rights, then loaded into the backseat of the patrol car. She leaned forward and yelled, "Get hold of Richard! He's in Milwaukee! His number is in my address book on my cell! Tell him to turn himself in, and while you're at it, get hold of Mr. McKenna and let him know what's goin' on!"

A couple of hours later Evangeline saw the headlights cutting through the darkness. With the Templetons gone, she grabbed Richard's weapon, not certain what to expect. When Dalton slammed the door to his SUV, the automatic floodlights illuminated his face, and Evangeline gave a sigh of relief, returning the weapon to the nightstand next to the bed.

After filling him in, Dalton was on the phone. "Yeah, it's me. Look, I need everything you got on a fella named Pantone, first name is Daniel. Lives in Grand Ledge. I'll send you the particulars. Encode what you got and send it to my cell."

After the call, Evangeline said, "I could have told you everything you want. Like I said, we went together for almost seven years."

Dalton didn't bother with a reply. Instead, he called his attorney, who was home, nursing a cold. Jazmine Fontaine was relatively new to the world of criminal jurisprudence, making a stab at respectability after years of working for an escort agency, where she provided wealthy clients with a variety of carnal pleasures. But working in the industry left her feeling hollowed-out, like a dead tree trunk, at least until Dalton McKenna showed up. He found her a job with Pokorney Industries, working as an analyst on an oil-shale project in northern Alberta, and although it wasn't something she would have gravitated toward, it did result in an opportunity to attend law school.

Fontaine sneezed, then sniffled. "Haven't heard from you in a spell. What's goin' on?"

"Busy like usual. Look, I got a coupla folks up here in Esky that were charged with aggravated battery and felony firearm. Both are currently in the Delta County lockup." Dalton described the altercation and concluded with, "They need some legal advice and thought you could help. Maybe you can talk to Andrews and see if she can backstop their bail. We're hoping for a PR bond, but it's a small community, and it could come down differently."

After providing the specifics, Dalton could hear his attorney scribbling down notes until she twanged, "Got it. Look, in the morning, I'll contact the Templetons and see if they want me to represent them. If they agree, I'll set up a Skype connection for their arraignment."

* * * * *

The *Agnes Bea* was sailing south at a steady clip when the helicopter approached from the northwest. The pilot was on a loudspeaker, and his voice boomed over the waves. "Cut your engines! This is the United States Coast Guard. Prepare to be boarded."

With gulls hovering high above, the scow turned to port in an attempt to flee while men onboard scrambled about, tossing bales overboard. Since the cargo was wrapped in dark plastic, they were partially buoyant, giving them the appearance of black ice cubes, floating in a sea of endless blue. The helicopter dropped a diver into the water who secured a bale and then placed it into an inflatable dingy. Off in the distance, a large white cutter approached, and its wake indicated it was traveling at top speed.

Four men were taken into custody, and the *Agnes Bea* was towed to the Coast Guard Station in Escanaba where several bales of marijuana were offloaded. Of the forty-some odd packages dumped into the lake, three were recovered, each weighing approximately fifty kilos. The owners of the *Agnes Bea,* John and Joe Steiner, were subsequently charged with drug trafficking and running a criminal enterprise under the Racketeer Influenced and Corrupt Organization Act (RICO) as defined under title 18 USC Section 1961-1968. In addition to their arrests, a civil suit was filed by the Department of Justice in US District Court, seeking asset forfeiture of the fishing trawler.

Meanwhile, Fontaine instructed Evangeline to file a counter-complaint against Pantone, alleging aggravated battery. Deputies from Delta County interviewed several neighbors who confirmed they heard gunshots several times over the past few weeks, but that sort of thing wasn't unusual. Complicating matters the slug that shattered Pantone's back window couldn't be located. Therefore, no ballistics could be performed to corroborate Pantone's assertion. Without any independent witnesses or physical evidence, the complaints against all three were dismissed without prejudice.

As Richard Templeton was being released from the Delta County lockup, the Steiners were being led to a holding cell, and when they passed in the hall, the three leered until Joe yelled, "You're a dead man, Templeton. Hear me? Dead man!"

CHAPTER NINE

*"It is the secret of the world that all things subsist
and do not die but retire a little from sight and afterwards
return again. Nothing is dead; men feign themselves dead
and endure mock funerals and mournful obituaries,
and there they stand looking out of the window, sound
and well in some new strange disguise."*
- Ralph Waldo Emerson

Late afternoon December 24, 1913

Being over six feet tall, Annie Clemenc pushed the crowd back and made her way to the stairwell, yelling as loud as possible. "There's no fire! You have to stop! Move back!"

A mass of people clogged the lone exit, and men were at the top of the staircase peeling off women and children from the mound of humanity. The screams by now had subsided and were replaced by moans, some deep within the pile. But the bodies were so tightly interlaced, unraveling them took time. The ones closest to the ticket counter were resuscitated, but further down, only breathless beings were recovered who were later placed into long rows. Most looked as if they had simply fallen asleep, giving rise to an allegation that poison gas was used. But the truth was the victims had simply suffocated.

* * * * *

With the arrest of the Steiners, life returned to normal out on Garth Point, and the reconstruction of the Templeton residence began in earnest. Meanwhile, Suzanne was vacuuming Tom Attwood's cottage, and the television was turned to a Marquette station when the news bulletin interrupted regularly scheduled programming. She turned up the volume.

106

We interrupt this program to bring you a news bulletin. Two local men were gunned down near the town of Garden this morning, and Kristen Bornhurst has a live report from the newsroom. What do you have for us, Kristen?

Well Shari, the Delta County Sheriff's Office is telling us that John and Joe Steiner were gunned down early this morning just outside Joe Steiner's rural home out on the Garden Peninsula. As you may already know, the two men were recently charged in federal court on drug charges and were out on bail at the time of the incident. The sheriff's office isn't releasing many details about the crime, but autopsies are planned for later today. When asked about possible suspects, Sheriff Wigglesworth said, and I quote, "We have a couple of individuals we need to talk to and believe these two murders are directly related to recent drug activity out on the Garden Peninsula." We'll have more details as they become available. Live from the newsroom, Kristen Bornhurst reporting.

Later that day, a patrol car pulled up to the back of the cottage, and Suzanne walked outside to greet them.

"Is your husband around?" was all the patrolmen said.

"He's at work. Should be back sometime after five. You wanna come in?"

Evangeline was at the sink, rinsing out a large roaster they had used the night before and took a seat at the kitchen table with Suzanne and the deputy at her side.

The officer removed his hat and inhaled deeply. "In case you haven't heard, Joe and John Steiner were killed this morning."

"Oh dear."

"And I'd like to know where you were during that time frame."

"Well, let me think." Suzanne took a moment to gather her thoughts and stroked her chin. "I slept in until about nine, then spent the remainder of the morning cleaning the house. And later, I went into town to run an errand." Before she could say anything more, the phone rang, and Suzanne was quick to answer. "Thanks for getting back with us, Ms. Fontaine. A deputy from the sheriff's department is here with us right now.

Here, I'll let you talk to him." Suzanne put the call onto speaker phone.

The officer snapped, "Who am I talking to?"

"Name is Fontaine, and I'm acting as legal council for both the Templetons and Ms. Attwood."

The deputy chuckled. "You're joking, of course."

"Hardly. Furthermore, my clients will not be answering any of your questions today, and unless they're being placed into custody, you are instructed to leave the premises immediately. Any further questions regarding the deaths of Joe and John Steiner need to be addressed to me personally. Any questions?"

Suzanne turned off the speaker, then put the phone to her ear. "Thanks, Ms. Fontaine. When Richard gets home, we'll give you a call."

After Suzanne put her phone aside, the deputy pressed on with splayed hands. "There's no need to get an attorney, Mrs. Templeton. We're here just to collect some basic information, that's all. You see, the victims were charged with drug trafficking, and several people overheard Steiner make a death threat to your husband while in custody. The DNR told us that it was your husband who called in that illegal netting operation, then before you know it, your house goes up in smoke. Coupla nights ago, this fella Pantone enters the fray for some reason or another, alleging you held a weapon to his head, and your husband shot out the back window of his pickup truck. Don't deny it. I saw the pictures." After a heavy exhalation through his nose, the officer said, "I think you and your husband have some serious explaining to do."

Suzanne took hold of Evangeline's hand.

With hands now folded, the deputy pressed on. "Now I'm not saying you didn't have a right to go after Steiner, considering what they did to your property, but I can arrange for the prosecutor to go light on you. You might even be able to argue self defense. What do you say? Help us out here."

Evangeline leaned forward and cleared her throat. "You were instructed to leave the premises by our attorney, and I'm giving you ten seconds to leave before I file trespassing charges against you and the Delta County Sheriff's Office."

When he rose, the chair legs growled along the pine flooring. He opened the screen door, turned and gave an exaggerated smile. "Have a nice day."

* * * * *

Indian Summer pulled into town like a long-lost friend, and the land was awash in a sea of crimson and yellow. Off in the distance, a downy woodpecker tapped away on a dead tamarack, and there was a light coating of ice along the shoreline. The lake steamed like a hot cup of Joe on a frosty morning. By mid-day, the autumn sun melted most of the shore ice, but frost remained inland where the forest canopy kept the sun's warmth at bay. Earlier that week, residents along Garth Point pulled their boats and piers from the icy waters. Later, storm windows were placed into service, and firewood was stacked into neat rows alongside various dwellings as folks prepared for the inevitable.

After filling the wood-box by the stone fireplace, Richard Templeton whisked his hands and heard an approaching vehicle. Suzanne swept back the curtain to the bedroom window and noticed the cloud of leaves that accompanied a pair of patrol cars. There were four uniformed officers in all, and when Richard exited the cottage, his first words were, "What can I do for you, fellas?"

A sheriff's deputy handed Richard the papers and said, "We have a warrant to search the premises."

"A warrant?" Richard used his index finger to scan the document. "Well according to this, you have the right to search my property, but my property is over there." The engineer folded up the paperwork, then swept his hand toward the new construction. "Knock yourself out, but just about everything we owned got burnt to a crisp and hauled to the landfill."

By now, Suzanne was standing next to her husband, and after explaining the matter, the deputy lifted his chin. "So, you're not going to let us in to this residence?"

"It's not mine," Richard replied with a shrug. "You'll have to talk to Tom Attwood who owns the place, or maybe you can get the judge to amend the warrant with a proper address. But as it stands right now, you only have the right to search my property over there." Richard pointed towards the north, then folded up the paperwork.

The officer's words were sharp. "Neighbors say your place was ransacked awhile ago, and you hired some ex-cop from downstate to go after Joe Steiner. Any truth to that allegation?"

"We didn't hire nobody," Templeton replied as he drilled his ear with an index finger, "and we haven't had any trouble since." Richard hocked up a wad of phlegm, depositing it into a blue handkerchief. "Ain't that right, sweetheart?"

Suzanne grabbed Richard's hand and was exceptionally saccharine in her reply. "I don't know what you're talking about, but we haven't had a lick of trouble whatsoever. We would have called you fellas if there was, but it's been real quiet."

"You know a guy named John Mosby? We believe he also goes by the name of Dalton McKenna."

Richard shrugged.

"He rented a helicopter over in Esky and paid the owner a grand for no more than a few hours work."

"So."

"We think someone hired him to scope out Steiner's house over on the Garden Peninsula. Pilot said he took several pictures and GPS coordinates."

Suzanne replied, "Look, we're sorry to hear about Joe Steiner and all, but I swear to God, we had nothing to do with it."

"Sheriff Wigglesworth says Steiner made a death threat while you were in the lock-up together." The officer snapped off his sunglasses, revealing a pair of bushy eyebrows. "Don't deny it because we got several people who'll swear to it."

"Look Officer," Richard squinted as he read the name tag, "Caspian. That just doesn't make any sense. Why would we hire someone to kill those boys?"

Caspian lifted his chin once again. "Maybe it's because the burned your house down. What do you have to say about that?"

"Look, putting a hit on someone costs big bucks, and you can check my bank account if you like. There hasn't been any big money withdrawn except for clothing we had to replace."

The officer clicked his ballpoint open and produced a brown notebook from his breast pocket. "What's the name of the bank?"

Templeton thought about the check he wrote to Dalton McKenna and cringed. "Well…ah…Wells Fargo. They got a branch office over in Esky."

He dutifully wrote the information down and snapped his fingers as he pointed to the lot next door, directing his officers to initiate the search.

While they examined the construction site, an amended warrant was issued, then brought out to the property a few hours later. Evangeline exited the guest house when they approached and said, "You're not going to go through my personal things are you?"

"A properly executed warrant allows us to examine everything on this property, including your personal possessions."

Afterwards, Richard got the phone from his truck and made the call. He cleared his throat and said, "Mr. McKenna?"

"Speaking."

"Rich Templeton here."

"You using a burner like I told you?"

"I am."

"Good."

Richard provided an update, then softly whispered, "Did you kill 'em?"

"Sorry, but since they made that death threat, I can understand why they consider you a prime suspect."

"So, what…what should we do?" Richard continued to pace about. "They served a search warrant this afternoon, and they're gonna check my bank account for any suspicious withdrawals." Richard gulped. "I hope you didn't cash that check I wrote?"

"Look, I'll be there tomorrow morning. Stay put."

* * * * *

It was difficult to accept, the prospect that the Templetons were the center of a double homicide investigation. So, as a means of coping, Evangeline went for a long drive. Several hours later she found herself at the museum in Calumet and stood before the paneled doors as she did before. Evangeline ran her fingertips over the coarse wood, feeling the rough and smooth areas where thousands of hands once touched. The white sheet of paper that listed the names of the deceased was still taped to the front, and Evangeline touched each one until she found what she was looking for. With her left palm upon her forehead, the vision gently unfolded. She could see a coal-burning stove in a meager kitchen with a copper kettle simmering on top. A scent of cinnamon caught her attention and eyed the apple pies cooling along the window sill where a set of checkered curtains flapped in the summer breeze. Off in the corner were a pair of work boots, soiled and stained brown. As Evangeline looked up, she saw the carbide lamp resting neatly upon a wood shelf near the coat hooks. Every detail came into focus: the wainscoting, the pine floor and all the scratches, the chipped plates and dishes stacked neatly in an open cupboard. She heard a siren off in the distance, and the clock above the cook stove read twelve-thirty. The sounds and sights evoked a sense of well-being, providing a certain connectedness to her humble surroundings, until she spied the rag doll off in the corner, looking forlorn and threadbare.

A docent interrupted her vision and said, "Can I help you with anything?"

It felt like her mind was being pulled in opposite directions, with one foot in the here and now and the other buried in the past. The transition was difficult, and as her pulse raced, sweat glistened from Evangeline's forehead.

"Sad story, eh?" the docent remarked.

The former teacher blew her nose, allowing time to gather her thoughts. "What do you think it was like for the families who lost loved ones?"

A strong inhalation across the docent's teeth sounded like bacon sizzling. "I'm sure it was pretty difficult. It's tough losing a child, but to lose one at Christmas…well, it musta been devastating."

"Do you know anything about the victims…I mean…like where they lived and next of kin?"

"Lemme think." The docent rubbed his forehead. "Well, the historical society published a book called, *Families Left Behind*, and we have a few copies for sale in the gift shop."

After purchasing the book, Evangeline donned a pair of reading glasses as she read the various stories on each victim and was surprised to find out no one had ever been charged for the seventy-three deaths. She thought about the irony of her neighbor being investigated for a crime he didn't commit and shook her head with disgust. But Evangeline did find a list of the victim's addresses and jotted a couple of names down on a scrap of paper.

Raymbaultown was only about a mile away and had been incorporated into Calumet Township years earlier. Here, Evangeline and Lucy walked about the empty lot on 'B' Street, kicking the tall grass, hoping to find something…anything. She found an old building stone half immersed in brown soil and extracted it from its muddy confines. There was a puddle out near the road, and as she washed the memento, Evangeline could feel the little girl's spirit. She looked up, expecting to see a child, but the only presence she could discern was a lone mourning dove, resting along a power line. Evangeline held her hand up as if she could touch the apparition, then closed her eyes once more, whispering, "I'm so sorry."

A car honked as it passed by, breaking Evangeline's reverie. She clapped her hands for Lucy to jump into the red Honda, where the two made the short trip to the Lake View Cemetery. Here, she stood above the grave marker with her hand to her throat while Lucy barked incessantly. She whispered, "Stop that! You're not supposed to be running loose out here, and I'm going to get into a peck of trouble if anyone sees us. So, knock it off."

Lucy came to Evangeline's side, nudging her with a wet nose, then returning to the spot she was sitting at an instant before. The tall brunette walked over and whispered irritably. "What?"

Suddenly, the same feeling as before descended. It too felt like a portal into another dimension, and she could see the man following close behind the caskets, plaintively calling his daughter's name.

"She's here, isn't she? They got the location wrong. That's what you're trying to tell me. Isn't that right, Lucy." Evangeline pondered the dilemma and sighed. "Come on. Let's get outa here. I'm starting to make stuff up. I don't know any of these people."

Afterwards, Evangeline stopped at Luigi's and was again their lone customer. She sat at the bar pondering recent events when a new vision emerged. She could see a man walking in through the front door, and for a second, she thought of Ulay, but his soiled boots and carbide lamp suggested he was a miner, not an artist. He was the same one from the vision before, a small man, about five-six, yet muscular. And when he talked, she could feel the immediate connection. The miner sat with others, and Evangeline could hear the laughter, but their discussion was in another language. She savored the moment like a prisoner on death row, enjoying a final sunset, until the bartender came by and said, "What can I getcha?"

"A cold beer would be nice," she replied with a smile.

As he grabbed a stein from the countertop, he looked up and said, "Hope you don't mind PBR. The beer man hasn't come yet, and it's all we got."

"That's fine."

He pulled the lever, and the fluid flowed like a stream of golden honey, filling her glass until the foam cascaded down the side. "Haven't you been in before?" he said with a slight squint. "If I'm not mistaken, you're from Esky, right?"

"You got a good memory. I'm just in town for a few days visiting...friends." Evangeline pulled her wallet out and said, "How much do I owe you?"

The bartender held his hand up as if to stop payment. "It's on the house. Last time you were in, you asked about places to visit. Didja check out the Vertin Gallery?"

"Indeed. The upper levels weren't open, but I imagine it was quite the department store back in its day." A sip of beer was followed by, "You got any other interesting places for me to visit?"

"Well. if you walk up and down Fifth and Sixth Street, you've pretty much seen all there is. Calumet is just a little town. As for interesting things going on, I got a group of paranormal investigators coming in next week."

Evangeline squinted.

"You see, there's a ghost that haunts the building, and a team of scientists down in Houghton are bringing their equipment in to see if we can detect whatever it is." He handed her the letter outlining their visit.

After scanning the correspondence, she said, "Have you... actually... seen the ghost?"

The bartender nodded, then pointed. "It always seems to hang out at the end of the bar. It's just a shadow that moves about and several other people have seen it too." He lowered his voice to a whisper and said, "Story has it that the upstairs portion was a boarding house, and someone related to the owner died up there. But nobody knows for sure." The bartender looked at his watch, then wiped his hands onto a rag. "Can I getcha to do me a favor?"

"Sure. What's up?"

"I have to run an errand." He took his apron off and tossed it aside. "Would you mind watching the place for me? Should be back in about fifteen minutes."

He headed towards the door with hat in hand until Evangeline called out, "But...but what if we have customers?"

He turned and grinned. "You'll figure it out. I trust you."

Now alone, she walked to the part of the bar where the apparition had been seen and stood before the old water closet. Evangeline whispered, "I'm not afraid of you. Whoever you are, you need to move on. The past isn't here." As she pondered the notion that a ghost haunted the establishment, the front door swept open, letting in a blast of warm air. Loud voices were accompanied by four men who took seats at the bar, and Evangeline set out several napkins. "What can I get you fellas?"

She served up a couple of pitchers of beer just as another group took seats at a booth by the jukebox. The middle-aged woman didn't know what to charge. So, she guessed and rung up about thirty bucks in sales. When the bartender returned, his first words were, "Holy shit."

Evangeline smirked. "Business picked up pretty quickly. Didn't know what to charge; so, I guessed. Put the money into your cash register."

Just then, a crew from the road commission walked through the front door, and one shouted, "We're thirsty. Don't care what you got on tap as long as it's cold!"

The bartender cocked his head to one side and said, "You need a job?"

* * * * *

Richard's voice rose a notch when he said, "I swear, I didn't have nothin' to do with killin' Steiner. I...I was over at my mother's, for Christ sake. You can ask her. She'll tell ya."

Dalton took a sip of beer, then blew his nose. "Didja tell the cops all that?"

"I did, but they found out about that damn helicopter you rented, and now they think I hired you to kill those two galoots. And sure-as-shit, they're gonna find out about that check I wrote, and it won't take long before someone makes the connection between you and that drug bust you orchestrated. And we better figure out damn quick who's responsible for killin' Steiner before we all end up taking our meals in Marquette!"

Dalton pulled out his cell and found his attorney's number.

After explaining the situation, Fontaine replied, "So you're thinking drug dealers are responsible?"

"Makes sense. They took a sizeable hit when their product was dumped into the lake, and from what the news was saying, upwards of two tons were lost. So, what's your professional opinion?"

"Considering the evidence, we have to be prepared that the prosecutor will press charges against you and Templeton. If that happens, we're going to have to establish reasonable doubt that someone else was responsible. Being a tight community like you say, it'll make it much more difficult, especially if the jury comes from the Garden Peninsula. Look, if you need help with this, why don't you get hold of Stuart O'Hare. Dana spoke to him the other day, and he might be able to offer some support."

Dalton McKenna recalled the time when O'Hare was charged with open murder. He chuckled at the thought and said to his attorney, "What's his number?"

* * * * *

The Templetons agreed to the interview, which was held at the Delta County Sheriff's Office in Escanaba. It was a small interrogation room with no windows, and a video camera was mounted near the ceiling. Caspian started out with the date and time, then began his questioning. "Mr. Templeton, please tell me about your relationship with a...," he flipped through a few pages until he found what he was looking for, "a Mr. Dalton McKenna."

Templeton's lawyer was present via a Skype connection and interrupted. "He's a close friend who has a camp up near the town of Ralph. Mr. Templeton employed him to help with a personal matter."

The sergeant pulled out a copy of the five-thousand-dollar check and held it up in front of the laptop. He turned towards Richard and said, "And what exactly kind of personal matter did you hire him for, Mr. Templeton?"

Richard tugged at his collar and replied, "Well, ahh..."

Fontaine interrupted once again, and her voice was resolute. "You need to direct your questions to me personally. Otherwise, we'll be terminating this interview."

Caspian snapped back into his chair, dropped his ballpoint onto a yellow legal pad, and then raised his hands as if

117

surrendering. "No reason to get upset, Ms. Fontaine. This is just a friendly little discussion. We just want to get to the bottom of all this. After all, we have two men lying in the morgue over at OSF."

"Don't go pulling that dumb-cop routine." Fontaine wagged her finger at the screen and said, "You know damn well this isn't a friendly conversation. You're investigating a double homicide, and my client is a prime suspect...innocent I might add."

The sergeant leaned forward with flared nostrils. "How 'bout I let you in on where we stand with this, sweetheart?" He leaned back into his chair with arms akimbo. "Templeton's house gets torched because he called in an illegal fishing operation out on the bay. The DNR confiscated a large net worth thousands of dollars not to mention the fish that were caught up in it. Not long after, your client hires a Mr. Dalton McKenna, who according to our records is a retired US Marshal. He uses an assumed identity by the name of John Mosby, then hires a chopper and according to the pilot, was interested in some growing operation out on the peninsula. Don't deny it because we have an affidavit from the pilot, who is willing to testify on our behalf. Now comes the good part."

Fontaine stifled a yawn.

"Your client lied to us about ever knowing this McKenna fella when we interviewed him a few days ago, and that alone is sufficient to charge him with obstruction. But it gets even better. You see, the *Agnes Bea* was carrying about two tons of Garden Gold when the Coast Guard received an anonymous tip. What you don't know is that they recorded that conversation, and we'll provide expert witnesses who will testify that the recorded voice belongs to your buddy, McKenna. Not only that, the two owners of the *Agnes Bea* are the same two guys who had their nets confiscated by the DNR. Am I going too fast for you, honeybunch?"

Richard cast his attorney a stern expression, but she ignored it.

"How did you find out the nets were owned by Steiner?" she asked pointedly.

The question caught Caspian off guard, derailing his monologue. "I...I'm not answering your questions. You're answering mine."

"How convenient."

"As it turns out, Templeton here was incarcerated for a spell. Apparently, a guy named Pantone filed a complaint, alleging that your client and his wife held a pistol to his head and shot out the back window of his pickup truck." Satisfied, Caspian clasped the back of his head with both hands, revealing sweat stains under his arms. "The charges were dropped for some reason or another, and when he was released, Mr. Templeton here passed the Steiners while they were being led to a holding cell, and a threat was made." The sergeant flipped a page and said, "And I quote, 'You're a dead man, Templeton. Hear me? Dead man!' Then a few days later, after they posted bond, their bodies were found face down on Steiner's driveway. Each shot a couple times with a .44 caliber revolver."

"So, what do you want from us?" Fontaine said clearly irritated.

"At minimum, I'd say we have a strong circumstantial case against your client." Caspian lifted his cleft chin and said, "Care to explain any of this, sweetheart?"

Fontaine cleared her throat, and her tone reflected more irritation. "Tell me, did you go to college?"

"What's that got to do with anything?"

"Because if you did, maybe it's not too late to get your money back. Because from where I stand, you don't know a damn thing about criminal jurisprudence!"

Caspian clamped his lips tight.

"Why aren't you going after the guys who owned all that pot that got dumped into the fucking lake?" The attorney hollered, "I'm sure they were less than thrilled with losing twenty-million bucks. Hell, here in Detroit, a drug heist of a few hundred will get you whacked. So, if you want to argue your case in front of a jury, be my guest, but we'll be presenting a rigorous defense. So, here's the short and tall of it, sonny. Our interview is over."

Dalton strolled into the DNR office, wearing a Hawaiian shirt that had green palm trees on the front along with several coconuts near the bottom. An elderly woman pulled back the sliding glass window that screeched in protest. "Can I help you?"

"Like to speak to David Fales. Understand he works in this office."

The woman craned her neck to see if she could spot the officer. "Hang on a sec. Lemme see if I can find 'im."

A moment later, the door creaked opened, and Fales extended his hand. The large man with a squeaky voice and full beard stood before Dalton McKenna and said, "I'm Officer Fales. How can I help you?"

Dalton accepted the hand and gave it a hardy shake. "Can we speak privately? I have some information about an illegal fishing operation in one of the inlet bays."

A heavy sigh preceded, "Why don't you come on back?"

The two snaked their way past various desks and file cabinets until they reached a conference room that overlooked the parking lot. Fales pulled out a metal chair and said, "What can I do for you Mr....."

"Dalton McKenna. I have a place up near Ralph."

Fales clicked his ballpoint open and scribbled down the name along with the date and time. "So, you said you had some information about an illegal fishing operation?"

"Not at all. What I really want to know... is... how long has Joe Steiner been paying you?" Off in the distance, Dalton could hear a chainsaw grinding away, and a door to a delivery truck slammed shut.

The DNR officer looked over the top of his wire-rimmed glasses and took a second to reply. "Pardon me?"

The former US Marshal pulled out a stack of papers from his briefcase, and after thumbing through several pages, he found what he was looking for, then scooted the documents across the table. "I highlighted the calls you made on your personal cell phone, and these are the ones you made to Steiner. Here's the list of callers to this DNR office, and if you look at the yellow highlighted item," Dalton tapped the paper with his index finger, "you'll see the call was made by Richard Templeton when he reported that illegal net out on the bay. Twenty minutes later, you were on the phone talking to Steiner, and I'd like to know the nature of that conversation."

By now, the color had drained from Fales' face. "Where did you get these?"

"That's largely irrelevant. Since Steiner went and got himself killed, I'd say you have some serious explaining to do. So, if I don't get some straight answers, all this is headed right over to the State Police."

Fales jutted his jaw as he stared at the conference table.

"You know how this turns out, Mr. Fales." Dalton whispered, "At best, you'll lose your job, but if they can connect you to those two murders…"

"I wanna talk to an attorney."

"Well sure." Dalton pulled out his phone and scooted it across the table. "Be my guest. But before you do, you might want to think about your family and what this will do to 'em. I think they'll have a hard time posting bond. Might even have to sell that nice house of yours."

The DNR officer bit his lower lip as he fidgeted with a ballpoint.

"Look, if you answer my questions, I'll see that all this," Dalton swept his hand over the various papers, "gets buried. But if you want to call your attorney, you might want to explain these bank statements." Dalton slid several more documents across the conference table. "They show some rather interesting deposits, almost twenty-grand by my reckoning." Dalton held his left hand to the side of his mouth and whispered, "Psst. You didn't declare any of this on your 1040s, and the IRS will weigh in on this most precipitously."

As Fales continued to fidget with his ballpoint, Dalton said, "Correct me if I'm wrong. You were a paid informant, and from the bank records I looked at, I'd say it was a modest sum of about a thousand a month, probably paid in cash. So, when Templeton called in the complaint about the illegal net, you called Steiner because he was the only one working that area. Furthermore, we suspect he told you what he was up to beforehand. So, when Templeton called, you knew exactly who to contact." Dalton was on the edge of his seat when he whispered, "That would make you an accessory to arson which is punishable up to fifteen years in prison, and you'd be on the hook for restitution."

A gulp preceded, "You a cop?"

"Private investigator."

"Look, I didn't have anything to do with that. I swear."

"Maybe not directly, but that call to Steiner incriminates you."

Fales' exhalation was like air being forced out of a steam vent, and his right knee pulsated like a jackhammer. "So, what do you want from me?"

"Cooperation. Any hesitancy on your part, and like I said, all this," Dalton wagged his finger at the scattered files, "gets sent on to the prosecutor. But…" There was a long pause until he added, "you can stay on their payroll for all I care as long as you give me the names of everyone involved, including your contact at the sheriff's department." Dalton pulled out some additional phone records and pointed to the call Fales had made to the Delta County Sheriff's office in Escanaba. With arms folded, he sat back into his chair "As you can see, this was made just after you called Steiner. So, who's your contact?"

By now, beads of sweat had formed along Fales' forehead. He looked up and rubbed his oversized neck. "How do I know I can trust you? I don't you from Adam."

"Look at it this way. If you think you can get a better deal with law enforcement or the drug dealers that hired you, feel free to give 'em a call. Just one other thing."

Fales lifted his chin, revealing a scar along his neck.

"Since law enforcement is involved, copies of all this have been sent on to several attorneys I work with, and if anything happens to me or the Templeton family, all this gets published in the local paper. Got it? So, if you want to avoid criminal prosecution, I need names and phone numbers, starting right now."

The DNR officer seemed smaller now, and his voice was a mere whisper. "OK."

CHAPTER TEN

*"Anything you lose
comes around in another form."*
- Rumi

December 24, 1913

Over the commotion, Peter heard someone say, "It's a stampede inside!"

Men ran to the front entrance, fighting their way to the door only to find a mass of humanity piled up on the staircase. Peter frantically called out, "Mary!!"

The fire department was now on the scene, and firemen pushed the crowd back. Peter was amongst them, striving to get closer and yelled, "Papa's comin',"

A couple of lifeless children were pulled from the mass stacked up on the stairwell and were placed along the sidewalk, where their clothing was loosened, hoping against all odds the victims might resuscitate. By now, the crowd was stirring like bees around an angry hive. Pushing and shouting gave way to wails of grief as parents collapsed over the bodies of their dead children. Fights broke out. At first, it was nothing more than the police pushing onlookers back, but soon striking union workers and members of the Citizen's Alliance entered the fray. Pushing gave way to fist and clubs, dotting the pavement with seething red blood.

Peter ran to the church where he had planned to meet up with his family, hoping they might be there waiting for him. But the church was nearly empty and fear set in. Meanwhile, the bodies were moved to the village hall and set out onto tables where parents came in with hopes their beloved children were not amongst the dead. Peter pushed his way to the front, and his words were quick, "Where's my wife and baby?"

"Name please."

"Elizabeth and Mary Kovarti. I'm Mary's papa."

He was led to a table, and the white linen cloth was removed, revealing his wife and daughter, side by side. Peter scooped up their lifeless bodies and wailed. The attendant restrained him, trying to pry the dead child from her father's embrace, but Peter continued to howl like a man being tortured by a relentless burn.

As townsfolk gathered, a call went out to other communities for caskets as there were simply not enough. There were seventy-three dead, fifty-nine of them children.

Meanwhile, a light snow started to descend, covering the streets and walkways with a white fluffy powder, obscuring the tears and blood, already shed.

* * * * *

"Hello?"

Evangeline cleared her throat and squeaked, "Hi, would this be Margaret Keillor?"

"Yes. Who's calling?"

"Hi. My name is Evangeline Attwood, and I understand this might seem odd, but are you at all related to a Mr. Roy Kincaid? He perished during World War Two."

It took a second before Evangeline heard, "Well, ah…yes. Roy Kincaid was my uncle. He was my mom's kid brother."

The two chit-chatted for a few moments until Margaret said, "So, why are you interested in my uncle? He's been gone like forever."

"Well, you see…."

Margaret broke in and said, "It just broke my mother's heart when he died." She sniffled, "We never brought him home, you know. The army thinks he's buried in a military cemetery somewhere in the Philippines."

124

"And you knew his wife, Emma?"

"Of course." Her voice was now light as a feather, and Evangeline strained to hear every word. "You see, my uncle died before I was born, but Emma sent a Christmas letter to my Mom every year. As I understand, she remarried a few years after Roy died and lived downstate. Was told she passed away recently. Are you related?"

"I'm not, but I have some material you might be interested in." And as Evangeline explained how she acquired Roy's letters, the former teacher could hear the sniffling. "I know this is hard, but I sent a letter to a laboratory, and they were able to extract a DNA profile from the stamps he licked. I was thinking maybe we could contact the military with this new information." There was nothing but silence until Evangeline said, "You still there?"

"Do you think it's even possible? I mean, after all these years, I'm not even sure there's anything left to compare it to. What's the army going to do…dig up all the unknowns? There must be thousands."

For whatever reason, Evangeline thought about the mass graves at Lake View Cemetery and the souls buried within. She lightly gasped at the mental image, then replied, "I was reading that the government was using this technique to bring home those that were unidentified, and some of them date all the back to the Civil War. I won't do anything, unless you say so, but it would only take a phone call to find out."

Margaret blew her nose, and when she spoke, her words were broken. "My…my Mom passed away a few years back, and she…m…made me promise never to forget Unka Roy." Margaret cried, "Oh…could you come see me? Maybe, you could show me his letters."

Evangeline pulled out a pen and a scrap of paper from her handbag. "I know where Luigi's is. Can you give me directions from there?"

"I live over on Pine Street, and if you take 5th all the way to the end, it'll take you right there. My house is just about a block from the Italian Hall Memorial. Do you know where that is?"

Upon arrival at Margaret's home, Evangeline poured some water into a dish, then patted Lucy's crown. "I won't be long, lamb-chop." She gathered up Roy's letters along with Emma's journals, making her way to the Victorian home with gingerbread trim and lace curtains. When she rang the bell, the curtains upstairs swept to one side, and the door creaked open a few seconds later.

There before her stood a short, middle-aged woman with a penetrating smile. Margaret extended her small delicate fingers and said, "You must be Evangeline. Come on in." She looked at the armful of books and said, "Are all those from Roy and Emma?"

"She was a prolific writer. Would you like to see a few?"

Pressing a hand to her heart, Margaret sniffled, "It would be an honor."

They sat at the dining room table, adorned with a lace runner and a bowl, full of oranges. With black reading glasses, Margaret perused each journal, and the two spent the better part of an hour reading Roy's letters to one another. The Calumet resident snapped her glasses off and walked into the kitchen, returning with a few letters of her own. "These were letters he sent to my Gramma. When she passed on, my Mom got them, and now they're here with me. Would you like to read a few?"

And with each letter, Roy came back to life; Evangeline could feel his personality emerge. The soldier had a sense of humor, and the two laughed when he wrote about the time he got caught sneaking Emma onto the base at Fort Custer. Since they weren't married, he got KP duty for a week, but as Roy put it, "…it was well worth it."

Margaret absentmindedly looked at her watch and sighed. "I didn't realize how late it's getting, and you have a long ride ahead of you."

"That's alright," Evangeline replied calmly. "Lucy and I were going to get a room at one of the motels here in town."

"A motel? You got to be kidding me. Why don't you stay out at our camp? It's only a few miles from here. It's right on Lake Superior, and nobody is using it. Besides," Margaret took hold of Evangeline's hand and patted it gently, "you're family now, and I wouldn't have it any other way."

* * * * *

It was a slice of heaven staying at Margaret's camp. It was right on Cedar Bay, and when she looked out onto the lake at night, Evangeline could see the lights from various ore boats en route to their southern destinations. She thought about the Carl Bradley and wondered what it was like for Richard's uncle as the ship broke apart in the cold waters of Lake Michigan.

In the morning, she lingered, walking the shoreline with a cool zephyr at her back, picking up colorful stones that caught her eye. It all seemed to fit together as if her time was destined and wondered, once again, whether acquiring Roy's letters was a mere coincidence. After all, without purchasing Emma's cedar chest, she would never have made the sojourn to the Copper Country and would never have met Margaret for that matter. With Lucy at her side, she spotted a couple off in the distance, walking the shoreline, holding hands. They were too far away to recognize, but Evangeline felt an element of sadness, wondering if she would ever fall in love again. Oddly, the sadness seemed to transform itself into something much more hopeful as if Lake Superior held some magic power, and as she pondered the possibilities ,a new sense of optimism ensued.

On the way back to Garth Point, Evangeline stopped at the Seaman Mineral Museum, where she brought along her specimen from the bottom of Lake Michigan. She asked the docent if there was anyone that could help identify its composition, and while she waited, the former teacher inspected a variety of display cabinets. Here, she read about minerals found in the Keweenaw and looked upon specimens of crystalline copper, along with a variety of half-breeds. Just as she was straining her neck to get a better look, a tall lanky fellow with a nimbus of bright orange hair appeared from behind a specimen cabinet. After introducing himself, Liam took hold of Evangeline's hand, pumping it like a hungry

127

politician. "Was told you have a question about a rock you have."

Once free of his grip, she shook her hand to get the blood circulating. "Yes, indeed. I was diving out on Little Bay de Noc," Evangeline fumbled with her backpack, then thrust the specimen forward with both hands. "I found this on the lake bottom. Careful, it's kinda heavy."

He inhaled abruptly, and the mineralogist's first words were one long exhalation. "Holy shit."

"A friend of mine said it was native silver, and supposedly, it came from this part of country. Just like to get another opinion, if that's alright."

"And your name is?"

"Evangeline…Evangeline Attwood." She swept her hair behind her ears and said, "I'm staying down on Garth Point. It's just east of Escanaba."

And within seconds, the mineralogist was on the phone, and Evangeline heard, "You need to come down here and check this out."

Meanwhile, Liam used a chrome-plated loop to further examine the specimen until the curator arrived and wasted no time in placing the rock on a triple-beam balance. Liam squinted as he read off the numbers. "Thirty-seven-hundred and seventeen grams. That's about one hundred and twenty troy ounces." He pulled out his phone and punched a few buttons. "At current market conditions, ahem, let me see here," He mindlessly scratched his temple. "Its scrap value alone would be around two-grand, but it's worth a lot more to a collector."

Evangeline whispered, "How much more?"

The mineralogist sucked air across his teeth and shrugged. "It's not an exact science, but large specimens like this are quite rare. And if I was to shoot you a number, it would just be just an opinion. So, don't go taking it as the gospel."

"Well?" Evangeline said impatiently.

"I'd say ten to fifteen-thousand. Maybe a tad higher."

Evangeline placed her hand at her collarbone and emitted a soft gasp.

With his head dipped towards a shoulder, the curator piped in. "Any chance you might be interested in donating it? We could give you a great tax deduction, and we'd place your name alongside the specimen when we display it."

She secured the rock into her pack, and then hoisted it onto her back with a groan. "I don't think that would be in my best interest right now, but I'll keep you in mind."

"Well then, at least let us get a couple of pictures. We'd like to post them at the entrance so our visitors can get an idea of the mineral wealth coming from this area. Maybe we can get a shot of you holding it. How would that sound?"

* * * * *

Meanwhile, new appliances and furniture were arriving daily at the Templeton estate. While carpenters added the finishing touches to the crown molding, Suzanne was on a ladder painting the trim around the kitchen cabinets. She didn't think anything about it when an SUV pulled up, as dozens of vehicles had made their way to the construction site over the past month.

A cold wind was blowing out of the northwest when there was a loud rap at the backdoor. "Hello! Anybody home?" the voice shouted.

Suzanne snapped off her latex gloves and held the door open, part way. "Can I help you?"

The young man standing before her was wearing a grey suit and looked out of place amongst the various construction workers and paint-spattered drop-cloths. He coughed a couple of times and said, "I'm looking for a Ms. Evangeline Attwood and was told she was living out here on Garth Point. Would you know how I might get hold of her?"

Suzanne recalled a legal matter she had with her ex-husband and how the papers were delivered by an officer of the court. With an air of suspicion, she cocked her head back and looked down her nose. "Uhm...what's this in reference to, if I might ask?"

"I represent a client from out of state, and he would like a word with her regarding a personal matter. It's most agreeable and involves a financial element."

Suzanne rubbed her forehead as if relieving a headache. "If you give me your name and number, I'll see she gets the message."

He pulled out an envelope from his suit jacket, and as he handed it to her, she got a glimpse of the semi-automatic, hanging from a holster under his left armpit. The visitor took off his sunglasses, revealing a scar that went from his right eyebrow to his cheek, and then forced a smile. "Please have her call us at her earliest convenience. It's written on the letterhead."

With Evangeline home from her trip to Copper County, Suzanne rapped loudly on the door of the guest house. "You decent?"

Lucy barked a few times, and when the screen door swept open, Suzanne produced a white envelope. "Got a letter for you."

"A letter?" Evangeline squinted, and then tore it open.

Carmine P. Langford
Attorney at Law
9835 Detroit Street
Escanaba, Michigan
Telephone 1-906-555-1913

Dear Ms. Attwood,

My client, a Mr. Carlisle Vernon, would like to schedule a meeting with you at your earliest convenience regarding your discovery of a silver specimen in Little Bay de Noc. Please contact my office directly. We can be reached at the number on top.

Sincerely,
Carmine Langford

How did he find out? Then, it dawned on her. Evangeline grew angry...angry with herself and angry with the curator at the museum. She knew it was a bad idea, having a photo taken of her holding that silver specimen, and now, everyone knew about it, creating worry. She didn't like notoriety, and the letter was an assault on her privacy. In time, Evangeline's anger abated and reminded herself that Langford's correspondence could actually be a God-send, especially if a monetary element was involved. Without a regular paycheck, a windfall of a few thousand dollars would come in handy, and she wondered if the curator's assessment was correct.

Langford's letter was a reminder that she hadn't picked up her mail lately which was being forwarded from downstate, and Evangeline made the drive to Escanaba about an hour later. As she waited at the counter, she fantasized about an imminent windfall until the postmaster produced a large parcel, and she tore the package apart in the privacy of her vehicle. There amongst the bills and solicitations was a package postmarked from Italy, and the return address was written in block letters.

Yastakovic
1708B
Via de Vallerozzi
Siena, Italia

Evangeline had written Ulay several times in hopes of reconnecting, even going so far as extending an invitation to come to America, but her letters went unanswered. She even hired an agency to find him, but after spending more than a thousand dollars with no results, she understood there would be no joyful reunion. Although her mind resigned to the inevitable, her heart still hoped to connect with the man who fathered Charlotte. Memories flooded in from every angle as she held the oversized parcel, hoping and remembering. After all these years, she wondered, what compelled him to communicate now? Evangeline tucked the package under the front seat, contemplating its contents, and drove home in silence, her heart racing.

* * * * *

The following morning, Suzanne Templeton and Evangeline Attwood entered The Ludington, an old established hotel that dated back to the 1920s. The exterior had seen better days as the white paint was peeling. Yet the building reeked of antiquity. Inside, the foyer was expansive, but few people chose to spend their time here, most opting for more modern accommodations. The front desk was rather ordinary, and the empty mail slots behind the counter were a testimonial to its economic decline. A sign announced, 'Free WiFi' in a feeble attempt to modernize, and the contrast between the hotel's past and its current condition reminded Evangeline of the city of Calumet. And the more she thought about it, the more she saw a similar comparison to herself, as someone who once was young and vibrant but had fallen upon hard times as well.

Upon receiving directions, the two knocked on the oak door, and a young man in a dark suit ushered them in. It was the same one that delivered the letter to Suzanne's new residence the day before. He acknowledged her with a polite nod and then announced, "Ms. Attwood is here to see you, Mr. Vernon."

Carlisle Vernon, a corpulent specimen with a double chin, was dressed impeccably in a black Armani suit and a burgundy-colored tie. He rose from an overstuffed chair, and as he did, the leather sighed with relief. Vernon extended his hand and smartly said, "Ms. Attwood. So nice to meet you." He turned to Suzanne and asked, "And you are?"

"This is my neighbor, Suzanne Templeton. She was the one that delivered Mr. Langford's letter. I'm curious. How did you find out about my silver specimen?"

Vernon released a barrel-sized laugh, and his face reddened. "I like a woman who gets to the point. So often, people beat around the bush and never establish real communication, and I tell you straight out, I like a woman who cuts the small talk and gets right down to business." With a gentle sweep of the hand and a million-dollar smile, he said, "Please ladies, have a seat." He turned towards the young man standing at the threshold.

"That'll be all, Clarence. Ms. Attwood and I have some business to discuss."

When his assistant closed the double doors, the locking mechanism gently clicked. Meanwhile, both chairs the two women sat in were enormous, engulfing their bodies in cheap brown leather. Vernon leaned up against the mahogany desk and said, "Can I get you ladies something to drink? Perhaps a glass of wine or maybe some iced tea?"

Evangeline's efforts to sit erect were thwarted by a chair that continuously sucked her in. Resting both hands on the plush armrests, she forced herself up. "No thanks. So, how did you find out about my silver specimen? Only a few people knew."

Vernon tossed a few ice cubes into a glass, then carefully poured an amber-colored fluid, giving the impression he was a man not easily rattled. He looked up and calmly said, "I have my sources. You see, I'm a businessman by nature and am willing to pay for information. Let's just say, your discovery has made the rounds. But the good news is, well...I'm willing to pay... ten thousand dollars in US currency for the specimen, sight unseen. How does that sound?" Vernon plunked a white envelope onto Evangeline's armrest. "You see, I'm a bit of a collector myself, and this sort of thing interests me terribly. Did you happen to bring the specimen along, per chance?"

"I placed it into a safe deposit box. Considering its value, I thought it would be best considering..."

Suzanne discreetly kicked Evangeline's foot, casting an icy expression.

"Perfectly understandable." Vernon took a sip from his glass, and the ice cubes clattered. "But I'd also like to make an offer for the exact location of your discovery. How would an additional fifteen-thousand dollars sound?" Another envelope was deposited similarly onto Evangeline's armrest.

As the unemployed educator thumbed through the stack of hundred-dollar bills, the color drained from her face. *That's twenty-five thousand dollars. Holy shit.*

Vernon returned to his chair, adjusting the cuffs of his crisply starched shirt. "I understand you quit your job recently, Ms. Attwood. Between your finder's fee and the silver specimen, you stand to gain twenty-five thousand dollars. All things considered, not a bad return on a day's worth of diving, and I'm sure it'll come in handy." He then cuffed his mouth with his right hand and whispered, "Don't worry, I won't send a 1099."

"But what if the location doesn't pan out? I've been down there more than once and haven't found anything. I'd hate to see you lose all your money."

Vernon pulled out a navigation map of the bay along with a felt-tip marker, handing the items to Evangeline. "Just mark the spot, and if nothing shows up, you're ahead of the game twenty-five thousand dollars, and I'm...outa luck."

Suzanne took hold of Evangeline's forearm and said, "This is all rather sudden. Why doncha give us a day or two to think it over, and we can get back to you."

The businessman emitted another barrel-sized laugh, then slapped his knees. "You're a shrewd negotiator, and I like that, Mrs. Templeton. I can see why Miss Attwood brought you along." After he picked up the two envelopes, Vernon deposited them into his coat pocket. "But my offer has a shelf-life of say... forty-eight hours? After that, I'll need to move on to more pressing business. I hope you understand."

On the drive back, Evangeline turned towards Suzanne and said, "Whatcha think?"

With a deep inhale, the woman with the curly blonde hair rolled the window down, and the cool Lake Michigan air rustled several papers along the dashboard. With hair blowing in all directions, she turned towards Evangeline and shook her head. "I don't trust 'im. I mean, how'd he know about you quitin' your job? And where did he get all that money? Somethin' just ain't right here, Ev." They sat in silence for a few minutes until she said, "Let's talk to Rich and see what he has to say."

When they arrived home, Richard was stoking the Weber grill, and Suzanne filled him in on their meeting along with Vernon's subsequent offer. Richard, wearing a Michigan Tech sweatshirt with a matching ball cap, slapped a couple of monster-sized steaks onto the grill that sizzled upon impact. As they talked, a cloud of white smoke drifted lazily towards the heavens, and just as Suzanne's husband flipped the meat, he said, "You know, if I were him, I'd be watchin' your every move. Wouldn't be surprised if he had somebody watchin' our shoreline this very minute."

Evie's mind was elsewhere. She was thinking about Ulay, wondering what was in the package but hadn't been able to muster sufficient fortitude to open it. It was easier pondering all the possibilities, and as her thoughts drifted into a fantasy, she could feel the power of his arms as they held her; never had she felt so secure. As she drifted away from the world of purloined silver and arson, an image of his strong weathered hands came to mind. For a brief moment, she could envision his face, his short beard with streaks of grey throughout along with his dark hair that was parted in the middle. She recalled the scar along the side of his forehead and wondered what had happened. Maybe, it came from a fight where he protected a loved one. She found the notion of her lover protecting her, even if it meant physical violence, quite seductive and alluring. Evangeline then pondered that scenario in detail.

"You think he's that diabolical?" Suzanne asked.

Richard cast a stern expression. "Look Ev, his assistant was carrying a sidearm. What kinda person does that?" He tested the meat with a finger, and the aroma wafted towards Lucy's olfactory neurons, who romped with excitement. Templeton called out, "Let's eat." With a platter in hand, Richard looked over his shoulder towards Evangeline and said, "You know, maybe tomorrow, you should give this McKenna fella a call? It wouldn't hurt lettin' him know what's going on. Maybe get his opinion."

"I don't think I can afford his services right now. After all, he is pretty expensive, and with me not working..."

"It's just a phone call, and it doesn't hurt to ask."

"Well. I don't know."

"Why don't you give him a call? I got his number right here."

CHAPTER ELEVEN

"There are claims in the parapsychology field which, in my opinion, deserve serious study, (with one being) that young children sometimes report details of a previous life, which upon checking turn out to be accurate and which they could not of known about in any other way than reincarnation."
- Carl Sagan Ph.D. astrophysicist

December 24, 1913

When Peter got home, he pulled out the package from the Christmas stocking that was wrapped in brown paper and held the new doll to his chest; his cheeks stained with tears. The Croatian immigrant walked about the modest flat and ran his fingers over his wife's clothing that hung neatly in the closet. Through the walls, he could hear the wailing coming from the neighbor's residence; their daughter had also been caught up in the crush of humanity. He hoped against all odds that this nightmare was just a dream; that a different reality would settle in once the sun came up, and his little girl would hug her new doll, a present from Saint Nicholas. He could imagine her small face, radiating joy and for a brief moment, he indulged in the illusion.

Outside, snowflakes were dancing as Peter looked towards town, where he could see the outline of church spires illuminated by the city lights. With the doll clutched to his chest, Peter fell to his knees bereft, his body trembling.

* * * * *

"Let see if I got this right." Dalton McKenna was on the speaker phone, and his voice was raspy. "So, you're telling me you found a piece of silver while diving, and some guy you never met wants to pay you fifteen-grand for the location. To make matters worse, his messenger is carrying a sidearm." Dalton barked, "And you're considering the offer?"

Evangeline whined, "Well, the money would come in handy. I quit my job this summer, and things are a little tight right now. So, you're implying that Mr. Vernon's offer might not be entirely on the up-and-up?"

Dalton exhaled loudly as if the discussion was tedious. "Look, I'll spell it out for you. What do you think is gonna happen when you give this fella the location, and he comes up with jack? I'll tell ya what's gonna happen. He's gonna think you gave him a load of bullshit, and it won't be long before that guy with the sidearm comes lookin' for ya." His words were now fast and direct. "Templeton is already the prime suspect in a double homicide. How do you think this turns out if there's more trouble coming from your property?"

Evangeline gasped, and her following words flew quick. "But...but maybe, Vernon will find more silver. It's not impossible."

"And how many times have you been out there?"

"A couple," she answered softly as if the volume would lessen its impact.

"And what did you find?"

"Well, I'm no expert. There were all kinds of rocks at the bottom." Evangeline continued to whine. "Just because none of them were shiny, doesn't mean there isn't more silver."

"Where you at?"

"At home, here on Garth Point."

"Look, I should be there in a couple of hours. I'm crossing the bridge right now. Don't do nothin' 'til I get there, hear."

It was late afternoon when he pulled in, and the construction crew was in the process of shutting down for the day. Dalton met the two women out on the drive, then walked about, examining the home's exterior. "So, when do you get to move in?"

"Hopefully, next week," Suzanne answered as she vigorously rubbed her hands together.

With a hint of a shiver, Evangeline stood next to Suzanne with her cap pulled down. "Why don't we go inside where its warm?"

They sat at the breakfast table in Tom Attwood's cottage, and Dalton noticed the boat tied to the pier, gently rocking side to side. "Surprised you haven't taken your boat in. It's getting late. Freeze up isn't that far off."

As Evangeline poured coffee into brown ceramic mugs, steam rose lazily. "I just haven't had time. Maybe next week I'll get to it. I checked the forecast, and it's supposed to warm up on Wednesday."

He pushed his cup aside, then rose from his chair. "Get your coat. I want to check somethin'."

As the three descended the narrow stairway that led to the dock, Suzanne turned to Evangeline and whispered, "What's he doing?"

Evangeline shrugged just as Dalton started inspecting the rowboat with a flashlight.

"What are you looking for?" Evangeline decried as she shivered in the cold rain. "I've taken anything of value inside."

There wasn't much to inspect, but amongst the cobwebs, Dalton saw the black square. He reached under the seat near one of the support struts, pulled the item out, and held it up to the light. As a steady rain descended, both women craned their necks to get a better look.

"It's a tracking device." Dalton pursed his lips tight. "I want you to go through your vehicle and clothing. We gotta make sure they didn't plant others."

McKenna placed the device back where he found it, then looked up at Evangeline, who was standing with hands plunged deep into her pockets. As Dalton yanked the pull-cord, the motor sputtered to life, and through a haze of white smoke and light rain, Dalton yelled, "I'm gonna take her for a spin. Be back in about an hour."

* * * * *

And so, it came to pass that Ms. Evangeline Attwood took the job at Luigi's, serving drinks and gossip to the residents of Calumet. At first, it seemed like an absurd idea. After all, the tavern was a good two-and-a-half-hour drive from her brother's cottage on Garth Point, but the owner offered an apartment above the bar to use whenever she was in town. Although it was just a bedroom and a bath, it didn't cost anything, making her meager employment more financially viable. She worked one week per month, and during her stint, business grew. On her first day, she wore a Mt. Rushmore t-shirt, and word spread, luring in a plethora of male customers.

Later that week, a cold rain descended in sheets, where dark angry clouds touched the ground like spirits from the past. Evangeline swept back the curtains to her apartment, and with Lucy at her side, she watched rivulets of water streak across the window pane. As she listened to the wind howl, her thoughts turned to Ulay, recalling how the steady tap of raindrops on his window in Verona made a similar sound, as if the pattern was composed just for them. Evangeline remembered them lying together. He hardly spoke; her fingers interlaced with his. With that memory firmly planted, she drifted off into a dreamless sleep.

When Evangeline awoke, she leapt down the stairs with Lucy leading the way. Since her shift didn't start for another few hours, she drove to the Quincy Mine; her windshield wipers slapping back heavy rain as they headed south on US-41. She dashed to the main hall, an old mine structure made of Jacobsville sandstone, and was greeted by an elderly volunteer who held the door open.

"Where's your umbrella, sweetheart?"

Evangeline pulled the hood back, exposing her damp tresses. "Left it at home. You still running tours this late in the season?"

"You're a little late, but if you hurry, we can catch the group that took off a few minutes ago."

After a dash to another old building, she joined about a dozen or so patrons who were gathered in a semicircle, listening to their tour guide explain how the steam-hoist operated. Later, they examined a mass of native copper dragged from the bottom of Lake Superior, along with several other specimens from the mine proper. The group was then ushered onto a covered tram and lowered down the side of the hill that overlooked the towns of Hancock and Houghton. Once at the bottom, they were ferried onto another vehicle that entered a drift, going nearly a half mile through solid rock. As the vehicle entered the side of the hill, a new world unfolded, filled with darkness and quiet. It was remarkably comfortable inside, and as Evangeline slipped her raincoat off, she listened to the guide explain how the various drilling methods were employed some hundred years ago. Before them stood a one-man pneumatic drill, and with a flick of a lever, the machine roared to life, creating an ear-deafening noise. As tourists protected their ears with fingers and hands, Evangeline eyed the rusted steel cart, resting neatly along the tracks.

After his demonstration, the tour guide yelled, "And if you look where the young lady is standing over there," he pointed in Evangeline's direction, "that device is called a tram, and the early miners would push it to the main shaft. Anyone interested in giving it a shove?"

A few men from the university put their shoulders to the half-empty cart, and it inched along the rails.

"Now, imagine it full of about three tons of rock, and you'll get some idea how difficult this work was." The guide smirked, then droned on.

As the former teacher ran her fingers along the corroded and bent metal, Evangeline fell into a reverie. In her mind, she could see the faint light off in the distance, and it was accompanied by the clatter of iron wheels grinding along a set of steel rails. In her mind, she watched the man stop to inspect his load, his headlamp shining bright, then looked over his shoulder to see if anyone was watching. He was a young man without a shirt, muscular with a carbide lamp atop his head, not unlike the one she imagined while at Luigi's. And as he picked through the rubble, the trammer held a fist-sized rock up to his carbide lamp, then tossed it aside.

140

Her reverie was broken when the tour guide called out, "We'll let you guys take a few minutes and explore the area. Stay on the marked paths and don't stray off into areas where there's no lighting. When you're done, we'll meet here at the tram."

Someone called out, "Can we take a couple of rock samples?"

"Sure. As you can see, we have plenty to choose from. Just no hammering on the walls. We wouldn't want anyone gettin' hurt."

Evangeline was mesmerized by the endless drifts and stopes, and as she wandered into the darkness, wearing a hardhat and an electric headlamp, she gazed at the endless rock walls colored brown with smatterings of green epidote, red feldspar and white calcite. She tripped over a rail but caught herself just before going down, and that's when she saw the glimmer. Recognizing its silvery sheen, Evangeline placed the small rock into her coat pocket, then returned to the tram where the tour guide was waiting.

* * * * *

After clearing his throat, he spoke clearly into the cell phone. "Hi, my name is John Mosby. Can I speak to Mr. Carlisle Vernon?"

"And what would this be in reference to, Mr. Mosby?"

"Ms. Attwood asked me to represent her interests regarding the silver specimen she found on the lake bottom."

"Are you a lawyer?"

"No, I'm just a friend, that's all."

"I see. One moment please."

Dalton McKenna paced back and forth in his motel room until the voice on the phone snapped, "Carlisle Vernon."

"Good morning, Mr. Vernon. My name is John Mosby, and Ms. Attwood asked me to represent her interests in regards to a silver specimen she found. As I understand, your offer was good for only forty-eight hours. Just wanted to know if you're still interested in my client's cooperation."

His voice was cold like stone when Vernon replied, "Well, I dunno. What do you have in mind?"

"I think we should discuss the matter in person. Are you available later today? Say at the city park in Gladstone?"

"Well, ah…"

"I think you'll like what I have to say."

A moment of silence was followed by, "How'll I recognize you? I have no idea what you look like."

"I know what you look like, and that's all that matters. Come alone. Say, one o'clock?"

He wasn't hard to find. Carlisle Vernon was sitting on a park bench overlooking the lake, broadcasting breadcrumbs to a flock of gulls. The sky and ground were heavy with birds when Dalton walked up and said, "Mr. Vernon…John Mosby."

The behemoth looked at his Rolex and said, "You're prompt. I like that quality. So often, people don't keep their word, and it reflects poorly on their character. You said you wanted to talk about Ms. Attwood's discovery. If you don't mind me being so blunt, what exactly does your client want?"

Dalton brushed aside a few crumbs that were quickly snatched up by their avian guests. He looked up and said curtly, "A million-five. Upon payment, she'll take you to the exact location." Dalton set the GPS he found on Attwood's boat onto the park bench. "I think this belongs to you."

"A million-five is a lot of money," Vernon said in one long exhalation. He looked down at the tracking device and said, "You know, Mr. Mosby, or whatever your name is, you should think carefully about the path you've embarked upon. I don't like high-handedness, and this is way out of your league." Vernon looked over his shoulder and snapped his fingers twice.

Dalton spotted a young man wearing a suit closing in from behind and pulled out his weapon. Upon eyeing the Colt, Vernon held up a couple of fingers whereby the suit stopped, hands deep in his trench-coat pocket.

"So, tell me. Why do you think your client's information is worth a million -five?"

"Just that we found more silver, and it seems to be strewn about an old shipwreck that's now almost entirely covered in silt. Thought that might be something you'd be interested in."

As Vernon stroked his chin, his face was without expression.

Just before leaving, Dalton said, "I'll give you forty-eight hours. You can call me at this number." He handed Vernon a slip of paper, and as he walked away, he bumped his shoulder into the young man wearing the trench-coat, then placed his hand upon the handle of his 1911 Colt that rested neatly in his waistband. "You ever make a move like that again, your family is gonna get a late-night call from the coroner's office."

On the drive back to his camp, Dalton updated Evangeline about the meeting. In response, she shouted, "A million-five! What the hell were you thinkin'?"

He slowed for a couple of deer, and said, "Well, it seemed like a good idea at the time. The good news is he didn't balk."

"But there's nothin' there," her voice filled with contempt. "What you're doing borders on criminal. Why dincha just tell him the truth?"

Dalton took a slug of bottled water to clear his palette. "First, we have to find out just how important your information is. You know, when someone is faced with an outrageous proposal, most folks just laugh. Lemme tell you somethin', Vernon wasn't laughin'. So, we know that whatever is at the bottom of that bay, is serious. Hang on. I got another call comin' in."

"Yeah."

"Mr. Mosby?"

"Speaking."

"Mr. Vernon would like to meet with you regarding your proposal. Say tomorrow morning at ten, at The Ludington. Please bring Ms. Attwood along as Mr. Vernon would like to speak to her privately."

"I'll see what I can do, but I'm not making any promises. Ms. Attwood has a couple of irons in the fire right now."

Dalton disconnected and returned to Evangeline with a chuckle in his voice. "Guess who that was? Don't bother, I'll tell ya. Carlisle Vernon wants to meet tomorrow morning."

She gulped audibly. "You're joking, of course."

143

"Do I sound like I'm joking? Asked that you attend personally, but considering his assistant carries a weapon, I'd prefer to leave you out of it. If we need your input, maybe a Skype connection would be in order."

"Look Mr. McKenna," her voice now plaintive, "this just isn't right. How can we seek a better offer when the negotiations are based upon deceit? If I paid that kind of money only to find …"

"Relax. I'm sure he has no intention of coughing up that kind of dough. You gotta understand, this is the only way we're gonna find out why that rock of yours is so important."

"I meant to ask you, why do you have two names, and which one is the real you? Are you Mr. McKenna or are you Mr. Mosby?"

An exhalation through his nose created a slight whistle. "They're both me."

"I don't understand."

"My name was Mosby in another lifetime, and I don his persona whenever I want to maintain a degree of anonymity."

"So, you're saying you've been… reincarnated?"

He replied with a resolute, "Many times."

"Are you putting me on?"

"Not at all," Dalton said firmly. "You see Ms. Attwood; death isn't the end of our story. We're sentient beings that transcend time. We don't have to get everything right in one incarnation; we're evolving with our real goal being true enlightenment."

There was dead silence until Evangeline said, "I'm curious. Do you think I've… been here before?"

She could hear the chuckle.

"Only you can answer that, but if it's true, I'm certain you've had some experiences that defy logic. When you experience things like coincidences and events you can't explain, it's usually about an issue that went unresolved in another lifetime. Now, I know what you're gonna say, that this is nothing but a bunch of crap, but I can tell you unequivocally, I've walked this earth many, many times."

"So, who were you back then?"

"A Confederate soldier, and in this lifetime, I've come back to continue my journey, by providing justice wherever I can. And if that means going after the likes of Joe Steiner, so be it. You see, death has no power over me."

Evangeline thought about the reverie she had deep within the Quincy Mine and her experience with the doors at the museum. She then ran her fingers over the unopened envelope postmarked from Italy, and Dalton could hear the sniffle.

CHAPTER TWELVE

"We are never so
defenseless against suffering as
when we love."
- Sigmund Freud

1:00 am December 25, 1913

As Christmas ushered in, a light snow continued to descend from the heavens as if it were an attempt to mask the suffering below, but the town of Red Jacket would have none of it. Peter walked aimlessly that evening, and with each block, he could hear the wailing coming from every corner of town as if it were a symphony all its own. He stood before the town hall, now acting as a temporary morgue, knowing his wife and daughter were inside. He attempted to enter through the large oak doors but found them locked. He pounded with his fists, hoping someone might answer. But no one did, and with both hands splayed over his head, he leaned on the entrance and wailed. "Elizabeth! Elizabeth!" He thought of his daughter lying next to her dead mother and cried, "Oh, Mary...papa comin'...papa comin'."

,

145

Evangeline was back at the post office in Escanaba where she picked up another batch of mail and noticed the magazine. It was odd. She hadn't ordered a subscription to *American Heritage* and tossed it aside without much ado, then noticed a letter from Calumet. Hastily, she used her fingers to rip it open.

Dear Evie,

Just wanted you to know, I called that number and sent on the DNA results you obtained from Roy's letter with hopes they might be able to identify his remains. I am indebted to you for all the thoughtfulness you have shown over these past few weeks. I'll let you know if we hear anything. If you're ever in the area again, please stop and see me.

As I Remain,
Margaret Keillor

A feeling of satisfaction swept over the former history teacher, knowing her efforts, at least in part, helped Roy's family, and with the letters Emma had saved, it seemed the old soldier might finally get a chance to come home. Evangeline petted Lucy's crown and said, "We did good."

Back at her brother's cottage, she pulled out Ulay's package from the nightstand and drifted into a world filled with possibilities. She recalled their time walking the streets of Verona, sharing a glass of lemoncello. She remembered how the streetlights reflected off the old cobblestones, giving them a silvery glow, and as they passed the Areni di Verona, it was busy with patrons, attending a performance of Rigoletto. A soprano's voice drifted over the ancient walls of stone, and as they listened, it was the most perfect evening. He slipped his hand around her waist, and when their heads came together, this time they did so gently, like they belonged there. That was her favorite memory, and she lingered, knowing it was a prelude to something more…something she would never forget.

As they ambled back to the hotel, the moon had risen just above the rooftops, looking like a giant pumpkin-head floating on a sea of dark purple. The lemoncello had checked her inhibitions hours ago, leaving Evangeline with a certain giddiness. Once inside, they fell upon the squeaky bed frame, tossing their clothes aside without concern, and as she relived the details, it left her breathless, remembering every second of their night together.

But as hard as she could, Evangeline couldn't understand why he distanced himself, never answering any of her letters. It infuriated her that their time meant so little as if a simple reply would have been too much of an effort, and she thought about burning the package. After all, it had been twelve years, and what could he possibly say after such an extended absence? As she fingered the unopened parcel, her phone sprang to life, pulling Evangeline back into the realm of form and substance, clutching onto a memory of a man she barely knew.

Dalton's first words were, "Look, I'm entering the hotel now. I'll leave my phone on so you can listen to the conversation."

Carlisle Vernon seemed angry and looked about with concern. "Ms. Attwood didn't accompany you?"

"She's out of town, and I'm authorized to negotiate on her behalf. I have her on the phone right now, and she can verify everything."

After briefly speaking with Evangeline, Vernon's nostrils flared. "And you have the location?"

"Ms. Attwood gave me GPS coordinates to the site." Dalton lifted his chin when he said, "So tell me, why are you interested in all this?"

"Well, I'm a bit of a history aficionado." Vernon poured himself a couple of fingers of bourbon from the bar situated in the corner, then looked over his shoulder. "I've been searching for a nineteenth-century shipwreck that went down somewhere near Little Bay de Noc."

Dalton leaned forward in his leather chair. "Tell me about it."

"I'm not sure that would be in my best interest," he said curtly. "See, if I tell you what I know, then you'll be inclined to circumvent our negotiations, and that makes little financial sense. No sir, I don't see how we can proceed along these lines whatsoever."

As Evangeline listened to the conversation via her cell phone, she idly thumbed through the *American Heritage* magazine she had picked up at the post office earlier that week, and there on page thirty-nine was an article, *The Calumet Tragedy*. With eyes wide, Evangeline stared at the photograph of the stairwell where seventy-three perished. She touched the portion of the picture where the fifth riser met the wainscoting and whispered, "Oh, my God."

Her reading was interrupted when she heard Dalton roar, "What kind of bullshit are you pullin'? You call me down here, waste my time, and got nothin' to say?"

"Calm down, Mr. Mosby."

Dalton stood and spat, "Look, if you want the location for that shipwreck, then you're gonna have to talk to us sooner or later because we're the only ones that have it."

Vernon rose from his seat and pointed towards the leather chair. "Mr. Mosby. Please, have a seat. I'm sure we can discuss this matter in a calm, rational order." He turned to his assistant who was hovering at the door's threshold. "Clarence, would you excuse us? Mr. Mosby and I have some things we need to discuss privately."

After Clarence left the room, Vernon leaned back into his leather chair, tapping his fingertips together. "Have you ever heard of the Silver Islet Mine, Mr. Mosby?"

Dalton tugged at his sleeves, took a seat and cleared his throat. "Can't say I'm familiar with it."

"It's an interesting story." Vernon took a sip of bourbon, leaned forward with an elbow resting on a knee, and whispered, "You see, back in the 1868, a rich vein of pure silver was located on a small islet in Lake Superior. But its location was in Canadian waters, a mere two-and-a-half meters above lake level. Apparently, when it was first discovered, waves had polished the vein into a mirror finish, and the first men on the scene chipped out large masses of native metal and filled their Mackinaw boat to capacity. To say the least, it was most profitable, producing millions of ounces, and at today's prices, that would translate into hundreds of millions of US dollars. But God only knows what the true wealth of that deposit was, as owners and workers alike lined their pockets with purloined metal. In spite of all the theft, a large shipment was loaded onto an old wooden schooner called the *Hudson Bay*. Its cargo was destined for the American mint in Philadelphia. And as you probably can surmise, the shipment...well, it never arrived." Vernon leaned back into his chair with glass in hand. "It's widely held that the schooner traversed Lake Superior, then onto Lake Michigan where its cargo was to be loaded onto a train for the remainder of the journey." Vernon looked both ways as if someone might overhear and whispered, "Considering the immense value of the shipment, only a few people knew its exact route. But as luck would have it, I found insurance records in Ottawa where a claim was paid back in 1880 under terms of absolute secrecy. To this day, no one knows for certain what happened to the *Hudson Bay* as there were no survivors, and some speculate, a storm sank her somewhere near Little Bay de Noc.

"Now comes the interesting part." Carlisle Vernon took another slug of bourbon, then leaned in. "You see, there was an old Menominee Indian chief who lived out on the Stonington Peninsula. He's long gone, but his descendents tell the story about a shipwreck right around the time the *Hudson Bay* went missing. As the story goes, several bodies washed ashore along with some wreckage."

"And the silver shipment?"

Vernon shrugged.

Dalton took a sip of bottled water, then whispered, "So, how much are we talking about here?"

"Hard to say," Vernon replied with another slight shrug, then leaned back into his chair with a satisfied expression. "But the amount of pure silver aboard the *Hudson Bay* was in excess of one hundred tons. Do you have any idea what that would fetch in today's market?"

149

"A tidy sum, I suspect."

Vernon slapped his knees, startling his lovebirds in the cage nearby. "That's to put it mildly. And to collectors, the specimen value alone would fetch upwards of ten times its value as scrap. Just think of it."

"So, you're thinking hundreds of millions in silver specimens are sitting on the lake bottom?" Dalton inhaled abruptly, then added, "That's a lot of money."

Vernon closed his eyes for a moment.

"If what you're saying is true, you have to know the State of Michigan holds all the salvage rights to the lake bottom. I'm sure they'll assert ownership."

Another shrug was followed by, "I can't see how anyone could say the State has a clear title when the ownership goes all the way back to those who owned the mine. And I found a couple of descendents of the original owner, a Mr. Alexander Sibley, who quitclaimed their interest. So, from where I stand, that silver belongs to me."

Dalton looked askance. "So, what are you proposing?"

"What would you say to ten percent of what's recovered? That could increase Ms. Attwood's portfolio by millions. Not a bad return on a day's worth of diving. I'm sure your client would agree."

"Just how do you propose we do all this?"

Vernon stood, then walked to the chair behind his desk where he poured more bourbon into a glass. After taking a healthy slug, Vernon looked up. "It doesn't have to be complicated. I can draw up the papers and have something to sign yet this afternoon."

"And you're willing to give Ms. Attwood ten percent of what's found?"

"Absolutely. And we'll handle all the salvage expenses."

A grin spread across Dalton's face just before he said, "I can get back to you just as soon as Ms. Attwood and I have the opportunity to discuss the matter."

It was a few hours later, and after talking with Evangeline, Dalton pulled out his phone. "Can I speak with Mr. Carlisle Vernon? This is Mr. Mosby, and he's expecting my call."

"One moment please."

A few seconds later, Dalton heard the click followed by, "Carlisle Vernon."

"Mosby here, and I've spoken to my client."

"Good. Good."

"I regret to inform you, but Ms. Attwood has decided to decline your offer and plans to seek other remedies."

Click.

* * * * *

Evangeline was putting up storm windows on her brother's cottage when the phone chimed, but the wind whipping off the lake made it difficult to hear. With a finger in one ear, she heard, "Ms. Evangeline Attwood, please."

"This is she."

"Ms. Attwood, my name is Howard O'Brien, and I'm a detective with the Meridian Township Police Department."

"The police department?" She envisioned a burglary back home and hastily said, "Did someone break into my condo?"

"Not that I know of, but that's not the nature of my call. I was told you dated a Mr. Daniel Pantone for several years."

She walked inside and poured a cup of coffee. "Well yes, I did, but we're no longer seeing each other. What seems to be the problem, detective?"

"Well, I hate to be the bearer of bad news, but Mr. Pantone has gone missing. His mom contacted our office a few days ago. Apparently, she hasn't seen him in over a week, and he hasn't reported in at work either. So, if you don't mind me asking, when was the last time you two spoke?"

After retrieving some milk from the refrigerator, the former teacher kicked the door shut, then began pacing about with cup in hand. "Well, like I said, it's been awhile. He came up here to my brother's home here on Garth Point, and we got into an argument." Slurp. "You see, Dan still wanted us to be together, and I asked him to leave."

151

"That's not what I read in the complaint. Your boyfriend said…"

Evangeline interrupted. "He's not my boyfriend."

"Said your neighbor Templeton shot out his back window of his pickup truck, and his wife put a gun to his head. Is there any truth to that allegation?"

"Look, if you have the report, then you know what was alleged." Evangeline slurped her coffee once more. "If you have any questions about the matter, you should talk to my attorney. Here, let me get you her number."

"That won't be necessary." O'Brien coughed a couple of times and said, "So, you have no idea where he is?"

"None whatsoever. Did you check with his friend, Norbert? The two have season tickets for Spartan football. He might know."

"You got a number?"

"Not offhand, but I'm sure his mother knows Norbert. Maybe, she can help."

"Well hopefully, he'll surface sometime soon. Maybe he's just recovering from a bender and is sleeping it off somewhere."

Another slurp of coffee was followed by, "Sorry, I couldn't have been more of a help, detective."

"If you hear from him, let me know. Got a pencil handy?"

* * * * *

The roads were filled with slush as Evangeline pushed her way north. It was the first snowfall, and the red Honda pulled into Calumet a few hours before her shift. With time on her hands, Calumet's newest bartender walked about town at a steady clip until she came upon a frozen puddle that blocked her path, and as she stepped onto the ice, it cracked loudly, breaking into a thousand shards. For that brief moment, it lifted her spirits, and when she looked up, the church spires could be seen off in the distance, separated by a myriad of cascading snowflakes.

As she walked towards the old church, it felt as if she was being drawn, and upon arrival, Evangeline placed her hand upon the large door and felt reassured, as if this were a place of refuge. She quickly entered and took a seat in a pew near the altar, bathing in a warm light coming from a stained-glass window off to her left. Here, the illumination from an ordinary street lamp transformed the window into a multitude of colors, depicting God the Father holding his beloved son. She made the sign of the cross and then closed her eyes. As the outside world with all its uncertainty faded away, she was transported to another time. It was the gentlest of transitions, and in her mind, she could see several closed caskets arranged in a semicircle about the altar; some were small and white, while others were long and black. Evangeline drifted further into the reverie, and the scent of pine boughs caught her attention. In her mind, she could see him sitting in a pew just a few feet away. He was the same one she had envisioned before, once in the mine pushing a cart-full of copper ore and also at Luigi's, drinking beer. His face was now flushed into a bright red color, and his eyes were puffy. Just as Evangeline was about to reach out, she felt someone place a hand upon her forearm.

"I thought that was you," Margaret whispered.

Evangeline recovered quickly and beamed upon seeing her visitor. "Mrs. Keillor."

"Hope I wasn't interrupting your prayers."

"Just daydreaming. That's all. What brings you to church so late?"

"I come down here once in awhile and pray. It seems to calm me when I think about bigger things than just Margaret Keillor. How've you been?"

"To be honest, not so well." She sniffled. "You see, I've been having these...visions, and I...I..." Evangeline covered her face with both hands.

Margaret pulled her close, gently caressing her right shoulder. "There, there now. Tell me what's going on."

With that one question, the flood gates opened, and years worth of grief surfaced. Evangeline broke down into loud mournful sobs and looked up with eyes red. "I don't know what's going on anymore. I...I see things."

As she explained the visions, Margaret continued to caress Evangeline's back. "Come on. Let's go over to my place. It's only a few blocks from here, and I'll put on a pot of tea. But first there's something I'd like to show you." And as they meandered through snow-covered streets, Margaret led her past another church where she pointed. "This use to be the old Apostolic Lutheran Church where many of the protestant victims were taken. Now it's a re-sale shop where old things get a new lease on life." She laughed at the irony.

"Did you ever attend services here?"

Like a schoolgirl, Margaret stifled a giggle. "I attended a wedding here back in the eighties. It was summertime, and the old church wasn't air conditioned. So, they left the front doors open, in order to get a little breeze. Nobody thought a thing about it, until a chicken from across the street followed the bride down the aisle. The congregation was reduced to gales of laughter."

Evangeline squealed.

As they continued their walk, Margaret took Evangeline's arm and said, "You know Evie, I think these visions you're having weren't intended to hurt you. It's just God's way of healing your distant past. Surprisingly, you're not the first one to make their way to Calumet. I have this friend who had visions not unlike your own. Lemme give her a call."

After hanging their coats up, the two sat about Margaret's dining room table like they had done during their first visit, and as they talked about Roy's demise, there was a knock on the door, followed by a gust of cold air.

"Anybody home?" the visitor called out.

Upon seeing Margaret's guest, Evangeline tipped her head slightly and said, "Wait a second. I've seen you before. You performed down at the Swallow Inn in Rapid River. You're that country and western singer." She extended her hand and said, "Hi, I'm Evie."

"Carol."

"Evie's been having these visions about the Italian Hall, and I thought the two of you should talk."

154

The country and western singer pulled a chair out, then tucked one leg under the other. "So, tell me, what kind of things are you seeing?"

Margaret uncorked a bottle of port wine and poured three glasses. "Maybe it would be more helpful if you first told her about your experience."

Carol shrugged, making her appear smaller, and her voice was soft and light. "I know this might sound odd, but I lived back then. I remember it quite well, and. I was tall and sort of a rabble-rouser."

Margaret took a sip of wine and elbowed her guest. "She hasn't changed all that much. She's still a rabble-rouser."

"So, what was it like when you... started to remember?" Evangeline stuttered, "I...I mean... did it come all at once or in bits and pieces?"

"Well, it's kinda hard to explain. It was as if it were a far-off radio station. Some days it would come in loud and clear while other days there'd be nothing but static. If I concentrate, I can still pick up the signal, but it now takes enormous effort. The reception has dropped off considerably over the past few years, and it's rare if I pick up on it whatsoever. Furthermore, I really don't care to connect with the past anymore." Carol lifted her head and proudly said, "I'm here, and that's all that matters. You know, most cultures embrace the idea of reincarnation, but here in the West, we're told that this life is all we get. So, it's exceptionally difficult for folks like us to accept the notion we've been here before."

With glass cupped with both hands, Evangeline leaned in. "Was it hard for you? I mean, when you first entertained... the notion."

"You have to understand I was raised a strict Catholic, and the idea of reincarnation was literally heresy. But I got over it. One time, I even went down to Chicago and saw my gravestone. It was a difficult life back then as there weren't many options for women like there are today."

With a warm smile, Evangeline said, "And now you're a country and western singer."

"But more importantly, I'm a sentient being, and I'm fully awake. You see, I was asleep for most of my life and struggled with almost everything and everyone."

Evangeline lowered her head. "I know what that's like."

"It doesn't have to be that way, sweetie." Carol took a sip of port wine and sat erect. "When I started to let go of my need to control people and outcomes, my life got better. But it really didn't take off until I was willing to send love to all those people who pissed me off. It's just so easy to hate, and you know why? Because we don't have to be responsible for ourselves. I told myself countless times that if it hadn't been for people like my boss or my ex, I'd be happy. By giving my power away, it kept me stuck as a victim of other people's cruelty."

Margaret's cat, Lola sauntered by when Evangeline said, "So how does this pertain to…?"

"Not unlike yourself, I too had visions. It was like a reoccurring nightmare, and I couldn't see how any of it fit into my life today. Eventually, I came to realize that in this life I was still trying to find resolution to all the issues of my distant past. Things didn't get better until I saw myself as a survivor rather than a victim. I now see myself as a sentient being on a path of spiritual enlightenment. By doing so, I've been able to break free from the limitations of my past and move on." Carol held up a hand as if stopping traffic. "Now, don't get me wrong. What happened back then was no doubt a tragedy, but I don't define my life by that sort of thing anymore, and when I decided to send love to those people who were responsible for that disaster, I broke free from that cycle of hatred."

"Don'tcha just love her?" Margaret said as she held Lola with both arms.

Carol took a sip of wine. "You see, if I want real love in my life, I must be willing to offer it, and for most of my life, I meted it out in exact proportion to the love I received. Is it any wonder that I experienced stinginess?"

Thoughts of Ulay came to mind just before Evangeline said, "And what about…the memories?"

"They're just memories, and they don't have power over me anymore. Yet on occasion, I have dreams about the Italian Hall, but when I do, I go to my inner sanctuary and send love." Carol laughed heartily. "It's a lot like the movie, *The Wizard of Oz.* We come to this world and have no idea what exactly we're doing and search for purpose and meaning along the way. But everything Dorothy wanted was within, and when she finally realized it, Dorothy got to go home to her loved ones. It's all about awakening, and the power we seek resides within ourselves."

Evangeline blew her nose into a tissue. "That's quite the analogy."

"Back in the early 1900s, all women could do was get married and have kids. I tried to change things, but our country wasn't ready for that kind of social justice. Now I have a career doing what I love. Since it doesn't pay all that great, I also work as a flight attendant and have travelled extensively."

The clock on the wall chimed eight times, and Evangeline cried, "Oh, shit. Look at the time. I gotta get to work."

"Work?" replied Carol.

"I'm tending bar over at Luigi's, and I'm already late. Why don't you guys come along, and we can talk along the way."

* * * * *

Dalton lifted Vernon's fingerprints from an empty whiskey bottle he obtained from a trash receptacle outside his suite and had it compared with the FBI's automated fingerprint identification system. Carlisle Vernon was one of several aliases. His real name being Conrad Jibril Omar, a Canadian national, and although he had never been convicted of a criminal offense, there were many charges that had been mysteriously dropped. Amongst the allegations included human trafficking, mostly Syrian refugees fleeing the conflict in the Middle East. His primary residence was Toronto, with domiciles on the Isle of Capri and the Grand Cayman Islands.

Upon receiving the information, McKenna placed the call. "Ms. Attwood?"

157

It was noisy in the bar, and Evangeline blocked one ear with the palm of her hand. "Yes."

"Just wanted to let you know, we did the right thing terminating contact with this Vernon fella. Did some digging around and turns out he's a scam artist operating under an alias. His real name is Conrad Omar. Got tons of money and doesn't mind bending the rules in order to get what he wants."

Evangeline spat, "That's just great. I told you we should never have baited him like we did. And now, he's pissed off. You know, you beat everything!"

No response.

"By the way, I got a call from a detective downstate." Evangeline paced behind the bar. "Says Dan went missing a few days ago. You don't think…" There was a moment of silence until she said, "You still there?"

"Omar could have found out about the complaint you guys filed against one another. With Dan missing, you'd be a person of interest, and if he doesn't surface, well…"

Her voice rose considerably. "You idiot! Why didja have to go tell him we found more silver? God, I won't forgive myself if his disappearance is because of that damn rock."

McKenna gave a rare sigh. "Look, I'm not trying to scare you, but we need to be prepared for the worst. I want you to make a spreadsheet with all the places you were during that time frame while it's still fresh in your head, then give a copy of it to Fontaine for safekeeping."

"And what about Dan?" she hollered.

"What's his phone number?" After writing it down, Dalton said, "Where you at currently?"

"I'm here in Calumet, and I plan to be back home in a coupla days."

"Good. I'll call you when I got something."

It was a few hours later when Evangeline noticed the lone text message. She was upstairs getting ready for bed and squinted to read the print.

Want 50 grand or we kill Mr. Pantone.
Will contact you with the time and location of the exchange.

Any attempt to bring in law enforcement will result in his death.

Three seconds later, she was on the phone. "Mr. McKenna!" she blurted. "I need help!"

Dalton was woken from a sound sleep and answered with a hazy, "Who's this?"

"It's me, Evie," she blurted. "I got a text message. Says Dan's being held against his will. Said they'd kill 'im unless I pay 'em fifty thousand."

Dalton recovered quickly, cleared his throat, and said, "Look, somethin's not right here. Why would they contact you and not his family?" Before she could answer, he said, "Got the number they called on?"

Her voice reflected urgency as she said, "It was blocked. Said they'd contact me to set up the exchange."

Evangeline could hear the yawn just before he said, "Look, I'll need the exact time of the message," and after receiving the information, he directed, "Stay put, and I'll see what I can do."

* * * * *

With the drilling assignment complete, Sam Carter found work with the Park Service, where he spent his days recording GPS locations for various mine sites throughout the Keweenaw Peninsula. It wasn't very challenging, but financial obligations required sacrifice. With school back in session, Travis wasn't able to accompany his father and stayed with his grandmother, who lived alone in a spacious Victorian home that overlooked the Menominee River.

For all practical purposes, mining in the Keweenaw had ceased by the late 1960s, leaving a plethora of derelict buildings, mine shafts, and rock piles. The tailings were exhausted of any marketable commodities by amateur prospectors shortly thereafter, using metal detectors, but occasionally large masses were still being found by road crews, gardeners, and excavators of every kind. A few years ago, a homeowner uncovered a thirty-ton mass of pure copper in the

159

glacial drift not far from the city of Hancock, creating quite the stir amongst local residents. When brought to market, it was rumored that it fetched two-hundred thousand dollars. For awhile, it was displayed in Presque Isle Park in Marquette, then later shipped off to China.

Knowing all this, Sam Carter brought along a metal detector in hopes of finding a piece of copper he might be able to sell, and since the geologist worked on a contract basis, he took an afternoon off when blue skies prevailed. He made his way to the confluence of the Eagle River; it was a place where he and his wife vacationed, and the two would amble every morning along the shoreline, perhaps picking up a colorful stone or a piece of driftwood.

Before they were married, Lori asked why he didn't change professions and find something more stable, but after walking the shores of Superior, she understood. His connection to the land was so primordial that to sever that connection would be like taking a duck out of water, and from that point on, she understood Sam Carter like never before. Now he stood there alone, looking out into the endless blue, thinking of better times and better people.

On the way out of town, he pulled into the Evergreen Cemetery, a bucolic piece of property carved out of the dense pine forest some hundred-and-seventy years ago. Here, he felt at peace amongst the towering pines and rock cliffs. As Sam Carter strolled amongst the old tombstones, he read off the names of miners who died a violent and untimely death. One stone in particular always beckoned. It was an old marker made of marble, the name almost entirely obliterated by the wind and rain, which simply spelled out, 'Our Baby.' This small tombstone drew him like no other, and as he stood there, Sam contemplating the death of an infant daughter and the family she left behind. And for whatever reason, it brought him to tears.

Afterwards, Carter took a leisurely drive along the Phoenix Farm Road, and his mood improved. Following a trail where he had previously met with success, he began walking in a field with his metal detector, setting the discriminator high. This way, smaller objects like nails and bottle caps would be ignored. Sometimes, a piece of charged conglomerate would set off his detector, and he'd add it to his collection. But it was a rare day when anything of value was found. To date, his best discovery was a nineteen-pound mass of float copper that sold for a hundred-and-twenty bucks. Not exactly a windfall, but Sam Carter kept searching in hopes of finding something better.

As he swept the detector from side to side, he got a glimpse of a dog running towards the woods. Intrigued, he hurried off in the mutt's direction and got entangled in briars. As he struggled with the dense vegetation, the detector screeched, suggesting a large metallic object was buried nearby. After clearing the area with a machete, he examined the ground, and the size of the anomaly was impressive, nearly ten square feet. Normally, something this size would suggest a large iron object, as the area was strewn with abandoned mining apparatus. It was frustrating to work so hard only to find a metal grate or a rusty barrel buried under four feet of earth. But it intrigued him nonetheless, and after digging down about a foot, he rechecked the chasm. The signal was now stronger than ever, and he got down on his hands and knees, looking for any signs of green. Even orange would be helpful, as it would indicate a mass of rusted iron.

Sam examined the excavation closely, and the ground seemed undisturbed, filled with pristine glacial debris. As the geologist dug further into the layers of the distant past, he found it satisfying. After three hours of digging, all he had to show for his efforts was a monster-sized hole. Carter rested his arm upon the end of a shovel, taking sips of bottled water and decided to abandon the site as storm clouds gathered. So, he returned to Calumet, where he ordered dinner from Jim's Pizza on Sixth Street.

By then, it was raining, and her gait was unmistakable. Evangeline Attwood was headed towards Luigi's at a quick clip, and she never noticed him. Sam Carter stood outside in the pouring rain with water dribbling down his nose and chin and thought about following her but couldn't muster the fortitude. On one level, he understood Evangeline had nothing to do with

Travis getting lost, but there was a resentment, its origins obscure. As he rested in his motel room that evening, listening to the steady pitter-pat of raindrops on his bedroom window, sleep proved elusive until around two that morning. When the storms finally abated, the middle-aged father fell into a deep slumber.

Oddly enough, he dreamt about a large copper mass he was working on deep within the earth's interior, where he chiseled away pieces, bit by bit. It was difficult work pounding on solid metal, but there was a method to the madness. Holes would be drilled into the mass using steel bits and sledge hammers, then packed with explosives. Sometimes, it was sufficient to break off a chunk, but the largest pieces were virtually impenetrable. Sam Carter saw himself working on such a mass and could feel the coolness of the breeze as it drifted through the dark adit.

Believing his dream to be an omen, Carter returned to his excavation just as the sun began to peek out from a bank of pastel-colored clouds. At the bottom of the hole was nearly six-inches of water from the previous night's storm. So, the geologist began bailing water with a coffee can, then commenced digging in earnest. The ground proved to be a worthy opponent with its coarse gravel and large glacial stones, making his progress difficult. But around nine that morning, he drove his shovel deep into the chasm and heard, "donk." Pushing the gravel aside, he saw the first glimmer of green, and adrenaline coursed through his veins. While sweat glistened from his neck and brow, swarms of black flies hovered. Using his fingers, Carter felt the edge of the buried mass, then used his trowel to further expose the copper mass.

"Gotcha," he mumbled as he wrapped a steel chain around an exposed corner and ran it to a hook under the front bumper. He started the engine, and the wheels on the old pickup spun wildly. So, Sam Carter dropped the transmission into four low, and the vehicle stuttered, tossing clumps of dirt high into the air, and the engine strained with increased acceleration. Suddenly, the truck broke free, sending a spray of mud and debris that cascaded down upon the cab. And there, standing in a clearing with a chain wrapped about, was a boulder mostly covered in brown goo. Green edges protruded from all sides, and Sam's heart raced as he wiped away the muck. The rock had three legs to it along with an appendage that stuck out of the side. And that's when he saw the dull grey. A rare smile engulfed the geologist's face which was quickly supplanted by a look over his shoulder to see if anyone was watching. But outside of a bald eagle circling above, he was alone. Getting it aboard the truck took over an hour and required the use of a come-along where it was winched up an improvised ramp made of downed timber. Once onboard, Sam hovered over the lagniappe, like a proud father. He poured bottled water over the edges, and as the dark-green color glistened in the morning sun, Sam ran a knife over a grey area, revealing a silvery sheen.

Sam Carter had several more stops to make before his assignment with the Park Service was complete. Even though the massive stone was too heavy for most people, keeping it in the back of his truck seemed risky as residents in the area would surely recognize its value. So, he called the Templetons who agreed to make the trip to Calumet, arriving about four hours later.

They were in the parking lot at the AmericInn as the three peered at the boulder in the back of Sam's truck. Richard whistled. "She's a real beauty. Whereja find her?"

"Up by the Phoenix location." With a grin and splayed hands raised high, Sam backed away. "Now don't go calling the DNR on me, pal."

Suzanne nudged him with an elbow and smirked.

"So, whatcha think it's worth?" Richard asked.

"Figure it weighs somewhere around two hundred pounds, maybe a little more." Sam pointed to the grey metal, then scratched at it with a pocket knife. "I think the silver comprises about a third of its mass. Whatcha think?"

A shrug was followed by, "Maybe."

"Bet there's nearly a thousand ounces here."

With his arms draped over the tailgate and his foot on the bumper, Richard whistled once more. "So, you still want me to take it back to Garth Point?"

"I got a little more work to do for the Park Service, and it shouldn't be left alone. Here, why doncha give me a hand, and we can transfer it over to your truck."

As the two men grunted with the load, Suzanne cleared her throat. "You know, Evie is working over at Luigi's tonight, and I said we'd stop in."

Sam looked up from the bed of Richard's truck with jaw muscles tight. Templeton stood erect and placed a hand upon Sam's shoulder. "Look, it wasn't her fault that Travis got lost. It was just an accident. Nobody's to blame." After climbing off the bed of the truck, Richard wiped his brow with a handkerchief.

Suzanne closed the truck's tailgate and said, "I bet she'd like to see what you dug up. Besides, the two of you now have something in common."

* * * * *

When Evangeline's cell phone vibrated, she didn't recognize the caller ID and answered with a cautious, "Hello?"

"It's me," Dalton said in a low tone. "Look, I got some bad news. You sittin' down?"

She turned her back to several customers with a finger in her ear. "What's goin' on?"

"Flew back home this morning to follow up on a lead, and found your buddy, Pantone."

Evangeline interrupted with, "He's not my buddy."

A sigh was followed by, "He's at a house here on the north side of town."

"But how didja find him? The phone number was blocked."

"I used your number and the time of the message, then followed it back to the originating tower. By using AoA technology, my contact was able to establish where your text message originated. Essentially, the tower acts like a locator beacon. To make a long story short, I found Pantone eatin' pizza and playing cards with a bunch of guys. Got video. Here, I'm sending it now."

164

Evangeline opened the attachments and mumbled, "What the...."

In the background, Dalton could hear a steel guitar. "I'm sitting right outside where Pantone is currently located. If you want me to confront him, he might reconsider. Last time I checked, extortion is punishable by up to twenty-five years in prison. Hope you kept that text message."

"I have it."

"You picked a real peach there, kiddo. Can see why you kicked his butt to the curb."

With her palm to her ear, she seemed distracted but managed a civil reply. "Look, how much is this all gonna cost? I don't have a lot of extra resources right now, and I can't afford to ring up an expensive bill for your services."

"I understand. Look, I feel somewhat responsible for baiting Vernon like I did. So, we'll call it even."

"I gotta get back to work." A customer held out his empty beer glass, and Evangeline raised a finger as she finished the call. "Do whatever you have to. I don't want anymore of this nonsense, understand?"

A middle-aged guy along with a few other musicians were in the middle of their set just as three familiar faces found seats by the old water closet. As a steel guitar wailed, Suzanne waved.

With a broad smile, Evangeline meandered through the crowd, greeting the Templetons with hugs, then turned and gave a rather tepid, "Mr. Carter."

"Ma'am."

Richard leaned in to get a better view of Mt. Rushmore and said, "Should see what we got out in my truck. It's the biggest hunka silver you've ever seen."

Sam and Evangeline turned towards the band and heard,

> *...Like a child who closes her eyes,*
> *to make everything disappear.*
> *My mind watches reruns,*
> *inside and alone...*

When the song ended, Evangeline tapped her order pad with a pencil. "And where's Travis? Hope you don't have him sitting out in the damn truck."

Carter jutted his jaw and answered with a snarky, "He's staying with my Mom just until I finish up here. I'll be home in a couple of days. Where's Lucy? Hope she's not sitting out in the damn car."

Richard interrupted, "Knock it off already. You guys are givin' me heartburn." Richard thumped his chest with a fist and then used his head to point towards the door. "Come on, let me show ya what we got." A few minutes later Templeton pulled the tarp back, revealing the large mass of native metal and pointed to all the grey areas. "That's pure silver. Ain't that right, Sam?"

The door to Luigi's swung open, and a blast of music accompanied a couple of men wearing plaid shirts. When they approached the pickup, a patron leaned in with a friendly, "Whatcha got dere?" Upon seeing the mass, their eyes widened as one whispered, "Is dat dere really what I dink it is?"

"You betcha. That's pure silver." Richard answered and then used his thumb to point towards Sam. "My buddy here found it."

With one foot on the rear tire, a patron turned towards Sam and whispered, "Whereja find 'er?"

"Rather not say."

Suzanne looked at her watch and cleared her throat. "Ahem. Look, we need to get going. Got a long drive ahead of us." She put her arm around Evangeline and said, "Give me a call when you get home. We'll have dinner together."

Evangeline turned towards Sam Carter and said, "Sorry about being so snotty back there. Congratulations on your discovery."

He turned his back to Evangeline, ignoring the apology and spoke to Richard directly. "Thanks for helping me out. Can you hold onto my rock for a few days?"

With the snub, Evangeline's face reddened. In response, Richard's wife took hold of Evangeline's hand and whispered, "Call me."

166

While heading south on US-41, Suzanne sat in the passenger seat with her arms crossed, silently fuming. "What's wrong with that guy?"

"I dunno," Richard replied as if the question caused discomfort. "He's going through a rough spell, I suspect. You know, he doesn't have a full-time job…"

"That doesn't give him a license to be mean. Did you see how he ignored her apology? You know, it wasn't her fault Travis got lost."

"I know."

"So, what's his problem?" Suzanne spat.

"You remember when Lori died. His life got turned upside down. Just think what it would be like if I kicked the bucket." Suzanne punched her husband in the shoulder. Richard mocked a fake injury and winced. "Now don't get me wrong. I ain't trying to make excuses, but ever since Lori passed, he hasn't been the same. You've seen it. When was the last time you've seen the guy laugh? For all I know, maybe he's feeling guilty about being attracted to her. Ever give that a thought?"

"Come on," Suzanne answered as if the explanation was less than plausible. She looked out the passenger window with arms tightly crossed. "It would serve him right if she never spoke to him again."

"I think he's afraid, that's all. Travis is getting attached to Lucy, and he doesn't want him to suffer another big loss. So, he's making sure nothing romantic kindles between the two of 'em."

"Well, I'd say he's sure doing a pretty good job."

CHAPTER THIRTEEN

"Truth is powerful and it prevails."
- Sojourner Truth

2:00 am December 25th, 1913

It was a small room in a boarding house above a saloon, and the tall, middle-aged man looked out of place with his crisply starched shirt and wool suit. Outside, snow was falling at a steady clip, covering the footsteps that led to the two story, wood structure. "That's him there," said McDonnell who was wearing a three-piece suit. It fit snuggly over his corpulent body, and he was exactly as he appeared; a tough leader of tough men who was hired to break the back of organized labor. Over the course of the last several months, his men busted many a head all in an attempt to suppress the revolt that all but crippled mine production. He liked cigars, and the room was filled with a white haze when his boss set his hat aside.

The well-dressed visitor stomped his leather boots to rid them of snow, then stood before the lump of a fellow who was resting on a cot. His words were barely audible when he said, "You know who I am? Got over seventy dead, most of 'em kids. Spent millions in this goddamn town, and now one fool could ruin everything. You have any idea of what you've done?"

No answer.

He turned towards McDonnell and said, "He one of yours?"

"Citizen's Alliance."

Off in the distance, church bells began to chime. McDonnell swept the white curtain back and looked at the spires off in the distance. "He was drunk and thought it would be fun to put a little scare into 'em. Had no idea it would cause a stampede. Unfortunately, the stupid son of a bitch was wearing a Citizen's Alliance button, and several people got a good look. A few might have even recognized 'im. This could mean the end, especially if they can tie this one," he pointed a thumb at the man sitting on the cot, "to C&H. Washington might get involved and you know what that means." McDonnell licked his dry lips, then asked, "What do you want me to do? All hell could break loose if someone identifies him."

A strong blast emanated from his thin nose just before he said, "Get him out of here. Now! The son of a bitch can board the train down in Houghton where there's less chance anyone

168

*will recognize him." He turned and faced the culprit directly.
"You're leaving town."*

"But I...I don't have anywhere to go."

*"Should have thought about that before you yelled, 'Fire.'"
McDonnell now loomed over his subject with his fingers on an
ivory-handled pistol. "If you're so much as utter a solitary
word about what happened here or this meeting, we'll be
paying you a little visit. You understand me?"*

His hands trembled when he nodded his assent.

*McDonnell's boss pulled out a couple of twenties from a
leather billfold, then looked at his watch that hung from a fob
made of solid gold. He whispered, "Get him a ticket to Chicago.
I want him out yet tonight and make damn certain he keeps his
trap shut."*

* * * * *

It was a ranch-style home, a massive set of garage doors
being the prominent architectural feature. With evergreens
under every window, it screamed middle-class as if boring was
a fashion statement all its own. Dalton stepped around the grill
that blocked the walkway, rang the buzzer, and a few moments
later the front door swept open. "Hi, Is Mr. Pantone available?"

A young man wearing a Lynyrd Skynyrd t-shirt cocked his
head to one side and answered, "And what's this in reference
to?"

"I have a copy of his ransom note right here on my phone,
and Ms. Attwood gave me explicit instructions regarding a
follow up. Tell Mr. Pantone, the penalty for extortion is twenty
years in federal prison, and I've forwarded her a clip of you
guys playing cards this evening."

A few seconds later Pantone came to the door with a
partially eaten bratwurst in his hand and mumbled, "What da
fuck is goin' on?"

"Nice to know you're alive and well, Daniel," McKenna
proffered derisively, "at least for the time being. Here's the
short and tall of it, son. I have a copy of that text message you
sent."

Pantone stuffed the last of his sausage into his mouth, and his words were garbled. "What are you talking about? What text…"

Dalton held his hand up. "Save your breath. We traced the message to this address, and it doesn't exactly look like you're being held against your will." He turned toward the other occupant and barked, "You part of this extortion?"

With raised hands, he backed away. "I…I don't know nothin' about no extortion."

Pantone attempted to slam the door, but Dalton thwarted his efforts, using his shoulder as a battering-ram. While two men fled out the backdoor, Dalton tackled Daniel in the kitchen. There was a brief struggle, but just as Pantone was about to deliver a blow, Dalton pulled his Colt, placing the muzzle up under his adversary's chin. A new attitude of cooperation settled in as Dalton rose from the floor.

"Have a seat." Dalton used his foot to scoot a chair across the linoleum.

Pantone held his shoulder as Dalton stood before him.

"It's your lucky day, Daniel. Under normal conditions, I'd have ended it right here-and-now, but Ms. Attwood gave me explicit instructions. Make any further attempts to contact my client, and I'll kill ya." With flared nostrils, Dalton placed the barrel of his weapon upon Pantone's forehead, pulling the trigger to a full-cocked position. "Are we clear on this?"

As Pantone was being let off the hook downstate, matters were somewhat less congenial on Garth Point. Richard Templeton was in the backyard, hosing off Carter's specimen when the patrol car approached. He held the garden hose between his legs and from a distance it looked as if he were taking a leak. The lead officer shook his head with amusement, and his first words were, "Mr. Templeton?"

"Yes."

"You're under arrest for the murder of Joseph and John Steiner."

* * * * *

"All rise!"

Judge Anthony Taggert pounded his gavel, then looked towards the bailiff. "Just this one case today, JD?"

JD Moorecraft, who was getting on in years, walked with an unsteady gait, and deposited the docket in front of Taggert. "Just this one here, but it's a goody."

Donning a pair of dark, horned-rimmed goggles that magnified his eyes, the judge reviewed the charges, then spoke into the microphone. "Ahem. Ms. Fontaine? How does your client plead to the charge of open murder?"

She rose from her chair, smoothed the fabric of her pleated skirt, and gave a resolute, "Not guilty, your honor."

"Very well. Mr. Collins, are you ready to proceed with your preliminary examination?"

"Indeed, your honor."

After presenting a largely circumstantial case which included a statement from a conservation officer with Michigan's Department of Natural Resources along with sworn affidavits from witnesses who overheard Steiner's death threat, Taggert turned and said, "Do you plan to call any witnesses at this time. Ms. Fontaine?"

"No, your Honor. Not at this time."

"Well, I believe the people have established probable cause. So, we'll go to trial. He covered the microphone and whispered to the bailiff, "What's the calendar look like, JD?" After the consultation, Taggert uncovered the mike and said, "I'm looking at the first week in January. Any objections?"

Both attorneys answered simultaneously. "No, your Honor."

With hands behind his head, Taggert lifted his double chin. "Now the matter of bail. What does our fine prosecutor have to say?"

"We're asking that bond be set at one million dollars, your Honor."

Fontaine rose from her wood chair and complained, "Your Honor, my client has lived in this area all his life, has a full-time

171

job and a spotless criminal record. On top of all that, he owns a home over on Garth Point…"

Taggert interrupted Fontaine's dispensation and leaned forward. "Were you the guy that helped organize that search when that little fella went missing about a month ago?"

Richard nodded. "That's me."

"Glad it turned out alright. How much you got in savings?"

"About ten grand, that's all."

Taggert slammed his gavel and said, "Bond set at one hundred thousand. You can post ten percent and be on your way. But let me warn you, Mr. Templeton. If there is so much as a lick of trouble coming from you, it's right back into the county lock-up. You understand?"

* * * * *

When Sam Carter came home, Travis ran from the living room, leaping into his father's arms with a smile as wide as a jack-o-lantern. "Didja bring me anything?"

"Well, lemme see." Sam pulled out a toy airplane from his backpack and dropped it into his son's hands.

Sam's mother was carrying a dust cloth when she walked into the living room and said, "So, how did it go?"

"Quite well actually. Made a couple of thousand surveying in some old mine shafts and found a mass of copper buried about four feet down. Wait 'til you see it. She's a real beauty."

Mrs. Eunice Carter wore a print dress that hung to her ankles along with a yellow cotton apron; her silver hair shimmering in the incandescent light. The octogenarian looked over the top of her bifocals, and her voice was dry like unbuttered toast. "Well, at least it's not more mineral rights that aren't worth the paper they're written on. How much did you pay for that last deed?"

The father with the dust-covered ball cap ignored the remark, arching his back after setting his son down. "How did Trav do?"

"Missed the bus a coupla times, but I drove him over. So, can you stay for dinner?"

Sam picked up the framed picture atop the Baldwin piano and reflected upon the happy couple. As he stared at Lori's picture, it seemed like another lifetime. It was the day they brought Travis home from the hospital, and the new mother radiated in the September sunshine. Travis broke the reverie and zoomed by with his new airplane in hand, interrupting his trip down memory lane. Sam inhaled deeply, then set the picture aside.

"Sorry, I already made plans for tonight." He gave his mother a quick kiss on the cheek and turned to his son. "Come on, Trav. We're heading over to Uncle Rich's for dinner. So, get your backpack."

With eyes wide, his son said, "Is Lu-tee gonna be dere?"

"Not sure. But we'll never find out unless you get your clothes packed. Aunt Suzanne is making macaroni and cheese...just the way you like it with the little hotdogs inside."

Sam's mother curled up her index finger a few times in a come-hither gesture and whispered, "Didn't know if you heard, but it was in the paper the other day that Richard got himself arrested. Said he killed those two dope peddlers out on the peninsula. Now I'm not saying he's guilty, but you sure it's OK for Trav to associate with folks like that?"

"Ah ma, he's a just a guy that's run into trouble not of his own making. You know, the two men who got killed burnt his house to the ground. Maybe you hadn't heard, but Suzanne was inside, and the neighbor girl pulled her from the inferno."

Eunice exhaled loudly.

"Trust me. Rich is a good man, and I can't think of a better person for Trav to be around. Was even thinking about having Richard and Suzanne be his Godparents in case something happened to me."

Eunice looked down her thin nose and snapped, "And what am I, chopped liver?"

"Come on, ma," her son pleaded as if her complaint was unwelcomed. "We've talked about this. You're getting on in years, and the burden shouldn't be placed solely on your shoulders." Sam placed his arm around his mother and said, "Besides, I'm healthy as a horse."

* * * * *

The Delta County prosecutor was working behind a desk when his secretary poked her head in. "Sorry to interrupt, Mr. Collins, but there's a gentleman here to see you. Says it has somethin' to do with those murders out on the peninsula."

Collins stuffed the Sudoku puzzle into the top drawer, and his voice was shrill. "Well, have him talk with the sheriff. They're the ones doing the investigation."

"That's what I told him, but he insisted on seeing you personally."

With pursed lips, the prosecutor shook his head, then inhaled abruptly. "Ah, shit. Give me a minute to straighten up, then show him in."

Upon entering, the two shook hands, and Collins pointed to a wingback chair that faced his desk. "Didn't catch the name."

"Dalton McKenna."

Collins did a double-take and tipped his head to one side. "Not the Dalton McKenna we got an arrest warrant out for?" Collins picked up the phone.

"Before you make that call, might want to hear what I have to say before you make a fool of yourself."

"Doreen!" he shouted. "Get Sheriff Wigglesworth on the blower!"

Dalton pulled out an envelope from his coat pocket and thrust it forward. "Here."

As the prosecutor waited for the connection, he perused the letterhead. "What the... So, you're saying you work for the Department of Justice?" Color faded from Collins' face when Wigglesworth squawked over the speaker phone. "Hey Bill, what da hell is goin' on?"

"Look, I'll get back with you. Something's come up, and we might have to rescind that arrest warrant for Dalton McKenna. I'll explain later."

Collins pressed the disconnect button and yelled, "Doreen!"

Doreen Dombrowski, a short, sixty-something grandmother, had worked as Collin's secretary for nearly nine years. As she

174

stood at the threshold, the prosecutor thrust the paper in her direction. "Get the DOJ on the line!"

A few minutes later, Doreen returned and whispered, "I have them on the phone, Mr. Collins. Apparently, Mr. McKenna is a retired US Marshal and occasionally works for the Department of Justice."

The Delta County barrister muttered, "This is just great. Nobody tells me a goddamn thing around here." He straightened his necktie, and when he picked up the receiver, his voice turned saccharine, like honey. "This is the prosecutor's office here in Delta County. Who am I speaking to?"

Dalton could only hear, "Well, ah…I see." There was a long period of silence where the ticking of the wall clock was the only sound. "And how long has Mr. McKenna been in law enforcement?"

More silence.

"Well…ah… thank you for keeping me apprised, and you'll fax us something yet today? Collins fiddled with the aging phone cord as he listened, then handed the receiver to Dalton. "He wants to talk to you."

After providing the Attorney General with an update, Dalton returned the phone to Collins who cleared his throat and said, "I know you must have a stable full of lawyers, but if you're ever in need of a good prosecutor, I would be more than happy to send my resume for your consideration."

More silence.

"I see. Well…ah…thanks anyway."

Click.

Dalton thrust his hands forward, exposing his wrists. "You wanna slap the cuffs on?"

Collins barked, "So, what can you tell me about this double homicide?"

Dalton took a seat and cupped the back of his head with both hands. "Well, for starters, at least two members of your fine sheriff's department are being paid a monthly stipend by the dope peddlers out on the Garden Peninsula along with a DNR officer over in Gladstone. Furthermore, just about everyone in town knows who's running that operation, and my question is this." Dalton lifted his chin. "Why didn't the sheriff's department do something about it?"

With flared nostrils, Collins said, "And you can prove it?"

"Yup."

"Doreen!" Collins hollered with a face flushed red.

Another trip to the office seemed irksome as she answered with a snotty, "Now what?"

"Get the sheriff back on the blower!"

* * * * *

Vernon's first words were, "So, did you pay her a visit?"

"She wasn't home," Clarence reported. "Went next door, and nobody was there either. Wandered around a bit, thinking that maybe they're working out back or somethin', and I ran across this." Vernon's assistant held his phone up and displayed a photo of Carter's rock, sitting outside Templeton's garage. "The fucker weighs a ton. Couldn't budge it an inch, and it's nearly pure silver. Just take a look."

Carlisle Vernon slammed his hand against the mahogany desk, and the boom startled the love-birds in a nearby cage, resulting in a bout of squawking. Vernon fumed, "That son of a bitch! If he thinks he can salvage that shipwreck without me, he's got another thing comin'. No sir, I'll have none of it!"

* * * * *

As soon as Travis got out of the car, his voice rang out. "Lu-tee!" But Lucy was no where to be found. Instead, Richard walked out of his newly constructed home and swung Travis by his arms, resulting in another bout of squealing. Upon setting the boy down, he looked up at the beaming engineer. "Unka Witch!"

"How's my little bean-sprout?" Richard lifted the boy off the ground once more, giving him a bear hug, then turned to Sam. "How was the drive over?"

"Not bad. Sorry to hear about your legal trouble. How you holdin' up?"

176

A gust of wind tousled Richard's hair just as he said, "Well, my attorney says we have good chance for an acquittal. Understand the prosecutor dropped charges against that McKenna fella, for some reason or another."

"So, is McKenna still assisting?"

"Haven't heard from him in a coupla days." Richard coughed a couple of times. "So, to be honest, I'm not sure what's goin' on."

And there resting on the concrete pavement near the garage door was Sam's specimen, encrusted in various shades of green and grey. As they walked over, Richard said, "I hooked up the hose the other day to rinse the mud off, and Jesus the piece is just loaded with silver. Didn't tell you, but I took it over to work and had it weighed." Richard arched his back after examining the specimen and said, "Had to use a forklift to get it out of my truck. Stuck it on one of our scales, and it clocked in at two hundred and thirty-one pounds."

When Suzanne walked out of the house, Sam kissed her on the cheek, and her first words were, "I have a bone to pick with you. You were awfully rude to Evie when we were in Calumet the other day. What the heck is wrong with you?"

Travis ran from Richard's hands and embedded himself into Suzanne's apron. "Ann Thuthan!"

"Hi sweetheart." She caressed the boy's crown, casting another stern expression toward Sam. "Well? She goes out of her way to make you dinner, and then you treat her like c-r-a-p."

Richard nudged Carter and said, "In case you forgot, this is what it's like being married."

Sam lowered his head.

"Come on," Richard said with a swat to Sam's back. "Let's get that rock of yours into the truck."

As the two struggled with the specimen, Richard looked to see if his wife was nearby, whispering, "Don't mind her. She's been like this ever since I got arrested. You know, we've been married almost ten years, but there are moments when I could… just strangle her." With jaw muscles tight, he added, "You haven't seen her daughter lately, but…" Richard emitted a hardy sigh.

"What?"

"Madison's a teenager now, and that pretty well says it all. Hormones are pounding like a bass drum. Kinda boy crazy if you know what I mean. On top of it, she's turning into a rather snotty little shit. Can't tell her a damn thing and hasn't looked up from her cell-phone since last summer. Always texting someone or checking her Instagram account. You know, it's a unique bond between mother and daughter, not unlike what you got with Trav. But not being the father, if I go sticking my nose into it, I end up sleeping on the sofa."

"So, how long you been in the doghouse?"

"Coupla days now." Richard sniffled with his arms draped over the side of the pickup. "Worked my ass off all my life. Went to college, paid off all my bills, even volunteer over at the fuckin' Lions club, and now I'm looking at life in prison. Not saying that the Steiners didn't need killin', but as God is my witness, I didn't do it." Richard sighed heavily.

"How's Suzanne holding up?" Sam asked.

Templeton replied, "Like I said, she's stressed out, and her dumping on you like that isn't really her. I spoke to her about it, but it led to another big argument, and that's why I'm sleepin' on the goddamn sofa."

CHAPTER FOURTEEN

"Regret is a form of punishment itself."
- Nouman Ali Khan

December 28, 1913

    The church was filled with mourners, and Mary's father sat near the caskets that were placed with others up by the altar. The service lasted nearly two hours, but it was mostly a blur. His body was present, but his mind drifted to another world. While a light snow descended, Peter thought about the day Mary was born and how his wife beamed with pride when she held her for the first time. She simply glowed. In contrast, the parish was cold, and the pews were hard like stone. As he ran his hand over the place where his wife and daughter once sat, he remembered the day when Mary was baptized. She fussed, but when the priest dribbled water over her head, the infant suddenly calmed. Peter then thought about the last time he saw her. Mary was sitting at the kitchen table eating breakfast and gave her a kiss just before heading into town, planning to meet later for Christmas Eve services. Torture would best describe his regret, knowing had he stayed with his family he would have protected them. But their well-being was taken for granted, and because of it, his wife and daughter were now up front in wood boxes.

    Afterward, Peter followed behind his daughter's casket, calling her name in a plaintive wail. It was a two-mile walk to Lake View Cemetery, and the streets were lined with thousands of mourners who stood like sentinels along the roadway, silently watching the procession. A few days before, striking miners employed their skill chipping out dirt and rock from the gravesite, bit by bit with pick and shovel. With the ground being frozen, the trenches were only four or five feet deep.

    There were five trenches in all; two located in the Protestant section while three were carved open in the Catholic portion of the cemetery. As a choir sang, 'Nearer My God to Thee,' the caskets were placed into pine boxes, then lowered with ropes into their final resting place, up to a dozen per trench with wood planking placed across the chasm. As the last box was lowered in the Catholic section, a cold wind howled out of the northwest as a priest offered a final prayer. "Dear Heavenly Father, we offer you our beloved children, knowing their

179

reward is with you in heaven. Look after them and never let them forget how much they were loved. And offer comfort and peace for those of us left behind. Help us heal our broken hearts. In your son's name we pray. Amen."

* * * * *

After finishing business with Pantone, Dalton drove north to his camp near Ralph, and mused out loud to his late wife in order to break the monotony of a long drive. As he approached Gene's Pond, he softly uttered, "Ah Addy, everything seemed to make more sense when you were around. Just don't understand why folks who have more money than they could ever possibly use, need even more. I know, you'd say it was greed, but what fuels it?" There was a moment of silence as Dalton listened. "So, you think it's an addiction to other people's energy?" Dalton paused to consider the notion, then whispered, "Interesting. I never would have thought of that."

He was just a few miles from home when he saw the flashing amber lights.

"Remember that time when we went to New Orleans for Mardi Gras?" Dalton chuckled. "What was the name of that bar we liked? Tipitina's? Served great hurricanes, and you looked stunning dressed in that red outfit of yours."

He saw the woman waving her arms with the hood wide open. McKenna pushed the switch on the arm-rest, and the passenger window whined down. The former US Marshal stretched his body so he could get a better view and said, "What seems to be the problem, ma'am?"

* * * * *

They were enjoying the last of their orange sherbet when they heard Lucy bark. Travis dropped his napkin, then bolted, sending the screen door slamming. Howls gave way to dog kisses, and a few seconds later, Evangeline walked out from her cottage only to find Sam Carter standing in her backyard. With arms akimbo, she stood still.

180

He nodded once. "Ms. Attwood."

"Mr. Carter."

"Look, I feel I owe you an apology. Just wanted to say I'm sorry about being less than cordial the other evening."

Her words were sharp like razor wire. "You know, it wasn't my fault Travis got lost!"

"I see."

On the verge of tears, she yelled, "No you don't see!"

Sam looked about and then furrowed his brow. "What's goin' on here?" he whispered sternly, as if the answer would invariably be unsettling.

It was as if the dam had burst, and the resulting tidal wave was about to carve a path of destruction that would run deep and far. "I come up here to get a little rest and to get away from all the crazy people in my life," the tears now unmistakable, "and find the same damn thing up here! And you're the worst!"

Lucy nudged Evangeline with a wet nose, then paced back and forth between the two. With his face flushed with embarrassment, Sam placed his hand on his son's shoulder and said, "Trav, why don't you go inside and see if Aunt Suzanne needs help with the dishes. You can come out and play just as soon as you get done. Me and Ms. Attwood have a few things we need to discuss."

Sam watched his son enter the back of Richard's home, and the two waited until the screen door slammed.

"What the heck is your problem?" he whispered.

"I've done everything to be civil and you…you treat me like crap! That's what the problem is!"

"Maybe, you'd feel different if you lost a child, but what would you know about that! You never had kids!"

It felt like a slap in the face, and Evangeline slowly boiled. "You insufferable bastard," her voice building into a crescendo. With searing tears and face red, she hollered, "You think you're the only one who has had it hard. Don't you EVER talk to me about losing a child! You don't know the first thing about what I've lost!"

Sam lowered his voice when he said, "What the heck are you talkin' about."

181

By now, Suzanne and Richard were looking out the kitchen window, craning their necks. Travis looked up to Suzanne and said, "Papa mad?"

With a reassuring caress, she replied, "It's just a little argument, that's all. Grown-ups have 'em all the time. Say, how would you like a horsey-back ride? Uncle Rich has been dying to give a little boy one, and as you can see, outside of you, we're fresh out."

As Richard galloped around the house with Travis draped over his shoulders, Suzanne continued to monitor the exchange from the kitchen window.

"And what would you know!" Her sobs were louder now. "Richard's been charged with murder all because of that damn net I found, and if that weren't bad enough, Travis goes missing, and you think I'm responsible." Her voice now elevated to a roar, and her carotid artery became prominent. "I tell you, I didn't have nothin' to do with any of that, and if you don't believe me, then you can go straight to hell because I'm done being nice!"

A few seconds later they heard the screen door slam. Sam walked in, and his face was bright red. "Did you... hear..."

Suzanne whispered as if there had been enough shouting, "Everyone heard. Your voices must have carried half-way to Esky. What the heck are you two arguing about?"

No answer.

Suzanne turned to her husband and said, "I'll be next door."

Travis squeaked, "Can I come thee Lu-tee?"

She took hold of Travis' hand, and with one long exhalation, said, "We won't be long. Besides, it'll give you a chance to cool off."

When the house quieted, Richard pulled up a chair and noticed Carter's trembling hand. After Sam settled, the engineer laid into him. "What da hell was that all about?"

With both arms folded across his chest, Sam answered, "I...I dunno. She just brings out the worst in me."

"But you guys hardly know one another, You sounded worse than my folks, and they've been waging war for nearly sixty years. So, tell me what da hell did she do that got you so all riled up?"

As Richard filled his mug with coffee, Sam's breath was staccato like. "I…it was like someone lit the fuse, a…and once it got going, I…I couldn't stop." Sam emitted a heavy sigh. "My mom has been ridin' my ass, telling me how I should move in with her. I'm having a hard time finding enough work to pay all the bills…raising Trav all by myself. It's been," Sam gulped, "hard."

"You're not the only one suffering, pal." Richard leaned forward with his hands wrapped around a coffee mug. "Heck, I could be spending the rest of my life in prison for a crime I didn't commit. But you don't hear me bitchin' about it, and my mother is a bigger pain in the ass than yours. You know, Evie didn't have nothin' to do with Travis getting lost. Why you dumpin' on her?"

Sam's eyes stared a hole into his coffee cup.

Richard gently swatted his guest with a hand. "I dunno about you, but I think she's positively stunning. Doncha find her at all attractive?"

It took a moment before Sam replied. "I suppose."

"I suppose?" he said with one eye closed. "What da heck does that suppose to mean?"

With head tucked low, the geologist looked older than his years, and his voice was thin, like a church supper. "I still think about… and entertaining any notion of me being with someone would seem like… I dunno…like I was being unfaithful."

Richard sat back in his chair, pursing his lips. "Ah, so that's what this is about. Let me tellya somethin'. You probably don't know this, but I stopped in one day to see how Lori's chemo was going. Must have been a coupla years ago now. You were out runnin' an errand or somethin', and we talked for the better part of an hour. Said she knew there wasn't much time left, and hoped you'd find someone new. You know, you're not being unfaithful if you started seeing someone." Richard whispered, "I'm not suppose to tell you this, and the ol' lady made me pinky swear, but Evie's had dreams about cha."

Sam squinted.

183

"Unfortunately, it was a nightmare, but you're in her head, and that's counts for somethin'. Why doncha come back in a day or two and get her a little somethin'. You know, a little peace offering. That's what I do when I'm in the doghouse."

The hum of the refrigerator was the only sound that could be heard until Sam replied, "You don't understand. I have Travis to think about, and I can't afford to have his heart broken. We're already squabbling, and we're not even seeing one another. You know, when Lori died, it broke the little guy's heart, and I don't think he can handle another big disappointment. His speech impediment is much worse now. Besides, I'm not certain I wanna spend time with someone who's has an unstable ex-boyfriend. I heard about the complaint Pantone filed; one of the cops over at Delta County told me about it. Did you guys really shoot out his back window?"

Richard flicked his hand and said, "Ah…it was just a little kerfuffle, that's all."

"So, tell me, you've been married a couple of times; you must have had some big arguments over the years."

"No shit." Richard took a slug of coffee, then pulled off a slice of coffeecake that sat nearby. "It was nothin' but one big fuckin' argument when I was married to Karen. Technically, they call it irreconcilable differences, which just about covers it. Now don't get me wrong, I was as much to blame as she was, but I became an expert in what not to do. So, when Suzanne came along, I had to change or end up with the same ol' bullshit. I love my wife, but there are times…" Richard clamped his lips tight. "Lemme give you an example. Just the other day, Suze recycled all my *Field and Stream* magazines. Had to go out to the recycling center in Esky and spent an hour crawlin' through the goddamn dumpster. You see, I squirrel away cash money in those magazines."

Sam squinted.

"You know, it's my little nest-egg, just for emergencies, like when I go to over to the Island Casino."

"So, how do you manage not killin' each other?"

"That's why I got a forty outside of town. When de ol' lady's driving me nuts, I go out dere and push dirt around with my

184

dozer. But my Dad uses it for the same thing, and sometimes we're both out dere at the same time."

Meanwhile, Suzanne was watching Evangeline pace back and forth with hands clenched tight. "That miserable…. Who the heck does he think he is?"

Suzanne put her hand onto Travis' shoulder and said, "Why don't you take Lucy out back and throw the stick for her? I bet she'd like that, but don't wander off. OK?" Once the screen door slammed, Suzanne patted the sofa. "Come, sit. All that pacing is making me dizzy. What's going on?"

Evangeline plopped herself down, silently fuming with arms crossed.

"I've been dumped on all my life, and I'm not taking it anymore."

"It's all about those letters, isn't it?"

"Huh?"

"You know what I mean. Sometimes, we romanticize how things should be rather than dealing with things the way they are." Suzanne exhaled forcefully through her nose, then sat erect, facing her neighbor. "It's terribly noble thinking about Roy who was shipped off to war. His letters are endearing, and the fact he died shortly thereafter gives them a certain ethereal quality. But had he lived, Emma might have ended up screaming at her husband not unlike you and Sam. This is years of experience speaking here. Thinking about a relationship is whole lot different than being in one. Some days, I'm ready to strangle the ol' man, and yet, I love him to pieces."

"But I'm not …"

"Oh really."

With a furrowed brow, Evangeline cast a sideways glance.

"But you have to admit that some of your anger doesn't have anything to do with Sam, at least directly. It's a whole bunch of things: Dan, your mom, and the charges against Richard, not to mention your financial situation. It all adds up."

The closet that held back the memories was about to burst open, and instead of stuffing her feelings like she often did, Evangeline resigned herself to the inevitable. "It's not that."

185

Evangeline stared at her now folded hands and sighed heavily. "I haven't said anything about this before, but … "

"What? Tell me."

Evangeline's voice elevated, and her voice was staccato like. "I…I had a daughter, a…and she died." It was as if she were gasping for air when she uttered, "Her name was Charlotte, and she was the most perfect little girl. I…I called her my little lamb-chop, and e…ever since…"

Suzanne lowered her head into a horizontal plane in order to better see Evie's face, and her voice was calm and reassuring. "Oh sweetie, you never said anything about this before."

A wave of grief was about to be released, and it seemed pointless to suppress what she had bottled up for so long. Images of her daughter, including her funeral, flickered before her, followed by the memories of Ulay. They all came rushing in from every perspective as if it had just happened, and Evangeline buried her head into her hands.

"Tell me about her."

After relaying what happened, Suzanne pulled herself close and whispered, "And what about Charlotte's father?"

"I never saw him again." Evangeline's voice strained when she said, "I tried to contact him through the address he gave me, but he never replied."

"Didja love 'im?"

This simple question evoked a wide array of emotions that including both anger and shame, but at the bottom of it was an undeniable connection. To be blunt, she was angry. Angry with various family members, who pointed out Charlotte's father didn't give a damn about her. That's why he never wrote, because Evangeline was nothing more than a notch on an Italian bedpost. So, she never mentioned his name to anyone, not even her family. She fumed at the injustice, and just before she replied, her lips were pressed into a solitary line.

"I don't even know what that means anymore," she looked away, avoiding eye contact. With arms crossed and looking out upon the lake, she continued. "Love and reality are absolute contradictions for me." Her voice was now building, and there'd be no going back. "The thought that we only have one person to

186

make our lives complete is absolute evil. I mean think about it. It's an insane notion! You finally meet someone who you want to spend your life with, and afterwards, you find out that you didn't mean shit to them. So now when I meet someone new, I don't even make the effort because I know how it's gonna turn out. You see, I'm dying inside. I don't feel pain or anger; it's as if I've become numb to it all, and then I think about my time in Verona, and I have these dreams…" Evangeline's sobs were now unmistakable. "…where Charlotte's father is sleeping next to me, and I can feel the warmth of his body, and I reach out to him, but when I do, there's nobody there. I wake up, and I'm trembling and drenched in sweat, and I know that something is terribly wrong. That's why I left Dan. I didn't want to end up getting divorced when I'm sixty years old, screaming that I never loved the man. So, to answer your question, yes I loved Charlotte's father." Evangeline spat, "Are you satisfied? And when my daughter died, it was clear that love wasn't meant for me."

Suzanne placed a reassuring hand upon Evangeline's forearm and whispered, "I'm sorry. I didn't know. It's been that bad, huh?"

No answer.

"But you must have had some feelings for Dan. After all, you were with him for almost seven years."

A few deep breaths helped restore Evangeline's composure, and her tone was conciliatory. "Dan had his moments when he could be charming. We did a few vacations together, but I never felt anything towards Dan like I did with Charlotte's father. I would have gladly of traded my seven years with Dan for just another night in Verona." She stared at her folded hands as a tear dripped off her cheek. "After my time with Ulay, everything else seemed rather shallow."

"Ulay?"

It was the first time in twelve years she had said his name out loud, and it felt as if a burden had been lifted from her shoulders. "That was his name. He was an artist traveling through Italy on vacation, and we met in Verona. We spent about three and a half days together, and it wasn't until I got back home that I realized I was…you know."

"Whew." Suzanne tucked her head once more into a horizontal plane in order to better see Evangeline's face. "Sounds like it must have been one torrid romance. Didja tell him about…?"

* * * * *

Fontaine was at her desk, flipping through pages of case law when the phone rang.

"Good morning, could I speak to Ms. Jazmine Fontaine, please."

"Speaking."

"My Name is Sergeant Bruce Howard, and I work for the Michigan State Police here in Iron Mountain. Do you know a Mr. Dalton McKenna?"

"Sure. I'm his attorney. What can I do for you, sergeant?"

His words were rote and without emotion. "Well, I regret to inform you, but Mr. McKenna passed away last night."

Jazmine cried, "He died?"

"We found your business card in his wallet and would like to know when the last time the two of you spoke?"

The sobs were unmistakable when she replied, "J…just the other day. Wh…what happened?"

"We're treating it as a homicide, but we're trying to locate his next of kin. Did he have a wife or children?"

The attorney's voice was no longer robust as she whispered. "He lived alone, and his wife died a number of years ago."

"Here's the problem. Once the autopsy is complete, we'll need to release the body. Does anyone down on your end have the authority to take possession?"

"Well, he has a trust registered with Ingham County, and I'm his successor trustee."

About the same time Jazmine Fontaine was talking to the Michigan State Police, a firestorm was brewing at Hunter's Bar, and Walt Pelligrini was on the line, calling a long-time friend from downstate.

188

"Pettigrew residence."

"Is James, dere?" Walt asked.

The housekeeper called out, "James, it's for you!"

James had worked as a geologist near Ralph years ago and recently, reconnected with Walt, a perennial resident at Hunter's Bar. James was married to Dana Andrews-Pettigrew who owned Pokorney Industries and employed both Jazmine Fontaine and Dalton McKenna.

A few seconds later, Walt heard a cheerful, "Hello."

"Hey dere, dis here Walt callin' from da UP. You sittin' down?"

"Walt, how you've been? What's goin' on?"

"I'm here at da bar in Ralph, and all hell's broke loose. Dats what's goin' on."

"What the heck are you talkin' about?"

"I'm talkin' 'bout your buddy dere, Dalton McKenna. Someone shot da ol' fart last night while he was sittin' in da car just sout of here."

James' reply came in one slow exhalation. "Holy shit."

"De road is swarmin' with cops. You tink it has somethin' to do with dat dere Templeton fella?"

"Templeton?"

"He's dat big fella down dere in Esky who got himself charged with dat dere murder. Works for da damn power company, eh?"

James whispered, "Is McKenna dead?"

"Connie says he was shot right trew da ear."

"Jesus, what the hell happened?"

"All we know is da MSP closed off da road sout of here, and dey ain't lettin' nobody trew. Ya know, McKenna and me worked together when dat dere kid got 'imself snatched a few years back, and let me tell ya, we liked da ol' bugger cuz he paid hard cash on da barrelhead. Whatcha dink we should do, eh?"

James exhaled loudly. "Lemme think...lemme think. Look, any security cameras in the area?"

189

"Well, da bar here has one ever since dat big fight we had dere out front a coupla years ago. You tink we should take a look?"

"You betcha and start askin' around if there's been any strangers floatin' about. It's not like this was a random act. How far back does the bar keep video?"

"I dunno. Lemme get back witcha on dat. Ya know, we're sure gonna miss da ol' fart. Just ain't right someone poppin' him in da head like dat."

* * * * *

Meanwhile over in Illinois, Stuart O'Hare was sitting in a classroom, listening to a professor pontificate about criminal law. It had sounded like a good idea at the time. Being retired, he didn't have much else to do and signed up for a class at the university with hopes of learning something. He sat in the back, trying not to be conspicuous, but being a good forty years older than the rest of the student body, he drew attention. Even the professor was younger than him, but that's not what bothered O'Hare. At first, he watched with amusement as the instructor called upon various students in an attempt to embarrass an ill-prepared participant, but by mid-semester, his banter and method of public humiliation had become tedious.

O'Hare had read the assigned case-study while eating breakfast and tossed it aside in disgust. He inhaled deeply, but he'd seen this sort of thing countless times before. On paper, everything seemed so black and white, but rarely did a criminal investigation come with easy to follow instructions. A slug of coffee made things more palatable, and he reminded himself he was just auditing the class, and his insights really didn't matter.

The former cop had a tacit agreement with the instructor, whereby he quietly listened to his ruminations without interruption. In return, he was never called upon, opting to sit back in his plastic chair, giving the impression that he wasn't an individual easily rattled by sophomoric banter. Meanwhile, nearby students sat erect, diligently typing notes into their laptops.

Stuart O'Hare was a formidable presence at six-foot three and two hundred and forty-five pounds. With a prominent chin and rugged complexion, he filled his chair completely, and rarely did anyone sit near him. But today was different. Maybe it was the case-study he had read or maybe it was a memory of his late wife that had surfaced, but whatever it was, it left him agitated. And when the law professor was pressing some obscure point about criminal law, O'Hare cleared his throat. Students turned as they never heard him utter a solitary word in the months they shared the classroom together.

"I see there's an element of discourse," the professor announced as he pulled out a seating chart, making a show of it by flipping through the pages. "Mr. O'Hare!" he barked. "Why don't you illuminate us with some of your fine legal interpretation? I assume you read the homework assignment."

Since O'Hare was auditing the class, formal admission into the School of Law was not required, and hence, his background was largely unknown. Of course, there were the occasional rumors that floated about. He had been seen around the lagoon with a young woman. Most thought she was a daughter, but someone reported they were holding hands which fueled speculation, at least amongst various co-eds.

When students heard Hartley's tone, they knew what was coming.

"So, Mr. O'Hare, what's your opinion regarding the allegation of prosecutorial misconduct as it pertains to the criminal complaint, State of Michigan versus Marsha Verlinden?"

His response was terse. "You don't want my opinion."

A soft chuckle was followed by, "Didn't read the homework assignment, huh?"

"I read it, but if you're really going to give these poor kids a proper education, you might want to offer them some relevant information about the extent of the criminal activity that was involved. From where I stand, the brief gives the reader the wrong impression."

Hartley now addressed the class like a Shakespearian actor. "Well by all means," sweeping his hand as if ushering him down. "Why don't you come on down here and…illuminate us with your… fine… legal… opinion?"

O'Hare slapped the top of his desk with a resounding whack, then ambled to the front where fellow classmates awaited the summary execution. One whispered to his neighbor, "This oughta be good."

Hartley leaned up against the blackboard with arms crossed and head lifted.

Stuart O'Hare pressed his lips tight and followed it by a deep inhalation through his nose. "You have to understand, life doesn't come in nice neat, orderly little packages like what you read in today's assignment. It's messy business when someone gets charged with a murder; it's often complicated. And sometimes, justice isn't always served. Some of you don't know this, but a few years ago, I was charged with open murder right here in DeKalb County. Maybe, some of you remember the Milo brothers." For a few moments, he silently paced back and forth with his hands cupped behind his back. "They had a pawn shop up on the north end of town, and both were murdered separately. One was shot in his store while the other was clubbed to death along the railroad tracks."

O'Hare could hear the whispering.

"Up until that point, I had spent the better part of forty years in law enforcement, only to be charged with a crime I didn't commit. Fortunately, we found evidence to refute the testimony of the prosecutor's main witness. All this took a great deal of resources, and rarely does the accused have sufficient assets to mount a credible defense. That being said, let me tell you a story that's a tad more relevant to today's assignment. It involved a child molester who murdered his girlfriend's daughter. Just for your edification, that girlfriend was Marsha Verlinden, and I was involved in that investigation. What your homework assignment doesn't tell you is that Ms. Verlinden's seven-year-old daughter had been sexually assaulted over the course of many years."

A few students whispered amongst themselves while others leaned forward.

"During the course of an unrelated homicide investigation, we found video documentation of the abuse. A digital photo of the girl was amongst the archive we recovered, and it had GPS coordinates attached to the file, which in turn led us to Marsha Verlinden's residence. As it turned out, little Aubrey hadn't been seen in over a year. Her mother had called the school and told them they had moved. So, nobody thought anything about it. During an interview, Verlinden and her boyfriend told investigators Aubrey had died in an accident, allegedly from a fall down a staircase. Since they were growing pot in the basement, neither reported it."

O'Hare noticed a young woman place her hand to her throat, stifling a sob.

"As for the video tapes, they were gathered without a valid search warrant, rendering them inadmissible. Compounding the matter, we didn't have the girl's remains, which left us with virtually nothing. So, without the videos or a body to submit as evidence, Verlinden's story that her daughter died by accident went unchallenged."

O'Hare continued to pace with hands cupped behind his back, and there was dead silence while Hartley leered from the blackboard. From the dark recesses of the lecture hall, a voice called out, "So, what happened?"

The room became still.

"Aubrey's remains were eventually located, but the medical examiner couldn't determine the cause of death because the body was in an advanced state of decomposition." O'Hare pulled from his pocket a picture and held it up. "This was Aubrey Verlinden!" he walked up and down the aisle in order for his classmates to see the photo of a smiling second grader.

"This sweet little girl endured some of the worst sexual abuse I'd seen in my forty-year career. We know what she endured because we have pictures of it, and not one person protected her," his voice now loud and shrill, "not her Mom... not her Dad...not the police, not a goddamn soul. Your reading assignment talks extensively about Aubrey's mother, and the confession she later recanted, but nowhere does it give the full measure of what was involved. Sure, the ol' lady lost custody of her remaining kids and plea-bargained the charges. Ended up getting twelve months in the county lockup for removing a body without approval from a medical examiner. I understand she's back working at the K-Mart in southern Michigan."

There was only silence until someone said, "What happened to Verlinden's boyfriend?"

"It was in the news. Some of you may have heard about it. You see, Crestwood's body was found right next to Aubrey Verlinden's. We're not sure what exactly happened, but the Washtenaw County Sheriff's Department got a tip and drove out to the Verlinden property. Apparently, Crestwood was in the process of digging up Aubrey's remains when an unknown assailant shot him in the forehead." O'Hare's nostrils flared, then looked towards Hartley. "But this is what really pisses me off. We spend good time studying poor ol' Marsha Verlinden and how investigators allegedly coerced a confession, but there's no mention of her daughter and the suffering she endured. As far as I'm concerned, our homework assignment is nothing but pure bullshit." O'Hare turned towards Hartley once more and lifted his head. "Put that into your fuckin' law book."

O'Hare stormed out of the lecture hall just as a text message arrived.

Captain, call when you can. Dana.

Dana Andrews-Pettigrew, the CEO and sole proprietor of Pokorney Industries, worked for O'Hare as a detective for a number of years before retiring and coughed up half a million dollars in bond money when he was charged with open murder.

O'Hare was out in the hall, calming himself when the connection was made. Pacing back and forth, he said, "OK, who died?"

"That's what I like about you, captain. No small talk and right to the point. It's Dalton," she said matter of factly. "Got the call this morning. Killed up near Ralph."

O'Hare exhaled strongly. "I knew it was only a matter of time. What the hell happened?"

"Not sure. Can you head up there and get a lay of the land? I can offer whatever support you need. Jazz is understandably upset."

O'Hare continued to pace, then looked at his watch. "Give me some time to pack a few things, and I can be there later tonight."

"You remember Walt?"

A derisive chuckle was followed by, "Like I could forget."

"Here's his number. I'm sending it as a text message. Give him a call when you get into town. Says he can put you up for a couple of nights. But…" her voice trailing off.

"What?" he said with irritation.

"I'm sure you remember. Dalton and I worked together several years ago finding Caroline Cannon, and we certainly had our differences. But he got justice for her parents and countless others." Her voice was now filled with contempt. "I want the sons of bitches that did this. Do whatever you have to, and I'll back you up."

* * * * *

Walt looked over Connie's shoulder as he viewed the video taken outside Hunter's Bar. She tapped the screen a couple of times with an index finger, leaving a grease stain. "Dat's dem dere. Dey ordered da Salisbury steak, eh?"

As Walt squinted at the image, his mouth was full of pasty, and his words were partially muffled. "Can't make da license plate, but it's a Jeep Cherokee, dat's for sure." After a slug of Old Milwaukee, his voice resonated. "De ol' lady has one just like it."

Connie looked up, then snapped off her reading glasses. "You know, Bernie Ostrowski videotapes right down dere off Spring Hill Road, eh? Ever since dose kids tipped over da shithouse, he's been running da video in hopes of catchin' the lil' buggers. Since we know da time when our buddy got himself kilt, maybe we could see if dat dere Cherokee shows up on da video."

195

An hour later they were in Ostrowski's basement, staring at a monitor, looking at scenes from the night before. After about forty minutes of viewing, Connie looked at her watch with irritation. "I can't sit here all day. Cancha speed 'er up?"

Ostrowski fast forwarded, and they saw a couple of deer amble across the road along with a few cars they recognized. Walt was in the process of putting his coat on when a dark SUV sped across the screen.

Connie yelled, "Hold it! Back 'er up!" Bernie obliged, and Connie spouted, "Dat's da same one we had over at da bar. Dats gotta be dem. Can you make a copy of dat?"

Seconds later, Walt was back on the phone and heard, "Pettigrew residence. How may I help you?"

"Needta speak to James. Tell 'im it's urgent, eh?"

"And who may I say is calling?"

"Dis here's his buddy, Walt, callin' from da UP."

A few seconds later, he heard, "Walt, whatcha got?"

"Dere was only one outa town car dat came trew Ralph, and we got da pictures of dere green Cherokee. Dey was headin' sout on Norway Lake right 'round dat time our buddy dere got popped."

"Any chance on a plate number?"

"Nah, it too dark. Whatcha want us to do?"

"Not sure yet. Got the wife working on it though."

"You knows, I spoke to your ol' lady just dis mornin' and can tell you straight out, she's what you call a real piece a work."

"You don't know the half of it," James whispered. "Look, I got some men coming your way and should be there in a few hours. Gave 'em your number and said they'd meet you at Hunter's Bar as soon as they get into town. Can you put 'em up for a couple of days?"

"Dat's what I talked to your wife about just dis mornin'. Doncha you guys ever talk to one another? Look, I got da ol' lady cleanin' up da deer camp but we gotta 'bout a truck-load of cabbage in da back bedroom, and if your buddy wants a place to sleep, he's gonna hafta help move it."

* * * * *

He looked out of place, standing at the door's threshold with his sunglasses and tan sport coat. There were only about a half-dozen patrons at Hunter's Bar, but every head turned when Stuart O'Hare made his entrance. Walt walked over, and the group relaxed, sensing their visitor was more a friend than an outsider. With a sock in the arm, Walt said, "Hey dere, Stewie. Good dey sent someone up here dat we know. Normally, we don't trust apple-knockers any furder dan we can trow 'em."

After Walt provided a physical description of the pair, O'Hare looked at the videos of the green Cherokee, then scratched the back of his big, melon-sized head. "Well, I have to admit it's an unusual coincidence having 'em drive down the same road around the time McKenna got shot, but it might be nothing." He turned to Connie and said, "Where did they sit when they came in?"

She pointed to a booth by the window. "If yous tinkin' 'bout prints, we wipe everyting down after each customer. De owner pitches a fit if de place is messy, eh?"

O'Hare exhaled forcefully. "Any trash they might have left behind?"

"We waltz it out in de afternoon, and da dumpster was emptied just dis mornin'."

"And what about a menu?"

Connie squinted at the ceiling and said, "Come to tink of it, dey did ask for a menu. We hardly ever use 'em cuz all our customers know da menu by heart. Now I remember. Da ol' man, pissed and moaned cuz it was stained. Said he wanted a clean one. Here, lemme get it."

Just as Connie was about to bolt, O'Hare grabbed her by the left arm, giving her a tug backwards. "I don't want 'em touched. We're gonna need your fingerprints so we can eliminate them."

* * * * *

While O'Hare was looking at video tape at Hunter's Bar, Evangeline Attwood was in Escanaba, loading her vehicle with groceries when she saw the little girl standing alone next to the cart corral, sobbing. The former school teacher approached and then squatted down to eye level. "What's wrong sweetheart? Where's your Mom?"

With cheeks red and tears dripping, the only thing she could make out was, "Mama!"

Evangeline looked about in hopes of finding someone who might be the child's mother, but outside of a few teenage shoppers, there wasn't anyone that looked remotely like the child's mother. The girl buried her head deep into the side of Evangeline's coat, and as Evangeline caressed her blonde hair, she thought about Charlotte and wondered what her daughter would have looked like had she survived. "What's your name, sweetheart?"

"Vivian."

There was a fleeting glimpse into that other world. Evangeline gasped ever so slightly as she peered down the rabbit hole, but the moment evaporated like a snowflake on a warm window pane. She gently rocked the girl from side to side and said, "Well that's sure a pretty name. What do you say we go inside and look for your Mommy? I'm sure she's beside herself wondering what happened to you."

The store manager was wearing a blue apron when she pressed the button on the microphone. "Attention Walmart shoppers, we have a little girl who is lost. Her name is Vivian, and she's about four years old. She was found out in our parking lot, and if this is your child, please come to the service counter. She misses her Mom very much."

As Evangeline waited, rocking the child side to side, she saw him. Sam Carter was sporting a blue vest and standing at the end of the aisle before her. Their eyes met briefly until a customer came running out of the produce section, and when she saw her daughter, the young woman broke into tears. Vivian continued to wail until her mother picked her up and explained what had happened. Bur Evangeline wasn't listening. Her mind was elsewhere. She craned her neck, looking for Sam Carter, but he was gone.

In today's top news, Delta County Prosecutor, Bill Collins told TV-6 that for the time being, he has dropped charges against a Rapid River man for the murder of Joe and John Steiner who, as you know, were gunned down last month outside of Steiner's home out on the Garden Peninsula.

Richard Templeton was initially charged with open murder, but with the recent death of a key witness, Prosecutor Collins decided to drop charges against Templeton, stating and I quote, "There doesn't seem to be sufficient evidence to proceed to trial, but the charges can and will be reinstated when and if additional evidence is uncovered in this ongoing investigation."

When asked, about the murder of a key witness, Collins refused to comment. But we have Avery Diebolt in Ralph, reporting on this grisly murder. What do you have for us, Avery?

Well Stephanie, it's been nearly fifty years since there's been a murder in this part of rural Dickinson County. I spoke to the Michigan State Police earlier this morning, and they aren't releasing any details or even the name of the deceased, pending notification of next of kin. We've talked to several people here at Hunter's Bar, and many of the residents in this area are scared, knowing a killer is running loose, and no one was willing to go on camera. Essentially, we're being told that the victim was a former US Marshal and worked for the Department of Justice where it's alleged he was investigating local drug activity. And I may add, Stephanie, there appears to be a direct connection between the murder here in Dickinson County to the murders out on the Garden Peninsula. Reporting live from Hunter's Bar in Ralph, Michigan, Avery Diebolt, TV-6 News; Marquette.

It was a long black bag with a zipper on top, filled with a human-shaped form. Jazmine Fontaine scribbled her signature onto the clipboard and said, "Do you mind if I have a minute?"

The young man who sported a mustache and goatee gave a sympathetic nod, then quietly exited. The crematorium was a small sterile room with a brown tile floor and bright incandescent lights that hung from round metal fixtures, resembling garbage-can covers, casting shadows here and there. She caressed the bag with her right hand and said, "You know, you were the only one who really understood, at least... before all this happened." Jazmine inhaled deeply, then pulled up a chair next to McKenna's body. "I never told you that when we were in Paris together, how much that meant. You treated me like an ordinary person, and not many men would have been so... respectful." She dabbed her nose with a tissue as she reminisced. "Remember that boat ride we took down the Seine? You brought along a bottle of French champagne, and it was the most perfect evening. I wonder if our lock is still there along that bridge near the Eiffel Tower?" Jazmine pulled up a picture on her phone where the two stood together with Notre Dame shining bright in the background. She patted the bag once more and said, "You were a good man, Dalton McKenna." Anger now coursed her veins, and her jaw muscles tightened, pressing her lips together. "And we're going to find the sons of bitches that did this. You can count on it."

The steel door creaked open, and she found the technician with his feet up on an old metal desk, reading a *National Geographic*.

"I'm ready now," she said plainly.

He tossed his magazine aside and looked at his clipboard until he found the entry. "Did you know... Mr. McKenna very well?"

She nodded. "He was my friend."

A few minutes later the black bag slid along steel rollers into the chamber. The door was clamped shut, and secured with an iron bar. Jazmine peered inside through the glass port just as the technician pushed the button, releasing jets of fire that engulfed its humble remains. She walked outside and could see a vapor trail coming from the stack. And for a moment, Fontaine thought she could make out a human-shaped image, dancing amongst the smoke and fumes.

Meanwhile out on Garth Point, the mood was more upbeat with a party in full swing, celebrating Richard's freedom. Amidst various neighbors and friends, Suzanne turned off the stereo and whistled, using her fingers. "Wanna thank y'all for coming out tonight and just wanted to say how much we appreciate your support." She hoisted her glass and shouted, "To freedom!"

The thirty-some celebrants rang a chorus of, "Here, here!"

After receiving several pats on the back, Richard walked across the room towards Evangeline who was leaning up against the kitchen countertop, sipping red wine from a long-stem goblet. "Glad you could make it. Suze told me about the text message you got."

"What a mess." Evangeline adjusted the sleeves to her black cocktail dress and said, "You know, I hired Mr. McKenna to help out with the matter, and it wasn't long before he found Dan playing cards with his buddies downstate. Even sent me a video clip. Here, let me show you."

After viewing the video, Templeton said, "So, you think Dan had something to do with McKenna's murder?"

"God, I hope not." A sip from her glass was followed by, "So, have you heard anything more?"

"Just what's on the news. Mr. McKenna's camp was only a few miles away from where he was shot, and considering the remoteness of the area, we figure someone must have planned it." Richard took a slug of scotch, then glanced at Evangeline's dress. "So, it'd be hard to believe Dan could have planned something like that. By the way, you didn't mention that ransom note to anybody, didja?"

Evangeline shook her head. "But why would someone kill Mr. McKenna? It doesn't make any sense."

"I dunno. Maybe he was getting close to finding out who killed the Steiners, but whoever killed the sons of a bitches, I'd like to shake their hand."

"Regardless, I'm happy how things turned out for you and Suzanne." Evangeline was scanning the crowd while Credence Clearwater Revival blared *Looking out my Back Door*.

Richard popped a few salted nuts and mumbled, "For your information, I invited Sam Carter. Should be here," he looked at his Shinola watch, "any time now. Is that gonna be a problem?"

Evangeline looked away.

"What the heck is going on with you two?" As Richard rinsed out his glass in the kitchen sink, he turned and said, "You guys hardly know one another, and you're already fighting like cats and dogs."

A moment later Sam Carter walked through the front door.

Evangeline spotted him and handed her empty goblet to Richard. "Look, I gotta run. Tell Suzanne I'll stop over tomorrow morning and help clean up." After ending her conversation with the host, she quietly slipped out the backdoor.

CHAPTER FIFTEEN

"What we think, we become."
- Buddha

December 29, 1913

After all the onlookers had gone home, the trenches at Lake View Cemetery were left open, as it was too dark to fill them in. The following morning was cold, and grains of snow blew hard across the snow pack, creating a constant growl as the wind swept through the open graves. But that was no deterrent. Peter stood above his daughter's pine box, offering a silent prayer, and here amongst the towering pines and tombstones, he wept.

202

They were at Hunter's Bar having a late breakfast when Stuart O'Hare pulled out a mug-shot from a manila folder. "The prints we got off that menu goes to this guy." As Connie put on her bifocals, she loomed from above. O'Hare looked up and said, "You certain he's the same one who came in?"

"Dat's him alright," she nodded agreeably. "He was with dat dere, snotty lil' bitch with da dyed hair."

At James Pettigrew's request, Harold Schmeltzer was summoned to assist in the investigation. Harold and his wife, Tricia had flown into Ford Airport earlier that day, then rented a car for the final leg. O'Hare and the Schmeltzers had worked together on prior investigations and enjoyed a cordial but sometimes tedious relationship. They joined Evangeline Attwood, Walt Pellegrini, and Connie Bilachek who had already assembled at Hunter's Bar in the small town of Ralph, Michigan.

They were sitting at a large round table when Harold Schmeltzer looked at the mug-shot O'Hare had provided, then flipped it over, inspecting the backside. "Any prior criminal record for this… Armand Hilbert?"

"Just hangin' bad paper, and he got a suspended sentence." O'Hare then passed out the rap sheet. "And as far as the green Cherokee goes, it took some effort, but we located it down in Green Bay."

"Howja you find it?" Connie asked.

"Since we knew the location and time the vehicle was in use, we looked for a similar GPS signature to any cell phone that was nearby. Turns out someone in that Jeep Cherokee had a cell phone, and it acted like a locator beacon. The vehicle was a rental, and they used an altered driver's license along with a pre-paid credit card. The rental company wasn't very cooperative, but I slipped 'em a coupla bucks and gotta copy of their paperwork." O'Hare slid the forms across the table.

Walt squinted as he perused the various papers. "Howja get all dis GPS stuff?"

"The woman I work with is connected to various government agencies, and she can access their databases, including cell phone locations."

"You mean James' ol' lady?"

O'Hare nodded.

"I hafta tellya straight out, she's what ya call a real piece a work, eh?"

"Tell me about it. As I was saying, the phone we're tracking made several calls during the period in question, and one was to a mining company up in Calgary."

Schmeltzer blew a long sigh and shook his head. "Not another mining company."

O'Hare put on a pair of reading glasses and gave a solitary nod. "The company's name is Tenet Gold, and interestingly enough, some of the calls we were tracking went to a Mr. Conrad Jabril Omar, one of their directors."

Evangeline stared at Omar's photo and said, "That's not his name. That's Carlisle Vernon, and I met him down in Escanaba."

"He was using an alias."

"But why? You don't think he's involved in Mr. McKenna's murder, do you?"

"The evidence points in that direction," O'Hare answered. "For what it's worth, I got a current location on that cell phone that we're tracking. It's a Chicago address."

Wearing a white apron with a pencil stuck behind her ear, Connie refilled their coffee cups and said, "Why doncha just let da cops handle it, eh?"

"Cuz," Walt replied with a sharp rebuke, "dere as worthless as hen shit on da pump handle. Remember when dat dere guy was breakin' in to all da camps up here a coupla years ago? Dey sent out dat dere, dumb cop from Iron Mountain, and da dumb bugger couldn't find a long-john in a doughnut shop."

O'Hare straightened the lapels, then managed a civil reply. "Look, you need to understand, I'm not here to put people in jail. I'm here to settle accounts."

O'Hare departed for the restroom whereupon Evangeline whispered to the Schmeltzers, "So, how did you guys meet?"

Tricia giggled like a schoolgirl, then looked at her husband. "You wanna tell her or do you want me to?"

With his palm facing up, Harold made a sweeping gesture towards his wife. "Be my guest."

"I was working for an escort agency out of Chicago."

Evangeline's scrunched her face as if tasting something bitter, then cocked her head to one side. "When you say 'escort agency,' you're not implying…"

"I'm not implying anything. I was a professional and worked the industry for several years. Turns out I had an assignment in Dexter, Michigan, and the guy who owned the place, unbeknownst to us, videotaped everything. He then used those videos to blackmail several clients. We knew nothing about it until a couple of our girls ended up dead along with the owner. To make a long story short, Stuart was a part of the investigation, and that's where I met my husband."

As the Schmeltzers gave each other a quick kiss, Evangeline said, "So, you're still….?"

"Not anymore. Now I work at an elementary school downstate."

What's the world coming to? Doesn't anyone do background checks, for heaven's sake? "Where do you work at?"

"Fairview Elementary. It's just a small school near the capital. I'm sure you never heard of it."

Evangeline snapped her head back and said, "I've been to Fairview Elementary. It's over on Wabash Street. I taught middle-school over at Pattengill for seventeen years, and some of my students came from your school." The two women gave each other a high-five. "So, do you know their principal, Mary Beth Mullins?"

"Of course," answered Tricia. "We've hung out a few times. Have you ever heard her sing? Lemme tell you, she got one amazing set of pipes. A while back, Mary Beth performed a gig with an entire orchestra out at Red Rocks west of Denver. How do you know MB?"

"Oh, we worked on a few projects together back when she was the school's literacy teacher. Small world. Never knew she had that kind of talent. When I get home, I'll have to ask her about her performance." By now, Evangeline had warmed considerably to Tricia and said, "So, tell me about this Stuart fella." Evangeline looked towards the restroom, craning her neck. "With that mouth of his, I'd imagine he's not married."

"He was, but she passed away a few years ago. Now he's dating a friend of ours. Wanna see the pictures?" Tricia fumbled through her purse until she found the phone and displayed an image of Stuart O'Hare with his arm around a woman's waist, both holding ice cream cones, with a rollercoaster in the background.

With a raised eyebrow, Evangeline said, "She's a lot younger than him."

"The first time they met, Jolene was ready to wring his neck, but one thing led to another and now...well, we'll just have to wait and see."

"And she's a..." Evangeline's voice trailed off.

"Well she was, but we all have a checkered past, including my dear husband here." Tricia gave her husband a poke in the ribs with an elbow. "This one got himself shot during that investigation in Dexter, and we nearly lost him. Show her the scar, sweetheart."

Harold unbuttoned the top of his shirt and exposed the bullet wound up by his collarbone. "Probably don't know this, but the three of us knew each other in another lifetime. It was right after the Civil War. You see, I was befriended by a Confederate soldier," Harold sat erect then adjusted his sleeves. "He took me in, and we ended up like family. Their daughter from back then was reincarnated and is the woman who's currently paying all our expenses. And from the," Harold used his fingers to make quotation marks, "what it's worth department, Mr. McKenna was Colonel John Mosby back during the great war. He went by the name of the Grey Ghost. You ever hear of him?"

"Mr. McKenna mentioned it, but it seemed pretty far-fetched at the time. So, you're absolutely certain, he's the Grey Ghost from the Civil War?" Filled with incredulity, Evangeline said, "What proof do you offer?" She looked over the top of her eyeglasses with anticipation.

Harold respired loudly. "I can't prove it, but if you spend time with him, you'd realize he's a force to be reckoned with. As you already know, he worked as a US Marshal but what you don't know is Mr. McKenna also served with the CIA. He retains many of those contacts and has access to all their databases because he holds dirt on just about everyone he worked with including our Attorney General. Lemme tell you somethin'. I have first-hand experience dealing with Dalton McKenna, and he's not a person you wanna cross not unlike Colonel Mosby." Harold shivered as he recalled the time when Dalton used a taser on him during an investigation into child abduction. "If my history serves me correct, Colonel Mosby was a constant thorn in the Union's flank and continues to do so in this life as well."

Evangeline recalled a lesson she taught on the American Civil War, and one of her students wrote a paper on Mosby. She looked at her watch, wondering what her former students were doing and realized they were all at lunch. In another twenty minutes, they'd be starting their afternoon session.

Stuart returned from the restroom, rubbing his hands onto his pants legs. He yelled, "The shithouse is outa paper towels!" He then turned to the group and said, "What are you guys kibitzing about?"

"Just telling Evie here about my time as a Union soldier."

Evangeline flared her nostrils. "And you're a part of ...?"

O'Hare emitted a rare wince and a took a seat. "I know it all sounds like a bunch of bullshit and understand the skepticism. But... I was Dana's father from back then. You haven't met her, but she's what you'd call a real piece of work. Has four-hundred-million in artwork hanging in a house worth, at most, a hundred-and-forty grand." O'Hare shook his head with derision.

"So, you're all saying that everyone here..."

Harold nodded.

"Then maybe you might appreciate this. You see, I've had some really bizarre things happen to me recently, and I'm wondering if they might be... a past life memory."

With a furrowed brow, O'Hare lifted his mammoth-sized noggin and said, "Tell me about it."

The container wasn't especially heavy, maybe four or five pounds. After going through the crusher, all that remained were some fine bone fragments that were stuffed into a metal tin. She placed the container on the passenger seat, then buckled the seatbelt as if McKenna was still embodied. Taking the back-roads, Jazmine Fontaine reminisced about their time together, vacillating between laughter and tears. She remembered the first time Dalton cooked her breakfast. It was at Schmeltzer's home in Skokie, and she snickered, remembering the apron he wore, embroidered with blue chickens. Few people knew he was a good cook, and they spent many breakfasts together, just talking. Sometimes, discussions were dark, like when she revealed her first paid sexual encounter and a subsequent suicide attempt. Yet, they also talked about ordinary things, like the weather or the latest news coming out of the Capital.

And when emotions became raw, the attorney would pull over and walk the shoulder of the county blacktop. Fontaine recalled a particular evening. The client's name was Alvin or was it Alex? After so many years, she simply couldn't remember. They were lying in bed together when he whispered, "It's only a paper moon sailing over a cardboard sea."

At the time, it seemed odd, considering they had just completed an hour-long session of rough sex. Normally, the men rolled over and fell asleep, but Alvin, or whatever his name was, was different. In the morning after she had showered and donned a leather skirt with a silk top, she asked him about it. He said it summed up his belief about life; that it was all make-believe, and the only thing real was love. Considering the source, she dismissed the notion as irrelevant, but now, many years later, she concurred.

Jazmine remembered their trip when they went to Paris. At first, Dalton seemed like all the rest, just a guy with deep pockets, trying to get some. But he didn't crowd her, and when they reached their apartment, he helped get her settled into her own bedroom. But as the days rolled into weeks, it seemed more and more peculiar, and she finally worked up the courage to ask him about it.

He explained the invitation to Paris wasn't about sex and plainly stated, "I'm just glad you're here," He then went into a monologue, explaining how sex was overrated. "You know what's more important than sex?" Jazmine recalled him saying. "It's the time people give one another. It's a slice of their life they're never going to get back. I can't think of a nicer gift a person can give to one another." As she reflected, Jazmine looked at the small tin next to her, buckled into the car seat.

She also recalled their discussion about death. It was a warm summer night; they were eating ice cream near the university, and the coolness of her raspberry sorbet felt heavenly. She had alluded to a prior suicide attempt, using a handful of sedatives flushed down with copious amounts of cheap bourbon. She laughed at the memory like a person whistling in the dark, hoping to keep the demons at bay, and after her disclosure, there was an awkward silence, sensing her revelation might not have been for the best.

But Dalton McKenna withheld judgment. "There are no free passes, kiddo," she recalled him saying. "If you decide to check out, that's really up to you, but you just end up right back here in the next life exactly where you left off." He reassured her that whatever she was going through had no real power over her unless she submitted to it. It was the first time anyone said her feelings weren't definitive, and under all that, he said confidently, was a divine spirit. And just like Alvin's lyrics, Dalton's assertion seemed preposterous, but in time, the attorney reconsidered the notion, and her perspective began to shift.

Jazmine had quit the escort agency several years ago and took a job with Pokorney Industries, where she worked as an analyst on an oil sand project. At first, it was rather dull, like a John Milton novel, but in time, she accepted, and sometimes actually enjoyed, the transition. But on rare occasions, she fantasized about her former life. It provided a certain element of duality that allowed her to express her darker nature. Jazmine liked having control over men, but she reminded herself that her lifestyle led to a suicide attempt and an addiction to sedatives. At times, she would drop the veil of secrecy and talk about it, whereby Dalton would offer an occasional shoulder to cry upon. He was steadfast and kind, qualities she'd come to admire more so now than before. Dalton had introduced her to Lenard Frank, who pulled a few strings and got her into law school, where she performed admirably.

Fontaine thought about the last few moments of his life, and her jaw muscles tightened. In her mind's eye, she could see Dalton pulling over to help a stranded motorist or something similar. Next came a bright flash, a sharp crack, followed by a scent of spent gunpowder, then an indelible darkness. She could envision the blood-spray pattern along the driver-side window and the lifeless body slumped down in the plush leather seat. And with that last image, she placed her left hand to her mouth and choked back a sob.

It never really seemed viable, but when Dalton outlined the likelihood of him dying from a violent act, she dismissed it as nothing more than male bravado. In part, because she really didn't want to accept the notion that the man she had come to respect might be targeted by a variety of people, including those working for the Department of Justice. Of course, she heard the stories and remembered the time when they had a guy hogtied in Schmeltzer's basement. Dalton told her it was better if she didn't know what had happened, but there was never any doubt. And then there was that incident in Dexter, Michigan. He told her the story about the young man who broke into the estate and how they dumped his body into the Huron River, but she never actually witnessed violence; she only saw a kind, gentle soul who was learning to play the oboe. She laughed when she thought about his first performance being filled with squeaks and missed notes. She was the only audience member and admired his perseverance.

Jazmine then thought about her own life, and to most, she came off as a confident professional who didn't put up with bullshit. But there was a more nefarious story, one that had led to a life of prostitution. With no family, she felt completely alone at times; that whatever she did, no one would possibly

210

understand. And then came Dalton McKenna who introduced her to Dana. Dana Andrews-Pettigrew was her employer who challenged the young woman at almost every turn, and with years of effort, Jazmine started to see things differently. Admittedly, she was a difficult person to persuade, none less assuage. In many ways, Dalton McKenna and Dana Pettigrew saved her life in every manner possible.

With only the hum of the tires to listen to, Jazmine pressed southward, where the moon was rising over a recently harvested cornfield. As the moonlight cast shadows long, there was a hint of frost in the air. It reminded her of the time they spent on Mackinac Island, where they would sit outside and watch the moon set.

As she passed through the towns of Mount Pleasant, then Alma and Ithaca, she thought more about the trip they made to Mackinac Island the year before. It was a last-minute decision; a friend of Dalton's offered the residence as partial payment for a debt once incurred. As she pressed southward through Saint Johns, she recalled the large Victorian home that overlooked Lake Huron. They would spend every evening outside watching the sunset, perhaps sipping iced tea, with only the sound of the wind rustling through the nearby willows. She learned from Dalton how to better appreciate silence compared to the radio and other mindless chatter, and as the attorney entered the city, everything seemed transformed, as if his death somehow made the town less complete.

Jazmine entered her condo and sighed when she slipped her shoes off, then stared at the pile of mail neatly stacked on her kitchen table. Sifting through the bills and flyers, she recognized the handwriting and flipped the letter over to see if there was a return address. The attorney used a dull steak-knife, ripping the envelope along the top, then put on her reading glasses, where she found a note written on plain yellow paper.

Dear Jazz,

Just sitting around waiting for my appointment with Vernon and thought I'd pen a few lines before I take off. I'd like to take this opportunity and write about a few things. First off, I want to thank you. You inspire me to see things differently, and because of that, I've changed. You helped me see the beauty in every day things and relish simple pleasures like a walk about town or maybe enjoying a bowl of popcorn. Just wanted to say how much I appreciate you and hope we can spend more time together once I finish business here in the UP.

One final matter, I spoke with Evangeline Attwood the other day, and something is going on here that runs deeper than the matter at hand. If you have time, talk to her. She has an interesting story. I've contacted Stuart O'Hare, and he may be of use to us throughout the investigation.

Talk soon.

Dalt

* * * * *

Jazmine Fontaine held her breath as she placed the key into the slot. Once inside, the attorney was surprised how quiet and orderly Dalton's home was. There was a mountain of mail stacked on the dining room table, not unlike the pile she found at her own residence. Apparently, the neighbor was bringing it in, and she made a note to stop next door and deliver the news.

There was a photograph on the fireplace mantle where a young Dalton McKenna had his arm around his wife; both beaming broadly in the bright summer sunshine. Fontaine noted the palm trees in the background and wondered where the photo was taken. She made her way to the bedroom and found their picture on top of the nightstand. It was of the two of them standing in the spot where Joan of Arc was incinerated, and the attorney enjoyed the irony. She held the picture with both hands, recalling the afternoon they spent exploring Rouen.

The silence in the small bedroom had a sound all its own where only a faint ringing sensation could be detected. As Jazmine stood in front of Dalton's bed, she could imagine him walking about the house as if nothing had happened or maybe making breakfast in the small kitchen down the hall. Fontaine remembered the last time he made breakfast for her, and for the briefest moment, she could detect the scent of bacon frying along with the sound of eggs sizzling in the cast-iron fry pan.

She eventually found her way to his office, a converted bedroom with a computer resting neatly upon an old mission-style desk. Jazmine started up the laptop and perused the various folders until she found what she was looking for. With a click of the mouse, the letter unfolded.

Dear Jazz,

I would imagine that if you are reading this, I am most likely dead or in a persistent vegetative state. Please, pull the plug, and let me die in peace. But do not be sad about my passing. I have lived many lifetimes and surely will return someday. I have had a full life and hope that my work helped alleviate suffering. I know what you're thinking. "How can I say that, considering all the people I've harmed over the years?" But I offer this humble explanation. Every one of those that I dealt with saved countless lives. Remember that guy from Chicago who killed your friend, April? Had we released him, how many other women would have suffered a similar fate?

But this is not my reason for writing. I want you, Jazmine Fontaine, to carry on. Alleviate suffering wherever you can and let no one stand in judgment of your actions. We have a moral responsibility to protect the innocent and offer assistance to those in need. Don't worry about making a mistake. We all do. Talk to Dana about it. You already know how we work, but with me gone, I'd like you to take my place in this on-going saga of settling accounts.

Thanks for your time. It's by far the most precious gift any person can give. Be of good cheer, my friend, and know that we shall meet again.

Your friend,

Dalton McKenna

Evangeline hesitated as she picked up the phone, and when the connection was made, her voice was soft and light. "Could I speak to Ms. Dana Pettigrew please?"

"This is she."

"Hi, my name is Evangeline Attwood, and I was told you worked with a Mr. Dalton McKenna."

A sigh preceded, "Then you know about…"

"Just wanted to offer my condolences. He was helping me with a matter involving my ex-boyfriend."

"What can I do for you, Ms. Attwood?"

"It's about something different. An acquaintance suggested I speak to you. His name is Stuart O'Hare and told me that he worked with you in law enforcement a number of years ago. He's the one who gave me your number."

Dana chuckled. "Boy, that brings back memories."

"Well, Stuart said you'd be a good person to talk to, regarding a topic that's… pretty unusual. *Go ahead and just say it.* Stuart said he was your grandfather back in another lifetime. Is that true?"

Amongst the barking dogs, Dana yelled, "Carly! You put that back! Sorry, I got four kids, and they're a handful at times. So, you we're saying something about my relationship with Stuart?"

"Precisely. I mean… is it true… that you were his granddaughter in another lifetime?"

"Hang on a sec. I'm going to take this into my bedroom where it's a bit quieter." There was silence for a few moments until Evangeline heard the click. "Now about Stuart and me. I know this is hard for most people to accept, but he was my grandpa back in the 1800s. My mom back then was his only child, and he lived near Dexter, Michigan in an old farmhouse." Dana could hear the sobbing and said, "Tell me. What's goin' on?"

There'd be no going back. Evangeline blurted, "I…I see things."

After describing her visions, Dana replied. "Don't be so hard on yourself. These things aren't intended to be harmful. They're there to help."

"So, what was it like when you first... remembered?"

Evangeline could hear a loud inhalation.

"It was rough to say the least. You see, I wasn't brought up believing reincarnation was even possible. But there were so many things that happened. I simply couldn't rule out the possibility."

"Like what?"

"Well for starters, I remember things from back then." In her mind, Dana could see the old farmhouse with its wood-burning stove. "You see, I fell in love with a boy when I was just a child, but he died of scarlet fever."

Evangeline thought about Charlotte and wondered if Dana felt similarly. "I'm sorry. I didn't mean to bring up such a hard topic, but if you don't mind me asking, how did you navigate all that?"

"It was hard to say the least." Dana sighed heavily. "And although it was unsettling at times, it finally worked out. You see, the boy who died back then is now my husband. And although he's an absolute goofball, I couldn't be happier."

"And he remembers back then?" Evangeline asked, hoping for a favorable reply.

"He remembers a few things, but not everything. Look, you just have to trust that things work out eventually. You know...be open to the idea that you can be healed in all of your relationships. I don't know if this helps any..."

Evangeline interrupted. "I just think about all those children who perished, and at times, I'm... I'm just overwhelmed."

"Oh sweetie, it doesn't have to be like that. You see, we provide all the meaning there is to everything in our life. Now I'm not saying it wasn't a tragedy, but it doesn't have to define you. Those children aren't suffering anymore. It's you who's suffering, and that too is a choice. I know it sounds harsh, but you could see things differently if you really wanted. You may not be able to do anything for those children who died, but you can love the children in your life right now."

Evangeline immediately thought about Travis.

"And when you honestly give of yourself, the universe responds with abundance. Trust me on this. Look, I know what it feels like to lose someone important. My first husband died on my living room sofa, leaving me with an infant son. Although it was terribly difficult, because of it, I got to meet my new husband, and like I said, I couldn't be happier."

Evangeline thought about Emma. She too lost a husband and then remarried. As a rare jolt of optimism coursed through her veins, she said, "You're not just saying all this just to make me feel better, are you?"

Evangeline could hear Dana breathing.

"It's just an opinion, and I wouldn't want you to accept anything without a healthy dose of skepticism. So, when are you coming back?"

"Maybe not for a while. I have to ask." Her voice now filled with incredulity, "Do you really have millions in artwork in your home? Stuart told me about it, but sometimes he seems to exaggerate."

"He also has a big mouth. When you get back, give me a call, and we can get together for coffee. I remember how hard accepting things like this can be, and you've got to understand that what you're going through is more of a blessing than a curse."

* * * * *

"You sure?" O'Hare asked as if the explanation was less than plausible.

"Look, all I can tell you is the phone is inside the building you're parked in front of and is currently operable. Can't tell what floor it's on, but if you dial the number, you might be able to hear it ring. The building has several companies associated with it; the largest is Emerald Realty. Their motto is, 'We'll help you find a real gem.' Kinda cute, doncha think?"

"How long before the batteries go dead?"

216

"Hard to say. It depends on the number of apps its running, but most burners can typically hold a charge from anywhere from two to five days, if its on standby mode."

Click.

Harold Schmeltzer tried to get a better look at the building in question, by craning his head. "How do you wanna do this?"

"Why don't you guys go on in and pretend you're looking for a house. Sometimes, the agents have their picture up by the reception area." He handed Harold the mug-shot of Armand Hilbert and said, "See if you can find anyone that looks similar. In the meantime, I'll check out the other businesses."

An hour later, O'Hare was tapping the steering wheel with his fingertips when the Schmeltzers entered the vehicle. "Where the hell have you been?" he barked as he looked at his Bulova. "Been sitting out here for over a goddamn hour."

"He's going by the name of Caypeck." Tricia handed O'Hare the business card that had the realtor smiling broadly, looking like Lorne Greene during his days on the set of *Bonanza.* "The wife is his tag-team partner going by the name of Rory. Here's her card."

O'Hare took a picture of Rory's business card and then called Connie at Hunter's Bar, where he had to speak up over the music playing in the background. "I'm sending the picture of both of 'em. Can you see it?"

"Turn da damn music down. I can't hear!" It took Connie a minute to find her glasses, and she replied with a resolute, "Dat's her alright. Dat's de snotty li'l bitch dat came in here with dat dere Hilbert fella. So now what?"

Later that evening, O'Hare found refuge in a utility closet down in the basement and waited until he got the call. Harold was across the street and reported through his cell phone. "The last car just left. So, we're ready on this end."

He emerged from the basement, and the three stood before the now darkened entrance of Emerald Realty, which was located on the ground level. The former cop was bent over with an LED flashlight in his mouth and used a variety of instruments to pick the locking mechanism. It took a couple of minutes to successfully gain access, and upon entering, O'Hare spied the alarm. Not having the code to deactivate, he whispered, "We gotta move. We only got five or ten minutes." He tossed Tricia the keys and said, "Pull the car up to the backdoor, and if we're not out in ten, take off."

Harold dialed the number, and in the distance, he could hear the faint sound of a phone ringing. O'Hare snapped his fingers and pointed.

There were nearly twenty offices to choose from, along with a reception area. But after four rings, the phone went silent. So, he repeated the process, leading the two men to an unlocked office near the back of the building. Once inside, Harold dialed the number once more, which in turn led them to a locked file cabinet along the far wall.

O'Hare looked at his watch; it wouldn't be long before someone responded to the silent alarm. He moved quickly, using a metal pick and a bobby pin to open the file cabinet. As he pulled out the SIM card, Tricia's voice squawked over the walkie-talkie. "Been listening to the scanner, and the call just came in. They're on their way. You only have a few minutes."

O'Hare looked at his watch, and as the SIM card was being copied onto his smart phone, he tapped his foot. "Come on. Come on." Once the process was complete, he tossed the phone back into its cabinet, slammed the door shut, and raced to the parking lot where the three took off down Mannheim Road, just as a patrol car passed with its red lights flashing.

* * * * *

It was November when the first snowfall dusted the ground with fluffy white flakes, but by evening, most had melted. Little Bay de Noc was still open, but to the north, a hoarfrost had settled in, and the edges of the Portage Canal were ice-bound. With the onset of winter came the heating bills, and since the Templetons had moved into their new domicile, Evangeline was now responsible for paying the utilities on her brother's cottage. Since the home was heated with propane, a full tank cost nearly four-hundred dollars, meaning she had to pick up additional hours, sending her back to the Keweenaw. The job didn't pay all that well, but tips from various customers, especially when she wore something colorful, made her employment more lucrative.

It was early evening, and with time on her hands, Evangeline walked the streets of Calumet with Lucy at her side. She enjoyed watching the snowflakes dance in front of the streetlights, and as she pulled her collar up, a 'For Sale' sign caught her eye. It was a large bungalow with tapered columns that supported the front porch, and as she stood on the sidewalk admiring its simple architecture, an elderly man with white hair walked out the front door, pulling his collar up.

He saw her standing there and said, "Lookin' for a home, eh?"

Evangeline tilted her head to one side, admiring the exposed rafters and the dormer on the second level, "Do you know how much they're asking?"

"One twenty-nine nine." Sensing an interested buyer, the realtor poured it on with fervor. "I'm their agent, and with a thirty-year mortgage, monthly payments could be as low as four-sixty-seven, depending on how much you put down. And don't forget, property taxes around here are dirt cheap. You want to come in and take a look? The owners have pulled up stakes, and the place is empty."

Evangeline glanced at her watch and replied, "Sure. But I don't want to leave Lucy outside in the cold. Think it'll be alright to bring her in?"

He curled his fingers repeatedly and said, "Sure. Come on."

Her imagination took over as she inspected various rooms and could see herself working at the granite countertop, preparing for a dinner party. The committee inside her mind was now in full session, debating the pros and cons of buying another home. As Evangeline made her way to the front entrance, she left with a promise to check back with the realtor in the next few days.

On her way back to Luigi's, Evangeline walked down Seventh Street where she passed the Italian Hall Memorial, now an empty lot with a salvaged arch placed in the center. Here, she read about the labor dispute in 1913, and a photo of Big Annie posted by the Park Service pulled her back in time. As she closed her eyes, Evangeline could feel the crush of humanity along with the moans from deep within the pile. She placed a hand to her collarbone and whispered, "Close your eyes lamb-chop. Just close your eyes."

* * * * *

O'Hare dialed the phone number Dalton had given him, and his first words were terse. "Need to speak to the Attorney General. Tell 'im it's urgent."

A woman responded with a high-pitched squeak. "Who might I ask is calling?"

"Name is Stuart O'Hare. We met a couple of times, and he knows who I am."

"I'm sorry, but he's not available at the moment. Can I take a message?"

He took a sip of Stroh's Bohemian and then pulled the lever back on his Barcalounger, hoisting his legs into a horizontal plane. "Let him know Dalton McKenna was murdered, and I got some information regarding those responsible."

O'Hare could hear the exhalation.

"Hang on. Let me see what I can do."

A few seconds later he heard a crisp, "Holden. Who's this?"

"Stuart O'Hare. Maybe you remember me. I was involved with that mess down in Dexter a few years back."

"You're that cop that got charged with open murder over in DeKalb County, right?"

He mumbled, "Forty years in law enforcement, and that's all anyone can remember."

The Attorney General replied with a snarky, "What do you want?"

"As you probably know, McKenna was shot the other night and being a former US Marshal, I thought you might be interested in what I've come up with."

Holden sighed.

Another slurp of beer was followed by, "Got evidence that implicates an Armand Hilbert and his wife who are both working under an alias. Names are Keith and Rory Caypeck, and they reside in the Chicago suburbs. Don't have an ID on the woman's true identity just yet."

"And?"

"Well, I got hold of the burner they were using the night of the murder, and there's several incriminating text messages."

"You work with Andrews, right?"

"Actually, she worked for me while I was chief of police over in Ingham County, but that's beside the point." O'Hare rose from his recliner and turned on the overhead light that illuminated a stack of papers resting neatly on the dinning room table. "You see, on the night McKenna got himself killed, the Caypecks sent a lone text message to a phone up in Calgary. Said, 'Mission accomplished. Send remainder to the account provided.' Also, we have eyewitness testimony, along with video, placing both of them at the crime-scene during the night in question."

"How didja find 'em?" Holden barked.

"GPS coordinates. Got 'em from some guy working at the NSA. Dalton gave me their number awhile back."

Holden emitted another heavy sigh.

"But here's the problem. As you know, none of it's admissible, and killing 'em didn't seem right." O'Hare took another swig of beer, then swiped his lips with a sleeve. "Want me to handle this or you want in?"

Holden's voice was sharp like broken glass. "If you haven't noticed, we're the Department of Justice, not the Gambino crime family. Look, nobody over here is particularly worked up, knowing the son of a bitch is dead. Just some friendly advice, O'Hare. You're walking on thin ice, and don't go expecting us to bail you out if you go taking matters into your own hands."

It was O'Hare's turn to sigh, and he did so loudly. "I figured as much. Look, I spoke with Andrews this morning, and she asked me to deliver a message just in case there was some sort of misunderstanding. You see, she still holds all those videos taken from that house down in Dexter. Says that if you renege on your agreement, she'll release those movies to the media, which includes one of your intelligence officers from the Joint

Chiefs pumpin' a coupla of hookers. If push comes to shove, says she might start talkin' about a whole bunch of other stuff."

"What are you getting at?" Holden barked.

O'Hare paused for a moment and said, "For starters, how about the relationship between the DEA and the murder of Marla Kemper? Andrews says one of your agents called Tony Zambrusko right after Marla reported her smuggling activity. A day later Tony put a bullet into her head. You should also know that Andrews uncovered a close-up video of your boss gettin' a blow-job from a coupla hookers. If you think that story with Stormy Daniels was salacious, wait 'til the press corps gets hold of this footage. Here, I'll send you a copy."

There was dead silence.

"You still there?" O'Hare asked.

* * * * *

"Can I speak to Carmine Langford, please?"

"Who may I ask is calling?"

"My name is Jazmine Fontaine. I've been trying to get hold of Mr. Vernon over at The Ludington but haven't had any luck and understand you're acting as his legal counsel here in Michigan."

"What can I do for you, Ms. Fontaine?"

"Ms. Attwood asked me to represent her in regards to a silver specimen she found while diving in your area, and your client expressed an interest in it. I'd like to schedule a meeting to discuss the matter. Is he available?"

Langford hemmed and hawed, like a used-car salesman. "Well...ah..., he's pretty busy right now. Ah... what exactly does Ms. Attwood want?"

"If you haven't heard, the man she hired to represent her interest was murdered the other night over in Dickinson County. Mr. McKenna and Mr. Vernon had somewhat of a cantankerous relationship as I understand, and we're concerned that your client may have information about his murder."

Vernon's attorney remained silent for a few moments until he barked, "Why don't we talk about your client for a change. I read the complaint, and her buddy, Templeton put a gun to her boyfriend's head and shot out the window in his truck." His voice now rose with anger. "Maybe you should be taking a closer look at your client's behavior, before accusing Mr. Vernon of misconduct!"

There was another pause until Fontaine said, "And why would you have copies of her boyfriend's complaint? Did Vernon hire you to look into it?"

"Well...ah..."

"Next, you're going to tell me that business was so slow, you had time to go over all the criminal complaints at the county courthouse. After all, it never even made the papers."

"Well...ah..."

"Save it. The only way you would have found out about that complaint was through Vernon, because he's got a couple of cops over at the sheriff's department who are on his payroll."

Langford shifted tactics quickly. "So, where's the shipwreck?"

"Look, there is no shipwreck. My client made it up in hopes of getting a better offer but realizes the mistake she made. If you like, I can give you the location, but you should know Ms. Attwood searched the area several times and didn't find anything of value. But there's one more order of business before I close. Lemme be perfectly clear. If Vernon had anything to do with the murder of Dalton McKenna, tell your client we'll hunt him down."

Click.

* * * * *

Dana Pettigrew-Andrews perused the vast library of videos she had archived on a server overseas, and as she watched Fontaine mount Alberta's Environmental Minister, she thought about Dalton McKenna. He was the one who urged her to employ Fontaine and smirked at the irony. After all, she was now an employee of the nascent Pokorney Industries, a Swiss company with corporate offices in Zurich. Its inception was derived through the Department of Justice who endowed it with funds confiscated from various drug cartels as a means of keeping Andrews' archive from being published.

With the help and consent of the American government, Pokorney was given dual identities. Here in the United States, she was a retired cop by the name of Dana Andrews-Pettigrew, wife and mother of four, living in a modest bi-level in southern Michigan. But she also held a Swiss passport that identified her as Mme. H. Pokorney, President and Chief Executive Officer of Pokorney Industries with assets measured in billions.

Dana downloaded the video and then performed a Google search, noting the address and phone number for Alberta's Environmental Minister. Once complete, she contacted her team of lawyers and analysts, seeking advice on how to best proceed.

* * * * *

Tenet Gold Corporation's (TGC) primary asset was the Cooperstown Gold Deposit in northern Alberta with proven reserves of over fifty million troy ounces. The operation was primarily open pit, but recently, underground adits were sunk in order to extract high-grade gold mineralization at depth. The Cooperstown provided a steady revenue stream to TGC stockholders that exceeded five-hundred million Canadian (CA) dollars per year. With two-hundred ninety million shares of outstanding stock, the market-cap exceeded fifteen billion dollars, resulting in lavish bonuses for executive management.

On Monday morning, TGC stock was trading on the Toronto Stock Exchange for $51.67 (CA) per share, and no one particularly noticed the ‚recent surge in future contracts. It happened rather quickly. A brokerage firm based out of Zurich began acquiring contracts, positioning themselves that TGC's price would plummet over the next three months. The firm had no shortage of investors/brokers who were willing to buy TGC options at $37.00/share, and as the day progressed, more than fifty percent of Tenet's stock was vulnerable to new ownership.

James Currant, Chief Executive Officer and President of TGC, was apprised of the situation later in the day, then called an emergency meeting of the Board of Directors. Here, their

Chief Financial Officer assured the board the company's financials were solid and noted the price per share had actually risen to $55.92, quelling all concerns.

But this optimism was quickly dashed when the Vice President for Acquisitions and Mergers passed out documents outlining the brokerage firm's position. His office had spoken to several analysts on the Toronto Stock Exchange (TSX), and Pokorney Industries was indentified as the financial motor behind the recent future contracts. Several years prior, Pokorney Industries had performed a similar maneuver and within a few days, had control of Timberlake Resources. That outcome resulted in a sale of their primary asset, oil-sand acreage, at discount prices. Recently, Pokorney Industries had sold their holdings throughout central Canada and profited handsomely. With this information, frantic calls were made to every analyst who consistently reassured the board TGC's financials were solid as bedrock.

The following day, smiles permeated the corporate office as stock prices rose to $61.34 per share, but it was only a lull before the impending storm. And this one hit quickly like a tsunami rolling over a flat landscape, offering little resistance. Overnight, Alberta's Environmental Minister issued a cease and desist order to the Cooperstown Project, citing a variety of environmental concerns: waters from the main pit were being discharged into the local watershed and contained unusually high levels of arsenic and lead. As a result, their water discharge permit was revoked. Management challenged the assertion and re-tested discharge waters in an attempt to assuage the minister's concern, with hopes of rescinding the order but to no avail.

With copious amounts of meteoric water and nowhere to pump it, the large open pit, which was now over eight-hundred feet deep, began to fill. The mine operator moved the haul trucks and portable equipment to higher ground, but stationary objects, like conveyor belts and rock crushers, soon become inundated, rendering them useless.

TGC's response was immediate. A flurry of lawsuits were filed with hopes of overruling the Environmental Minister's decision, citing damage to equipment and impending layoffs. While lawyers argued amongst themselves, a team of engineers descended upon the Office of Environment and Climate Change with hopes of rescinding the decree. Meanwhile, the pit continued to fill, and with all the water descending from various cracks and fissures, walls began to collapse, while employees watched helplessly from offices above.

As water levels rose within the pit, stock prices moved in the opposite direction. By the end of the week, TGC was trading at $41.19 per share, but when news of layoffs reached the press, stock prices tumbled to $6.41/share. At this point, Pokorney Industries asked for a meeting to address TGC's Board of Directors.

PI's CEO, along with her legal team of lawyers and financial analysts, explained their position via a Skype connection. "Good morning, gentlemen," Pokorney said in a taciturn voice. "I'll make this brief, but as of this morning my company holds a majority interest in Tenet Gold. Being the primary shareholder, my first order of business is to relieve James Currant and Conrad Jibril Omar from all duties, effective immediately."

Heads swiveled from side to side, and there was a stir of hushed voices upon hearing the announcement.

With splayed hands, Currant called out, "You can't be serious. But why?"

Pokorney leaned forward, and her answer was succinct. "Armand Hilbert." A din rose from the table until she posted a photograph of a middle-aged man and a woman walking out of an office building near Chicago. "Let me give you some background information for your edification. These two people were hired by Director Omar to kill Mr. Dalton McKenna, who was representing a woman who found a massive silver specimen while diving in Little Bay de Noc. As you well know, Tenet recently acquired all rights to the Silver Islet property located on the north shore of Lake Superior." Pokorney held up a quitclaim deed, then flashed an old photograph of a head-frame with Lake Superior looming in the background. "Being so remote, the ore was taken by ship to various markets back east. Enter the *Hudson Bay.*" Pokorney then displayed a photograph of the wooden schooner and several directors sat erect. "The *Hudson Bay* was a 19th century vessel carrying a load of silver ore to Chicago when it went down in northern Lake Michigan, and its contents, which were never recovered, are estimated to be in excess of one-hundred-million US dollars. Now, I want you to take a close inspection of this next photograph. This is your good director, Mr. Conrad Jabril Omar. While in Escanaba, he assumed the identity of a Mr. Carlisle Vernon." A picture of the corpulent director was displayed where he walked along a street in downtown Escanaba, eating a hotdog during a warm summer day.

Omar rose from his leather chair with face red. "This is bullshit. I'll sue you for everything you got!"

A fellow TGC director took hold of Conrad's arm and assisted him back into his chair.

"Let me continue. In order to persuade Ms. Attwood to divulge the location of her silver discovery, her representative, Mr. Dalton McKenna, was murdered, and we now have enough evidentiary material to have those responsible charged." She reposted the photograph that showed a couple walking out of an office building where Pokorney pointed. "Meet Keith and Rory Caypeck. These are assumed names, and this one here," she used a red laser to circle the person of interest, "is a Mr. Armand Hilbert." The next photograph was a mug-shot taken nine years earlier, a grey image of a middle-aged man holding a placard that spelled out, 'Orlando Police Department.' "And here is the data we took off Mr. Hilbert's SIM card, showing various text messages to a phone owned by Director Omar." If you don't believe me, we're going to call that number right now." Pokorney nodded to her assistant who made the call, and a few seconds later, Omar's phone vibrated from his coat pocket where he attempted to muffle the sound. A few directors stared with mouths agape.

"Here's the deal, gentlemen. I own over fifty percent of Tenet's stock, and I'm taking over as of right now. I've notified the RCMP regarding this company's involvement in the murder of an American citizen, and we are seeking extradition. For what it's worth, everyone in this room who was even remotely involved in hiring Hilbert will be going to prison."

When the Skype connection went blank, the CEO of Pokorney Industries looked at the blank monitor with a satisfied grin. "That should shake things up," she whispered.

* * * * *

Later that morning, the two sat in a coffee shop, and when Currant spoke, his voice was strained. "I've spent years building this goddamn company and because of your bumbling, all that becomes meaningless!"

With eyes wide, Omar looked visibly shaken and ran his fingers through his thin hair, then rubbed his corpulent neck.

Currant's eyes were wide too and seemed out of breath when he uttered, "You told me you had everything under control. For Christ's sake, didn't you even check to see if they had a criminal record? What the hell were you thinking when you hired 'em?"

"I thought they were professionals."

"If they were so goddamn professional, how come they got caught?" Currant calmed himself by taking a gulp of Columbian roast, spilling some into his saucer. "If we don't get this matter resolved, and I mean quick, there are going to be some serious consequences." A quick exhalation was followed by, "So this is what I want you to do. Get the Caypecks out of town, some place they can't be reached. If they're not cooperative, settle accounts." Currant pulled out his checkbook and started writing. He ripped out the slip and thrust it towards Omar. "Here."

The former director placed the check into his breast pocket and then gave a solitary nod.

While Omar and Currant were strategizing, Harold Schmeltzer and his wife were sitting outside the Caypeck residence just north of Chicago, using binoculars to get a better look. They had positioned themselves in a parking lot that supported a ballpark in north Wilmette, and the sunshine was streaming from behind a bank of dark purple clouds. Stuart

O'Hare was parked next to them with his window rolled down, engine running.

"You sure this is gonna work?" Schmeltzer asked with an eye clamped shut.

No answer.

"You gotta remember, I'm married now, and I got responsibilities."

"Remember Tony Zambrusko, doncha?"

Tricia leaned over to get a better look at O'Hare. "Who's Tony Zambrusko?"

Harold turned towards his wife and replied, "A guy we had in custody. He killed a mother of three because she would no longer assist in a drug operation. You see, the woman worked for an airline as a flight attendant, and she had a way of getting drugs onboard her airplane without anyone knowing about it. Anyways, Tony tried to escape, and one of the guys we worked with… stopped him. Put a bullet right into his forehead. God, what a mess." Harold briefly shuddered when that mental image flashed before him.

"And you were…" Tricia tipped her head to one side and squinted.

Harold nodded

O'Hare tapped his side mirror with his fingertips. "And don't forget your buddy, Tom McCoy." He stretched his neck in order to look at Tricia directly, and his words were sharp. "You remember him I'm sure."

"What's your point?" Harold replied defensively, trying to protect his wife.

"We made sure you guys didn't end up in Waupun's Correctional Facility when you killed the son of a bitch back in that stinkin' farmhouse in southern Wisconsin, and no one is gonna get locked up over this either." As the garage door growled, a black BMW pulled out. O'Hare put on a pair of sunglasses, dropped the shifter in 'drive,' and said, "Well, let's get to it."

CHAPTER SIXTEEN

"Destiny dictates the reunion of soul mates.
You will meet again. Read the signs
...follow your heart...trust your intuition."
- Brian Weiss, M.D.
Chairman Emeritus of Psychiatry
Mount Sinai Medical Center

December 31, 1913

The following week, Peter entered the Italian Hall, still littered with upended chairs and clothing. The Christmas tree on the stage was standing, and bits of hard candy were scattered about. As he stood on the lone staircase, he found his daughter's rag doll. The Croatian immigrant clutched it to his chest and closed his eyes, envisioning Mary's final moments. He could hear the screams and feel the weight of the crowd bearing down upon his daughter. And then came the anger for those responsible: Calumet & Hecla, the Citizen's Alliance, and of course his wife, Elizabeth for not protecting his little girl.

That evening, Peter wandered aimlessly through town until he stood before the large wood doors. The Croatian immigrant removed his hat, then took a seat in a pew near the stained-glass window, closing his eyes with hopes of finding relief, but the grace of God he so desperately sought remained elusive. Instead, rage coursed his veins, all encompassing like a relentless burn. With jaw muscles tight, he pulled a jackknife from his pocket, and began the desecration with hard violent strokes. When complete, he whisked the wood chips aside with his hand, revealing a solitary word. He kissed his fingertips, and then wiped them upon the oak pew.

* * * * *

The cold marched through northern Michigan like a Yankee invasion, starting north, then moving south with a fury. Winter overcame the Keweenaw as well, and Lake View Cemetery was covered with a fresh six inches of white granular snow. Charlie Tassanare, the sexton, was standing before an open grave, inspecting the final resting place of a new arrival. It would be one of the last. With winter came hundreds of inches of snow, making it impossible to locate proper grave markers. Hence, caskets were stored in an innocuous brick building where sometimes a dozen or more local residents awaited their final journey to a plot of earth where they would spend eternity.

Charlie had seen them before; the tracks in the snow that led nowhere. It had been several years since his last encounter, and he followed them until he came upon a snow angel. To the casual observer, it was nothing more than a child playing outside, but the shoeprints ended abruptly. And it was always the same. Small shoeprints that led to the section where the mass graves were located. Some of the victims had gravestones, but many were without any marker whatsoever. And in the waning sunlight, he could hear the faint sounds of children playing.

He never told anyone about what he had seen for fear they would assume he suffered from delusions or early-onset dementia. Nor did he mention it to his wife of forty-three years, but he knew. They were still here, and when he heard the laughter, he grinned pensively, knowing they were nearby. Yet, it also came with a certain element of sadness, realizing their lives had ended abruptly and tried to imagine their last few moments on earth.

His grandmother was at the Italian Hall that afternoon, and when he was a mere boy, she would talk about that Christmas Eve. She told her grandson how they lowered the dead down a ladder, then placed them along the walkway below. Now, Charlie was charged with overseeing their graves and took a degree of satisfaction, knowing they were under his protective care.

231

With hands sunk deep into his coat pockets, Charlie's hopes for continued solitude were dashed as the visitor approached. Dealing with the living was much more tedious than dealing with the dead, and as she got closer, he muttered under his breath. "Ah, shit." He cleared his throat and offered up an exaggerated smile, like a used-car salesman trying to sell a clunker. "We'll be closing up soon."

"It'll only take a minute." As Evangeline kicked the snow away from the granite marker, he noted the date of their death and said, "Did you have family who died in the Italian Hall?"

She didn't answer. Instead, Evangeline pulled out the solitary rose from its plastic wrapper, placed it onto the headstone, and whispered so no one could hear. "Know that you were cherished."

The words were automatic after so many years of working at the cemetery. Charlie cleared his throat and said, "Sorry for your loss." Cold winter air filled his lungs when he inhaled sharply. "I've never shown anyone this before, but would you like to see something interesting?"

A flick of a tear was followed by, "Sure."

They walked together, and he pointed to the tracks in the snow. "See, the big ones are mine, and I was following them and look." Charlie pointed to the snow angel.

"That's nice," she said, trying to be polite.

"You don't get it, do you?"

"Get what?" Evangeline replied with a furrowed brow.

"The tracks...look carefully." As she reexamined the snow angel, he said, "They lead here, but there aren't any footprints that lead out. Where did they go?"

They heard the faint laughter of children, and after scanning the tree line in hopes of locating the source, Charlie whispered, "That's them. Don't know why they're showing up right now, but that's them."

Evangeline bit her bottom lip just before she whispered, "Who...who are you referring to?"

"The children ... you know...from the Italian Hall."

As she placed a hand upon her chest, a chill embraced her. "Have you... heard them... before?"

Charlie pressed his lips tight, then nodded.

As Evangeline stood there, she drifted into a reverie, and in her mind, a group of children could be seen playing in a grassy field, laughing and chasing one another amongst wildflowers of daisy and Indian paintbrush. As she watched the scene unfold, a girl walked towards her. She thought the child might be Charlotte, but as she neared, it became obvious it was someone else. As Evangeline watched, a little girl kissed her fingertips and with her right hand, blew a kiss. It felt like a slap across the face, and when Evangeline regained her composure, she cried out, "Please don't go!"

* * * * *

Around the time Mme. Pokorney was talking to the Board of Directors, Stuart O'Hare walked into Emerald Realty with a toothpick in his mouth and found the receptionist painting her fingernails fluorescent green. The young woman with ebony hair sported a heart-shaped tattoo on her exposed left shoulder and looked up to see a towering specimen, wearing a tan sport coat with an American flag attached to the lapel. O'Hare pulled his toothpick from his lips and served up his best smile. "Hi, I'm looking for a home in the area. Wife and I just moved here from Omaha, and it was suggested I talk to a Mr. Keith Caypeck. Office downtown said he's quite good. Is he available?"

A few seconds later a middle-aged man munching on a handful of almonds approached. For a split second, O'Hare thought about Caypeck's hand wrapped around a pistol, standing along a dark stretch of blacktop south of Ralph.

He took hold of O'Hare's giant-sized mitt and pumped it a couple of times. "Understand you're looking for a house."

"Got relocated and I need to find something quick. Can you help me out?"

Realizing he still had salt on his hands, Caypeck whisked them a couple of times and said, "Sorry. Didn't catch the name."

"Stuart…Stuart DuMont."

"Nice to meet you Stuart. Why don't you come on back, and I can show you some of our listings?" As they walked down an antiseptic corridor painted in white, Caypeck looked over his shoulder and said, "What kind of price bracket are you looking at, Stu?"

"Well, I'd like to keep it under a million-five. I can do a cash sale."

They entered a large office done in Danish Modern, and O'Hare noticed the framed picture of Caypeck's wife that graced the Borge Mogensen desk. The ex-cop suddenly thought about a case in southern Michigan a few years back where they had found a woman in the basement freezer. She had been missing for over a year, and during that time, her husband ran the household as if nothing had happened. When he was asked about her absence, he seemed genuinely concerned, even helped pass out flyers that asked for information as to her whereabouts. O'Hare looked at Caypeck and saw a man not unlike the one who killed his wife and stuffed her into the basement freezer, no conscience whatsoever.

"Please have a seat," Caypeck said agreeably, sensing an impending sale. "Can I get you something to drink? Maybe a cup of coffee…tea…water?"

O'Hare closed the door, then sat before the agent with head tipped to one side, eyes penetrating.

The odd behavior piqued the realtor's curiosity, and he asked, "Is there something wrong? Do I have a spot on my tie?"

"Are you an idiot?"

Caypeck's nostrils flared. "Pardon me?"

O'Hare exhaled forcefully, then leaned forward with both elbows on his knees. "I'll spell it out for you, Dumbo. They probably didn't tell you this at the time, but the guy you killed up near Ralph was a former US Marshal and CIA operative. Do you have any idea what happens when one of their agents gets whacked?" O'Hare didn't wait for a reply. "Lemme set this straight for you. They assume there's been a security breach, and the government throws every resource possible into finding answers."

Caypeck gulped, then shook his head as if he had water in his ears. "I...I don't know what you're talking about."

"I think you do. You see, we were here in your office the other night and copied the SIM card from that cell phone stored in your file cabinet." O'Hare pointed, "The one over there." The former cop pulled out the mug-shot from a brown manila folder, sliding it across the desk. "You see Mr. Hilbert, we found text messages from one of the directors at Tenet Gold, alluding to," O'Hare used a pair of fingers to make quotation marks, "business up in Ralph."

Caypeck cradled his head with both hands.

"That's why I asked if you were an idiot. Anybody who knew what they were doing woulda ditched the damn burner, not stuff it into a goddamn file cabinet."

O'Hare sensed panic as Caypeck licked his dry lips.

"We also found pictures of McKenna's vehicle on your cell." With head lifted slightly, O'Hare said, "Care to explain?"

No answer.

"I figured as much. For your information, we took over Tenet Gold the other day and had a little talk with their Board of Directors. We showed 'em our evidence regarding the murder of Dalton McKenna, including the information taken off your SIM card, and there's little doubt, some of 'em will be extradited and charged accordingly." O'Hare slapped his knees with amusement.

The realtor gently slid open the top drawer to his desk, and O'Hare lunged, sending Caypeck to the floor where they struggled briefly. As the former cop stood with fist ready, Caypeck covered his face with both hands. Instead of landing a blow, O'Hare grabbed Caypeck by the lapels, stuffed him back into his swivel chair and then removed the Beretta pistol from the desk drawer, placing it into his coat pocket.

The commotion caught the attention of another realtor down the hall who stuck his head in, and said, "Heard a crash. What's going on? You OK?"

Caypeck forced a smile and said, "Just leaned back too far in my chair and went topsy-turvy. Mr. DuMont here was just giving me a hand." He brushed his Canali wool suit with both hands and said, "I'm fine though."

The realtor extended his finger toward Caypeck and gave it a crisp snap. "Gotta be more careful, bud. Wouldn't do the company any good having our top seller ending up in the hospital."

With their visitor gone, O'Hare took a seat and straightened his attire. "So, both Omar and Currant are on the run, and they both know the only thing between them and a lengthy prison sentence is you and your stupid wife."

Caypeck glared.

"So, with a personal fortune measured in millions, I figure they should have you and the missus disposed of promptly. Furthermore, I spoke to the Attorney General this morning about your involvement."

The color had drained from Caypeck's once robust looking face, and he looked grey and deadpan. "You FBI?"

"Private investigator, but here's the deal, Dumbo."

Caypeck gulped, then licked his dry lips once more.

"Like I said, there's ample evidence of your involvement in Dalton McKenna's murder, but since it involved foreign nationals, it could be construed as a terrorist attack, meaning you'll be afforded little constitutional protection. You see, we have eyewitness testimony that places you and your ol' lady up in Ralph, along with video of your rental car roaring down Norway Lake Road the same evening McKenna got killed. Add that to the text messages we took from your cell phone, and no doubt when it goes to trial, you'll be convicted of premeditated murder." O'Hare adjusted the collar to his white shirt and said, "But..."

Caypeck sat up with eyes wide.

"Here's the deal. You give the DOJ complete and forthright information on the people who hired you and become a prosecutorial witness in every matter they deem appropriate, and they'll stick you into witness protection."

"But you're just a private investigator. You don't speak for the DOJ."

O'Hare barked, "Would you like me to get 'em on the line?"

"Shhh." Caypeck ducked his head, then looked around, hoping no one overheard. He whispered, "Then... then why aren't they handling this?"

"Because if we can't come to some sort of agreement, they just as soon let nature take its course. It's a lot cheaper and less paperwork. Furthermore, not being a federal employee, I don't have to follow judicial protocol." O'Hare pulled out Caypeck's Beretta and pointed it. "No Miranda rights...no nothin'. You follow me?"

The realtor rubbed his sore wrist and bemoaned, "And what about my wife?"

"She'll be offered a similar deal, but any deception on your part, and the offer gets rescinded. So, we'll be interviewing you separately and better pray your stories line up."

"But I...I can't remember everything, and my wife she...she's getting a tad absentminded."

O'Hare had been down this path many times and wasn't about to allow Dalton's killer any negotiating power. "If you don't like our deal, why don't you call Omar and see what he has to offer? I'm sure he'd love to hear from you." With his left hand pointing towards the door, O'Hare said, "So, if you want to take off, be my guest. But before you part, you should know as of this morning, Homeland tagged your passports, your credit cards have been cancelled, and the IRS has frozen your bank account. You see Mr. Caypeck, you messed with the wrong people, and if we don't get your full cooperation, a whole bunch of people will be waiting in line to settle accounts, and I'll be one of 'em."

Caypeck sat back in his swivel chair, biting the tip of an index finger.

"Now there's one more matter we need to talk about." O'Hare's lips were pressed tight, and his face reddened considerably. "Dalton McKenna was a friend, and if I had my way, I'd strap you and your stinkin' wife into the electric chair and personally pull the switch." O'Hare calmed himself and continued to smooth his attire. "But apparently, the DOJ has other plans for your sorry ass. What I need to know is this."

O'Hare's brow was now deeply furrowed. "Did you kill Steiner?"

"Who the hell is Steiner? Look, I know a little about this McKenna fella, but the person you should talk to is Omar. He's the one who orchestrated this bullshit."

O'Hare pulled out his phone, and his instructions were crisp. "Pull the car around back. We're heading out."

* * * * *

It was late November, and the wind drove steel-colored clouds over the rocky cliffs of the Keweenaw. Superior's waves crashed ashore, making the beach stones rattle as the wind numbed both mind and spirit. It started out as a cold rain, but as the day progressed, arctic winds howled, and hard granular snow swept across the peninsula in sheets of white, cutting and biting everything in its path like a thousand razorblades. The most timid residents huddled indoors, but for a hearty few, it was an opportunity to start up their snowmobiles and wax their cross-country skis. As the icy winds cut through the town of Calumet, residents fought back in every manner possible. Copper World set out their Christmas decorations along with a few other merchants on 5th Street, and several homeowners along Pine strung out Christmas lights onto their bushes and trees in an attempt to infuse some color into the rather bleak landscape. Meanwhile, plows kept the main thoroughfares open while the constant din of snowblowers could be heard throughout the area, where homeowners made quick work of snow covered walks and driveways.

Meanwhile, business at Luigi's was brisk, and its tiled floor was spoiled with melted snow and ice. While the jukebox played *Kathy's Song*, Evangeline filled orders, mostly for draft beer and a few shots of Yukon Jack. There was a run on frozen pizzas, and the pool table had a line of steady customers. Rumor had it that a construction company from downstate was going to open an office in Laurium, but town folks had heard these types of speculation before, only to have them dissipate like steam on a cold winter's night.

The owner of Luigi's came in around eight, and Evangeline tossed him her apron. "Gonna take the dog for a walk, then get something to eat." Once business with Lucy was complete, she brought her companion to the apartment above the bar, then hiked a couple of blocks to the church with muffler wrapped tight. It was a snowy evening, and with the holidays approaching, she wanted a quiet place to reflect. Evangeline lit a small votive upon the altar, said a silent prayer for Charlotte and then took a seat on a wood pew near the side.

As Evangeline rested, her mind drifted into another world. She wondered what Charlotte would have looked like by now. Her daughter would have been in sixth grade, and just starting to notice boys. At times, Evangeline would dream that her daughter was still with her and remembered the smile that engulfed the little girl's face. She would carry that image to the grave and cursed the infection that took hold shortly after birth. She wondered how God could allow a light so wonderful to be so quickly extinguished. And as she pondered her past, Evangeline felt the faint impression on the wood pew. It was almost gone now, worn away by countless years of people attending services, but it was unmistakable. It was a solitary word crudely carved. Maybe it was done with a pocketknife, but the edges had smoothed over time, and it piqued her interest. The 'M' was almost completely worn away, but the letters, 'a,' 'r,' and 'y' were unmistakable: Mary

Her thoughts whirled like dervishes and kept at bay the peace she so desperately desired. The only thing that quieted the cacophony of inner dialogue was sitting alone in church. Here, she could rest without judgment or guilt. And as Evangeline thought about the demise of Dalton McKenna, she felt the blast of cold air as the large entrance door opened. She sat in the shadow, preferring isolation to being seen and watched a man light a candle. Calumet's newest bartender strained to get a better look, and when she recognized the parishioner, Evangeline placed a fingertip to her mouth; her breath as soft as a whisper.

Sam Carter looked small amongst the muralled apse and vaulted ceiling, and as she craned her neck to get a better view,

Evangeline wondered if he was thinking about his late wife. But Carter was on the move, and he headed for the exit. Evangeline decided to follow, lagging well behind. Upon arriving at the entrance, she was greeted by another blast of cold air, and Sam Carter was gone.

She returned to Luigi's shortly thereafter and meandered toward the cash register with order pad in hand. The owner yelled, "Didja get somethin' to eat?"

As Evangeline put on an apron, she yelled back. "I'll toss a pizza into the oven."

A giant of a man wearing a plaid shirt and a Detroit Lions ball-cap held his glass up and commanded, "Need a refill here!"

As she worked the tap, he said, "Can I buy ya a drink?"

Damn that sounds good! Evangeline slammed a bottle of Yukon Jack onto the bar, then grabbed a shot glass from the sink below. After the incident at church, she simply had enough. Enough of Sam Carter, enough of the God-awful memories, enough of Joe Steiner, and enough of the goddamn Italian Hall. Evangeline Attwood thought about how she placed everyone else's concerns above her own, and how her own family offered nothing; instead, they sucked the life out of her, leaving behind a hollowed-out heap. And then there was the package from Ulay that brought back a flood of memories, and it took effort to blot it all out.

The snow outside blew sharp ice pellets not unlike the thoughts swirling through her mind. The cacophony of inner dialogue made Evangeline's head spin, whereby she poured herself a couple of fingers of Yukon Jack, downing it like a sailor on leave.

"Easy does it dere." her admirer said just before taking a long draw from his stein. The two laughed until he said, "What's your name?"

"Evie," she shouted.

He extended his monster-sized paw and said, "Pete. Work for de road commission. Got all our plows out tonight, and I'm sure I'll be fixin' everythin' again tomorra mornin'. Everything is held together with nothin' but balin' wire and duct tape, if you know what I mean." He looked about, leaning back onto the

240

bar with arms splayed like the crucifixion. "Good crowd tonight. Haven't seen it this busy in quite some time."

The next hour was accompanied by a few shots of Yukon Jack, and after closing, the two were alone. As she placed a chair on top of a table, Evangeline stumbled.

"Here, let me help you with dat." Pete placed his hand upon her waist and ran his index finger over an exposed forearm.

A cold gust of wind accompanied the now open front door, and Evangeline called out, "Sorry, we're ..." her voice trailing off.

There stood a tired-looking Sam Carter, his blue scarf encrusted with snow. He stomped his brown work boots, then stood mute, eyes penetrating.

The mechanic broke the silence, and his words were quick. "Last call was twenty minutes ago, bucko."

Evangeline approached and whispered, "What are you doing here? It's after two."

"Just thought I'd come down and see if you were still working. But it looks like ..."

"Damn right you're interruptin'." The mechanic pulled Evangeline into a side embrace, letting Carter know she was spoken for. But Evangeline squirmed, and her smile was as artificial as an aluminum Christmas tree. "Maybe some other time."

As Evangeline struggled with the restraint, Sam Carter leapt, landing his fist alongside the mechanic's jaw. It drove the behemoth backwards into the jukebox which suddenly sprang to life, playing *Streets of Bakersfield*. But Sam's punch was absorbed without much effect, and in an instant, just as the Buck Owens got into the chorus, the mechanic charged with his head down, aiming directly at Sam's mid-section. Not being under the influence, Sam's mobility was unimpaired, and the middle-aged father easily sidestepped the assault. The mechanic charged again, but this time Pete's neck landed flush inside Sam's elbow. As he tightened the grip, chairs flew, and a half-empty pitcher crashed to the floor, sending glass shards and beer foam in every direction. As the seconds ticked away, the mechanic flailed in a feeble attempt to break the choke hold. In response, Carter launched his feet backwards, applying his entire weight onto Pete's oversized neck. The two dropped to the floor with the mechanic's head leading the way.

As the struggle ebbed, Sam released his grip, only to see Evangeline holding a cell phone. All that could be heard was, "Big tall guy named Pete. Full beard and plaid shirt. Works for the road commission. He's down on the floor fighting with a customer."

It was only seconds before they could hear the siren off in the distance, and a few moments later, a cold blast of arctic air swept in as a pair of Houghton County deputies entered through the front door. By then, the mechanic was on his hands and knees gasping for air, spitting blood. After the bartender explained what happened, the officer barked, "You wanna press charges?"

She looked at the heap struggling on the floor as if it were an animal foraging. "If he leaves and promises not to come back, I won't."

One of the deputies looked at Carter and snapped, "And what's your story?"

Evangeline placed herself next to Sam, then took his hand. "He helped me. If he hadn't intervened, I...I don't know what would have happened."

Meanwhile, Pete sucked blood from his lip and offered up a few select curse words. Sam gathered his fingers into a fist, and one of the deputies pushed him back. "Easy does it, fella."

She took Sam's hand once again and whispered, "It's OK," then turned toward one of the deputies and said, "Do what you like with him," using her head to point towards the mechanic, "but get him outa here."

Pete grabbed his coat off the table, then gave Sam a parting shove.

After another round of taunts and curse words, a deputy stepped between the two, pushing the mechanic to the door. "Go on home and sleep it off. Any more of this bullshit, and you'll be coming with us." He turned toward Evangeline and said, "He's one of our frequent flyers."

242

After Pete and the two deputies left, Luigi's took on a different atmosphere. As Evangeline swept up the broken glass, Sam slipped a quarter into the Wurlitzer, and a few seconds later, he walked over and said, "I wanna dance."

As she swept, Evangeline looked up and chortled.

"It's the least you owe me for getting that gorilla off ya. You sure can pick 'em, you know." He snapped his fingers and said, "Come on."

Partially under the influence, Evangeline stumbled once again. Catching her by the arm, Sam pulled her erect.

"Thanks," she said, clearly embarrassed.

With one hand on her waist and the other clasping her right hand, Sam instructed, "Keep your elbows stiff so I don't walk into you, understand?"

It was awkward, letting him have his way, and his leads were strong and dominant. The two twirled about the empty tables to the melody of the *Tennessee Waltz*, periodically crunching broken glass, and when Evangeline looked at her feet, he said, "It'll go easier if you keep your eyes up here."

By the time the music ended, Evangeline felt secure in his grasp, and not only that, she felt a certain connection as if Ulay was holding her. When the tune ended, all she could muster was, "That was nice."

The jukebox had gone cold, and as gale-force winds continued to howl across the entrance, there was silence within. The kind of comforting silence that was always there but never given much attention. It had a music all its own, and for a brief moment, the world with its endless storms and confusion, became still, like leaves gently settling on a warm fall afternoon.

As Evangeline continued to sweep the floor, Sam placed several chairs upon the various tabletops, and they worked together until Evangeline said, "Would you like something to drink?"

"I'll take a ginger ale if you have one handy."

"A ginger ale? Are you serious?"

"Well, that's all I drink these days. I gave up liquor awhile ago. Just figured it wasn't in alignment with being a good father. Travis deserves someone who's fully present."

Evangeline set her broom aside and said, "So, why didja come here tonight?"

"I dunno." With his shoulders pulled in close, Sam Carter seemed smaller now. "Saw you in town earlier and wanted to…you know, apologize for… you know." With hands sunk deep into his pockets, his eyes avoided hers. "Don't know what came over me, but the thought of losing my little boy…"

She nodded, then took a dust pan full of broken glass to the wastebasket in back, and when she returned, Sam Carter was gone. With a furrowed brow, Evangeline spied the rag doll sitting on top of the wood table where her broom rested. It was a threadbare little thing with brown hair and a button nose, and when she picked it up, she felt a similar sensation like the one she experienced when caressing the wooden doors at the museum.

CHAPTER SEVENTEEN

"Blessed are those who hunger and thirst for justice.
They shall have their fill."
- Matthew 5:6

January 21st, 1914

With only a suitcase in hand, Peter boarding the coach in Calumet and found a window seat near the back. He had sold all his earthly possessions and purchased a train ticket to Chicago, hoping to start anew. As the train pulled from the station, he looked out the window one last time and could see the church spires off in the distance. He thought about his wife and daughter; they would never have the chance to leave. He opened his suitcase and removed the rag doll, held it to his chest and closed his eyes.

* * * * *

Evangeline didn't recognize the phone number and answered with an apprehensive, "Hello."

"Stuart O'Hare. You busy?"

"Just cleaning up, that's all. What's going on with the investigation? Did your lead pan out?"

Upon hearing the Attorney General's offer to place the Caypeck's into witness protection, she said, "I can't believe they get to walk."

"The DOJ wants their cooperation, so they can pursue those who hired 'em. It's the price of doin' business. Look, while I gotcha on the line, I've been lookin' into your story about the Italian Hall. Was up your way recently and talked to a buddy of yours...a Ms. Margaret Keillor."

"Sure. I know Margaret. What did she have to say?"

"Just that no one was ever apprehended. After looking over the coroner's transcript, I'd say no one was terribly interested in finding those responsible."

"Tell me about it. Whoever did it got off Scot-free, not unlike the Caypecks. I dunno. Just doesn't seem fair, that's all."

His question was hard like a slap. "You're Elizabeth Kovarti. Aren't you?"

Evangeline's words were broken, and her eyes filled with tears. "H...how...could you p...possibly know that?"

"Came to me when I read the list of those that had perished. It was the oddest thing; your daughter screamed her name inside my head, and I could see the two of you climbing a flight of stairs."

Evangeline whispered, "This can't be happening..."

"Maybe this might help. Several years ago, I was looking into a pair of homicides downstate. The perpetrators worked for an oil and gas company where they brought their clients to an upscale home they owned in southern Michigan. Lacking any moral compass, they hired hookers for entertainment and videotaped their activity, using it later to extort favors."

"I've already heard this story. Harold and Tricia told me about it."

O'Hare forcefully exhaled through his nose, giving a slight whistle. "Well, here's a part that you probably haven't heard. You see, one of the victims turned out to be a seven-year-old girl, who was sexually abused, and somewhere along the line, she ended up dead. We know about the abuse because we had the videos taken of her."

O'Hare could hear the gasp.

"What's the point you're trying to make?"

"The point is this. Her spirit, not unlike Mary Kovarti's, came to me while I was using the men's room at work. I know what you're thinking, but it's the god-honest truth. You see, she was with one of the hookers we fished out of the river, and if it hadn't been for her assistance, the child's remains might never have been found."

Evangeline's sobs were now unmistakable.

"You OK?"

She sniffled, "It's hard for me. You see, I lost… my daughter several years ago to an infection. H…her name was Ch…Charlotte."

"Look, I'm not tellin' you all this to make things worse. Just wanted you to know, that death isn't the final answer."

Her voice was now soft and light. "Didja ever lose anyone close?"

"Just my ex ..." he whispered.

"And you still loved her?"

A moment of silence was followed by, "Very much so."

There was dead silence until Evangeline said, "I'm so sorry."

"Don't be. She taught me a lot. You see, when you graduate from 'being in love' to loving someone, you understand that love is not about owning. It's about wanting the best for them. It's about helping them achieve greatness with or without you. Love isn't what you say, rather it's about what you do."

Sniffle. "Your ex sounds like she was a very special person. I'm sorry for your loss."

"I'm at peace with it. Like I said, I've walked this earth many times, and I'm certain we'll meet again. And that goes for you too. So, if there's any truth to you being Elizabeth Kovarti, I think you'll be afforded an opportunity to heal some of this."

A gulp preceded, "So, you think it's true?"

"It really doesn't matter what I think, but you have to admit there are some interesting parallels between then and now. You know, when I was going through something similar, I was given a piece of advice that you might find worthwhile. You see, the past really isn't here. When we live in the past, we're really not living at all, and the challenge we face is to let go of what happened and embrace the moment we have."

"And what about those that created... all the hardship?"

"All I can say is justice eventually prevailed for the little girl who got murdered." O'Hare let out a deep sigh, as he recalled the night when Fred Abrams put a .45 caliber slug into Crestwood's head. As he dwelled on that image, a new call announced its arrival on Evangeline's phone.

"Look, I gotta 'nother call coming in. I'll talk to you tomorrow." She recognized Tom's number and blurted, "What the hell is goin' on?"

His words were lifeless. "She's gone."

It felt like an express train approaching. Evangeline gripped the bed frame with her left hand, bracing for the impact.

"It's Mom."

Evangeline's mother lived with her son, and with those few words, she was swept up in strong emotions. The first wave was guilt; later, anger would surface. She whispered in one long exhalation. "Oh God, what happened?"

Tom was slow in his response. "We were out having dinner, and when we got home, we found her in the basement. Apparently, she had a heart attack. By the time the paramedics arrived, she was long gone."

"I'm on my way!"

She didn't bother to stop, opting for the most direct route to her brother's home with Lucy at her side. As the yellow lab

247

rested her chin on Evangeline's lap, her mind drifted toward a distant memory. She recalled her mother taking her to the Adler Planetarium in Chicago when she was about seven or eight years old. It was just the two of them and a time when her mother seemed content with her position in life. But as she aged, the light that she admired, darkened so completely hospitalization was necessary. With the aid of anti-depressants, her depression abated, but her demeanor had become deadpan, and her interest in matters outside the home waned, content in watching endless episodes of *The Price is Right.* Her mother's depression of late had worsened, drawing everyone into the abyss.

It was difficult fully absorbing the impact of her mother's death, but for the most part, the wake felt like a high-school play where corny actors attempted to be someone else. And now amongst family friends and various relatives, Evangeline was cast as the grieving daughter, knowing full well she hid the difficulties she endured.

The funeral was held the following day, and the former teacher tried to focus on more pleasant memories, and as she sat in a metal folding chair, listening to the preacher ramble on, she pulled the rag doll to the top of her purse. Evangeline caressed the doll's head and thought about the child who loved it so much, it became threadbare.

Afterward, it was a Godsend having a place to go, and with every passing mile, her spirits lifted. It wasn't like she didn't love her family, but after a few days with them, she could feel the darkness settle in like a blanket of heavy fog, clouding her senses and perspective.

As she crossed the Mackinac Bridge, she felt new life coursing through her veins, and it felt invigorating. When she passed through Houghton, even the Christmas decorations seemed to welcome her. In response, Evangeline rolled the passenger window down, and Lucy hung her head out, barking incessantly at the Portage Lake Bridge. It made her laugh, and she realized just how long it had been since she had done so.

While downstate, Evangeline put her condo up for sale, and the realtor offered assurance that her residence would sell quickly. So, her first order of business was a second look at the home on Pine Street. Evangeline parked in front, and with its large front porch and mature maple trees that canopied the front yard, it simply looked inviting. She envisioned the home decorated with white Christmas lights and maybe a large wreath on the front door that would welcome a plethora of guests. But the warmth of that reverie was offset by a distant memory, and when she peered down Pine Street, looking to the west, she could envision the funeral procession, heading to Lake View Cemetery. For a brief moment, she felt like she was there, but instead of feeling grief, a sense of connection set in, bringing a new feeling of completion.

* * * * *

Stuart O'Hare walked into the DNR office, tapped on the sliding glass window with a set of keys, and was greeted with a snotty, "What?"

"Need to see David Fales. Was told he works here."

Wearing the standard brown shirt with a pair of green cargo pants, the DNR officer emerged from behind the steel door and extended his big hand. "I'm Officer Fales. How can I help you?"

"Name is Stuart O'Hare, and we need to talk."

The DNR officer lifted his chin and gave a puzzled expression.

"Probably don't know, but the guy who got murdered over in Dickinson County the other day was a former US Marshal. So, if you don't want to talk to me, I'm sure the FBI would love to hear what I gotta say."

A gulp was followed by, "Why don't you come on back."

Fales closed the door to his small office, then pulled the lone chair in front of the metal desk. "Here, have a seat." As O'Hare parked himself, Fales said, "So, you're telling me McKenna was a US Marshal?"

"Yup, and furthermore, I have his files."

The DNR officer kept glancing out the window as if he'd rather be somewhere else. "Hope you understand I had nothing to do with any of that."

O'Hare took the direct approach. He cocked his head to one side and said, "So, who's paying you now that the Steiner's are dead?"

"Huh?"

"Cut the bullshit." O'Hare raised his head a few degrees and looked down his nose. "I've seen your bank statements, and the deposits are ongoing." His voice was now loud and shrill. "I'll ask you just once more, where's the money coming from?"

Fales looked about as if he were drowning, searching for any type of flotsam to grab hold of.

O'Hare dialed a number and placed the call on speaker phone, where a voice squawked, "Michigan State Police."

"I'd like to talk to whoever is in charge of investigating the Joe Steiner murder."

"One moment, please."

As O'Hare waited for the connection, Fales raised his hands in a conciliatory gesture, and his words were quick. "OK...OK. Look, the guy you're interested in goes by the name of Carlisle Vernon."

After O'Hare disconnected, he pulled up a photo of Conrad Jabril Omar on his phone. He held it out and said, "This him?"

Fales nodded.

"And the Steiner boys were doing business with Vernon?"

"Not sure to what extent."

"So, when was the last time you two spoke?"

"Maybe a coupla weeks."

"And what the hell did he want?"

"Just wanted me to keep an eye on McKenna. That's all. It seemed harmless enough. Look, I didn't have anything to do with this bullshit. I just followed him around a coupla times." Fales looked back toward the parking lot as perspiration beaded along his forehead.

A chain saw buzzed away in the background when O'Hare said, "Maybe you don't know, but Vernon and his boss are on the run." He found the RCMP website and displayed the two photographs. "See for yourself."

Fales squinted. "Conrad Omar?"

"He's been using an alias here in Delta County. Since Omar has fled the country his minions are attempting to silence everyone involved. And the way I see it, with his money, you won't make it through the week." O'Hare whispered, "Maybe, they'll make it look like an accident, or maybe you'll simply disappear by stuffing your fat ass into a wood chipper." The sound of a chain saw was louder now, grinding away. "Either way, your days are… numbered." O'Hare used his phone once again and played an audio clip where Keith Caypeck outlined his involvement in the murder of Dalton McKenna. "See, we have this pretty well nailed down, and the Caypecks were given immunity in exchange for their full cooperation against the men who hired 'em. To top it off, we have text messages from your cell, giving locations as to McKenna's whereabouts."

Fales cradled his head with both hands and said, "What about my family?"

"The guy who paid you uses hired killers, and your testimony could send him to prison. Figure it out."

Fales picked up the phone, and in seconds O'Hare heard, "Hi, it's me. Look, I need you and the kids to go to your Mom's for a couple of days." His voice now resonated when he barked, "Don't ask why. Just pack a few things, but I need you get out, and I mean right now." There was some silence as O'Hare tried to hear the other side of the conversation, but all that could be heard was a tinny noise that emanated from the receiver. "Look, I'll explain later, OK? Call me when you get there."

After Fales disconnected, O'Hare cracked his neck, whispering, "That won't help. They'll find you one way or another."

The DNR officer got his coat from the hall tree, and as he started to work the zipper, O'Hare looked up and squinted. "You know, if we can get to Omar before he gets to you, we can end this bullshit. You have a way of contacting him?"

Out in the parking lot, there was a sharp crack when the door to a delivery truck slammed shut, and Fales put his hand upon the semi-automatic that hung from his hip. He pulled down the blind and emitted a sigh of relief. "Just a cell phone number."

* * * * *

The realtor was laying it on thick by pointing out all the recent upgrades that included new kitchen cabinets and granite countertops. As he droned on, Evangeline ran her fingers over the cold stone that surround the copper-lined sink, pondering what her financials might look like after selling her condo downstate. After paying the commissions and moving expenses, she felt there would be sufficient funds to purchase the Calumet home outright with enough left over to purchase essentials like a snow-blower and kitchen appliances. Without a job that offered benefits, life in the Keweenaw could be precarious. But the home had possibilities, and she liked the idea of living in an area regulated by the Park Service. After all, not many people could say they lived inside a national park.

As they walked outside, the realtor buttoned his coat, lit up a Camel, and blew a long column of smoke. "You know, you could make an offer contingent upon selling your home downstate, and if it doesn't sell, you could get most of your down payment back." He then cupped his mouth with a gloved hand as if conveying a secret. "They're asking one twenty-nine-nine, but you could make a counter offer and see what they say."

Attwood inhaled deeply, and numbers spun through her head like a ride on a tilt-a-whirl, spinning, twirling and endless. "I could do one-ten," she said in a low whisper as if the tone would lessen its impact. "Do you think that would be alright? I...I could secure the offer with a thousand-dollars in earnest money."

A thousand-dollar smile emanated from the realtor's face, and a string of orange-colored teeth glistened from the street light above. "Come on. We'll go back to my office and write it up. "A shrug was followed by, "The worst they can say is, 'no,' and if that happens, you're no worse off than you are right now."

Later that evening, Evangeline was in her apartment above the bar when the dreams rolled in like a storm out on the bay, and as Evangeline rested in bed with Lucy at her side, her mind produced more vignettes from the past. The first dreamscape was of her childhood home and her mother frying pork chops on the kitchen stove. She could hear the meat sizzling along with the tangy scent of roasting pork, and the sensation brought a joyful, yet rare memory of her mother. Evangeline was just a teenager at the time, and whispered, "Please forgive me." Her mother dropped to the floor, clutching her heart, and Evangeline screamed, "Mama!! Mama!"

Suddenly, another dreamscape crashed ashore, and in an instant, she was home with her father. He had just walked into the kitchen after cutting the lawn and with a sweaty brow, poured himself a glass of lemonade. Evangeline's father was the glue that held the family together, and after his death, she felt adrift in a world that had, for the most part, lost warmth and meaning. As her father quenched his thirst, Evangeline took his hand and could feel his wedding ring. "I miss you," was all she said.

"I miss you too, paczki. Now don't get me wrong, I adored your mom, but at times...." With lips drawn tight, he shook his head. "Well, let's just say, we didn't always see eye-to-eye on everything." The old man with the speckled hair pinched his daughter's chin and said, "Do whatever you need in order to be happy and screw the rest of 'em."

Evangeline's last dreamscape was of Ulay. They were lying in bed together, and she could feel the warmth from his body. He took hold of her hand, then whispered into her ear. "I love you." And with that last vision, she bolted upright.

* * * * *

Carmine Langford was the quintessential ambulance chaser, having no moral compass, and his sole allegiance was to his checking account at the Delta County Community Bank. The attorney was an average-sized man with an inflated ego, who could polish almost any situation into a buff shine so bright it

253

was hardly recognizable. And when Stuart O'Hare entered his office, he was greeted with a hardy handshake and a couple of platitudes. When asked about Carlisle Vernon, he replied matter-of-factly. "Well yes, he's a client of mine."

"Know how to get hold of 'im?"

And in true lawyer form, he replied with a question. "Do you know Mr. Vernon?"

"Not directly, but I was told you could get a message to him. Apparently, he's not answering his phone."

The attorney cracked open the window, as if a blast of fresh air would add to his credibility, but instead, the room grew cold not unlike the tile floor that seemed unusually antiseptic. O'Hare eyed the law degree prominently hung on the adjacent wall and noted the university. It was from the same one he was attending in Illinois, and he thought about Hartley. Both had egos the size of a blue-ribbon hog, and with that knowledge, O'Hare shook his head with disdain. "Something has come up, and I need to speak to him directly. It's about the *Hudson Bay*."

Langford sat back in his chair as if his own personal *Hudson Bay* had docked right next to his office door, then cracked his knuckles. "Ah, you know about that, huh?"

"Just wanted to let him know a team of divers I hired identified a debris field along with some rather large silver specimens." O'Hare pulled out his phone and displayed the giant half-breed Sam Carter had found, now buffed into a bright silver sheen. "We polished some of it, but it's a monster of a rock weighing in at over two hundred pounds. Lemme tell ya, it was a real bugger hoisting it from the lake bottom."

The attorney started taking notes on a legal pad, flipping pages periodically. He looked up and said, I assume you're working with Ms. Attwood then?"

O'Hare tugged at his collar and replied, "Bought controlling interest from her and can provide the contract."

"You know, her attorney called a while ago. Said the whole thing about finding a shipwreck was nothing more than a scam. Said their sole intention was to get Mr. Vernon to up his offer. She then went into this tirade, accusing my client of being involved in that murder over in Dickinson County."

"That's lawyers for ya. Here, take a good look at this picture." O'Hare held out his phone once more and displayed several close-up photos of Carter's boulder.

"Impressive."

"Must be over three-thousand troy ounces of pure silver. Despite the weather, I have a crew out on the site as we speak, and I was told just a few minutes ago that they found another monster-sized chunk. We can make arrangements if you'd like to see it."

"At this point, I don't think it'll be necessary." With a pair of folded hands resting upon a yellow legal pad, Langford said, "So tell me, what exactly do you want from Mr. Vernon?"

"Tell him, I need a partner." O'Hare inhaled deeply and then unbuttoned his sport coat. "There are going to be substantial costs involved and wanted to see if he'd be interested in purchasing a one-third interest."

Langford scribbled down a few more notes, then looked up. "And what are the terms?"

"We're looking at selling a one-third interest for a million-five. If costs exceed that, then the partners pay a prorated share of expenses based on ownership or face dilution."

O'Hare could hear the scratch of Langford's pencil as he wrote down the particulars.

"And of course, I can provide a Heads of Agreement along with the conveyance for your client to review during due diligence. The remainder we'll have to work out later. But if this is something he'd be interested in, have someone get back to me. I'd like to start the salvage operation in earnest just as soon as possible."

"If the shipwreck is the *Hudson Bay*, you should know Mr. Vernon owns the cargo as he obtained a quitclaim deed from the owners of the Silver Islet Mine. Therefore, I doubt your agreement with Ms. Attwood holds water, considering she doesn't have clear title. Compounding the matter, the State of Michigan will assert ownership, as they claim salvage rights to all shipwrecks within its territorial waters."

O'Hare lifted his head, and his tone was indignant. "That's a buncha crap, and you know it, or your client wouldn't have

255

offered Ms. Attwood ten percent of the salvage rights. Look, if Vernon wants in, convey the terms and get back to me. Here's my number."

A few minutes later, O'Hare was on the phone standing on the sidewalk outside of Langford's office, talking to Dalton's contact at the National Security Agency.

"Heard about McKenna. A real shame," the voice said over the phone.

"Yeah, I know. I'm sure you're really choked up."

A sharp inhalation was followed by, "What can I do for you Stuart?"

"I'm sending you Langford's number as a text message and want to see if he makes any calls from his business line. I'm also sending you his e-mail address. He might use it to contact Omar. If he does, I'll need an IP address."

"What time frame are we looking at?"

"For the next coupla days, I'd say." O'Hare's words were crisp. "Can you handle something like that?"

"I'll see what I can do, but you should know, you're not at the top of my list in terms of priorities. So, it might be awhile before you hear back from me."

It was about an hour later, and as O'Hare walked into Rosy's Diner in downtown Escanaba, his phone rang. "Yeah," he snapped.

There was no greeting whatsoever. The voice said, "Langford just made a call to a burner. The phone's transponder was turned off. So, we're not certain as to its location. I'm looking into tower activity now. Should have something shortly."

Click.

O'Hare ordered lunch and pulled out a book on the copper mine strike of 1913. When the phone sprang to life, O'Hare had a mouth full of chili-dog and mumbled, "What's up?"

"The signal is running through a tower in Rome."

"Rome?"

"Yup. But in order to get an exact location, I'll have to use a stingray."

O'Hare thumped his chest from indigestion, then took a slug from his chocolate shake. "Refresh my memory. What's a stingray?"

"It's a cell-site simulator that mimics cell phone towers in order to get the burner to emit a ping. We have an operative in the general vicinity, and it might take an hour or two to get hold of him. I'll send you the location as soon as I have something."

A grin spread across his face when he replied, "Think it's Omar he's talking to?"

"Maybe. McKenna sent a sample of Vernon's voice pattern, and I'll compare the two when I have the chance. So, were you a friend of his?"

"Worked together a couple of times, but I'm retired now."

"Ah. Just so you know, the DOJ approved our sessions. Don't know how you managed, but I'm providing them with the information you requested. If you have a problem with that, you should take it up with whoever is your contact. Look, I'll call when I got something."

Less than thirty minutes later, his phone rang once more, and O'Hare set aside his book, snapping forth his usual salutation. "Yeah."

"Carmine Langford here."

"That was quick. You get hold of Mr. Vernon?"

"Indeed. I spoke with my client and regret to inform you Mr. Vernon has decided to pass on your proposal. I want to wish you the best of luck with your venture, but I should remind you that Michigan holds title to all ship wreckage within their territorial waters, and that might impact your salvage operation."

"Thanks for the heads up."

"Not a problem. If you need any legal assistance, don't hesitate to call."

* * * * *

It was dark when they pulled into Rapid River. The wind was coming off the lake, and the air was heavy with the scent of fish and seaweed. As the couple walked from the parking lot

257

towards the Swallow Inn, the smell evoked a pleasant memory for Richard Templeton as he recalled the time when he and his grandfather fished together along the shores of Little Bay de Noc. Richard wondered what his grandfather would have said, regarding the destruction of his home and the criminal charges levied against his grandson.

The Templetons joined Sam Carter who was sitting at the bar, and after exchanging pleasantries, Suzanne nudged him with an elbow and said lasciviously, "So I hear you danced with Evie the other night."

Sam sighed. "News travels fast I see."

"So?" the word drawn out like a string of mozzarella.

Richard pulled away from the memory of his grandfather, then pumped his fist. "Did ya...you know."

His wife gave him a shot with her elbow, and the rotund engineer winced.

"It was just a waltz for heaven's sake."

"We want details," Suzanne asserted, then whispered, "Evie says you beat the crap out of some gorilla over at the bar she works at. What the hell is going on, and how come we're the last ones to find out?"

As the three meandered their way towards an open table, Richard pressed the interrogation further. "What the heck were you thinking? You want to end up in the slammer like me? You got responsibilities."

Richard held the chair for his wife, and after they were seated, Suzanne leaned in, and the floodgates opened. "I'm not supposed to tell you this, but I had a long chat with Evie right after your little kerfuffle." Her voice now strong and acrid. "Did you know Evangeline had a daughter? Well let me tell you, the poor thing was only about five weeks old when she died. So, when you told her she didn't know what it was like to lose a child...well let's just say, it hurt her badly. What the heck were you thinkin'?"

Sam stared at his folded hands.

"And what about that doll you gave her? What was that all about?"

It felt like a sucker punch, staggering about in a ring with no ropes. His voice strained as he pleaded his case. "Travis and I were at an auction awhile back, and I bought a whole box full of stuff for a couple of bucks. And inside a strong box was this rag doll." Sam leaned forward and said, "I know you're gonna think it's crazy, but when I took it out, I thought of Evie."

Suzanne wiggled in her seat, then leaned in.

"Thought I'd give the doll as a sort of peace offering like you suggested. Figured it couldn't do any harm." Sam whirled his index finger around his ear and said, "Pretty crazy, huh?" After placing their order for three smelt dinners, Sam cautiously asked, "So what did she have to say about the gift?"

Suzanne answered, "Well, I think it made quite the impression as she keeps the dumb thing with her wherever she goes. So, you gonna ask her out?"

No answer.

"Well, why not?"

"Cuz I got a dog now."

With eyes piercing, she replied with a sarcastic, "A dog?"

"I know it sounds lame," Sam nervously scratched at the back of his neck, "but I found her when I was working up in Calumet. She's the cutest little thing. She's a cocker spaniel, at least in part, and Travis named her, Mimi."

As Suzanne tossed her hands into the air, Richard said, "So, who's watching the damn dog while you're sittin' here?"

"My mom."

"And your mom can't watch Mimi for a couple of hours when you're out havin' dinner?" Suzanne then continued with a whiney tone, as if sniffing something foul. "You know, if you don't want to go out with Evie, then why did you dance with her?"

Suzanne's phone rang, and she covered the receiver with the palm of her hand. "It's Ev." She then returned to the call and said, "You must have ESP. We were just talking about you."

"Who's all there?" the voice on the phone squeaked.

"Rich and Sam. We're over at the Swallow Inn. Where you at?"

"Home here on Garth Point. Saw that the lights were out at your place and was wondering where you were."

"Look, why don't you come on down to the Swallow Inn. It's all you can eat, and the smelt dinner is to die for."

* * * * *

It was evening, and O'Hare was sitting in his Barcalounger, reading *Death's Door*, a book about Michigan's largest mass murder. The only illumination came from a bridge-lamp set along side his chair, leaving the remainder of the home in virtual darkness. As he took a sip of Stroh's Bohemian, the doorbell chimed. He set aside his reading, then cracked the front door, where he was greeted by a blast of cold air.

A shadowy figure lurked before him, and O'Hare turned on the porch-light only to find a weathered-looking old man with a thin pate, wearing a trench coat. "Can I help you?"

With his head lifted, the visitor said, "Stuart O'Hare?"

"You're a cop, right?"

He displayed his detective's shield and said, "How could you tell?"

"The coat. Looks like something that fell off the discount rack at JC Penney." O'Hare inspected the shield and said, "Washtenaw County? This is a little out of your jurisdiction doncha think?"

The cop exhaled loudly.

O'Hare handed him the badge and said, "What can I do for you, detective?"

"Can I come in?"

O'Hare held the door open, then turned on a few lights, revealing a rather barren decor, "This is about Aubrey Verlinden, isn't it?"

The old man in the worn overcoat looked tired and hacked from a two pack-a-day habit. "Got a call saying you had information about Aubrey. Wanted to call, but we didn't have your number. Apparently, you told a bunch of budding ambulance chasers that Aubrey was a victim of some sort of sexual assault and had videos to back it up."

It was his first laugh of the day, and O'Hare showed little restraint. "Hartley, right?"

The detective spit a wad into a red handkerchief, then wiped his mouth, "Apparently, you're taking a class of his."

"Yeah, I'm taking a class of his. A real piece of work if you ask me."

The old detective attempted to hide the grin and gave a deadpan, "So, we need to see the videos."

O'Hare sighed. "I don't have 'em."

"But you've seen them."

"In part."

A deep respiration was followed by, "So, where are they?"

"I really don't know. We were investigating a homicide that led to your jurisdiction. The owner of the home video-taped several sexual encounters for extortion purposes. Unfortunately, one of their guests was a high-level government employee, and before you know it, Homeland stepped in and confiscated everything, alleging it was a matter of national security. So, from where I stand, you're kinda barkin' up the wrong tree, detective."

"You have anything to do with Corey Crestwood's murder?"

"Nope."

"The guy I spoke to…."

"You mean Hartley."

The detective flared his nostrils and said, "He seems to think you knew details about the murder scene that no one else would know. Care to explain?"

"What's to explain?" O'Hare shrugged. "Just reiterated facts that are a part of the public record. I didn't have anything to do with Crestwood's demise. You know, there must have been at least a dozen guys who confessed to Crestwood's murder. Why aren't you pestering some of them?"

"Because you were close acquaintances with the two primary suspects." He flipped through a small notebook and said, "Mr. Fred Abrams and a Mr. Lenard Frank. Even though they're both deceased, the case is still an open murder investigation, and this Hartley fella seems to think your description of the crime scene implicates your involvement."

O'Hare shook his head with lips drawn tight. "Let's just consider for discussion purposes, I really did kill Crestwood." The two walked towards the kitchen where O'Hare flipped the switch to the overhead light, revealing a stack of dirty dishes in the sink. "Remember that YouTube video where the killer detailed the specifics of the crime? How the hell you ever gonna get a conviction when it was viewed some forty thousand times? Hate to say this detective, but your trip out here was poorly conceived."

"So, if we issued a search warrant, what would we find?"

"I dunno. Maybe you can find my virginity. Lost that about forty-five years ago and haven't seen it since."

The old detective emitted a reluctant grin

O'Hare swept his hand towards the remainder of the home and said, "Look, if you want to search the place, go ahead."

"Where's the house where all this videotaping took place?"

"Can't help you with that. Like I said, Homeland declared it a matter a national security, and I'm not allowed to discuss the matter."

"Got a name who can corroborate your story?"

"Talk to our illustrious Attorney General. Holden knows."

The detective leaned up against the new refrigerator, then let out a heavy sigh. "I'm told you worked law enforcement."

"Yup. For the better part of forty years. You wanna beer?"

Their dialogue began to soften with O'Hare's offer, and the detective said, "Nah, I gotta long drive ahead of me. Besides, it wouldn't look good if I got pulled over." The old cop saw the books on the kitchen table. "Whatcha readin'?"

"Just looking into a cold case. In 1913, some jerk yelled, 'Fire!' in a crowded hall during a Christmas party, and seventy-three people got smothered in a stairwell."

"Ah, the Italian Hall."

O'Hare tipped his head to one shoulder. "You know about that?"

"My grandma lived up in Red Jacket at the time."

"Red Jacket?"

"That's what they called it before the city changed its name to Calumet. They incorporated and named it after their primary employer, Calumet and Hecla. My mom's family is from that area. My Gramma was just a kid when it happened. She passed back in the eighties, but she told me all about it. Apparently, one of her friends from school was crushed to death along with her mom. You know, the good ol' days weren't always so good. So, why all the interest? Whoever did it, has to be long dead."

O'Hare took a seat at the kitchen table, and the detective did likewise. After a sip of beer, O'Hare said, "Client of mine has had some visions from back then, and it piqued my interest. Understand they never apprehended those responsible." O'Hare stated matter of factly.

"Not unlike Crestwood's killer."

"Yeah, but Crestwood was a child molester who, in my opinion, got what he deserved. Those that perished in the Italian Hall were just kids trying to have a little Christmas fun. Seventy-three dead and nobody is held accountable."

The old detective spit another wad into his handkerchief, then pulled out a package of Lucky's. "Do you mind?"

"Suit yourself."

After taking a long drag, the detective relaxed as he exhaled smoke through his nose. "My Gramma knew who did it. Said she saw him at the Italian Hall that day and recognized him as a guy living above a saloon down the street. But being a kid, nobody listened to her."

O'Hare slid a coffee cup over, and said, "So, what happened to him?"

"Thanks." The detective flicked an ash into the cup, and it sizzled when it touched the left-over coffee. He leaned back and said, "Grams said he lived with a bunch of other guys in a boarding house and disappeared right around that time. Said she never saw 'im again."

"Huh." O'Hare lifted his big head once more. "You have dinner yet?"

Another long drag was followed by, "Nah, I was just going to grab a hotdog or something and head on back."

As O'Hare got his coat from the hall closet, he turned and said, "Come on. We can head over to Tom and Jerry's. It's right on Lincoln Highway, and you can tell me more about your grandma. You wouldn't happen to have an address where she lived by any chance?"

"Well, lemme think." With a cigarette dangling from his lips, he mumbled, "You know the area?"

"Somewhat."

"My gramma lived right off Portland Avenue, near a tavern called Luigi's. I think it's still in business. Why do you ask?"

* * * * *

He was standing alongside Trevi Fountain, and the sound of splashing water coalesced with hundreds of young voices that gathered about. Some tossed coins over their shoulder into the churning water while a few couples nestled together, holding hands. Street vendors were out in force, selling flowers and souvenirs. When the young woman approached, he was sitting on a stone bench eating a lemon gelato. She asked where he had gotten it, and before long, the two struck up a conversation. Both were traveling alone, and the man mentioned his trip to Florence the following day.

She swooned, "God, that's sounds nice. I've never been to Florence before."

"Well, why don't you come with? This way I'll have someone to talk to while I'm driving."

"Well, I don't know."

"Come on," he prodded. "I can get you back to your hotel by late afternoon, and if you come with me, you won't have to contend with the god-awful bus."

It was a spring morning in Florence, and the birds were fluttering about, looking for nesting material. The cathedral of Santa Maria del Flore was just waking up as the two stood in front of the church where they admired the massive stonework and stained-glass windows. She suggested it, and although he was initially reluctant, the man consented with reservations. After all, climbing hundreds of feet of stairwell was no easy task when one weighed over three hundred pounds.

They were the first to arrive that morning. Inside the sanctuary, the air was heavy with moisture, and the smell of damp stone emitted a certain earthiness. After paying their admission fee, they started their assent to the top of the Duomo. There were four hundred and sixty-three limestone steps in all, and iron handrails offered support to the thousands of visitors who wanted a great view. Outside, the city was alive with spring, and the ascent to the observation platform seemed, at first glance, rather simple. Electric lighting made the passageway more navigable, but being grossly overweight, Conrad Jabril Omar needed to stop regularly in order to catch his breath. As perspiration beaded along his forehead, he rested near the top. Bent over with palms on his knees, the woman placed her hand along his back and whispered into his ear. With eyes wide, Omar stood erect just before he felt the shove. He stumbled, and the former director of Tenet Gold lunged, his outstretched hands finding only damp Italian air. Fontaine watched him cartwheel down the steps where his head banged hard against the cold stone with every tumble. She took a deep breath, then descended herself, and when she passed the silent body of Conrad Jabril Omar, she pulled up her collar, bent down to one knee, and whispered once more.

* * * * *

Spring had come to northern Illinois, and O'Hare was back home after his lengthy visit to Michigan's Upper Peninsula, chuckling derisively as Hartley droned on about constitutional law. He sat in the shadows, silently watching the debacle unfold, while some thirty prospective lawyers dutifully pecked away at their laptops. Hartley, a tenured law professor, called out a few names and asked questions about a case-study, resulting in more public humiliation. O'Hare hadn't bothered to read it, opting for an early morning walk by the lagoon. It was a time when he did his best thinking, and on this early spring morning, O'Hare thought about Jolene Grey, who had become a steady fixture in his limited social life. They were an odd fit, but for whatever reason, it pleased him. He thought about their dinner plans later that evening. Maybe they'd get take-out and go for a drive. He had a blanket in the back of his SUV and imagined them wrestling under the stars; her giggling like a teenager. Just as the reverie shifted into third gear, Dennis Hartley barked at a student for a wrong answer. The banter temporarily derailed O'Hare's carnal images, and as he listened to the instructor pontificate, his mind drifted again towards a prurient fantasy. Maybe this time Jolene would be wearing leather or was it spandex? As his heart-rate climbed, he thought about the absurdity: an ex-cop once charged with open murder and a former hooker who spend time together like a pair of adolescents, stealing kisses here and there, along with an occasional poke in the arm. He liked that about Jolene. On one hand, she could be quite cerebral, while at other times, she could be playful, something O'Hare missed ever since his ex-wife packed up and called it quits.

His fantasies were interrupted by a loud voice, jolting him awake.

Hartley shielded his eyes as he peered into the shadows where O'Hare rested. He called out with a derisive, "So nice of you to grace us with your presence, Mr. O'Hare. Understand you've had a little legal trouble of late."

Students gawked at O'Hare, expecting fireworks.

O'Hare descended the stairs towards the podium, and when the ex-cop arrived, he said, "You don't scare me. You might be able to intimidate these poor kids because they don't know no better. But let me tell you somethin', your bullshit ain't cuttin' it."

He turned to the class and said, "I'm sure many of you remember me from last time. But what you don't know was our good Mr. Hartley here…"

"It's *Professor* Hartley."

O'Hare used his thumb to point him out, "Our boy, Denny over here called the Washtenaw County Sheriff's Department and reported my little story. Even sent some cop out to talk to me, and it got nothing more than a big laugh. You see, all those details I spoke about came from a YouTube video the killer made right after Crestwood's demise, and there were over forty thousand hits." He turned to Hartley and said, "You should have done *your* homework." O'Hare tipped his big head and looked

266

down his flared nostrils. "But apparently, you have some legal issues of your own, *Professor* Hartley. Made a few calls, and lo and behold, a prosecutor down in Biloxi, Mississippi says you stole a few items from the Winn Dixie back some twenty-odd years ago. Apparently, you never showed up for your court date, resulting in a bench warrant. When I talked to 'em the other day, I was told the warrant is still valid. What's the old adage?" O'Hare stroked his chin and looked up at the ceiling. "Something about people in glass houses?"

It got a snicker from a few students, just as Hartley stormed out.

"Sorry about that," O'Hare said as he addressed classroom. "Seems we're a little short on instructors today."

"Tell us another story," a student shouted which was followed by several voices. "Yeah!"

O'Hare paced in silence as he thought about the request, then turned towards his audience who were now sitting attentively. "Don't get me wrong, I'm not trying to impugn the legal profession, and I hope y'all have productive careers, providing sound legal counsel. I tell you, there's nothing more satisfying than helping someone find justice. But I would be remiss if I didn't talk about the bigger picture. As I said before, justice and the law don't always go hand in hand."

A few minutes later, Hartley re-entered with a campus police officer and yelled, "I want this guy removed from my classroom!"

O'Hare pulled out his cell, then put it on speaker. As the security officer took hold of O'Hare's arm, he heard, "Biloxi Police Department."

"Hi, my name is Stuart O'Hare. I'm up here in Illinois and understand you have an outstanding warrant for a guy named Dennis Hartley. It was issued from your jurisdiction some twenty-three years ago. He's standing right before me along with a uniformed police officer. Do you want him placed into custody?"

"One moment please."

The campus cop whispered, "You're going to have to leave. I'm asking you nice...OK?"

The phone sprang to life, and a shrill voice with a strong southern accent announced, "This is Captain Pulaski. Who am I speakin' to?"

"Stuart O'Hare. You still have a warrant out for a Dennis Hartley? It was quite some time ago."

"You're the guy who called here before, right?"

"Yeah. That's me."

"Well, the warrant is still outstandin'."

"Look, I have police personnel with me right now. Do you want him taken into custody and extradited?"

"Are you kidding?" Pulaski laughed shamelessly. "It was just a shoplifting charge. So, we're not gonna pop for any extradition-related expenses."

"I'll pay for it."

There was another burst of laughter before O'Hare heard, "You're joking of course. Y'all gonna have to fly him on down here, and that's two tickets not to mention personnel costs. In the end, it could run into the thousands."

"Consider it my civic duty."

"Well, it's your money. Maybe, the judge'll include reimbursement upon sentencing. If y'all give us a number, I'll forward a copy of the warrant to the appropriate authority."

O'Hare turned to the campus police officer. "You heard him. There's a warrant out for Hartley's arrest, and if you don't place him into custody this very instant, I'm going to file a complaint. So, you better call dispatch and let 'em know you're bringin' someone in for processing." He turned to Hartley and gloated. "I think this has been a most productive lesson for your students. Maybe we could do this again sometime."

It only took a few moments until several officers arrived, and upon reviewing a .pdf file of Hartley's warrant, they escorted the instructor to the door, leaving O'Hare alone in front.

"I'm sorry about all this," O'Hare said apologetically. "You kids deserve better. You pay top dollar to be here and end up listening to a bunch of horseshit. But I'll let you in on a little secret. Hartley ain't a bad guy, he just made a dumb mistake. Sooner or later, we all do. I'm sure he thought it was no big deal, skipping out on a PR bond. After all, it only involved about fifty-bucks worth of stolen groceries. But let me tell you somethin', if you don't deal with your past, it has a way of haunting you later on. Had he just showed up on his court date, he'd have been given a fine and sent on his merry way. But he skipped out, and the fine State of Mississippi doesn't take kindly to folks who thumb their noses at 'em. It's all so unnecessary." O'Hare yawned, then looked at his watch. "Looks like we have about twenty minutes of lecture left, and I hate to see you guys get short-changed. If you like, I could fill you in on a cold-case I've been working on, but if you want to take off, be my guest."

No one moved.

O'Hare walked about the front gallery with his hands clamped tight behind his back, and then raised his big skull. "So, let's talk about the law. After all, that's why we're all here." O'Hare resumed his pacing, and several students closed up their laptops.

"It was Michigan's largest mass murder. Back in 1913, it started out as a labor dispute up in the Copper Country. Anyone know where that is?"

A student raised his hand, and O'Hare pointed.

"It's the northern-most tip of Michigan that juts out into Lake Superior."

"Good to know the university is teaching geography as well as law." It got a few polite chuckles, and when it died down, O'Hare said, "But let me give you some background information. Back then, mine owners were only payin' their workers about three bucks a day, and that was for a ten-hour shift. Working in the copper mines was dangerous, where a week didn't go by without someone being killed. And if you got killed or hurt, the mining company had no further obligation to your family and frequently tossed them out onto the street because they owned all the houses in the area. So, the Western Federation of Miners came in to organize labor, and you can imagine how well that went over. It didn't take long before a strike was declared, and the mines were shut down, leaving some thirteen-thousand families without a source of income. In response, mine owners, along with county officials, brought in muscle from out of state with the sole intention of breaking the back of the newly formed union. And with their financial wealth, they had just about everyone in their pocket, including the churches, merchants, the police, and most of the newspapers, leaving a largely immigrant work force without any protection or legal recourse.

"Now I want you to close your eyes for just a minute. And imagine it's Christmas, and you haven't seen a paycheck in six months. You're taking your kids into town to see Santa. There's no extra money for presents, just a stick of hard candy from a guy wearing a scraggily beard. To make matters worse, tensions between workers and merchants were pretty bad. You see, the mines had been closed since July, and shopkeepers were suffering from the lack of business, holding labor responsible for their economic woes. So, in the midst of this bloody strike, a little party was planned for the kids at the new Italian Hall. The old one burnt to the ground some years prior, and the new hall was a two-story brick structure with a fire escape. Nearly seven-hundred showed up for the party. Everything was going well until some punk yelled, 'Fire!' There wasn't any fire, but it created a stampede nonetheless, and seventy-three people were suffocated in the lone stairwell, mostly children."

As O'Hare paced to and fro, he took a moment to gather his thoughts. "Now granted, this wasn't premeditated murder but rather manslaughter where the person responsible knew, or should have known, their actions were extremely reckless. As you can probably guess, no one was apprehended, and to this date, it's still an open murder investigation."

The room drew silent.

"An inquest was held by the coroner a week later, and not much came from it, even though there were eyewitnesses who saw the perpetrator. But a coroner's only function is to determine the cause of death, and everyone knew how the victims died. You see, the sheriff of Houghton County was responsible for investigating the crime, but he was in the pocket of the mining companies, like so many others. So, the coroner did a half-assed investigation of his own. Most of the witnesses spoke poor English and weren't afforded a translator. Hence,

270

important evidence was lost, which is exactly how the mining companies wanted it. I read the transcript the other day, and it was so poorly done, it's hard to find words that adequately express the outrage. So, my question is this. How do we seek justice for those that have no voice? As I said before, justice and the law do not always go hand in hand."

A young law student raised a couple of fingers, and O'Hare pointed. "Question."

"So, are you suggesting vigilantism is justified?"

O'Hare shook his head. "No, not at all. What I'm saying is, there's a higher law that goes beyond the one you're currently studying. You know, it's like the old adage, 'What goes around comes around.' Want to be a liar, cheat, and a thief? Fine, then the only folks who'll have anything to do with your sorry ass are liars, cheats, and thieves. It's called the law of attraction."

Another student called out, "Back to the Italian Hall, if you don't mind. That was over a hundred years ago. Surely, those responsible have long passed on. Why all the interest?"

O'Hare exhaled forcefully through his nose, and for a moment, there was absolute silence. "Children are pure innocents needing protection, and I've spent my career finding justice for kids like little Aubrey Verlinden. Some of them who perished at the Italian Hall were only a couple of years old, and whatever problems the mine owners were having with organized labor, had nothing to do with those kids. But not unlike so many other cases, they're the ones who pay the price." O'Hare continued to pace with his hands clamped tight behind his back. "Why don't you close up your laptops because what I'm about to say, isn't something that needs to be copied down. You see, all bills eventually get paid, just like with our good buddy, Professor Hartley."

A student in the front row squinted.

"Let me be specific. You're right. The person responsible for killing all those kids is dead, but death doesn't close out accounts. There's such a thing as karmic justice. Maybe it won't happen in this lifetime but surely it will happen in the next."

Another student hollered, "So you're saying, you believe in... reincarnation?"

"Maybe."

A low din came from the classroom until someone said, "Care to elaborate?"

Another long exhalation was followed by more pacing. "I'm not here to convince you one way or another. Right now, most of you are being introduced to the process called, 'deductive reasoning' with the intention of becoming a well-paid divorce attorney or something similar and hopefully, pay back the mountain of debt you've incurred."

The classroom erupted in laughter.

"But life doesn't always come in nice, neat little packages where everything is self explanatory. As you age, you start to ask better questions like: 'Why am I here?' Or maybe you ask yourself, 'What'll it be like when death comes knocking on my door?' Or maybe it's something more sublime like, 'Will I ever see my relatives again?' All I can tell you is if I end up seeing my relatives after I die, I'll know where I'm at."

More laughter.

"I've been in law enforcement for over forty some odd years, and I can tell you with absolute certainty life is a complicated mess and yet at the same time, a wonderful gift. You have to figure out for yourself what it means."

O'Hare nodded once, pressed his jaw muscles tight, then added, "And that ends today's lesson."

CHAPTER EIGHTEEN

"There is no death...
Only a change of worlds."
- Chief Seattle

April 21ˢᵗ, 1941

He was an old man surrounded by family, and as he lay near death, his thoughts went back to the Keweenaw. He never said much about it to his new family; they only knew the general details, as any discussion about his time near Lake Superior evoked regret and sorrow. But his thoughts could not be willed away nor forgotten. Peter could still remember the color of his daughter's green eyes and how she giggled when he tickled her tummy. By now, it all seemed like a dream; that maybe his time working underground didn't really happen. He kept a strongbox beneath his bed, and when he questioned the reality of his past or simply couldn't remember, he would open it. Inside was a piece of native silver and of course, the beloved rag doll Mary adored. And when he held the doll close, he could still detect the sweet scent of his daughter, and it soothed him.

"What's wrong papa?" she asked as tears coursed down her cheeks. "Is it about, Mary?"

With eyes red, Peter said, "I should of..." his words trailing off.

His oldest daughter sat on the edge of the bed with hands folded. "Tell me, papa. Tell me about her."

The years of inhaling rock dust had taken its toll, and his body, once strong and vibrant, had now become broken, ridden with frailty and emaciated. With every cough, his life force seeped away. There was little semblance to the robust miner who pushed tons of copper ore through the dark drifts and adits deep within the earth's interior.

He sobbed, "Do you think... God will forgive me?"

She caressed her father's thin hair, then took his hand; his fingers now cyanotic. "Do you want to talk about it? They say talking is good for the soul."

He had his daughter fetch the box beneath the old iron bed and pointed to the bureau where she found the key. Once opened, the old man clutched the doll to his chest.

She placed her hand upon his wrist and said, "What is it papa?"

"Just...just want a chance to make it right. Do you...think...that God will give me... another..."

And with these final words, the old miner closed his eyes one final time.

* * * * *

She was in her apartment above Luigi's with Lucy at her side, holding the unopened parcel postmarked from Siena. She looked at her canine companion and said, "Whatcha think?" Evangeline retrieved a steak knife from the sink and then flopped back into bed, donning a pair of red reading glasses. "Well, here goes nothin'."

As her hand trembled, she tore open the large package and inside were the letters she had sent, neatly tied together with string along with two long envelopes. She sat up with her knees to her chest and pulled the first one apart.

Dear Ms. Attwood,

I am writing you on behalf of my brother, Ulay who passed away earlier this year due to advanced liver disease. He asked me to write you and to return your letters. My brother spoke of you fondly during the last few months of his life and asked me to send on the attached letter. We shall miss him.

Sincerely Yours,

Amadeo Yastakovic

With her hand atop her heart, tears cascaded. She held the letter simply addressed, 'To Evangeline.'

My Dearest Evangeline,

As I sit here at my desk, I'm not sure what to write, but feel compelled to pen a few lines for you to read when I am no more. There's something I hid from you and should have said

274

something early on. You see, I am a heroin addict. When we met in Verona, I had been clean for almost a year, but it was an addiction I wasn't able to overcome until these past few years. My addiction drove me into homelessness, at times sleeping under bridges and panhandling money from complete strangers. That's one of the reasons why I didn't write. I wanted you to remember me like I was in Verona. I now recognize the error of this decision.

I've been clean for several years now, but the decades of abuse have taken a toll upon my body, and as a result of sharing needles with other addicts, I contracted hepatitis. I need a liver transplant, but having only a short time in recovery, I am relegated to the bottom of the waiting list.

Please don't feel sorry for me. In spite of my difficulties, I met a wonderful woman, and we married a few years ago. She works as a nurse here in Siena, and has been my steadfast companion, helping me in variety of ways as my health declines.

So, by now, you're probably wondering, "Why am I writing?" As I close out this incarnation, I have a strong desire to settle accounts. My time is coming to an end, and as I hold your photograph, I remember how much I loved you. I've asked my brother to write after I've passed and return your letters. During my darkest days, I would hold them against my heart, and they inspired me to be a better man. So, in many ways, you saved me.

Please think of me fondly but let there be no tears of sadness. Do whatever you need in order to find your heart's desire. You're worthy of all these fine things.

Your devoted,

Ulay

Enclosed was a photograph of a much older Ulay standing on a stone bridge overlooking the Adige. Here, they had stood many years prior, and she remembered how he wrapped his arms around her and how safe she felt in his strong embrace.

275

As a cold rain tapped against her window, strong emotions washed ashore, and they slugged it out with one another, like a pair of prize fighters in a desperate battle of wills. The first wave pummeled her with an all-encompassing grief, where she buried her face into her hands. Lucy responded, nuzzling her with a wet nose, and Evangeline took hold of her soft yellow fur. But grief was pushed aside by remorse, knowing that Ulay never knew about Charlotte. She chastised herself for being so stubborn. Why didn't she mention their daughter in the numerous letters she wrote? It came to her, she recalled, that announcing her pregnancy might have made her seem desperate or worse, like a gold-digger, looking for a meal ticket. Evangeline thought about sending him a picture of his daughter after Charlotte was born, but she never heard a word from him during the entire pregnancy, and his silence bred resentment. After her daughter died, what could she possibly say? So, she said nothing, opting to play it safe over the risk of experiencing his wrath or worse, his indifference.

* * * * *

Spring was in full bloom on Garth Point, and the land was awash with new growth. Geese were seen crossing the bay, enroute to their summer nesting grounds, and trilliums dotted the forest floor like little patches of white hope. Off in the distance, a pileated woodpecker could be heard tapping away on a dead spruce tree while homeowners set out lawn furniture, and boats filled the marina in town.

After a full day of yard work, the Templetons enjoyed a quiet evening in front of their new fireplace. Suzanne had her feet up on the coffee table with an afghan pulled over her legs, while Richard thumbed through an old issue of *Field and Stream*. Suzanne turned to her husband and said, "You know, I was thinking; why don't we go up to Calumet and see Evie this weekend?"

Richard turned a page in his magazine and replied with a mindless, "Uh-huh."

"What did I just say?"

276

He turned a page and replied with another, "Uh-huh."

Suzanne took hold of his reading material and scooted over. "Look, there's something I want to talk about. I found a box full of pictures up in the closet. Where did they come from?"

The engineer cleared his throat and then gulped. "They were over at my parents, and my Mom thought I should have 'em, considering everything got burned up in the fire."

"There were several pictures of you before we were married. How come you never say anything about your first wife?"

"You mean, Karen?"

"Who else do you think I'm talking about, dummy? You've never really said much about her in all the years we've been together. How come you never mention her?"

He grabbed another issue of *Field and Stream* from the coffee table and as he flipped a few pages, Richard replied with a mindless, "I dunno."

"Come on." Suzanne whined, "Tell me about her."

"What's there to say. We got divorced, and then I met you."

"But she must have spent time out here at Garth Point, and I was wondering what she was like, that's all."

Templeton licked a finger, then flipped a page in his magazine. "I don't spend much time reminiscing about that sort of thing. We didn't end on a positive note."

"But how come you never want to talk about it?"

Richard looked over the top of his reading glasses and inhaled sharply. He walked into the bedroom, returning with the box his mother had given him days earlier. Suzanne sat close as he rummaged through the various pictures and documents, then showed his wife a photo of Karen taken right after they got married.

"She's pretty."

No answer.

"So, where did you guys go on your honeymoon?" Suzanne asked.

"Aruba. I think there's a picture here somewhere." He continued to fumble through the stack of papers and muttered, "If I can only find it."

While Richard continued to sort through the stack of photos, Suzanne went to the bedroom and returned with an album of her own. With one leg tucked under the other, she said, "I saved this from the fire," then displayed all her vacation pictures.

Upon flipping through a few pages, Richard asked, "Where were these taken?"

"Sephoria. That's where the Virgin Mother spent her childhood, at least that's what the tour guide said. My ex and I vacationed there before Madison was born."

Richard bolted erect. "Wait a second." There was a large photo taken of the tour group, and he tapped it with an index finger. "That girl in the front row sorta looks like Evie."

"Lemme see." The two were now cheek to cheek examining Suzanne's photograph. "Well, it kinda looks like her, but…"

Suzanne's husband sat close to his wife and squinted at another couple standing in the back row with arms around one another. "Wait a second. Isn't that's Sam and Lori?" With eyes wide, Richard uttered, "Wh…what the heck are they doin' in your picture album?"

* * * * *

When Roy licked the stamps on the envelopes he sent to his wife, minute amounts of DNA were deposited that were matched to a set of remains buried at the American Military Cemetery in Manila. Subsequently, Roy's body was flown home where a service was performed at Lake View Cemetery. An honor guard of former soldiers escorted the casket to a cemetery plot where he would be buried next to his mother. As a lone trumpet sounded, Evangeline thought about all the letters he had written to his beloved wife, and because of those correspondences, Roy got to come home, at least what was left of him.

As Evangeline looked up from her seat near the casket, the markers for the Klarich children could be seen off in the distance; three stone crosses, now turned grey with age, bearing the names of each victim from the Italian Hall. Evangeline thought about the snow angel the sexton had pointed out some

278

months prior, then dabbed her nose with a white-laced handkerchief.

As speaker after speaker talked about Roy's service, Lake View Cemetery was astir with various politicians, along with local media who attended the ceremony. Margaret, dressed in black, sat with her husband in a folding chair next to the metal casket, and when an Army officer presented the American flag, now folded into a crisp triangle, she wept. Her husband put her arm around her as cameras recorded the event from afar.

But spring was in the air. Crocuses were seen throughout the community, and in town, a few tourists were spotted walking along Sixth Street. With the onset of warm weather, the Quincy Mine resumed their underground tours with an abbreviated schedule, and outside of the fanfare associated with the internment of a World War II veteran, life was blossoming.

Evangeline Attwood moved into the home on Pine Street, and a few days after Roy's service, her possessions from downstate arrived in a large van. It took all morning to unload a lifetime collection of household goods and memorabilia, and when they approached with Emma's cedar chest, she had them place it at the foot of her bed. After the last of the boxes were stacked in the living room, the siren in town went off, and she swept back the curtain to take a final look at the semi-trailer parked out front. As they pulled away, Evangeline slipped the picture of Ulay back into the photo album next to the sole photograph of her daughter, placing the folder at the bottom of Emma's cedar chest where she whispered, "Look after our little girl. She needs a good father."

Lucy whined as the scent of hyacinths wafted through the open window, suggesting a walk was in order. The temperature was in the low seventies, and when they passed an ice cream store, Calumet's newest resident went inside and ordered a chocolate malt. When she finished, Evangeline noticed him sitting at the counter alone and approached. "Sam?"

He turned and gave a tepid, "Hi."

"What are you doing here?"

"Just having a soda, that's all." He drew on his straw until the beverage slurped, then wiped his mouth with his sleeve.

"Got hired by a Canadian company to look at a few sites up near the Phoenix Location, and Calumet is the only place with year-round accommodations."

She swiveled her head back and forth. "And where's Travis?"

"With my Mom. She's taking care of him until I head back on Friday."

"That must be hard for the two of you."

"Well, we Skype every day, but I miss the little guy. Things are kind of tight right now, and I gotta accept work wherever I can. I'm fortunate I get to go back on the weekends."

She dipped her head slightly, looking over the top of her sunglasses. "Did you sell your rock? I thought that might help out at least financially."

"I placed an ad on eBay and started the bidding at ten thousand but couldn't muster even one bid. So, I was thinking I'd take it to Tucson when they have their big, rock and gem show next February. If you like, I could try to sell your specimen, but the market right now isn't the best."

"So, what did you do with it?"

"It's sitting in my living room, collecting dust." Sam collared his mouth with his right hand and whispered, "To tell you the truth, I wouldn't mind keeping it. It's a real beauty."

Evangeline looked at her watch and said, "Look, I gotta run. I got Lucy tied up outside, and she needs some attention." After an awkward moment, she said, "Nice seeing you again, Mr. Carter."

And as she untied Lucy from the parking meter, she heard a voice. "Go ask him," was all it said. Evangeline looked about as if the source was nearby, but the sidewalks were empty. She dismissed the thought until the voice repeated itself and then felt the presence of the old soldier as his spirit passed.

The door had a small bell atop, and whenever a customer walked in, it would provide a merry rhythm. When Evangeline reentered, Sam turned. She tipped her head to one side and said, "Would you like to join us? We're just going to walk around town. It would be nice having the company."

With those few words, the two ambled down Seventh Street, absorbing the warmth of a beautiful spring day. When they passed the Italian Hall Memorial, Evangeline read the historical marker, then slipped her hand into his. And at that exact moment, a mourning dove, hidden in the underbrush, took flight.

If you would like to leave a comment or contact the author, you may do so at www.Facebook.com/Richard Lassin Author. To listen to the original music to *Red Jacket,* go to YouTube and type in the search box: Red Jacket Video Richard Lassin.

If you would like to read more about Stuart O'Hare and Dalton McKenna, *Reflections* is a novel about going home, and is the prequel to *Red Jack*et. The book along with *Red Jacket* will be available soon. Stores that carry these books will be listed on the Facebook page cited above.

Made in the USA
Monee, IL
04 November 2019